Penguin Books
The Joke

KU-048-590

Milan Kundera was born in Brno, Czechoslovakia, in
1929. He studied philosophy and musical composition
before joining the Film Faculty at the Academy of Music
and Dramatic Arts in Prague as an assistant, lecturing in
world literature. *The Joke*, his first novel, appeared in
1967, and he has also written plays such as *The Owners of
Keys,* poems, short stories, a book of essays on the art of
the novel, and translations from French (Apollinaire)
and Ukrainian. He has won several literary awards in his
own country.

Milan Kundera

The Joke

Translated from the Czech by
David Hamblyn and Oliver Stallybrass

Penguin Books

Penguin Books Ltd, Harmondsworth,
Middlesex, England
Penguin Books Australia Ltd, Ringwood,
Victoria, Australia

Originally published in Czechoslovakia
by Verlag Ceskoslovensky Spesovatel
First published by Macdonald 1969
published in Penguin Books 1970
Copyright © Milan Kundera, 1967
English translation © Macdonald & Co. (Publishers) Ltd., 1969

This edition follows the text of Milan Kundera's novel as originally
published and reinstates the passages omitted
from the hardback edition

Made and printed in Great Britain
by C. Nicholls & Company Ltd
Set in Linotype Times

Part I: Ludvik

Here I was – back in my home town after all these years. I stood in the main square, which I had crossed times without number as a child, as a boy, and as a young man, feeling no emotion at all; indeed I mentally compared the flat square to a huge parade ground, and the Guildhall spire jutting up over the rooftops to a soldier in some antique helmet, and reflected on how the military past of this South Moravian town, which had once formed a bastion against Magyars and Turks, had imposed a stamp of irredeemable ugliness upon its features.

After the long years there was nothing to draw me back to this home town of mine. I told myself that I had grown indifferent to it, and that this was hardly surprising: after all I hadn't lived here for fifteen years, I had very few remaining friends or acquaintances here (and preferred to avoid even these), and my mother was buried among strangers, in a grave I did not tend. But I was deceiving myself: what I had called indifference was really hatred. I could not put my finger on the reasons for this, for good things as well as bad had happened to me here, as in all the other towns, but the hatred was there none the less. It was the circumstance of my journey here that had made me conscious of it: the job I had come to do could, after all, have been attended to in Prague, but I had suddenly begun to feel an irresistible attraction towards the opportunity of completing it in my home town, precisely because this was a prosaic and cynical mission which derisively removed any suspicion that I was returning for nostalgic reasons.

I gave the unlovely square a final scornful glance and turned my back on it, walking down the street to the hotel where I had booked a room for the night. The porter gave me a key attached

to a pear-shaped lump of wood and said: 'Second floor.'
The room unprepossessing: a bed up against the wall, in the
middle a small table with one chair, by the bed an ostentatious
mahogany bedside table with a mirror, and a tiny cracked
wash basin by the door. I put my briefcase down on the table
and opened the window: it looked out over a yard onto some
houses displaying their bare grubby backs to the hotel. I
closed the window, drew the curtains, and went over to the
wash basin, with its two taps, marked red and blue; I tried them
and cold water trickled from both. I looked at the table: it
was just about adequate, and a bottle with two glasses would
have gone quite 'well on it, but the trouble was that only
one person could sit at it, as there was only one chair in the
room. I drew the table up to the bed and tried to sit at it, but
the table was too high and the bed too low: the latter, moreover, apart from making a rotten chair, sank so much under
me that its performance as a bed at once became equally
suspect. I leaned my fists on it; then I lay down on it, carefully
raising my feet in the air so that my boots should not dirty
the (cleanish) coverlet and quilt. The bed sagged so that I lay
as if in a hammock or a narrow grave; it was impossible to
imagine anyone else lying in that bed with me.

I sat down on the chair, stared at the threadbare curtains
and began to think. Then I heard steps and voices in the passage. It was a man and a woman, whose every word I caught:
they were talking about some Peter who had run away from
home and some Aunt Clara who was a fool and had spoilt the
boy. Then I heard a key being turned and a door being opened,
and the conversation continued in the room next door; I could
hear the woman sighing (yes, one could even hear her sighing!)
and the man resolving to give Clara a good talking-to.

I made my decision: I stood up, washed my hands again in
the wash basin, wiped them on the towel, and walked out of
the hotel, without even knowing where I was heading. All
I knew was that unless I wanted this unsuitable hotel room to
jeopardise the entire object of my long and laborious journey,
then I must, however repugnant the idea, find someone here
to whom I could go with a confidential request. I passed in

rapid review all the faces I remembered from my youth, rejecting each in turn through my aversion for the business – which the nature of my request would necessitate – of attempting to bridge the long years of separation. Then I recalled that there was probably one man living here, a newcomer for whom I had once been instrumental in finding a position, who would, if I knew him at all, be only too glad to repay one favour with another. He was an eccentric, scrupulously moral yet strangely unsettled and feckless, whose wife, as far as I knew, had divorced him years ago because of his living anywhere and everywhere except with her and their son. Then with a shock I wondered whether he might have remarried, for that would have complicated my request, and I hurried on towards the hospital.

The local hospital is a complex of buildings and pavilions straggling over a large expanse of garden. I entered an unsightly shed by the gates and asked the porter behind the table to connect me with the virology department; he pushed the telephone over to my side of the table and said: O-Two. I dialled O2 and learned that Dr Kostka had left only a few seconds before and was on his way to the exit. I sat down on a bench by the gates so as not to miss him and stared at the men loafing around in their blue and white striped hospital gowns, and presently I saw him: he was walking along deep in thought, tall and thin, ugly in an agreeable sort of way, and quite unmistakable. I got up and walked right up to him, as if wishing to collide; he looked at me in annoyance, then suddenly recognized me and thrust out his hand. His surprise seemed almost like a good omen and I was pleased by the promptitude with which he greeted me.

I explained that I had arrived less than an hour before on some unimportant business which would keep me here for two days, and he expressed gratified surprise that my first move had been to come and see him. I suddenly felt guilty at not having done so for his own sake, and because the question I was now asking him (I boldly inquired whether he had married again) was inspired by calculation, not by genuine interest. He told me, to my satisfaction, that he was still by himself. I said there must be a lot of things for us to talk about. He agreed, and regretted that he had only just over an hour now before returning to the hospital, and that in the evening he had to make a bus journey out of town. 'Don't you live here?' I asked in consternation. He assured me that he did and that he had a bedsitter in a new block but that 'a man doesn't feel right on his own'. It turned out that Kostka had a fiancée in another town twelve miles away, a schoolteacher with a two-room flat of her own. Will you be moving in with her eventually?' I asked. He said it would be hard to find a position in the other town as interesting as the one I had helped him get, and his fiancée would have difficulty finding a job here. I began, quite sincerely, to curse the ineptness of our bureaucracy, which cannot even help a man and woman to live together. 'Calm down, Ludvik,' he said indulgently, 'it's not quite as intolerable as all that. The trip does cost me a little money and time, but my solitude remains untouched, and I remain free.' 'Why do you need freedom so much?' I asked him. 'Why do *you*?' he countered. 'I'm a lady's man,' I replied. 'I don't need freedom for women, I want it for myself,' he said, and went on: 'I'll tell you what – come round to my place for a while until I have to leave.' I could have wished for nothing better.

We left the hospital and came presently to a new housing estate, its blocks projecting disharmoniously upwards one after another from an unlevelled dusty terrain (without lawns or pathways or a road), a depressing piece of scenery on the town's edge, where it bordered on the empty flatness of the far-flung fields. The lift was out of order, so we climbed the narrow stairway to the third floor, where I saw Kostka's name written on a card. As we crossed the vestibule of his room I felt highly satisfied: in the corner stood a wide comfortable divan covered with a red patterned blanket; besides the divan his room had a table, easy chair, large bookcase, gramophone and radio.

I expressed my approval of Kostka's flat and asked what his bathroom was like. 'Not very luxurious, I'm afraid,' he said, flattered by my interest, and ushered me into the vestibule, off which there was a door into the bathroom, small but very agreeable, with bath, shower and wash basin. 'Looking at this nice flat of yours makes me wonder,' I said, 'what you're doing tomorrow afternoon and evening.' 'Unfortunately,' he apologized, 'I have to work late tomorrow and won't be back till around seven. Have you got a free evening?' 'I may well have the evening free,' I replied, 'but I wonder if you could lend me your flat just for the afternoon?'

My question surprised him, but he replied at once, as if eager to show his willingness to help: 'I'd be very glad to share it with you.' And he went on, as if deliberately not trying to guess my purpose: 'If you have trouble finding accommodation you can always sleep here tonight. I shan't be back till tomorrow morning, and even then I shall be going straight to the hospital.' 'No, there's really no need. I've booked at the hotel. The thing is, the hotel room's not very nice, and tomorrow afternoon I need some pleasant surroundings. Not just for myself, you understand.' 'Of course,' said Kostka, meekly lowering his head, 'that's what I guessed.' After a while he added: 'I'm glad to have the chance of doing you a favour. That is, if it really is a favour I'm doing you.'

Kostka made coffee, and we sat and chatted for a while. I tried the divan and discovered with delight that it didn't sag or even creak. Presently Kostka announced that he must be getting back to the hospital, and gave me a quick initiation into some of the mysteries of the household: the bathtaps had to be tightened well, hot water in defiance of all conventions flowed from the tap marked C, the socket for the radiogram was hidden under the divan, and there was an almost full bottle of vodka in the cupboard. Then he gave me a ring with two keys and showed me which was for the outside door and which for his flat. During a lifetime of sleeping on various beds and sitting at various tables I have developed a special cult of keys, and I slipped Kostka's into my pocket with quiet glee.

As we left, Kostka hoped his flat would bring me luck. 'Yes,' I said. 'It will help me do a splendid demolition job.' 'What's splendid about demolishing things?' he asked, and I laughed inwardly, recognizing in this question, mildly put yet intended as a challenge, the Kostka I had first met fifteen years ago. I liked him, but at the same time he amused me, and I replied: 'I know you're a quiet toiler on God's eternal building site and don't like hearing about demolition, but I'm not one of God's masons. Mind you, if God's masons built real walls, I doubt if our demolitions could harm them. But instead of walls all I can see everywhere is theatre curtains, and the demolition of curtains is merely justice.'

We were exactly where we had parted ways last time, some nine years before. Abstract as our argument was, we were well aware of the concrete base beneath it and we had no need to repeat ourselves; all we needed to repeat was that we had not changed, we were as different as ever – and of course it was this very difference that endeared Kostka to me and made me love these arguments, which gave me the chance for another perfunctory clarification of who *I* was and how *I* thought. So as to leave me in no doubt he replied:

'What you've just said sounds fine. But tell me: if you're such a sceptic, how can you be so sure of telling a curtain from a wall? Have you never doubted that the illusions you ridicule *are* only illusions? What if you're wrong? What if they're real values that you're busy demolishing? The disparaged value and the debunked illusion have the same miserable substance, and there's nothing easier than getting them mixed up.'

I accompanied Kostka back through the town to the hospital, playing with the keys in my pocket; I was happy to be with my old friend, ready as he was at all times to convince me of his rightness, even now on our way across the bumpy surface of the new estate. Of course he knew that tomorrow we had the whole evening in front of us, and after a while he turned from philosophizing to more mundane matters, making sure once more that I would wait for him in the flat till seven tomorrow (he had only the one set of keys) and asking me if there was really nothing else I needed. I put my hand up to my face and said all I needed now was a visit to the barber's, for I was disagreeably stubbly. 'Excellent,' said Kostka, 'I shall arrange for you to have a personal shave.'

I accepted his patronage and let him take me to a small barber's shop with three revolving chairs towering before three mirrors, two of them occupied by men with heads bent forward and faces covered in soap. Two women in white coats were leaning over them. Kostka approached one of them and whispered something; the woman wiped her razor on a cloth and called something to the back of the shop; out came a girl in a white coat and took charge of the abandoned gentleman, while the woman Kostka had spoken to motioned me to sit down in the third chair. I shook hands with Kostka as he left and sat down, leaning my head back on the headrest and letting my eyes wander over the blotchy white ceiling. I avoided the mirror, since after all these years on earth I still have a horror of looking at my own face.

I still kept my eyes on the ceiling even when I felt the hairdresser's fingers on my neck as she drew a white sheet over the collar of my shirt. Then she stepped back and all I heard was the movements of the razor on the leather strop, while I remained sunk in a sort of delicious immobility filled with agreeable indifference. Presently I felt fingers on my face, wet slippery fingers smearing soap cream on my skin, and it occurred to me what a strange and ridiculous thing it was to have some unknown woman, who meant nothing to me, and to whom I meant nothing, gently caressing me. Then the woman started to spread the soap with a brush, and it was as if I was no longer sitting there, as if I had sunk in the blotchy white expanse on which my eyes were fixed. I pretended – for my mind never stops playing games even in moments of repose – that I was an unarmed victim who had just been handed over to the mercies of this woman, now busy sharpening the razor. And, with my body dissolving in space and feeling only the touch of her fingers on my face, it was easy to imagine her hands lovingly holding my head, turning it and fondling it, as if they had no interest in the body apart from the head, and that the sharp razor now waiting on a nearby table would merely consummate that wondrous independence.

Then the touch ceased and I heard the woman step back; now, no doubt, she was taking the razor in her hand. I told

11

myself (for my mind was still playing its games) that I must see how she looked, this woman holding and lifting my head, this tender assassin. I lowered my eyes from the ceiling to the mirror, and as I did so the game I was playing for my own entertainment became uncannily real: I seemed to recognize this woman who was leaning over me in the mirror.

With one hand she held the lobe of my ear while the other was carefully scraping soap off my face; I gazed at her, and the likeness, so dreadfully certain a moment before, began slowly to dissolve and disappear. Then she leaned over the wash basin, flicked the ball of foam off the razor with two fingers, stood up and gently turned the chair round; for an instant our eyes met and again I knew it was her. Admittedly the face was different, rather as if it belonged to an older sister, greyed and faded, slightly sunken; but it was fifteen years since I had seen her last. During that period time had masked her real face; but luckily the mask had two holes through which her old eyes could look at me once more, and they were just as I remembered them.

Then the trail became confused again. A new customer came into the shop, sat down behind me to wait for his turn, and presently started talking about the fine summer we were having and the bathing pool which was being built outside the town. The woman shaving me answered. I paid more attention to her voice than to the words, which were of no great significance, and I was sure that it was not a voice I recognized; it sounded matter-of-fact, careless, unconcerned, almost rude – the voice of a stranger.

Now she was rinsing my face, pressing her palms into it so that, in spite of the voice, I again began to believe that this was her, that after fifteen years I could once more feel her hands on my face, stroking me long and tenderly; for I had completely forgotten that she was not in fact caressing me but rinsing me. Meanwhile her stranger's voice was directed to the talkative customer, replying to something he had said, but I didn't want to believe the voice, I wanted to believe the hands, to recognize her by the hands; by the measure of tenderness in her touch I tried to make out whether it was her and whether she had recognized me.

Then she took a towel and dried my face. The prattler was laughing loudly at one of his own jokes and I noticed that the woman was not laughing; she had probably stopped listening to him. This disturbed me – it seemed to prove that she had recognized me and was secretly upset. I resolved to say something to her as soon as I got up from the chair. She removed the cloth from my neck. I stood up. I took a five-crown note from my breast pocket. I waited for our eyes to meet again so that I could call her by name (the other fellow was still gabbling on about something), but she kept her head turned unconcernedly away, and took the five crowns in such a brisk and matter-of-fact way that I suddenly felt like a madman suffering from illusions, and could not find the courage to speak.

I left the shop strangely shaken; all I knew was that I knew nothing and that it was a sign of callousness to be uncertain of recognizing a face which I had once loved so dearly.

Of course it was not difficult to get at the truth. I hurried to the hotel – on the way I saw my old boyhood friend Jaroslav, leading fiddle in the local cymbalo band, but avoided his eyes as if fleeing from his intrusive noisy music – and telephoned Kostka; he was still at the hospital.

'That hairdresser you left me with – might she be called Lucie Sebetkova by any chance?'

'She goes under a different name now, but that's her. How do you know her?' asked Kostka.

'It was ages ago,' I replied.

I didn't even go in to dinner; I walked out of the hotel in the gathering dusk, and began wandering round again.

Part II: Helena

1

Tonight I'm going to bed early. I don't know if I'll get any sleep, but I'm going early all the same. Pavel left for Bratislava this afternoon, I'm off to Brno tomorrow by plane and the rest of the way by bus. Zdenicka will be here on her own for two days, but she won't mind that. She doesn't like our company much, or my company rather – she adores her father, Pavel is the first man in her life, and he knows how to handle her, as he always did with women, as he did with me – and still does. Only this week he was his old self again, stroked my face and promised to look me up in Southern Moravia on his way back from Bratislava. He said we had a lot of things to talk over. Perhaps he's seen it was no good the way things were going and wants them to be the way they were before. But why now, now that I've met Ludvik? It's getting me down, but I mustn't be depressed, I mustn't. *Let sadness not be linked with my name* – those words of Julius Fucik's are my motto, and I don't care if they *are* out of date now. Maybe I'm silly, but the ones who say I am are silly themselves. They've got their slogans and mottoes, 'absurdity', 'alienation' and the rest, and I don't see why I should trade in my silliness for theirs. I don't want to split my life in two, I want it to be one life, one from beginning to end, and that's why I like Ludvik so much, because I don't have to alter my ideals and tastes when I'm with him. He's ordinary, straightforward, cheerful, says what he means, and these are the things I love, the things I've always loved.

I'm not ashamed of the way I am. I can't be different from what I've been and what I am. Until I was eighteen all I knew was being cooped up in a convent, T.B., two years in a sanatorium, another two years catching up on the schooling I'd

15

missed. I didn't even go dancing, all I knew was the tidy flat of a tidy Pilsen family and endless swotting for school. Life passed me by, then in '49 I went up to Prague, and all of a sudden it was like a miracle, I was so happy, I shall never forget it, and that's why I can never erase Pavel from my heart, even though I don't love him, even though he hurt me so much, I just can't. Pavel is my youth, Prague, the university, and most of all the Fucik Song and Dance Ensemble. Nowadays no one knows what all that meant to us. That's where I met Pavel, he sang tenor and I sang alto. We did hundreds of concerts and shows, we used to sing Soviet songs, our own building songs, and of course folk songs. Those were what we liked singing best, and I fell so much in love with Moravian folk songs that even though I was Pilsen born and bred I used to think of myself as a Moravian lass, and they became the leitmotiv of my life, and for me they merge with the whole of that time, with my youth, and I hear them every time my sun comes out, and I can hear them now, these last few days.

As for how I got to know Pavel, I can hardly bring myself to tell anyone these days. It was like something out of a school reader. It was the anniversary of the liberation and there was a big demonstration in Old Town Square. Our ensemble was there, we were always together, a little handful of people among the tens of thousands, and up on the rostrum there were politicians, speeches, applause, and then Togliatti came to the microphone and made a short speech in Italian, and the audience responded as usual by shouting, clapping, and stamping their feet. Somehow it happened that Pavel was standing right next to me in that enormous crowd, and I heard him shout something different, something of his own into that great clamour, and I looked at his lips moving and realized he was singing, or rather shouting, a song. He wanted people to hear him and join him in singing an Italian revolutionary song that was in our repertoire, and very popular at the time:

> *Avanti, popolo, a la riscossa,*
> *Bandiera rossa, bandiera rossa ...*

That was Pavel all over, he was not content with merely attacking one's reason, he wanted to strike at people's feelings as well. I thought it was marvellous to be greeting an Italian workers' leader in a Prague square with an Italian revolutionary song, and I longed for Togliatti to be moved, just as I had been moved. So I joined in with Pavel as loud as I could, and others joined in until the whole of our ensemble was singing it. But the clamour in the square was terribly loud and we were only a handful, fifty of us and more than fifty thousand of them, horribly outnumbered, fighting a hopeless battle. After the first verse we thought we would go under, that no one would hear us singing, but then the miracle happened. Gradually more and more voices joined in with us, people began to understand what was going on, and the song slowly wound its way out of the pandemonium on the square like a butterfly out of an enormous clamouring chrysalis. At last the butterfly, the song, or at least the last few bars, reached the rostrum and we gazed up eagerly at the Italian's face under his greying hair. We were happy when we thought we saw him respond to our singing with a movement of his hand, and I was even sure, although I couldn't possibly have seen from that distance, that I saw tears in his eyes.

And in the midst of that excitement and emotion, somehow, I don't know how, I suddenly gripped Pavel's hand, and Pavel replied by squeezing mine, and when the square was quiet again and someone else took the microphone I was afraid he would let go of my hand again, but he didn't. We stayed holding hands till the end of the demonstration, and didn't let go even afterwards. The crowds broke up and we spent several hours strolling together through a Prague decked with flowers.

Seven years later, when Zdenicka was five, he told me, and I shall never forget it, that 'we didn't marry for love, we married for Party discipline'. I know it was only said in the heat of an argument, I know it was a lie, I know Pavel married me for love and it was only afterwards that he changed. But even so it was a dreadful thing to say, because he was the one who was always arguing that love today was different from what it used to be, that it was not an escape from people but a support in the battle, and indeed that was the way it was for us. At midday we didn't even have time for lunch, all we ate were two dry rolls in the Youth League secretariat, and then we might not see each other again all day. I would wait for Pavel to come home around midnight from his endless six- or eight-hour meetings. In my spare time I typed the reports he had to read at all sorts of conferences and political instruction classes. He attached no end of importance to them, only I know how much store he set by the success of his political speeches. A hundred times he'd repeat in these speeches that the new man was different from the old in having abolished the distinction between his private and his public life. And now, years later, he suddenly complains that the Comrades in those days wouldn't leave his private life in peace.

We went around together for almost two years and I was getting a little impatient. There's nothing odd in that, no woman can remain content with just a student friendship. Pavel was, however, he'd got used to its convenient lack of ties. All men have a selfish streak, and it's up to the woman to stand up for herself and her mission as a woman. Unfortunately Pavel didn't appreciate this. The Comrades in the ensemble did, though, especially some of my girl friends, and they put their heads together with some of the others and finally summoned Pavel before a committee. I don't know what they said to him, we've never discussed it, but I don't imagine they made things too easy for him. Morals were very strict in those days, exaggeratedly so, but I dare say it's better to exaggerate morality than immorality, as they do today. Pavel kept out of my way for a long time and I thought I'd ruined everything. I was beside myself, I wanted to kill myself, but then he came to me, and my knees were trembling, and he asked me to forgive him, and gave me a locket with a picture of the Kremlin on it. It was his most treasured possession and I never take it off, for it means a lot more than just a keepsake of Pavel's. I cried with happiness and a fortnight later we were married, and the entire ensemble was at the wedding, and it went on for almost twenty-four hours, with singing and dancing. And I told Pavel that if we betrayed each other we would be betraying all the people who celebrated the wedding with us, betraying the demonstration in Old Town Square, betraying Togliatti. Today it makes me laugh to think of all the things we afterwards *did* betray . . .

2

Let me see, what shall I wear tomorrow? I think the pink cardigan and the plastic mac, they suit my figure best. I'm not the slimmest woman in the world nowadays, but maybe I've a different sort of attraction in return for my wrinkles, something the young girls don't have, the charm of experience. I know that's what I have for Jindra, poor lad, and I can still see his disappointed look when he heard I was flying off next morning and he would be going by himself. He's happy when he can be with me, and demonstrate his nineteen-year-old maturity in front of me. He'd do eighty with me, I'm sure, just for me to admire him. He's a plain sort of lad but an excellent mechanic and driver, editors like having him out in the field on small reporting jobs. Anyway, why not, it's nice to know there's someone who likes having me around – these last few years I haven't been too popular at the radio station. They say I'm a nuisance, a fanatic, a dogmatist, a Party bloodhound, and I don't know what else besides, but I don't see why I should feel ashamed of loving the Party and sacrificing all my spare time to it. What else have I left in life anyway? Pavel has other women, I never bother to check on them any more. My daughter adores only her father. My work has been exactly the same for the last ten comfortless years: reports, interviews, programmes about targets being met, cow sheds and milkmaids. Home is equally hopeless. It's only the Party that's never done me any harm, nor I it, not even in '56 when almost everyone wanted to desert it, when it all came out about Stalin, and people went mad and dropped everything, and said our papers told lies, our nationalized shops were no good, our culture was in decline, the collective farms should never have been set up, the Soviet Union was a slave state, and the worst thing was that even the Communists used to say these things at their own meetings, and Pavel used to say them and they would all clap him once more. Pavel was always being clapped, ever since he was a child he's been clapped. He was an only child, his mother took his photo to bed with her, her wonder child, though he's only an average husband, a non-smoker and a non-drinker, only he can't live without applause, that's his alcohol and his nicotine, and so he was glad to have the chance to pull at people's heart strings again, and he spoke about those dreadful executions with such feeling that people all but wept. I felt how much he enjoyed being indignant, and I hated him.

Luckily the Party rapped the hysterical ones over the knuckles and they grew quieter. Pavel calmed down too, his post as university lecturer in Marxism was far too cushy for him to risk it. But something remained in the air, a germ of apathy, mistrust, misgiving, a germ that went on quietly and secretly multiplying. I didn't know how to counter it and I clung to the Party more tightly than ever, and now it's as if the Party was a living being, something human, something special, more female than male, a wise woman to confide in, at a time when I have nothing to say to anyone, and not just to Pavel – the others don't care for me either. That became obvious at the time of a worrying episode when one of our editors, a married man, was having an affair with a young girl on the technical staff, irresponsible and cynical, and the editor's wife in desperation turned to our committee for help. We spent hours discussing the case and interviewing the wife, the girl and witnesses from her department, one after the other. We tried to see every point of view and be fair. The editor received a Party reprimand, the girl was admonished and they both had to promise to split up. Unfortunately words are merely words, and they only said it to keep us quiet and went on seeing each other. But truth will out and we soon learned about it, and I took the hard line and proposed that the editor be expelled for deliberately deceiving and misleading the Party. After all, what sort of a Communist is it that would lie to the Party? I hate lies. But my proposal was not accepted and the editor escaped with another reprimand, while the girl had to leave the company.

They really got back at me for that, making me out to be a beast and a monster. They led a regular campaign against me and began prying into my private life, and this was my Achilles heel, because no woman can live without emotion, otherwise she wouldn't be a woman. Why deny it? Since I didn't have love at home I'd looked for it elsewhere, and even so had looked in vain. They laid into me at a public meeting and called me a hypocrite, trying to pillory other people for disrupting marriages, trying to expel and dismiss and destroy when I myself was unfaithful to my husband whenever I had the chance. That was how they put it at the meeting, but behind my back they said even worse things. They said I was a nun in public and a whore in private. As if they were incapable of understanding that it was my unhappy marriage which made me strict towards others, not from hatred towards them, but from love, from love of love, love for their homes, for their children, because I wanted to help them, and because I too have a child and a home and am afraid for them.

But then again maybe they are right, maybe I really am just a malicious old woman, and people really should be allowed their freedom, and no one has the right to meddle in their private affairs. Maybe we did have our picture of the world all wrong and I really am just a horrid commissar sticking my nose into things which are none of my business. But that's what I'm like and I can only act as I feel. It's too late to change now. I've always believed that people are one and indivisible and that only the petty bourgeois is hypocritically divided between his public self and his private self. That was my credo and I've always acted on it, and so I did in this case.

And if they say I'm spiteful, then I readily admit that I hate these young girls, these raw brats with the cruelty of youth, without an ounce of compassion for older women. They'll be thirty one day, and thirty-five and forty. And don't let anyone say that she loved him. What does she know about love? She'll sleep with any man the first time, she's got no inhibitions, no sense of shame. I feel insulted to the core when anyone compares me with girls like that just because I as a married woman have had affairs with other men. I've always looked for love and if I made a mistake and didn't find it I shrank away and went elsewhere, even though I knew how simple it would be to forget my girlish dreams about love, forget them and cross the frontier into the land of wondrous freedom, where shame and inhibitions and morals no longer exist, the land of strange, disgusting freedom, where everything is permitted, where men and women turn into beasts.

And I know too that if I crossed that border I'd cease to be myself, I'd become somebody else, I don't know who, and I'm terrified of it, that dreadful change, and that's why I'm looking for love, a love into which I could enter just as I am, with my old dreams and ideals, because I don't want my life split in two, I want to keep it one from beginning to end, and that's why I was so fascinated when I met you, Ludvik, oh Ludvik ...

3

It was really rather funny the way I first walked into his office. He didn't make much impression on me and I got down to business straight away. I told him what I needed to know, and how I saw the feature shaping. But when he started to talk to me I suddenly found myself confused and tongue-tied, and when he saw my embarrassment he turned the conversation to general topics, asked whether I was married, whether I had any children, where I went for my holidays. And he said I looked young and pretty. He wanted to help me get over my shyness and that was nice of him. I've known egotists galore who aren't a tenth as clever as he is. Pavel would have talked entirely about himself. But it was really funny the way I spent a whole hour with him and knew no more about his institute at the end than I did at the beginning. Back home I threw something together but it just wouldn't come right, perhaps I was glad it didn't, at least I had an excuse for telephoning him and asking him if he'd be so kind as to read over what I'd written. We met in a coffee house and my unfortunate feature was only four pages long. He read it and smiled gallantly and said it was excellent, and made it clear from the start that I interested him as a woman and not as a journalist, and I didn't know whether to feel pleased or offended at this, but he was nice to me and we seemed to get on. He wasn't a wishy-washy intellectual of the kind I dislike. He had a full life behind him, had even worked down the mines, and I told him that those were the people I liked, people whose lives were straight out of Gorky, but what shook me most was that he was from Southern Moravia, had even played in a cymbalo band. I couldn't believe my ears, I recognized the leitmotiv of my own life, saw my youth across a great gulf, and felt my heart going out to Ludvik.

He asked me what I did all day, and I told him, and he said – I can still hear his voice, half-joking, half-sympathetic – 'My dear lady, that is no sort of a life.' And then he said it must be changed, I must start living differently, paying a little more heed to the joys of life. I told him I had nothing against that, joy had always been my creed and there's nothing I loathe more than all these fashionable mopings and bore-doms, and he said it was of no account what my creed was, because those who profess joy are usually the saddest people of all, and I felt like shouting 'You're right! Oh, you're so right!', and then he said straight out that he'd call for me the next day at four o'clock outside the radio building and we'd take a trip together into the country. I protested that I was a married woman, that I couldn't just go out into the woods like that with a strange man, and Ludvik answered jokingly that he wasn't a man, only a scientist. But how miserable he looked as he said it! Seeing him look so miserable made me all hot with joy that he wanted me and wanted me all the more because I was married, because it set us further apart, and men always want most what is most unattainable, and I eagerly drank in all the sadness in his face and saw in that instant that he was in love with me.

And next day the Vltava murmured on one side of us and

the forest rose sheer on the other, and it was all utterly romantic. I love things to be romantic and I behaved like a silly girl, not like the mother of a twelve-year-old daughter. I laughed, I skipped about, I took him by the hand and made him run with me, and we stopped and my heart was beating, and we were standing close together face to face, and Ludvik bent down slightly and kissed me gently, and I pulled away from him and took him by the hand and we ran on again. I have a spot of bother with my heart, it beats like mad after the slightest exertion, I only need to run up a flight of stairs, so I slowed down a little and gradually my breathing became quieter and I began humming the first two bars of my favourite song, 'The sun shone out over our garden'. . . . And when I felt he was with me I began singing it out loud, quite uninhibited, and I felt all the years, cares, worries, thousands of grey scales falling off me. And later we sat in a little inn at Zbraslav and ate bread and sausage, and everything was quite simple and ordinary, with a surly landlord and a stained cloth, and yet such a lovely adventure. I said to Ludvik: 'Do you know I'm going to South Moravia for three days to do a feature on the Ride of the Kings?' He asked me where exactly, and when I told him he said that was where he was born, and it was such a coincidence that it took my breath away. He said: 'I'll take some time off and come with you.'

I was alarmed when I thought of Pavel and that little spark of fresh hope he'd kindled in me. I'm not cynical about my marriage and I'm ready to do anything to protect it, for Zdenicka's sake, or, more truthfully, for my own sake, for the sake of everything that ever was, the memory of my youth. But I didn't have the strength to say no to Ludvik, I just didn't have the strength, and now the die is cast. Zdenicka is asleep and I'm frightened. Ludvik is already in Moravia and tomorrow he'll be waiting for me when my coach arrives.

Part III: Ludvik

1

Yes; I began wandering round again. I stopped on the bridge across the Morava and gazed downstream. What a repulsive river the Morava is – brown as if running with mud instead of water – and how dismal its banks look: a street of five single-storey middle-class houses, each standing on its own, eccentric and forlorn. Perhaps they were intended as the basis of a river-side prospect whose proud lines had never been realized. Two of them have angels and small scenes carved in ceramic and stucco, which today of course are chipped and cracked: the angel is wingless, and the scenes have been stripped in places down to the bare brick and lost their continuity. Then the street of orphan houses peters out, and there are only iron electricity pylons, grass with a few straggling geese, then fields, fields without horizons, fields stretching to nowhere, fields in which the liquid mud of the Morava is lost to sight.

Towns are well known for their ability to produce mirror images of each other, and this view, which I had known since childhood and which had nothing new to tell me, suddenly reminded me of Ostrava, that mining town full of deserted houses and dirty streets leading nowhere, like a huge make-shift doss-house. I had been decoyed; I stood there on the bridge like a man exposed to machine-gun fire. I could not bear to look at that woebegone street with its five solitary houses because I could not bear to think about Ostrava. So I turned round and looked upstream.

Along the bank there was a path, flanked on one side by a thick row of poplars to form a narrow promenade, from which the bank dropped down to a surface overgrown with grass and weeds; across the river, on the opposite bank, could be seen the stores, workshops and yards of several small factories. On the other side of the path there was first a sprawling rubbish tip, then again open fields punctuated by iron pylons. I went over it all along the narrow pathway as if stepping across a long footbridge over the waters – and if I liken the whole scene to wide expanses of water it is because it blew cold on me, and because I was walking along that path as if at some point I might suddenly plunge off it. I realized at the same time that the particular ghostly atmosphere of the landscape symbolized everything that I had not wanted to recall after my encounter with Lucie; it was as if the suppressed memories were being projected onto everything I saw, onto the desolation of the fields and yards and storehouses, onto the murk of the river and onto that ubiquitous chill which gave unity to the whole scene. I knew that there was no escaping the memories; that I was surrounded by them.

2

The events leading to my first major disaster – and through this harsh agency to Lucie – would be easy enough to relate in facetious tones and even with some amusement; the cause of it all being my fatal predilection for stupid jokes and Marketa's fatal inability to understand them. Marketa was serious in all things (and thus in perfect harmony with the spirit of the age), as well as being amply endowed with credulity. This is not a euphemistic way of suggesting that she was stupid; on the contrary, she was gifted and bright and in any case young enough, as a first-year student of nineteen, for her naïve trustfulness to number among her charms rather than her defects, particularly as it was accompanied by an indisputable physical attractiveness. In the faculty we all liked Marketa and we all more or less made a pass at her, which did not prevent some of us, at least, from making gentle and unmalicious fun of her at the same time.

Of course fun went down badly with Marketa, and even worse with the spirit of the age. It was the first year after

February 1948; the new life had begun, a completely different life, and the features of this new life, as I remember them, were rigidly serious – though the seriousness took the surprising form, not of a frown, but of a smile; yes, those years proclaimed that they were the most radiant of all years, and anyone who failed to rejoice was immediately suspected of lamenting the victory of the working class, or, equally sinful, of being *individualistically* submerged in his own inner sorrows.

I had few inner sorrows at that time, moreover I had a considerable sense of fun; yet it cannot be said that I was accepted without reservations by that radiant age. My jokes were not serious enough, and the joyousness of the time did not take kindly to irony or practical jokes. It was, as I have said, a very serious kind of joy, proudly entitling itself 'the historic optimism of a victorious class', an ascetic and ceremonial joy; Joy, one might say, with a capital J.

I remember how in those days the entire faculty was organized into so-called study groups, which met fairly frequently for mutual public criticism and self-criticism, and to work out an assessment of each of its members. At that period, like any other Communist, I had plenty of responsibility (I held an important post in the League of University Students) and, as I was also a good student, it was hardly likely that these evaluations would affect me adversely. But the sentences acknowledging my efficiency, my correct attitude to the State, my work and my knowledge of Marxism were usually followed by one about my lingering 'traces of individualism'. A qualification of this kind need not have been dangerous, as it was customary to include some critical remark in even the best testimonials, to castigate 'lack of interest in revolutionary theory', or 'coldness in dealing with people', or 'lack of alertness and vigilance', or even 'an incorrect attitude to women'; but whenever these were not the only factors involved, when a further note of reservation was sounded, or when one was involved in some sort of conflict, or under suspicion or attack, 'traces of individualism' or 'an incorrect attitude to women' could become the seeds of one's

27

destruction. And there was a particular fatality about the fact that every one of us, yes, every single one of us, carried such a seed around with him in the form of his Party card.

Sometimes, more in fun than from any real concern, I would defend myself against the charge of individualism and ask my colleagues for proof. Their evidence was not particularly concrete; they would say:

'It's the way you behave.'

'How do I behave?' I would ask.

'You always have that strange smile.'

'So what? I enjoy life.'

'No, you smile as if you were thinking to yourself.'

When the Comrades classified my conduct and smile as intellectual – another notorious pejorative of those days – I actually came to believe them, since it was beyond the limits of my audacity to imagine that all the others could be wrong, that the Revolution itself and the spirit of the age could be wrong, or that I, a mere individual, could be right. I began to exert some constraint over my smiling, and presently to feel a tiny crack opening up between the person I was and the person who (according to the spirit of the age) I ought to be and tried to be.

But which of them was really me? To be completely honest, I was the man with several faces.

And I acquired more and more of them. About a month before the vacation I began to get friendly with Marketa (she was first year while I was second) and, like any young man of twenty, I stupidly tried to impress her by donning a mask: I pretended to be more mature and experienced than I was, I assumed an air of aloofness, I put on an act of looking down on the world from above, and wearing an additional layer of skin, invisible and impenetrable. I thought, quite correctly as it turned out, that humour would reinforce my aloofness, and, even though I had always been one for a laugh, the banter I carried on with Marketa was particularly forced, affected and tedious.

But which was the real me? I repeat: I was the man with many faces.

At meetings I was earnest, enthusiastic and convinced; among my closest friends I was teasingly provocative; with Marketa I was cynical and fitfully scintillating; and when I was alone, and thinking of Marketa, I was as helplessly excited as a schoolboy.

Was this last face perhaps the real one?

No. All the faces were real: I did not, as hypocrites do, have one real face and various false ones. I had several faces only because I was young and did not know who I was or who I wanted to be. But the difference between all these faces frightened me; none of them seemed to fit properly and I changed from one to the other clumsily and haphazardly.

The psychological and physiological machinery of love is so complex that at a certain period in his life a young man has to give his almost exclusive concentration to the mere business of mastering it, and in this way he misses the actual content of love – the woman he loves. (Just as a young violinist cannot concentrate properly on the content of a work until he has mastered the manual technique well enough to play without having to think.) If I have spoken of a schoolboyish excitement in my thoughts of Marketa I must supplement this by saying that the excitement sprang not so much from the degree of my infatuation as from the awkwardness and uncertainty whose weight I could feel and which came to rule my emotions and thoughts much more than did Marketa.

To ease the weight of my embarrassment and awkwardness I showed off in front of Marketa, disagreeing with her at every opportunity, or just poking fun at her opinions, which was not all that difficult, for despite her intelligence (and her beauty, which, like all beauty, suggested to those around an illusory inaccessibility) she was a girl of trusting simplicity, who could never look behind anything, and saw only the thing itself. Thus she had a remarkable understanding of botany, but frequently failed to see the point of a funny story. Similarly, though she allowed herself to be carried along by all the enthusiasms of the time, when confronted with some political action carried out on the principle of the End justifying the Means she would become as hard of understanding as when told a joke. From this the Comrades concluded that she needed to fortify her enthusiasm with knowledge of the strategy and tactics of the revolutionary movement, and resolved that during the vacation she should take part in a fourteen-day course of Party instruction.

This did not suit me at all, as I had intended being alone with Marketa in Prague for this fortnight in order to put our relationship, which up to then had consisted of walks, talks and a few kisses, on a more definite footing. I had only that fortnight – I had to spend the next four weeks on an agricultural work party and the last fortnight of the vacation with my mother in Moravia – and I reacted with painful jealousy when Marketa, so far from sharing my annoyance about the course, told me she was looking forward to it.

From the course, which took place in some castle in Central Bohemia, she sent me a characteristic letter, full of earnest agreement with everything happening to her. She liked it all, even the early morning P.T., the speeches, the discussions, the songs; she described the 'healthy atmosphere' which prevailed there, diligently adding her opinion that the Revolution in the West would not be long in coming.

As far as that goes, I agreed with everything Marketa said; I even believed in a speedy revolution in western Europe. There was one thing, however, I did not agree with: that she should be so happy and contented when I was missing her so much. So I bought a postcard and, to hurt, shock and confuse her, wrote:

> Optimism is the opium of the people! The healthy atmosphere stinks! Long live Trotsky!
> Ludvik

3

Marketa answered my provocative postcard with a brief letter-card bearing a few trite words, and made no reply to the other letters I sent her during the vacation. I was somewhere in

Sumava, raking hay with a students' work party, and Marketa's silence put me in very low spirits indeed. I wrote to her almost every day, letters full of a pleading, mournful infatuation; couldn't we, I begged her, at least see something of each other during the last fortnight of the vacation? I was willing to give up my trip home, forego seeing my poor deserted mother, do anything to see Marketa; not merely because I liked her but because she was the only woman on my horizon, and being a boy without a girl was an unbearable state of affairs. But Marketa didn't answer my letters.

I couldn't understand what was going on. I arrived in Prague in August and managed to catch her at home. We went for our usual walk along the Vltava, on to the island – the Emperor's meadow, that dismal field with its maple trees and empty playgrounds; and Marketa told me that nothing had changed between us and acted accordingly – but with that unwavering *sameness* (sameness of kiss, sameness of conversation, sameness of smile) which I found so depressing. When I asked her for a date next day she told me to phone her and we would arrange things then.

I phoned – and an unfamiliar woman's voice told me Marketa had left Prague.

I was unhappy as only a womanless young man of twenty can be; a young man, that is, who was rather shy, who had brushed with physical love on only a few occasions, and then fleetingly and clumsily, but whose mind was constantly preoccupied with it. The days were unbearably long and useless; I couldn't read, I couldn't work, I went to the pictures three times a day, to one performance after another, just to kill time, and to drown the owl's screech that kept issuing from somewhere inside me. I, whom Marketa regarded, thanks to my own laborious attempts at showing off, as a man almost totally blasé about women, did not even have the courage to speak to the girls in the street, girls whose beautiful legs pierced me to the marrow.

And so I was heartily glad when September came at last, and with it the university term; also, a few days earlier, my work in the League of Students, where I had a room of my own and plenty to do. However, on the second day there was a telephone call summoning me to the Party secretariat. From that moment on I remember everything in complete detail: it was a sunny day, and as I left the League of Students building I felt the low spirits which had haunted me all the vacation slowly dissolving. It is fortunate that one's private passions are matched by a passion for public work; I was glad that this passion was drawing me into its embrace again, and I walked towards the secretariat with an agreeable feeling of curiosity. I rang the bell, and the door was opened by the committee chairman, a tall thin-faced youth with fair hair and ice-blue eyes. I gave him the standard greeting, 'Honour to Labour', but instead of responding he said: 'Back there – they're waiting for you.' In the last room at the very back of the secretariat I found three members of the Party University Committee waiting for me. They told me to take a seat. As I sat down I could sense something ominous in the air. The three Comrades, with whom I was on terms of the utmost familiarity, had all adopted an unapproachable sort of manner; true, they used the familiar form of 'you' (as is the rule among Comrades), but this was an official and menacing brand of familiarity rather than an amiable one. (I confess that from that time on I have had an aversion to this form of address; it is supposed to express confidence and intimacy, but if the people using it are strangers it comes to express rudeness instead, so that a world in which people use it as a general rule is not a world of general amicability but one of general disrespect.)

I sat in front of those three students and they asked me the first question: did I know Marketa? I said I did. Had I written to her? I had. Did I remember what I had written? I said I didn't, but as I did so the postcard with its provocative text popped up in front of my eyes and I began to have some idea of what this was about. 'Can't you remember?' they asked me. I said I couldn't. 'And what did Marketa write to you?' I shrugged my shoulders, as if to imply that she had written about intimate matters which I couldn't possibly discuss there. 'Didn't she write anything about the course?' they asked. 'Yes,

she did,' I said. 'What did she say?' 'That she was enjoying it.'
'And?' 'And she wrote that the speeches were good and the
staff were good.' 'Did she tell you there was a healthy atmosphere prevailing on the course?' 'Yes,' I said, 'I believe she
did write something of the sort.' 'Did she tell you she was dis-
covering the power of optimism?' they continued. I said she
had. 'And what do *you* think of optimism?' they asked. 'Optimism? What am I expected to think of it?' 'Do you consider
yourself an optimist?' they persisted. 'Yes,' I said with some
diffidence. 'I like a bit of fun, I'm a man who likes having a
good time,' I added, trying to lighten the tone of the interview.
'The lover of life can be a nihilist as well,' said one of them.
'He may even enjoy a laugh at the expense of those who suffer.
He can be a cynic as well,' he went on. 'Do you think Socialism can be built without optimism?' asked another of them.
'No,' I said. 'Then you're opposed to Socialism being built
in this country,' said the third. 'What do you mean?' I said
defensively. 'Because for you optimism is the opium of the
people.' They were on the attack. 'What do you mean, opium
of the people?' I was still on the defensive. 'Don't try and
dodge the issue – that's what you wrote. Marx called religion
the opium of the people, but you think our optimism is
opium! That's what you wrote to Marketa. I should like to
hear what our workers would have to say, those shock-workers
busy over-fulfilling the plans, if they were to learn that their
optimism is opium.' Another one had taken it up. And the
third added: 'For a Trotskyite constructive optimism is always opium. And you are a Trotskyite.' 'For heaven's sake,
where did you get that idea?' I asked. 'Did you write it or
didn't you?' 'I may have written something of the kind as a
joke. Anyway it was two months ago and I don't remember.'
'We can remind you,' they said and read my postcard aloud:
'Optimism is the opium of the people! The healthy atmosphere stinks! Long live Trotsky! Ludvik.' The words sounded so awful in the little room belonging to the political
secretariat that I was afraid of them and felt they had a destruc-
tive power against which I was powerless to resist. 'Comrades,
it was meant as a joke,' I said, feeling no one could possibly

believe me. 'Do you consider it funny?' one of the Comrades asked the other two. Both shook their heads. 'You'd have to know Marketa,' I said. 'We do,' they replied. 'Well then,' I said, 'Marketa takes everything seriously, and we've always made fun of her and tried to shock her.' 'Interesting,' said one of the Comrades. 'We wouldn't have thought from your other letters that you didn't take Marketa seriously.' 'Do you mean you've read all my letters to Marketa?' 'So it's because Marketa takes everything seriously,' said the second one, 'that you make fun of her. But tell us, what is it that she takes seriously? The Party, optimism, duty, wouldn't you say? And all those things she takes seriously are one big joke to you.' 'Look, Comrades,' I said, 'I don't even remember writing it, I dashed it off, just a couple of sentences, as a joke, without thinking what I was writing. If I'd had some sinister motive I wouldn't have sent it to a Party School!' 'It's immaterial how you wrote it. Whether you write it quickly or slowly, on your knee or on a table, you could only have written what you felt. Perhaps if you'd thought more about it you wouldn't have written it. As it is, you wrote without any dissimulation. As it is, we know who we're dealing with. We know at least that you're two-faced, one face for the Party and one for the rest.'

I felt I'd run completely out of arguments. I went on repeating the same things over and over again: that it was all a joke, that the words were meaningless, that it was just the way I felt at the time, and so on. I made no impression on them whatever. They said I had written my sentences on an open postcard and that anyone could have read them, that the words had an *objective* content and that they were not accompanied by any explanatory notes on my mood at the time. Then they asked me how much Trotsky I had read. I told them none at all. They asked who had lent me the books. I said no one. They asked me to name the Trotskyites I had meetings with. I said I didn't know any. They told me they were relieving me as from that moment of my post in the League of Students and demanded the keys to my room. These were in my pocket and I handed them over. Then they told me that my case as a Party matter would be decided by my branch at the Natural

Sciences Faculty. They stood up and looked right through me. I said 'Honour to Labour' and left.

. Then I remembered that I had a lot of my own things in my room in the League offices. I have never had much idea of tidiness, and my desk drawer contained my socks as well as various private papers, while nestling among the official documents in the cupboard was a cut plum cake which my mother had sent me. I had just given up my key, but the porter on the ground floor knew me and gave me the master key, which used to hang with a lot of other keys on a wooden board. I remember every detail: the key of my room was attached by a strong hempen cord to a small wooden board, on which the number of my room was written in white. With this key I unlocked the door and sat down at the desk; I opened a drawer and removed all my things from it; I worked slowly and with concentration, because I was trying in those few moments of relative peace and quiet to work out what had happened to me and what I had better do.

It was not long before the door opened, and in came the same three Comrades from the secretariat. This time they could hardly be described as looking cold or reserved; this time their voices were loud and excited, particularly the shortest one, the committee personnel officer, who snapped at me: how had I got in? What right did I have there? Did I want him to have the police take me away? And what was I doing ransacking the desk? I told him I had come for my plum cake and my socks. He told me I had no right whatever to come here even if I had a whole cupboard full of socks. Then he went to the desk and scrutinized paper after paper, notebook after notebook. They were in fact my own private belongings, which he finally allowed me to pack in my case while he watched. I put the socks in as well, crumpled and dirty, and the cake which was lying in the cupboard on a sheet of greaseproof paper covered in crumbs. They watched my every move. I left the room with my bag, and as I did so the personnel officer told me not to show my face there again.

As soon as I got out of range of the men from the District and the invincible logic of their interrogation, it appeared to me that I was innocent, that there was nothing evil in what I had written or said, and that I ought to go and see someone who was well acquainted with Marketa, someone whom I could confide in and who would understand that the whole business was ridiculous. I looked up one of the students from our faculty, a Communist, and when I told him the whole story he said the District was too bigoted, they had no sense of humour, but that he, knowing Marketa, had a shrewd idea of what it was all about. In any case I should go and see Pavel Zemanek who was to be this year's Party chairman of our faculty branch and who knew both myself and Marketa very well.

4

I had had no idea that Zemanek was to be branch chairman, and it struck me as excellent news, as I knew him very well indeed and was moreover confident that he would be entirely sympathetic on account of my Southern Moravian origins. For Zemanek loved singing Moravian songs; at that time there was a great vogue for singing folk songs, and for doing so not in a pedantic or reverential fashion, but with one's hand above one's head in a rather harsh sort of voice, with the air of a really folksy character whom his mother has delivered into the world during some folk dance, to the sound of the cymbalo.

In the Natural Sciences Faculty I was the only genuine Moravian Slovak and this brought me certain privileges; on every formal occasion, at meetings, celebrations or on the First of May, the Comrades invited me to take my clarinet and join two or three other amateurs among my fellow students to produce an imitation Moravian band. In this way (with clarinet, violin and bass) we had for two years marched at the head of the Mayday procession; and Zemanek, being a handsome young man who loved to perform, would march with us dressed in a borrowed folk costume, would dance in the procession and wave his arms in the air and sing. This Prague boy born and bred, who had never been near Moravian Slovakia in his life, greatly enjoyed acting the village swain, and I regarded him in a friendly light because I was happy that the music of my homeland, long the El Dorado of folk art, should be so much loved and favoured.

And Zemanek knew Marketa, which was another advantage. The three of us often found ourselves together at student functions; and on one occasion, among a rather larger group, I had invented some nonsense about tribes of dwarfs living in Sumava, illustrating it with quotations from an alleged scientific work on this remarkable topic. Marketa was astonished that she had never heard of these dwarfs. I said it was not surprising: bourgeois science had deliberately suppressed their existence, as the capitalists had bought and sold them as slaves.

'But someone ought to write about it!' cried Marketa. 'Why isn't there anything written about it? It would make a very strong case against the capitalists!'

'Perhaps we don't write about it,' I pronounced thoughtfully, 'because the whole subject is rather delicate and scandalous: the dwarfs had an extraordinary capacity for the act of love, and that was why they were so much sought after and why our Republic secretly exported them for fat sums of foreign currency, particularly to France, where they were engaged by ageing capitalist women as servants – though naturally destined for another use altogether.'

The others stifled their laughter, which was aroused not so much by any particular wittiness in my invention as by Marketa's absorbed expression, her perpetual readiness to show enthusiasm for (or against) anything and everything; they bit their lips so as not to spoil Marketa's joy in acquiring knowledge, and some of them, Zemanek in particular, joined in and confirmed my account of the dwarfs. When Marketa asked what they actually looked like, I remember Zemanek with a serious expression telling her that Professor Cechura, whom Marketa and all her classmates had the occasional honour of seeing behind his professorial desk, was of dwarfish stock, possibly on both sides, certainly on one. Zemanek had apparently been told by one of the lecturers how he had once spent a holiday in the same hotel as the Cechuras, who between them were not quite nine feet in height. One morning he had entered their room without realizing they were still asleep, and was horrified to find them lying in the same bed, not side by side but one below the other, Cechura huddled in the lower half of the bed and his wife in the upper.

Yes, I confirmed: this proved beyond doubt that both Cechura and his wife were Sumava dwarfs by origin, because sleeping head to toe was the atavistic custom of all the dwarfs in that region, and in earlier days they would never build their huts on circular or square plots but always on extended rectangles, since not only husband and wife but entire clans were accustomed to sleep in a long chain, one below the other.

Recalling this little piece of nonsense on that black day, I seemed to see in it a faint glimmer of hope. Knowing my sense of humour and knowing Marketa, Zemanek would understand that the postcard was merely a joke aimed at provoking a girl whom we all admired and, perhaps for that very reason, liked to belittle. And so at the first opportunity I gave him an account of my misfortune; Zemanek listened attentively, then frowned and said he would see.

Meanwhile I lived in a state of suspended animation, attending lectures as before, and waiting. I was hauled before numerous party commissions which were attempting to establish whether or not I belonged to a Trotskyite group; I tried to prove that I had no real idea even of what Trotskyism was. I met the glances of all those looking into my case and tried to read belief into them; sometimes I succeeded, and then I would carry the look with me for a long time, trying patiently to kindle a spark of hope from it.

Marketa continued to avoid me. I realized that this was on account of my postcard, and I was too proud and sensitive to feel like seeking her out. One day, however, she stopped me in a faculty corridor and said: 'I'd like to talk to you about something.'

And so we went out together for the first time in months. It was already autumn, and we were both wearing long trench coats, really long ones reaching below the knee, in the fashion of those inelegant days; there was a thin mist and the trees on the embankment were leafless and black. Marketa told me how it had all happened: while she was still on the course the Comrades running it had suddenly summoned her and asked her if she had received any mail there. She replied that she had. They asked where from. She said she had had letters from her mother. No one else? Oh, another student, she said. Could she tell them the name? She gave my name. And what did Comrade Jahn write? She shrugged her shoulders, not wanting to recite the words on my card. Had she written to him as well? She said she had. What had she written? Nothing much, she said, just about the course and things like that. Was she enjoying the course? Yes, she loved it. And had she told him that in her letter? Yes, she had. And what had he said? Marketa hesitated. 'He's a bit funny, you'd have to know him.' 'We do know him,' they replied, 'and we'd like to know what he wrote. Can you show us this card?'

'You mustn't be cross with me,' said Marketa, 'but I had to show them the card.'

'You don't need to apologize,' I told her. 'They knew all about it before they saw you – or they wouldn't have asked to see you.'

'I'm not apologizing,' she protested, 'and I'm not ashamed of having given them the card to read. You mustn't make it sound like that. You're a Party member and the Party has a right to know who you are and what you think.' And then she told me she had been horrified by what I had written: after all, we all knew that Trotsky was the arch-enemy of everything we were fighting for and everything we lived for.

What could I say to Marketa? I asked her to continue and she told me what happened next.

Marketa said they read the card and were shocked. They asked her opinion of it. She told them it was disgraceful. They asked her why she had not brought it along herself to show them. She shrugged her shoulders. They asked her whether she knew what alertness and vigilance meant. She looked down. They asked her whether she knew how many enemies the Party had. Yes, she knew, but she did not believe that Comrade Jahn ... They asked her if she knew me well, and what I was like. She said I was a bit funny – I was a staunch Communist but sometimes I would come out with things that a Communist ought not to say. They asked her for examples. She said she could not remember any specific instances, but that for me nothing was sacred. They said my postcard had made that abundantly clear. She told them that she often had arguments with me, and that I talked in one way at meetings and in another way with her. At meetings I was enthusiasm itself, whereas with her I would mock and disparage everything. They asked her whether she thought a man like me should be a member of the Party. She shrugged her shoulders. They asked her whether the Party could build Socialism if its members went about proclaiming that optimism was the opium of the people. She replied that a Party like that would never build Socialism. All right, they said, that would do. For the time being she was to tell me nothing about the interview, because they wanted to see what else I would write. She told them she never wanted to see me again. They said that this would be a mistake and that on the contrary she was to write to me, so that they could find out more about me.

'And so after that you showed them all my letters?' I asked, blushing to the depths of my soul at the recollection of my romantic effusions.

'What else could I have done?' said Marketa. 'But I simply couldn't go on writing to you after that, just to set a trap for you. I wrote you one more card and called it a day. I didn't want to see you because I wasn't supposed to tell you anything, and I was afraid you'd ask me questions and I wouldn't be able to lie to you, because I don't like telling lies.'

I asked Marketa what had inspired her to see me today.

She told me that Comrade Zemanek was responsible. He had met her after the vacation in the corridor of the faculty building, and had taken her into the little room where the Natural Sciences Faculty Party branch had its secretariat. He said he had heard about a postcard I had sent her containing anti-Party statements, and asked her for the words. She told him. He asked her what she thought of them. She said she condemned them. He told her she was right to do so and asked if she was still going around with me. She was embarrassed and answered evasively. He told her that the faculty had received very favourable reports about her from the summer school and that the faculty branch thought highly of her. She said she was glad they did. He told her that he did not want to interfere in her private life but that in his opinion a man is judged by the company he keeps and it would not be exactly an advantage for her to choose me.

This had apparently weighed heavily on Marketa's mind for weeks afterwards. She had not in fact seen me for several months, and Zemanek's suggestion was therefore quite superfluous; indeed, the very cruelty and moral inadmissability of suggesting to someone that she should desert her boyfriend just because he had made a mistake made her wonder whether she had been unfair when she stopped seeing me in the first place. She visited the Comrade who had been in charge of the vacation course and asked him whether the injunction of silence about the events surrounding the postcard still held; and on learning that there was no longer any reason for secrecy she had stopped me and asked to speak to me.

She then confided in me all the things that had been worrying her. She agreed that she had behaved badly in deciding not to see me any more; no man is completely damned, whatever the gravity of his mistakes. She said she had remembered the case of Alexey Tolstoy, who had been a White Guard and an emigré but who in the end had become a great Socialist writer in spite of this. She had also recalled the Soviet film *Honest Justice*, at that time very popular in Party circles, in which some Soviet medical scientist places his discovery at the disposal of another country before his own – an action smelling of 'cosmopolitanism' and treason. Marketa was visibly moved as she made her main point, the way the film ended: though the scientist is finally condemned by the honest justice of his colleagues, his wife does not desert her erring husband, but tries to inject her strength into him and help him to atone for his great wrong.

'So you've decided not to leave me,' I said.

'Yes,' said Marketa, and took me by the hand.

'But Marketa, do you really think I've done something seriously wrong?'

'Yes, I think you have.'

'Do you think I still have the right to remain in the Party, or not?'

'I think not, Ludvik.'

I knew that if I had been willing to enter into the spirit of the play which Marketa was living out I would have succeeded where months ago I had failed: impelled as she was by the pathos of her chosen role of redeeming woman, like a steamship by its steam, she would doubtless have given herself to me body and soul. But this would, of course, have been on one condition: that her salvationist urge should be fully gratified by the object of redemption – in other words myself – conceding its own profound guilt. And that was the one thing I could not do. I stood inches from the much-desired goal of Marketa's body, and yet I was unable to take it at that price, because I was unable to concede my guilt and bow before an intolerable verdict; I could not bear to hear anyone with whom I was intimate acknowledging this guilt and pronouncing verdict on it.

I did not give in to Marketa, I refused her, and so I lost her. Did I then feel myself blameless? Certainly I kept assuring myself of the stupidity of the whole affair, but even as I did so (and today, after all these years, this seems the hardest and strangest thing of all) I started seeing those three sentences on the postcard through the eyes of the men who had interrogated me; I began to feel outraged by the words, and to fear that behind the façade of my humour there did in fact lurk something serious and sinister, that I had never really been one with the body of the Party, never been a true proletarian revolutionary, but had 'gone over to the revolutionaries' on the basis of a mere personal decision. (I may say that we felt our revolution to be less a thing of choice than of essence: a man is either a revolutionary, in which case he merges with the movement into one collective body, thinks with its head and feels with its heart, or he is not, in which case he can only *wish* he was one. But then he is constantly guilty of not being one; he is guilty in being on his own, in being different, in not merging.)

Looking back on my state of mind at that time I am reminded of the enormous analogous power of Christianity to persuade the believer of his own fundamental and unceasing sinfulness. I stood, we all stood, before the Revolution and its Party with our heads continually lowered; and so, as I gradually came to accept the idea that my message, however jokingly intended, was still a matter for guilt, a reel of critical self-denunciation wound itself through my head. I told myself that those words of mine were no mere incident, but exemplified all too well the 'traces of individualism' and 'intellectual tendencies' with which the Comrades had formerly chided me; that I had taken to preening myself too much on my education, my undergraduate status and my future as a member of the intelligentsia; and that my father, an ordinary working man who had died during the war in a concentration camp, would have found it hard to understand my cynicism. I reproached myself with the fact that his working-class outlook had, apparently and lamentably, died in me; I reproached myself on every possible score and even became reconciled to the necessity for some form of punishment. One thing, however, I did resist, and that was my expulsion from the Party and consequent branding as its enemy; to live as the branded enemy of everything I had chosen as a boy, and to which I had clung so closely, seemed to me a hopeless sort of existence.

Such was the self-criticism – at the same time a kind of whimpering self-justification – which I recited a hundred times to myself, at least ten times before various committees and commissions, and finally at the decisive plenary session of our faculty organization, when Zemanek delivered his brilliant and unforgettable opening address on myself and my errors, and proposed on behalf of the committee that I be expelled from the Party. The discussion which followed my piece of self-denunciation went against me; no one took my part, and finally the meeting – there were about a hundred people present, including my teachers and my most intimate friends – decided by a unanimous show of hands to approve not only my expulsion from the Party, but – and this I had not expected – my enforced departure from the university.

That same night I got on a train and went home, but home brought me no comfort, because for several days I could not pluck up the courage to tell my mother, who took a proud interest in my studies, what had happened. Then on the second day Jaroslav called round, a school friend who had also played in the same folk ensemble at that time, and was delighted to find me at home: it seemed he was to be married in two days' time and wanted me to attend as 'witness' according to the traditional local wedding rites. I couldn't refuse an old friend; and so I found myself celebrating my downfall with the festivities of a wedding.

Jaroslav was in all things a dyed-in-the-wool local patriot and Moravian folklore expert, and he even put his own wedding to the service of his beloved lore, cramming it with old popular rights: national costume, a cymbalo band, a 'giver' pronouncing florid speeches, the carrying of the bride over the threshold, songs, and an entire day of ceremonies which, of course, he had reconstructed more from books than from any living memory. But one curious thing caught my attention: my friend Jaroslav, the enthusiastic leader of a thriving song and dance ensemble, while retaining every possible old custom, was, it seemed, sufficiently mindful of his career, and obedient to atheistic slogans, to give the church a wide berth, although a 'traditional' wedding without priest or God's blessing was unthinkable; similarly he had the 'giver' utter all the popular ceremonial speeches, but carefully omitting any biblical motifs, although it was precisely these which constituted the principal imagery of the traditional formulae.

The low spirits which prevented me from joining in the drunken wedding festivities made it possible for me to scent chloroform in the spring-water of the traditional rites, and beneath the apparent spontaneity I detected a streak of falsehood. And when Jaroslav asked me, as a sentimental reminder of old times, to take my clarinet and sit in with the other players, I refused. I remembered the last two Maydays, when Prague-born Zemanek danced along beside me in national costume, throwing his arms in the air and singing; I could not take up my clarinet, and the whole business of high-pitched folk squealing suddenly made me feel sick, sick to the very soul . . .

5

By forfeiting my right to study, I forfeited also my right to defer national service. To fill in the period of waiting for the autumn draft I did two long stints with a labour gang: first on road repairs somewhere near Gottwaldov, and at the end of the summer on seasonal work with Fruta, the fruit processing plant. Finally autumn came, and one morning, after a sleepless night on the train, I made my way to the barracks in a grim and unfamiliar suburb of Ostrava.

I stood in the barrack square along with other young lads drafted to the same regiment. We were complete strangers to each other. In the gloom of this initial mutual unfamiliarity the harshness and the strangeness of others shows sharp in the foreground; so it was then, the only human bond between us being our uncertain future, about which brief conjectures fluttered to and fro. Some maintained we were in the 'black' division, others denied this, others again did not even know what it meant. I knew all right, and these surmises filled me with horror.

Then the sergeant came for us and led us away into one of the blocks. We poured along the passageway and into a large room with enormous posters and slogans, photographs and primitive drawings all over the walls. On the end wall was pinned up a large inscription WE ARE BUILDING SOCIALISM, cut in red paper, and under this inscription there was a chair with a wizened little old man standing beside it. The sergeant pointed at one of us, who then had to sit on the chair. The old man tied a white sheet round his neck, put his hand in a bag which was leaning against the chair-leg, drew out an electric hair-cutter and plunged it into the lad's hair.

The barber's chair inaugurated a production belt designed to turn us into soldiers: from the chair on which we forfeited our hair we were hustled into another room, where we had to strip down, pack our clothes into a paper bag, tie this with a string and hand it in at a window; then, naked and shorn, we proceeded along the corridor to the next room, where we were issued with nightshirts; in our nightshirts we made our way through another door, where we received our heavy boots; in boots and nightshirts we marched across the square to another block, where we were given shirts, pants, socks, belts and battle dress (there were ominous black facings on the tunics . . .); finally we reached the last block, where an N.C.O. read out our names, divided us into companies and assigned us rooms and bunks in the barracks.

Thus, with remarkable speed, each of us was stripped of his own will and became something externally resembling an object (dumped, disposed, despatched, consigned) and internally something like a man (suffering, irritated, apprehensive). That same day we were ordered on parade, then to supper, then to our bunks; in the morning we were woken up and taken out to the mines; at the pithead we were assigned to production gangs by companies and issued with tools – drill, shovel, safety lamp – which none of us knew how to use; then the cage carried us below ground.

When we surfaced again with aching bodies the N.C.O.s were waiting for us, assembled us and marched us to the barracks for dinner. After dinner there was drill, and after drill kit-cleaning, political instruction and compulsory singing. Our every human activity was replaced by the impersonal, prescribed functions we carried out. For private life we had a twenty-bunk room. And so it went on from day to day.

The depersonalization which had overwhelmed us appeared in those first days to be utterly opaque. The impersonal, prescribed functions we carried out replaced every human activity. The opaqueness, of course, was only relative, being caused not so much by the actual conditions as by the eye being unaccustomed to them (just as when one enters a dark room after being in bright daylight). After a time it slowly began to grow clearer and in that twilight of depersonalization the men's humanity began to show. I have to admit that I was one of the last to accommodate his vision to the altered light.

This was because my entire being refused to accept its fate. The soldiers with their black facings among whom I found myself were drilled in only the most perfunctory way, they had no weapons, and they worked in the mines. They were paid for their work – and indeed paid better than other troops – but for me this was a very poor consolation. We consisted entirely of those whom the young Socialist republic was unwilling to entrust with arms because it regarded them as its enemies. Obviously this led to rougher treatment and the threat of our military service stretching on longer than the normal compulsory two years; but what horrified me more than anything was finding myself in the midst of men I considered my own mortal enemies as well as the State's and knowing that I had been assigned to them, definitively and irrevocably, by my own Comrades. I spent the early period in the black or penal division as a stubborn recluse; I did not want to get used to my enemies, I did not want to become acclimatized among them. At that time the question of any time off was a very tricky one indeed (the private had no claim to leave but received it merely as a *reward*, which in practice meant that he got out once a fortnight, on alternate Saturdays), but on those days, when the soldiers surged out in gangs to the bars and after the girls, I preferred to be left on my own. I would lie down on my bunk in the hut, trying to read or even to study (for certain branches of mathematics all one needs is pencil and paper), and drawing nourishment from my nonconformity. I took the view that I had only one job to do there: to continue the fight for my political honour, for my right not to be regarded as an enemy, my right to be somewhere else.

I paid several visits to the company's Political Officer and tried to convince him that my presence in the penal corps was all a mistake; that I had been expelled from the Party for intellectualism and cynicism but not as an enemy of Socialism. For the umpteenth time I recounted the ridiculous story of the postcard, a story which now was by no means so funny and which in the context of my black epaulettes had become even more suspicious and appeared to harbour something which I was suppressing from my account. I am bound in all fairness to say that the Political Officer heard me out patiently and showed a somewhat unexpected understanding of my desire for justice; indeed, he made some inquiries about my case higher up (an indeterminate and invisible place); finally, however, he summoned me and said with unconcealed resentment:

'Why try to fool me? I've discovered you're a Trotskyite.'

I tried to grasp the fact that there was no power capable of altering the image of my own person as it was deposited somewhere in the supreme hall of decision governing human destinies; I understood that this image, however unlike me, was much more real than myself; that I was its shadow rather than it being mine; that its non-resemblance to myself was my fault and mine alone; and that this dissimilarity was my cross, which could not be shifted on to anyone else, but which was mine to bear.

Nonetheless I was unwilling to capitulate, I really wanted to bear the burden of my dissimilarity, and furthermore to go on being the person who it was decided that I was not.

It was about a fortnight before I became accustomed to the hard labour down the mines, holding the heavy drill whose vibrations I felt pulsating through my body even in my sleep. But I worked with a sort of diligent fury; I wanted to produce exceptional outputs, and soon I began to have some success.

Except that no one saw this as an expression of my conscientiousness. For we were paid piece rates – deductions were made for board and lodging, but that still left us plenty of spending money; and so many of the others, whatever their way of thinking, worked with considerable verve in order at least to wrest something worthwhile from those otherwise wasted years.

Even though everyone regarded us as violent enemies of the regime, all the forms of public life that are customary in Socialist collectives were maintained in the barracks; we, the enemies of the regime, were given ten-minute P.T. sessions under the eye of the Political Officer, we had political pep talks every day, we had to look after the notice boards, on which we pasted photographs of Socialist statesmen and painted slogans about the radiant tomorrow. At first I volunteered almost demonstratively for these tasks. But no one saw any evidence of conscientiousness in this either; all the others volunteered as well when they needed to be noticed by the Commanding Officer and granted an evening's leave. None of the men saw this political work for what it was, only as an empty tribute which had to be rendered up to those in power over us.

Then I saw that this defiance too was useless: that my 'dissimilarity' was noticed by myself alone, and that for the others it was invisible.

Among the N.C.O.s into whose tender mercies we were delivered was a dark-haired Slovak sergeant who was distinguished from the others by his mildness and complete lack of sadism. He was popular among us, though there were some who said maliciously that his kindheartedness sprang only from his stupidity. The N.C.O.s, of course, in contrast to ourselves, carried arms, and from time to time they went off for target practice. On one occasion the dark sergeant came back covered with the glory of having been placed first in marksmanship. A number of us were loud in our congratulations – which were half good-natured, half mocking; but the sergeant merely blushed.

Later that day, finding myself alone with him, I asked him, just for something to say: 'How do you manage to be such a good shot?'

The sergeant gave me a quizzical glance and said: 'It's a special dodge I've worked out. I pretend the tin target's an imperialist. And I get so angry that I hit the bull.'

I was about to ask him how he imagined this imperialist as looking (what sort of nose, hair, eyes and hat he had), but he stopped me dead by saying, seriously and thoughtfully: 'I don't know why you all congratulate me. If there was a war on I'd be shooting at you.'

Such a remark, coming from this goodhearted fellow, who never even shouted at us, and was later transferred for this reason, showed me that the threads connecting me with the Party and my Comrades had been broken beyond repair. I found myself left outside the main stream of my life.

6

Yes. Every thread was cut: my studies, my part in the Movement, my friendships, love and the quest for love, everything that had made life meaningful. I had nothing left but time. Time I came to know intimately as never before. It was not the time with which I had previously had dealings, a time metamorphosed into work, love, effort of every kind, a time I had accepted without interest because it was unobtrusive and kept itself decently out of my affairs. Now it came to me in all its starkness, in its true and original form, and forced me to name it by its real name (for now I was living sheer time, sheer empty time), so that I should not forget it for a moment, so that I should be constantly mindful and aware of its pressure.

When music is playing we hear the melody and forget that this is only one of the forms of time; when the orchestra ceases to play we hear time and only time. I was living in the pause. Not in the orchestral general pause whose dimensions are firmly set by the pause sign, but in a pause without ordained end. We could not, as they did in all other regiments, shave slivers off a tailor's measure to see the two years' service growing shorter with every day; the length of time the men in black could be kept in uniform was completely arbitrary. Forty-year-old Ambrose from B Company had been here four years already.

To be in the army at that time and to have a wife or fiancée at home was a very harsh fate indeed. Not only did your imagination stand permanently and uselessly on guard over her unguardable existence, keeping constant watch over her fateful inconstancies, but you were in a state of constant anticipation about her occasional visits, mixed with fear less on the appointed day the company commander should refuse leave, and she should come to the camp gates in vain. With a humour as black as their epaulettes, the men used to tell stories of officers lying in wait for these frustrated wives, and reaping the fruit of desires which rightly belonged to the privates confined in their barracks.

And yet for those with a wife or girl at home there was a thread stretching across the abyss, a desperately thin and fragile thread perhaps, but still a thread. I had no such thread; I had broken off all relations with Marketa, and the only letters I received came from my mother. . . . But wasn't this a sort of thread? No, it was not; home, the parental home, is not a thread. The letters received from parents are messages sent from a stronghold from which one is continually receding, and serve only to make you conscious of your alienation, because they remind you of the haven out of which you set sail under conditions so honestly, so unselfishly created; yes, such a letter says, that haven is still here, still thrives, secure and resplendent in all its former glory, but the way back to it is lost.

Slowly I grew used to the idea that my life had lost its continuity, that it had fallen from my hands, and that it only remained for me to commit my spirit to its inescapable destiny. Gradually my eyes grew accustomed to the dim light of reality, and I began to notice the people around me; later than the others, but luckily not so late as to be estranged from them altogether.

The first to emerge from the murk was Honza from Brno, who spoke the almost incomprehensible patois of that city, and who had been posted to the penal division for assaulting a policeman. He had thrashed him as an old schoolmate with whom he had had an argument; but the court did not see it in this light. Honza had served six months in jail and then come straight to us. He was a skilled fitter but was openly indifferent to whether he would ever return to his craft, or what he would do; he had no ties, and his indifference to the future was the true source of his impudent and carefree independence.

The only one who could measure up to Honza in this rare sense of freedom was Bedrich, the most eccentric inmate of our twenty-bunk room. Bedrich had come to us two months after the regular September draft, having originally enlisted in an infantry regiment, where he had stubbornly refused, on strict religious grounds, to be issued with a rifle. The authorities did not quite know what to do with him, especially after intercepting letters he had addressed to Truman and Stalin with an impassioned appeal to both statesmen to disband their armies in the name of Socialist brotherhood. In their confusion they even permitted him, for a time, to go on drill parade, where he was the only man without a weapon, and executed the commands to slope and order arms perfectly but with empty hands. He also took part in the early political sessions and joined eagerly in the discussions, inveighing against the imperialist warmongers; but when, off his own bat, he made a poster calling for total and universal disarmament, and hung it in the barracks, he was court-martialled for mutiny. The court, however, was so nonplussed by his pacifist harangue that they had him examined by a psychiatrist and after further dithering withdrew their charge and transferred him to our mob. Bedrich was delighted. This was the remarkable thing about him: he was the only man there who had deliberately earned his black epaulettes and took pleasure in wearing them. That was why he felt free – though in his case, unlike Honza's, independence took the form, not of insolence but of quiet obedience and contented industry.

The others were all much more weighed down by their cares and sorrows. There was the thirty-year-old Hungarian, Varga from Slovakia, who, oblivious of national prejudices, had fought during the war in several armies and been captured several times by both sides. There was the red-haired Petran, whose brother had escaped across the border, shooting a frontier guard as he did so. There was the simple-minded Josef, a rich peasant's son from a Polabian village, who was so accustomed to blue horizons and soaring skylarks that the infernal labyrinth of shafts and galleries oppressed him with a suffocating terror. There was Stana, a twenty-year-old madcap from Prague's East End, on whom the local council had passed a savage sentence for getting drunk in a Mayday procession and *deliberately* urinating on the edge of the pavement in full view of the cheering citizens. There was Pavel Pekny, a law student, who at the time of the *coup* had demonstrated against the Communists with a handful of his fellow students; he soon discovered I belonged to the same camp as those who had subsequently kicked him out of the faculty, and he was the only one who made evident his malicious satisfaction that I had ended up in the same boat as himself.

There are several other men I could recall, among those who shared my fate at that time, but I want to stick to essentials: the one I liked best was Honza. I remember one of our first conversations together; it was during a short break in a pit gallery where we found ourselves side by side munching some food, and Honza slapped me on the knee and said:

'Hey, you, are you deaf and dumb or something?'

I was indeed at that time deaf and dumb, or rather permanently withdrawn into my shell; and I found it difficult, when we got talking, to explain to Honza, in words which immediately struck me as unpleasantly affected and artificial, how I came to be there and why I ought not to be there. He said: 'Do you think any of us ought to be here, you fool?' I wanted to explain my position again, but as I searched for more natural words Honza swallowed his last crust of bread and said slowly: 'If you were as tall as you're daft you'd have the sun burn a hole through your skull.' These words, with their urban, demotic brand of mockery, made me feel suddenly ashamed of fretting over my lost privileges – I whose convictions had been based on antipathy to privilege and self-indulgence.

In time I became very friendly with Honza, who respected me for my skill and speed at mental arithmetic, an ability which on several paydays prevented us from being given short measure. On one occasion he called me an idiot for spending my free evenings in camp and dragged me out with the rest of the gang. I remember that outing vividly. There were quite a few of us, about eight in all, including Varga the Hungarian and Stana the Mayday urinator. There was also Cenek from B Company, a failed industrial art student who had been posted to the penal division for persistently doing cubist paintings at college, and who now sought to ingratiate himself by doing great charcoal drawings of Hussite warriors with mace and flail all over the barrack rooms.

Our choice was strictly circumscribed: the centre of Ostrava was out of bounds, and we were allowed only in certain districts of the city, and then only in certain public houses within those districts. We got as far as the next suburb and struck lucky, for there was a dance in progress at a former drill hall, to which none of our restrictions applied. We paid the nominal entrance fee and surged in. The hall contained plenty of tables and chairs but rather fewer people – about ten girls and perhaps thirty men, of whom half were soldiers from the artillery barracks nearby.

The moment the gunners saw us they were on the alert and we could feel them eyeing us and counting heads. We sat at a long empty table and ordered a bottle of vodka, but an ugly-looking waitress announced sternly that she was not permitted to serve alcoholic drinks. Honza thereupon ordered eight lemonades, collected a banknote from each of us, left the hall, and presently returned with three bottles of rum. In topping up our glasses of lemonade under the table we employed the utmost circumspection, knowing full well that the artillery-men were watching us and that they were perfectly capable of reporting us for illegal consumption of liquor. The armed forces all detested us: on the one hand, brought up on the spy stories of the day, they viewed us as suspicious elements, criminals, assassins, monsters ever ready to murder their sleeping families in their beds, while on the other, and perhaps more seriously, they envied us for having so much more money to spend than they themselves could afford.

This was the curious thing about our position: we knew only toil and sweat, we had our heads shaved clean every fortnight to keep our hair from giving us any unseemly self-confidence, we were the disinherited of the earth, with nothing in our lives to look forward to; but we had money. We were not millionaires; but in those few hours of freedom two nights a month, and in those few permitted places, we privates could behave like millionaires and compensate for the chronic frustration of the rest of our long days.

Up on the platform an indifferent dance-band alternated between polkas and waltzes. A few couples whirled about the floor, while we coolly ogled the girls and sipped our lemonade laced with rum, which assured us a certain immune superiority to the others in the hall. We were in excellent spirits; I felt an intoxicating conviviality rise to my head, a feeling of companionship I hadn't experienced since the last time I played with Jaroslav and the rest in the cymbalo band. All the while Honza had been devising a scheme to whisk as many girls as possible away from the gunners. His ploy was admirably simple, and we lost no time in putting it into effect. Cenek, that extrovert comedian, took the lead, and to our delight carried out the plan in the most striking fashion. Having invited a dark, heavily made-up girl for a dance and then brought her over to our table, he had a rum lemonade poured for himself and one for her, saying to her significantly: 'Let's drink to it then!' The girl nodded and clinked glasses with him. At that moment a young artillery corporal sauntered up and said to Cenek in as offhand a tone as he could manage: 'All right if I . . .' 'Go on, friend, have a waltz if you want one,' said Cenek. While the girl and her corporal were skipping to the inane rhythm of the polka, Honza was phoning for a taxi, and as soon as it arrived Cenek went over and stood by the exit. His girl finished the dance, told the corporal she was going to the ladies – and the next moment we heard the taxi making off.

Old Ambrose from B Company was the next to achieve success, finding himself an older girl whose miserable appearance did not deter four gunners from vainly circulating round her; ten minutes later Ambrose rode off with his girl and with

Varga (who, it seemed, was diffident about his own chances) to rendezvous with Cenek in a bar at the other end of the town. Presently two more of our number managed to get a girl between them, which left just three of us: Stana, Honza and myself. By now the gunners were looking at us more and more ominously as they began to realize the connexion between our diminished number and the disappearance of the three women from under their very noses.

We tried to look innocent but we could feel a fight was in the air. 'One more taxi now for an honourable retreat,' I said, looking wistfully at a blonde I had managed to dance with earlier on. I had hoped during the next dance to pluck up the courage to lure her away, but the gunners had mounted such a guard on her that I was unable to get near her. 'It's no good,' said Honza, getting up to phone. As he walked across the hall, the gunners all got up from their tables and closed in on him. There was a fight brewing, and Stana and I had no choice but to get up and force our way through to our threatened companion. The crowd of gunners was standing round Honza in menacing silence, broken presently by the appearance of a soldier who was far from sober – he too probably had a bottle under the table. This character launched into a sermon about how his father had been unemployed in the First Republic and how he wasn't going to stand by while these bourgeois with their black bands lorded it over them, no he wasn't going to stand for it, so his mates had better watch out in case he smacked that one (meaning Honza) across the jaw. Honza kept quiet and at the first pause in the trooper's speech asked civilly what the Comrades of the Artillery wanted from him. 'We want you to get out at the double,' one of them said, and Honza explained that that was just what we were doing and that if only they would let him go he could phone for a taxi. When he said this it looked as if the trooper was going to have a fit. 'Bloody hell,' he shouted in a high-pitched voice. 'Bloody hell, here's us slogging away and not able to get out, working our fingers to the bone and no money for it, and these capitalists, these saboteurs, these bastards, are going by taxi! Taxi, they're not leaving here in a taxi, not if I have to throttle them with my bare hands!'

The others all joined in the argument; a number of civilians crowded round the soldiers, including the drill-hall staff, who were anxious to avoid an incident. Suddenly I caught sight of my blonde; she had got up from the table where she had been abandoned and was now on her way to the toilet, quite indifferent to the fracas. As inconspicuously as possible I detached myself from the group and followed her into the vestibule where the cloaks and toilets were, and a solitary cloakroom attendant. I had been thrown in at the deep end and had to learn to swim. Shy or not, I plunged my hand in my pocket, brought out a few crumpled notes and said: 'Why don't you come with us? We'll have a better time than you can in here.' She looked at the notes and shrugged her shoulders. I said I would wait for her outside and she nodded, slipped into the ladies and emerged a moment later with her coat on. She smiled at me and announced that she could tell straight away that I was different from the rest. This pleased me greatly, and I took her by the arm and led her across the street and round the corner, where we watched the entrance to the drill hall, lit by its solitary lantern, for Honza and Stana to come out. The blonde asked me if I was a student, which I confirmed. She then told me that she had just had some money stolen from her in the factory cloakroom, that it was the firm's money and that she was desperate they might sue her for it: could I lend her a hundred? I reached in my pocket and gave her two crumpled hundred-crown notes.

We didn't have long to wait before out came our two friends with their caps and coats on. I whistled to them, but as I did so three other soldiers, coatless and capless, came rushing out of the hall and dashed up to them. I heard the menacing inflection of their voices, and though the words were lost I could guess their meaning: they were looking for that blonde of mine. Then one of them took a swing at Honza and the fight was on. Stana had one of the gunners on him while Honza had the other two; they had almost forced him to the ground when I arrived and laid into one of them. The gunners had assumed that they would have the advantage in numbers, and as soon as the balance was restored they lost their confidence; finally, when one of them folded under Stana's fist and sank moaning to the ground, we took advantage of the confusion and beat a hasty retreat.

The blonde was waiting obediently for us round the corner. When my friends saw her they went wild with joy. They swore I was one of the best, they were all over me in fact, and for the first time in ages I felt genuinely and hilariously happy. Honza brought out a full bottle of rum from under his coat – how he had managed to keep it intact during the fight is beyond my understanding – and swung it over his head. We were in roaring spirits except that we had nowhere to go: we had been thrown out of the one neighbouring establishment that was not out of bounds, our indignant rivals had denied us our taxi and might at any moment threaten our existence with a punitive campaign.

We set off hurriedly down a narrow alleyway between houses for a short distance, until presently there was only a wall on one side and a fence on the other. A ladder loomed up against the fence, and close to it some sort of grass-cutting machine with a tin seat. 'A throne,' I said, and Honza sat the blonde down on the seat, which was about three feet off the ground. We passed the bottle from hand to hand and all four of us drank freely. The blonde soon became voluble and started on Honza: 'Could you lend me a hundred?' The magnanimous Honza slipped her the hundred, and presently the girl had her coat turned back, her skirt lifted up and her knickers down. She took my hand and pulled me towards her, but I took fright and broke away, whereupon Stana thrust up to her, showing not the slightest hesitation, and resolutely entered between her legs. Their clinch lasted for barely twenty seconds, after which I wanted to give precedence to Honza, partly because I fancied playing host, partly because I was still scared. This time, however, the blonde was more determined and pulled me hard against her, and when, aroused by her touch, I was quite ready to oblige her, she whispered softly in my ear: 'I only came because of you, silly.' Then she started to make such moaning noises that I suddenly felt this was a really nice girl who was in love with me and whom I loved. She went on murmuring and sighing, and it was not until I heard Honza's voice pronouncing some obscenity behind me that I discovered this was not the nice girl I wanted to be in love with. I broke away from her without finishing, so violently that the blonde was almost frightened and said 'What's the matter with you?', but Honza was already on her and the moaning began afresh.

That night we got back to camp around two in the morning. At half past four we had to be up for the voluntary Sunday shift, for which our Commanding Officer received a bonus and we our fortnightly Saturday passes. We were sleepy, the alcohol was still inside us, and although we resembled wraiths as we moved about the gloom of the gallery I enjoyed reliving in my imagination the evening we had just spent.

The Saturday a fortnight later was not so good; Honza had had his leave stopped over some incident, and I went out with two young blokes from another company whom I knew only slightly. We headed straight for a woman who because of her monstrous height was known as the Candelabrum. The compulsion to put their brief and infrequent free periods to use at any price caused the men to go for an available woman rather than a bearable one. In time, by comparing notes they formed a pool of those females who, however hideous, were at least more or less definitely available for general use.

The Candelabrum belonged to this pool. Not that I minded this; indeed, when the other two started joking interminably about her abnormal height and about us having to find a brick to stick under our feet when the time came, in a curious way I found myself rather enjoying this gross and tedious humour, and getting support from it for my fierce lust for a woman. For any woman – the more depersonalized, the more soulless, the better; all the better if she was just *any* woman.

But even though I had had plenty to drink the fierceness of my lust soon subsided when I actually set eyes on the Candelabrum. Neither Honza nor Stana nor anyone I liked was there, and everything seemed vile and pointless. Next day I had a terrible hangover feeling which in retrospect encompassed even the events of a fortnight back, and I swore I would never again desire either the girl on the grass-cutter seat or the drunken Candelabrum.

Was this some moral principle speaking out in me? Of course not; it was mere disinclination. But why disinclination, when only a few hours before I had experienced fierce desire for a woman and the fury of this desire had gone hand in hand with a complete indifference as to who this woman might be? Was I perhaps more squeamish than the others, or did I have an aversion to prostitutes? Not at all: I had suddenly felt acutely sorry for myself.

Sorry because I saw quite clearly that this situation was not something exceptional, a form of excess, or a whim, or an urge to know and experience everything, both the sublime and the vile, but that it had become the basic, characteristic and normal situation of my present life; that it had defined exactly the range of my opportunities, had drawn precisely the horizon of the love life which was to be mine from now on; that it was not an expression of my being *free* (as I might have seen it had it arisen, say, a year earlier), but rather an expression of my being predestined, restricted, *condemned*. And I felt afraid – afraid of this miserable horizon, afraid of the destiny which was mine. I felt my soul contract, felt it begin to flinch from all this, and realized with horror that there was no place it could escape to from the encircling chains.

7

This depression induced by our pitifully limited love life was experienced, with varying degrees of consciousness, by nearly all of us. Bedrich, of the peace manifestos, resisted it by a contemplative withdrawal into the depths of his being where his mystic God evidently resided; the erotic counterpart of this pious inwardness being the masturbation which he practised with ritual regularity. The others exhibited a much greater degree of self-deception, complementing their cynical whoring expeditions with romanticism of the most sentimental kind.

Some had a love at home whose memory they polished industriously till it shone with the greatest brilliance; some believed in Eternal Faithfulness and Faithful Expectation; others would secretly persuade themselves that the girl they had picked up drunk in a bar cherished sacred feelings towards them. Stana had two visits from a girl in Prague whom he had known before he was called up, and whom he had certainly not taken very seriously at the time; and suddenly Stana went all soft and with characteristic impetuosity determined on an immediate marriage. He made out that he was only doing this for the two days' marriage leave, but I knew this was merely a cynical façade. It was early in March when the C.O. actually gave him the two days' leave, and Stana went off to Prague for the week-end to get married. I remember this perfectly, because his wedding day became a day of great significance for me also.

I had been given leave for the day, and being in low spirits still after that last free evening which I had wasted with the Candelabrum I avoided my messmates and went out by myself. I took the suburban line and boarded an ancient narrow-gauge tram linking the outer suburbs of Ostrava and let it carry me away. I got off the tram on impulse and boarded the first tram that came along on the other track. The whole milieu, those endless Ostrava backwoods with factories and fields, meadows and rubbish tips, copses and slag heaps, tenement blocks and rustic dwellings, all mingled in the weirdest harmony, attracted and unsettled me in a curious way. I got off the tram and set off on a long walk, taking in the strange landscape almost with passion and trying to plumb the very depths of its spirit, to name in words what it was that gave a scene composed of such diverse elements its unity and order. I worked my way past an idyllic old-world country cottage overgrown with ivy, and it occurred to me that it was *because* of its utter incongruity with the crumbling tenements in its vicinity, with the silhouettes of pitheads and chimneys and furnaces serving as a back-cloth, that it really belonged. I walked past some squat temporary dwellings, a sort of colony within a colony, and a little way off I saw a bungalow, dirty and grey but surrounded by a garden and an iron fence; a large weeping willow grew in the corner of the garden, a sort of stray which had wandered into the district – but which, I said to myself, *for that very reason* belonged there. I was disturbed by all these minor manifestations of incongruity, which I saw not only as the common denominator of the entire region but as an image of my own fate, my own exile in this city. And, of course, the projection of my own fate onto an entire, impersonal city did something to reconcile me to it: I realized that I did not belong here, any more than the weeping willow and ivy-covered cottage I had just passed belonged here, or the ill-assorted houses and stunted streets that led nowhere, or the monstrous estates of squat prefabs usurping a region once pleasantly rural; and that it was precisely because I did not belong here that I was fated to be here, in this appalling city which clasped in its ruthless embrace everything alien to it.

Presently I found myself in a long street in Petrkovice, once a village and today one of Ostrava's inner suburbs. I stopped outside a fair-sized single-storey building with the inscription CINEMA fastened vertically down one corner. I speculated, like any idle passer-by, on why the cinema had no name; I looked at it closely, but there was no other inscription anywhere on the building, which incidentally looked singularly unlike a cinema. Between it and the next building there was an alleyway, about six feet wide; I walked down this and reached a yard and a low-lying extension of the building, with glass cases on the walls for advertisements and stills. I went up to these but once again was unable to discover the name of the cinema. Looking around, I saw behind a wire fence a little girl in a neighbouring back yard, and asked her what the cinema was called; she looked at me in surprise and said she didn't know. I grew resigned to this anonymity: in the banishment of Ostrava even the cinemas had no names.

I drifted back to the glass case and noticed for the first time the title of the film announced by the poster and two photographs: *Honest Justice*. This was the Soviet film to whose heroine Marketa had alluded when she had taken it upon herself to play the role of grand commiserator in my life, the very film whose most severe aspects had been referred to by the Comrades when they instituted proceedings against me; the whole affair had made the film highly distasteful to me, and I had hoped never to hear of it again. And now even here in Ostrava I could not avoid its finger raised in admonition. Still, if we do not like the finger, we can turn our backs on it. I did just that and made for the alleyway leading back to the street.

And that was when I first set eyes on Lucie.

She was walking towards me, making for the back yard of the cinema; why didn't I walk past her and away? Was it because of the curiously haphazard nature of my entire outing? Was it because of the peculiar late afternoon light in the yard that I stayed there another minute instead of going out into the street? Or was it something in Lucie's appearance? Yet her appearance was perfectly ordinary. Later on it was this very ordinariness which touched and attracted me; but how was it that she caught my eye and halted me in my tracks this first time I saw her? Hadn't I seen plenty more of these Ostrava nonentities out on the streets? What was so extraordinary about her ordinariness? I do not know. I only know that I stood where I was and watched the girl as she passed. She walked slowly and unhurriedly up to the glass case and stood looking at the stills from *Honest Justice*; then she turned slowly away and passed through the open doors into the vestibule containing the box-office.

I believe now that it must have been that singular slowness of Lucie's which captivated me so much, a slowness suggesting a resigned consciousness that there was nothing to hurry for and that impatience gets you nowhere. Yes, it was probably that melancholy slowness which kept my eyes fixed on the girl as she made her way to the box-office, took out some change, bought a ticket, glanced into the auditorium, then turned back and came out into the yard again.

I never once took my eyes off her. She stayed with her back to me looking out over the yard to where the garden plots began, enclosed by their wooden fences, and the cottages which continued until they were hidden by the outline of a lignite quarry. I shall never forget that yard, I remember every detail: the wire fence with the little girl gawping at us from the steps of the house, the steps themselves, flanked by a low wall with two empty flower vases and a grey washbowl on top, the smudgy sun edging down towards the quarry on the horizon.

It was ten minutes to six, which meant that it was ten minutes before the performance was due to begin. Lucie turned and strolled across the yard and out into the street. I followed her, and ravaged rural Ostrava was replaced by the city street. Fifty yards away there was a small square, neatly laid out, with benches and a little garden, and behind the square a pseudo-Gothic structure in black brick, with a clock-tower. I watched Lucie sit down on a bench, her slowness never deserting her for an instant; she even sat down slowly. She did not once look round her, she did not even let her eyes wander; she just sat there, as people sit when they are waiting for an operation or for something which absorbs them so much that they do not look around but have their gaze turned inwards; perhaps it was this circumstance that made it possible for me to stroll near and look her up and down without her being aware of it.

People speak of love at first sight – but I am only too well aware of love's retrospective tendency to create its own legend, to turn its own beginnings into myth, and I hesitate to assert that this was a case of being suddenly in *love*. But some sort of second sight there certainly was: the essence of Lucie's being, or, to be precise, the essence of her meaning for me, I sensed and understood in a flash of intuition akin to that epiphany by which religious truth is revealed to some men.

I looked at her and took in the countrified home perm crumpling her hair into a shapeless mass of curls, I took in the wretched brown overcoat, ragged and rather too short. I took in her face, unobtrusively attractive, attractively unobtrusive, and felt that this girl could supply the calm, simplicity and modesty that I needed. It seemed that we were very close in other ways too, and that, strangers as we were, we had a mysterious shared gift of self-evidence, so that I need only go up to the girl and start talking to her, for her to look me in the face and smile as if she suddenly saw standing before her a long-lost brother.

Presently Lucie raised her head and looked up at the clock-tower; even this movement is fixed in my memory, the movement of a girl who has no wrist-watch and who instinctively sits facing a clock. She got up and walked over to the cinema. I wanted to join her, but suddenly found I lacked, not courage so much as the right words; my heart was filled with emotion but my head was empty of even a single syllable. Instead I followed her as far as the vestibule containing the box-office; from here I could see into the auditorium, which was yawning and empty. There is something repellent about an empty auditorium, and Lucie stopped and looked about her with an air of embarrassment. At that moment several people entered the vestibule and began surging towards the ticket office. I nipped in front of them and bought a ticket for the atrocious film.

Meanwhile the girl had entered the auditorium. I followed her to the same row – for in the half-empty hall the number on the ticket lost all relevance and everyone sat where they liked – and sat down in the next seat. At that moment there was a squeal of music from a worn record, the lights dimmed and advertisements appeared on the screen.

Lucie must have realized that it was no accident for a soldier wearing black insignia to have sat right next to her, and she was certainly conscious of me the whole time and of my proximity – all the more, perhaps, because I concentrated entirely on her, and enjoyed a slightly childish revenge by paying no heed to what was happening on the screen, and letting the film so frequently quoted at me by moralists flash past without my paying it the slightest attention.

As the film ended, the lights went on, and the meagre audience got up from their seats. Lucie got up, lifted the folded brown overcoat from her lap and put one arm in the sleeve. I quickly put on my cap to hide the clean-shaven skull, and without a word began helping her into the other sleeve. She glanced briefly at me and gave a barely perceptible nod, which I was uncertain whether to interpret as a bow of thanks or a purely instinctive gesture. Then she picked her way out of the row of seats. I quickly put on my green coat (which was too long and probably did not flatter me) and followed her out. We were still inside the auditorium when I spoke to her.

It was as if for those two hours I had been sitting beside her, and thinking of her, I had been attuning myself to her wavelength; I was able to start a conversation with her as if I knew her well. For once, I was able to start a conversation without a humorous or paradoxical remark, without my usual compulsion to burden myself with disguises; in fact I was perfectly natural – and this surprised me, as up till then I had always stumbled around in front of girls under the weight of several disguises. I asked her where she lived and worked, and whether she went to the pictures often. I told her that I worked in the mines, that it was hard work and that it wasn't often I was able to get out. She said that she worked in a factory and lived in a hostel, that she had to be in by eleven and went to the pictures a lot because she didn't care for dancing. I told her I'd be glad to go with her any time she was free. She said she preferred going on her own. I asked her if that was because she felt depressed about life. She said it was. I told her I was none too happy either.

There is nothing which brings people together so quickly (even if the closeness often proves illusory) as a shared melancholy, a quiet mutual sympathy and understanding, that most elementary form of rapport, which lays to sleep all misgivings and inhibitions and is intelligible to the fine and coarse soul alike, the educated and the simple, and which is yet so rare; for one has to lay aside cultivated restraint, cultivated gestures and mimicry, and be oneself. How I managed, suddenly and with no preparation, to do this, I who had always fumbled blindly behind my masks, I do not know; but I felt it like an unexpected gift or a miraculous liberation.

We told each other the most commonplace things about ourselves; our confessions were brief and to the point. When we reached her hostel we stayed outside for a while; light from a street lamp fell on Lucie and I looked at her brown coat and stroked her, not her cheeks or her hair, but the ragged material of this pitiful garment.

I still remember the swaying of the lantern and the unpleasantly loud laughter of the young girls who kept passing us and opening the hostel doors. I remember looking up the wall of this building where Lucie lived, a wall grey and bare, with unrecessed windows. Above all I remember Lucie's face, which, unlike the faces of other girls I have known in similar situations, was calm and ingenuous, like the face of a school-girl standing by the blackboard and reciting what she knows obediently and guilelessly, seeking neither attention nor praise.

We agreed that I should send Lucie a postcard to let her know when my next leave would be and when we could see each other. We said good night, without kissing or cuddling, and I walked away. After a few steps I turned round and saw her standing in the doorway, making no attempt to unlock the door, just standing and watching me. Only then, when I was some way off, did she drop her reserve and allow her eyes, which until then had been rather timid, to fix me in a long stare. Then she lifted her hand like someone who has never waved and does not know how to do so, who only knows that it is the proper thing to do at such a moment, and is awkwardly attempting to make this gesture. I stopped and waved back; we looked at each other from this distance, then I walked on again, stopped again – Lucie was still waving her arm – and in this manner made my slow retreat until finally I turned the corner and we vanished from each other's sight.

8

From that evening I was transformed, *re-inhabited*. I was no longer just a pitiful emptiness shot through, like junk in a ransacked room, by longings, reproaches and complaints; the room within me had suddenly been tidied up and someone was living there. The clock which for months had been hanging on the wall with its hands motionless had begun to tick. This was significant; time, which till now had flowed like an indifferent stream from nothingness to nothingness (for I had been living in the pause!), without articulation, without measure, had begun once more to acquire its humanized face, to dissect itself and measure itself out. I began to live for the passes out of camp, and the days between became the rungs of a ladder up which I climbed after Lucie.

Never in my life have I devoted so much silent, concentrated thought to a woman as I did to Lucie. (Though it must be admitted that never have I had so much time for it either.) To no other woman have I ever felt so much gratitude.

Gratitude? For what? First and foremost for releasing me from the bounds of that pathetically limited romantic horizon by which we were all surrounded. The newly married Stana, it is true, was another who had found a way of breaking these bounds: at home, in Prague, he now had a woman of his own to love and care for, could sketch to himself the long future of his married life, and take pleasure in the knowledge of being loved. But he was not to be envied. By marrying he had set in motion a destiny over which, the moment he boarded the train and returned to Ostrava, he had lost all influence whatsoever; and so, as the weeks and months went by, more and more disquiet dripped into his initial contentment, more and more helpless anxiety about his life in Prague, a life from which he was cut off and to which he had no access.

I too in meeting Lucie had set my destiny in motion; but I did not lose sight of it. Our meetings may have been infrequent but at least they were more or less regular, and I knew she was capable of waiting a fortnight or longer for me and then meeting me as if we had parted only yesterday.

But Lucie did not only rescue me from the bitter taste my bleak erotic adventures in Ostrava had left in my mouth. At that time I knew full well that I had lost my fight and would not be allowed to change the black insignia of my corps. I knew it was senseless to alienate myself from people with whom I had to live for two years or more, senseless to be constantly advertising my right to my original career, the privileged nature of which I was only just beginning to grasp; yet at the same time this realization was a matter of the intellect and the will only, and was powerless to deliver me from my inner lamentations over my lost destiny. On this inner sorrow Lucie had a miraculous alleviating affect. It was sufficient just to feel her beside me with the whole warm circumference of her life, a life in which there was no room for questions of cosmopolitanism and internationalism, alertness and vigilance, the definition of the dictatorship of the proletariat, the whole gamut of politics with their strategy, tactics and 'personnel policy'.

These were the concerns – so much a part of the age that their jargon will soon become incomprehensible – upon which I had come to grief, and to which I clung. I could have gone before various commissions and trotted out dozens of reasons why I had become a Communist, but the thing that had attracted, even infatuated me about the Communist movement was the feeling, however illusory, of being close to the *helm of history*. In those days we really were making big decisions about the fate of men and things – not least in the universities, where there were as yet few Communists among the professors, so that in the initial years the Communist students ran the universities almost unaided, making the decisions on academic staffing, on teaching reform and on the curriculum. The elation we experienced is commonly called the intoxication of power, but, with a little good will, I could choose a rather less severe way of putting it: we were bewitched by history, intoxicated at having jumped on its back and being able to feel it beneath us. Admittedly, in most cases this did develop into an ugly lust for power, but all the same, just as all human dealings are ambivalent, there was at that time, and with us youngsters in particular, an altogether idealistic illusion that we were inaugurating a human era, an era when man – every man – would be neither outside history nor under the heel of history, but would direct and create it himself.

I was convinced that outside the radius of that helm of history, to which I made such frequent and heady allusion, there was no life, only vegetation, boredom, banishment, Siberia. And then suddenly, after six months of Siberia, I saw a completely new and unexpected opportunity of life: before me there had opened out the forgotten pastures of ordinary everyday life, previously hidden under the soaring wings of history, and in these pastures stood a poor, unhappy but very lovable woman – Lucie.

What did Lucie know about those great wings of history? She would hardly have heard of them; she knew nothing of history, she lived under it, she did not want it, it was alien to her. She knew nothing of the *great problems of the age*. The problems she lived with were trivial and eternal. And suddenly I had been rescued; it seemed to me that she had come to me in order to lead me into her grey paradise, and the step which a short while ago had seemed unthinkable, the step by which I was to make my exit from the stage of history, was suddenly a cause for relief and rejoicing. Lucie held me shyly by the elbow and I allowed myself to be led . . .

Lucie was the commonplace girl sent to usher me away. But who in more factual terms was Lucie?

She was nineteen but in reality much older than that, as women always are when they have had a hard life and been flung headfirst from childhood to adulthood. She told me that she came from Cheb, that she had left school at fifteen and taken up an apprenticeship. She didn't like talking about her home and only did so when I made her. She had not been happy there. 'They didn't like me,' she said, and gave several instances. Her mother had married again and her new stepfather drank and treated her badly; once they had suspected her of concealing some money from them; and they used to beat her. When the discord reached a certain pitch Lucie took the first opportunity and left for Ostrava. She had been there a full year; she had a few girl friends but preferred going about on her own. Her friends went dancing and brought boys back to the hostel. This she refused to do. She was a serious girl: she preferred going to the pictures.

Yes, she actually described herself as 'serious' and associated this quality with her visits to the cinema. Best of all she liked war films, of which there were any number showing at that time. This may have been because she found them exciting, but more probably because the great accumulation of suffering they contained made her feel sad, and she thought that this elevated her and confirmed her in the 'seriousness' she so much valued. Once she mentioned to me that she had seen ever such a nice film; it was Dovzhenko's *Michurin*. She said she liked it very much and proceeded to tick off the reasons: it gave ever such a nice picture of how beautiful nature was; also she had always loved flowers; and a man who didn't like trees wasn't a nice man at all.

It would not be quite fair to suppose that Lucie attracted me by the exotic quality of her simplicity; her simplicity, her fragmentary education, did not prevent her from understanding me. This understanding consisted, not in any experience or knowledge, any skill in debate or capacity for giving advice, but in the anticipation and receptiveness with which she listened to everything I said.

One summer day I had managed to get out before Lucie had finished work; so I took a book with me, sat down on a garden wall and started reading. I had not been doing much reading, as I had little time and no real links with my friends in Prague; but on being called up I had taken three books of poetry with me, which I read over and over again and which brought me comfort: they were poems by Frantisek Halas.

These books played a special part in my life – special, because I was not a great reader, least of all of poetry, and these were the only books of verse that I had ever grown fond of. I had come to them just after my expulsion from the Party, when Halas's name was regaining its notoriety, a leading ideologist having accused the recently dead poet of faithlessness, morbidity, existentialism, everything which in those days had the ring of political anathema. (The book in which he had summarized his opinions on Czech poetry and on Halas had been published in a huge printing, and thousands of youth groups had it as a set book to be sifted through at their seminars.)

In moments of unhappiness man seeks solace in associating his own grief with the grief of others; and although there is something rather ridiculous about this, I admit that I had sought out Halas's verse in order to acquaint myself with someone else who had been excommunicated, and to discover whether my mentality resembled his. I also wanted to see whether the sorrow proscribed by that high and mighty ideologist as morbid and harmful would afford me some joy by striking a note to which I could respond; for in my situation I hardly expected to find joy in joy. Before leaving for Ostrava I had borrowed all three volumes from a former fellow student, a great lover of literature, and finally I managed to persuade him not to expect them back. And so the verses came with me.

When Lucie found me at the appointed place with a book in my hand, she asked what I was reading. I showed her the open book, and she said in some surprise: 'But that's poetry!' 'Do you find it funny for me to be reading poetry?' I asked. She shrugged her shoulders and said: 'No, why should it be?' But I think she did, because in all probability she associated poetry with school readers. We strolled through the strange soot-filled Ostrava summer, that black summer through which, instead of floating white clouds, coal trucks shunted along overhead cables. I saw that Lucie was still in some way drawn to the book in my hand. So when we sat down in a little wood just outside Petrvald, I opened the book and asked: 'Are you interested in this?' She nodded.

I had never recited poetry to anyone before and I have never done so since; I have a kind of built-in reserve which prevents me from being too open with people, from proclaiming my feelings to others; and reading verse seems to me more than just talking about my feelings, it is as if at the same time I was standing on one leg. There is a certain unnaturalness in the very principle of rhyme and rhythm, and it would embarrass me greatly to have to apply myself to it except in solitude.

But Lucie had the miraculous power, which no one else has ever had, of breaking down this reserve and relieving me of my burden of shyness. I could permit myself anything in front of her: candour, emotion, pathos.

So I read:

> 'Your body is a lean ear
> From which the grain has fallen and will not sprout.
> Your body is like a lean ear.

> Your body is a skein of silk
> Written in longing to the last fold.
> Your body is like a skein of silk.
>
> Your body is a burnt sky
> Dreaming watchful in a tissue of death.
> Your body is like a burnt sky.
>
> Your body is hushed and quiet.
> Its tears quiver in my eyelids.
> Your body is hushed and quiet.

I had my arm round Lucie's shoulders, which were protected by a thin, flower-patterned dress, and I felt this in my fingers and succumbed to the suggestion that the lines I was reading were all part of the sorrow of Lucie's body, a quiet resigned body condemned to death. And I read her some more poems, including the one which to this day evokes a picture of her, and which ends with the lines:

> 'Foolish words, I do not believe you, I
>   believe silence –
> Above beauty, above everything
> The triumph of understanding.'

Suddenly my fingers felt Lucie's shoulders tremble; she was crying.

What had made her cry? The meaning of the words? Or the nameless sorrow which wafted from the melody of the verse and the *timbre* of my voice? Had she, perhaps, been exalted by the triumphal elusiveness of the poems and been moved to tears by this very exaltation? Or had the verse simply opened a mysterious sluice within her?

I do not know. Lucie held me round the neck like a child, with her head pressed against the sweaty cloth of the green uniform spanning my chest, and cried and cried and cried.

9

How many times in recent years have women of the most varied temperaments reproached me, when I was unable to reciprocate their feelings, with being conceited? This is nonsense, I am not in the least conceited, but, if the truth be known, it does cause me pain to think that ever since I became fully mature I have been unable to establish a real relationship with any woman, that I have never, as they say, loved a woman. I am not sure that I know the reasons for this failure, whether they lie in some inborn emotional deficiency, or whether they are rooted in my life history. I do not wish to sound pathetic but that is the way it is. Again and again in my reminiscences I return to that hall with its hundred people raising their hands to vote and giving the word for my life to be smashed. Those hundred people had no idea that one day there would be a 1956 and that conditions would gradually change. They could have had no inkling of this and they counted on my being an outcast for life. Not for masochistic reasons, but from some malicious streak in my make-up, I have often composed imaginary variations on this theme, speculating, for instance, on what would have happened if it had been moved that instead of being expelled from the Party I should be hanged. I can never imagine but that in this case too they would all have raised their hands, especially had the desirability of my hanging been passionately urged in the opening address. From that time on, whenever I have met new men and women who might become my friends or lovers I have mentally transported them to that assembly hall and asked whether they would have raised their hands. No one has ever passed this test: they have all raised their hands, just as those one-time friends and colleagues of mine, willingly or unwillingly, from conviction or from fear, raised theirs. And take good note of this: it is a hard thing to live with people who would have sent you to exile or death, it is hard to put your trust in them, it is hard to love them.

Perhaps it was cruel of me to submit my acquaintances to an imaginary trial of this kind when it was highly probable that they would live close to me in a more or less quiet and ordinary fashion, beyond the limits of good and evil, and would never find themselves in a real hall where hands are raised. Some may even say that this procedure of mine had only one purpose: to elevate myself above all others in my moral complacency. But such an accusation of arrogance would not really be justified. I have never myself raised a hand to vote for anyone's destruction, yet I know full well that this is of fairly questionable merit, since I was deprived at an early stage of any right to raise my hand. I have tried for a long time to convince myself at least that if I had had the opportunity I would not have taken it; but I am honest enough to laugh at myself for this. Would I have been the only one not to raise his hand? Am I the one just man? Alas, I found no guarantee within myself that I would have been any better than the rest; so where do I stand in relation to others? But this consciousness of my own deplorable state in no way reconciles me to the same things as others. I detest with all my heart fraternal feelings based solely on mutual recognition of a similar baseness, and have no desire for this kind of slimy brotherhood.

How is it, then, that I was able to love Lucie? Happily the speculations on which I expatiated a moment ago date from a later period, so that I was still able (for this was in my youth, when I still *worried* about things rather than *thinking* about them) to accept Lucie eagerly and trustingly as a gift from heaven – a heaven that was cheerful in a subdued sort of way. This was a happy time for me, possibly my happiest: I was worked to death, beaten and pushed around, but from day to day my skies became bluer and bluer. It's funny really: if the women who dislike me today for being conceited and suspect me of regarding everyone else as idiots were to meet Lucie, they would sneer at *her* as an idiot and quite fail to understand how I could have loved her. I was so fond of her that I could not permit the thought that we might one day split up; we never talked about this but I was always quite seriously under the impression that one day I would marry her. And if it ever occurred to me that this was an unequal match then the in-equality attracted rather than repelled me.

For those few happy months I ought to be grateful to my Commanding Officer as well: the N.C.O.s pushed us around as much as they could, searched for specks of dust in the folds of our uniforms, rumpled our bunks if they found the slightest crease in them – but the officer was a good man. He was get-ting on in years and had been transferred to us from an in-fantry regiment; this was said to have meant a loss of status for him. So he too had been in trouble, and, unconsciously perhaps, this may have predisposed him in our favour. Ob-viously he wanted us to keep order, do what had to be done, and put in a voluntary Sunday shift now and again, to give him some political activism to show his superiors; but he never had us running around for nothing, and he issued our fort-nightly Saturday passes without reluctance. I even believe that that summer I managed to get out and see Lucie as often as three times a month.

When I wasn't with her I would write to her. I sent her in-numerable letters and cards. Today I find it hard to imagine the things I wrote to her and how I expressed myself. I would like to reread those letters now, but at the same time I am glad that I can't. A man has a great advantage in not being able to meet himself in his more youthful edition; I am afraid that I would dislike myself and that I would even tear up this narra-tive because I would see that the testimony I am giving about myself is over-saturated with my present views, my present way of thinking. But what recollection is not at the same time, and beyond our control, a retouching of an old painting? What recollection is not a simultaneous revelation of two faces, the present and the past? What sort of person I was yesterday can never be discovered, without the help of what I remember to-day. But in any case – to return to the matter in hand – it is not so important what my letters were like; I propose merely to mention the fact that I wrote Lucie a lot of them – and that Lucie did not write me one.

I could not induce her to write. Perhaps I shouted her into silence with my own letters; perhaps she thought she had nothing to write about, that she made spelling mistakes; perhaps she was ashamed of the artless handwriting which I knew only from the signature on her identity card. It was not within my power to indicate to her that it was precisely her artlessness and ignorance which made me so fond of her – not that I respected primitiveness for its own sake, but because they bore witness to Lucie's innocence and gave me the hope of becoming more deeply, more inextricably involved with her.

Lucie used just to thank me shyly for my letters and presently came to long for some way of repaying me for them; and since she did not want to write she chose to give me flowers instead. It started like this: we were strolling through a little copse when Lucie suddenly bent down for a flower – may I be forgiven for not knowing its name; it had small violet leaves and a thin stalk – and handed it to me. This struck me as rather touching and didn't bother me at all. But when, on our next date, she met me with a whole bunch of them I began to feel a little embarrassed.

I was twenty-two and avoided like the plague anything that might cast doubts on my virility or maturity; I felt embarrassed if I had to walk up the street carrying flowers, and I did not like buying them, still less receiving them. In my embarrassment I suggested to Lucie that flowers are given to women by men, not to men by women; but then I saw she was nearly in tears, hastened to add how nice they were, and took them from her.

There was nothing to be done. From then on there were flowers waiting for me at every date, and finally I resigned myself to the situation, disarmed by the spontaneity of the gifts and realizing that they meant a lot to Lucie. Perhaps in her inarticulateness she saw in flowers a form of speech – not the rigid symbolism of the ancient flower language, but rather an older, less concrete, more instinctive, *proto-language*. Perhaps, being on the silent rather than the talkative side, she instinctively longed for that stage of evolution when there were no words, when people communicated by simple gestures: they pointed out trees with their fingers, they laughed, they touched one another ..

Whether at that date I had already grasped, or failed to grasp, the essence of Lucie's flower-giving, I was touched by it and wanted to give her something in return. Lucie had in all three sets of clothes which she wore in regular alternation, so that our dates followed one another in the rhythm of the three-beat bar. I liked all her clothes, precisely because they were worn and not very tasteful. I liked the brown coat, too short and worn at the cuffs, which I had caressed before I had caressed her face. Still, I thought I would buy Lucie some clothes, some nice clothes, and plenty of them. I had stopped throwing my money away in bars, which meant I had ample funds and no desire to save. So one day I took Lucie along to an outfitter's.

At first Lucie thought we were just going to have a look round and watch the people streaming up and down the stairs. On the second floor we stopped by a long rail on which women's dresses were hanging in dense array, and when Lucie saw me looking inquisitively at them she came nearer and began commenting on some of them. 'That's nice,' she said, pointing at something with a neat pattern of red flowers. There were not, in point of fact, all that many nice dresses, but there were one or two things which were not too bad. I pulled one out and called to the assistant: 'Could the young lady try this one on?' Lucie may have wanted to resist but didn't dare in front of a stranger, and so, before she knew what had happened, she found herself behind the curtain.

After a while I lifted the curtain to see how Lucie looked. Although the dress she was trying on was nothing exceptional I almost stopped dead in my tracks: its modern cut had quite transformed her. 'May I take a look?' asked the assistant standing behind me, and his admiration was eloquent as he took in Lucie and the clothes she was trying on. Then he looked at my regimental insignia and asked if I was a political. I nodded. He winked and smiled, said 'I might have one or two better-quality things over here – would you like to see them?' and in a trice produced a few summer dresses and some smart evening clothes. Lucie tried them on one after the other, and every single one suited her. She looked different in each, while as for the evening dresses I would not have recognized her in them at all.

Twists and turns in the course of affections are not always the result of dramatic events, but often of matters which at first glance are of no consequence at all. In the development of my affection for Lucie these clothes played such a part. Until then she had performed every possible role for me – a child, a source of affection, a source of comfort, a balsam and an escape from myself – everything, that is, except a woman. Our love in the physical sense of the word had not extended beyond a few kisses. And in any case the way Lucie kissed was that of a child. (I had fallen in love with those long, dry, chaste kisses, in which the mouths are closed, and as they rub together they put their soft lips to account with such feeling.)

In short I had until then felt affection for Lucie, but no sensual desire; indeed, I had become so accustomed to the absence of sensuality that I was not even conscious of it. My relationship with her seemed so perfect that it could never have occurred to me that there was something missing from it. Everything blended harmoniously together: Lucie – her monastically grey clothes – and my monastically innocent relations with her. The moment she put on other clothes the entire balance was destroyed: she immediately escaped from my impression of her, and I realized she had before her other possibilities and other forms than those touchingly rustic ones. I suddenly saw her as an attractive woman with a good figure and with legs alluringly outlined under the well-cut skirt, a woman whose drab protective colouring melted away in these clothes with their striking colours and subtle lines. I was utterly captivated by the sudden revelation of her body.

Lucie lived in the hostel in a room which she shared with three other girls. Visitors were allowed only two days a week and even then for no more than three hours, from five till eight; they had to sign in at the concierge's desk, hand in their identity cards and check out as they left. Added to all this, each of Lucie's room-mates had a young man (or more than one), and each of them needed the intimacy of the hostel room for dating purposes, so that there were constant bickerings, feuds and recriminations over a single minute that one of them might have taken from the others. All this was so unpleasant, not to say humiliating, that I had never attempted to visit Lucie at the hostel. But I knew that in about a month's time all three of her room-mates had to go off for a three-week agricultural work party. I told Lucie I wanted to take advantage of this and see her in her room. She did not take too kindly to this; she looked mournful and said she preferred being with me out of doors. I told her that I longed to be with her somewhere where no one and nothing could disturb us and we could concentrate entirely on each other, and that I wanted to see how she lived. Lucie could find no answer to this, and I remember to this day how excited I was when she finally agreed to my proposal.

10

I had now been in Ostrava for almost a year, during which the military routine, initially so unbearable, had become habitual and ordinary; it was still harsh and unpleasant, but I managed to live with it, to make a few friends, and even to be happy. For me, indeed, this was a fine summer – the trees were full of soot and yet they still seemed the purest green when I viewed them with eyes just delivered from the darkness of the pit – but, as is so often the case, the germ of unhappiness was concealed in the midst of happiness: the gloomy events of that autumn were conceived in that green-black summer.

It began with Stana. Within weeks of his marriage he began getting word that his wife was hanging around the bars. He took it very much to heart and wrote her letter after letter, to which he received placatory answers. But then, one Saturday early in the summer, he had a visit from his mother; he spent the whole day with her and returned to camp pale and taciturn. At first he was too ashamed to tell anyone, but the next day he confided in Honza, then in others, until soon we all knew. As soon as Stana realized this he started talking openly about it, every day and almost nonstop, saying that his wife was sleeping around and that he would go and wring her neck. He went direct to the Commanding Officer to ask for two days' leave, which the C.O. was loath to grant him, since he was always getting complaints, both from the mines and from the barracks, about Stana's preoccupation and irritability. Stana then asked for a twenty-four hour pass, which the C.O. took pity on him and granted. Stana left and we never saw him again; what happened to him I know only from hearsay.

Apparently he got to Prague and went for his nineteen-year-old wife, who admitted everything quite readily, perhaps even with relish. He started hitting her and she fought back, he tried to choke her and finally smashed a bottle over her head; the girl fell to the floor and lay there motionless. Stana came to his senses and fled in panic. Somehow or other he managed to get hold of a shack in the Krusny mountains and lived there in terrified anticipation of being caught and strung up for murder. Two months later they found him and put him on trial, not for murder, but for desertion. The girl had come round soon after he had left, and apart from a bump on the head had suffered not the slightest damage to her health. While he was serving his time in the glasshouse she obtained a divorce, and today she is the wife of a famous Prague actor, whose shows I see to remind me of my old friend and for no other reason. For Stana afterwards came to a sorry end: when his military service was up he stayed on in the mines, where an accident cost him a leg, and the amputation his life.

That woman, who by all accounts still shines in bohemian circles, brought misfortune not only on Stana but on all of us. At least that is what we all assumed, though we can never be certain whether there was any real connexion between the scandal surrounding Stana's disappearance and the ministerial committee of inspection which shortly afterwards visited our barracks. Whether there was or not, our C.O. was replaced by a young officer, hardly more than twenty-five at the most, with whose coming everything changed.

He looked even younger than he must have been, like a little boy in fact – which made him all the more anxious to acquit himself in the most impressive manner possible. We used to say among ourselves that he rehearsed his speeches in front of the mirror and learned them off by heart. He was not one for shouting; he spoke drily, letting us know with the greatest composure that he regarded us all as criminals. 'I know you'd like to see me hanged,' this child said to us the first time he addressed us; 'but if anyone is going to hang it will be you, not me.'

The first clashes were not long in coming. The incident with Cenek has stuck in my memory most, perhaps because we found it so uproariously amusing. I cannot resist telling it now. During his first year of service Cenek had done a large number of murals which, under the old C.O., had always received due recognition. Cenek, as I mentioned before, had a predilection for Hussite warriors and their commander Jan Zizka, but to give pleasure to his messmates he always liked to throw in a few naked women, whom he represented to the C.O. as symbols of Liberty or the Motherland. The new C.O., also wishing to make use of Cenek's services, summoned him and requested him to paint something for the room where political instruction classes were held. He took the opportunity of telling him to 'leave all those Zizkas alone' and 'take more account of modern conditions', and that his picture should depict the Red Army, its alliance with our working class, and its significance for the victory of Socialism in February 1948. Cenek said 'Will do!' and set to work, spending several afternoons on the floor and using large sheets of paper which he then tacked up all over the end wall of the room. The finished work was a good five feet high and twenty-five feet long and our first view of it fairly took our breath away. In the middle stood a warmly clad Soviet soldier in a heroic posture, with a sub-machine gun slung from the shoulder and a shaggy fur cap over his ears; while all around him were some eight or nine naked women. Two were standing by his side and gazing up at him coquettishly (he had an arm round each and was laughing exuberantly); the rest were ogling him, stretching out their arms towards him, or just standing there (in one case lying down), showing off their handsome proportions.

We were waiting for the Political Officer to arrive and had the room to ourselves. Cenek took up a position in front of the mural and began expounding it along these lines: 'You see this one here on the right of the sergeant, that's Alena, lads, she was the first woman I ever had, she had me when I was sixteen. She was an officer's wife so this is just the place for her. I painted her the way she looked then, I don't suppose she looks half as good now, and even then she was a bit on the bulky side as you can see here' (pointing) 'round the hips. She was a lot better from behind, so I've done another one of her over here' (walking to the edge of the mural and pointing at a bare backside). 'You see her royal behind just a little oversize, but that's the way we like them. I was a bit daft in those days, and I remember she used to love being beaten on the behind and I didn't know what it was all about. One Easter she kept on at me not to forget to bring my whip with me, and when I came she said "Beat me, beat me, and you'll get an Easter egg," so I whipped her over the skirt sort of symbolically, and she said "What's the good of that? Pull my skirt up," so I had to pull her skirt up and take her drawers down, and I just went on like a bloody fool hitting her like before, and she kept shouting "Hit me properly, you little monkey!" Anyway, that was all bloody stupid, and this one here' (pointing at the woman on the sergeant's left) 'that's Lojzka. I had her when I was more grown up. She had small breasts, long legs and a very pretty face' (pointing at each item as he named it) 'and she was in the same year as me. This one's our model from art college. I know her inside out and so do twenty other lads, because she always used to stand in the middle of the classroom while we learned how to paint the human body, but none of us ever touched her. Her mother always used to wait for her in front of the classroom block and take her straight home. So she used to show herself off to us, God bless her, with all due propriety. And this one here, gentlemen, she was a right scrubber.' He pointed at a woman lolling on a sort of stylized couch. 'Come up and have a look at her.' We did. 'See that mark on her stomach? That's where she was burnt by a cigarette and they say it was some jealous

83

woman that did it, some woman she went with because, you see, this little lady used to have it both ways, she had a cunt like an accordion and you could get the whole world into it, all the lot of us, with our wives, our girls, our children, our ancestors ...'

Cenek was evidently approaching the climax of his exposition when the Political Officer entered the room and told us to sit down. The Political Officer, who was used to Cenek's pictures, gave the new work no attention and began reading aloud from some pamphlet elucidating the differences between Socialist and capitalist armies. Cenek's commentary faded away in our ears and we were just settling down to a quiet nap – when the boy commander suddenly appeared in the room. He had obviously come to check up on the lecture, but before he could receive the Political Officer's report and motion us to sit down again he stood transfixed by the mural; he did not even permit the Political Officer to carry on with his reading, but pounced on Cenek and asked what was the meaning of this. Cenek leapt to his feet, struck a pose in front of the picture and began: 'Here we have an allegorical representation of the significance of the Red Army for the struggle waged by our nation; here' (pointing at the sergeant) 'is illustrated the Red Army; at his side' (pointing at the officer's wife) 'is symbolized the working class, and here on the other side' (pointing at the girl in his class at college) 'is the symbol of the month of February. These others' (pointing at the other ladies) 'are the symbols of liberty, victory, and equality; and here' (pointing at the officer's wife displaying her hind quarters) 'we see the bourgeoisie making its exit from the stage of history.'

The C.O. let Cenek finish his speech; then he announced that the picture was an insult to the Red Army and must be removed immediately, and that Cenek would have to take the consequences. *Sotto voce*, I asked why. The C.O. heard me and asked if I had any objections. I stood up and said I liked the picture. The C.O. said he could quite believe this, as it was just the sort of picture masturbators would like. I told him that Myslbek had painted Liberty as a nude woman as well, and Ales had even sketched the river Jizera as *three* nude women; this kind of thing had been done by painters throughout the ages.

The boy commander looked at me dubiously and repeated his order for the picture to be taken down. Nevertheless, we may have managed to confuse him, because Cenek was never punished for it; but the C.O. had taken a dislike to Cenek, and to me as well. Cenek was soon up on a charge, and a little later I was on one too.

It happened like this. Our unit was working with picks and shovels in an out-of-the-way part of the camp, under an indolent corporal who didn't bother to watch us too closely. We were leaning on our shovels, nattering among ourselves, and failed to notice the boy commander standing quite near, observing us. We only discovered this when we heard his stern voice saying: 'Private Jahn, come here!' I seized my shovel energetically and stood to attention before him. 'Is this your idea of work?' he asked. I can't remember how I replied, but I certainly wasn't insolent, because I had no intention of making life in the barracks any harder for myself or of needlessly antagonizing the man who had complete power over me. I doubtless gave him a perplexed and meaningless reply; at all events, his eyes hardened and he stepped quickly up to me, seized my arm and hurled me over his shoulder with an expert ju-jitsu throw. Then he squatted down beside me and pinned me to the ground; I made no attempt to resist, but just lay there in astonishment. 'Is that enough?' he asked, raising his voice for the others to hear. I said it was. He ordered me on my feet and announced to the assembled unit: 'I am giving Private Jahn two days' detention. Not because he was insolent. His insolence, as you saw, I dealt with personally. I am giving him two days for idleness, and I shall make it hot for the rest of you as well.' Then he turned on his heel and stalked off.

At the time my feeling towards him was one of unqualified hatred, and hatred throws too bright a light on things so that all their plasticity is lost. I saw him merely as a vindictive, wily rat. Today, however, I see him above all as a man who was young and acting a part. The young cannot help acting; they are immature but they are placed in a mature world and have to act as if they *were* mature. So they put on the masks and disguises which appeal to them and can be made to fit them — and they act.

Our Commanding Officer was such a one. Suddenly he found himself in command of our unit, of a crowd of men he was incapable of understanding; but from what he had read and heard he knew what to do, and he had his ready-made mask for this sort of situation: the coldblooded hero of the cheap thriller, the young man of iron nerve who outwits the criminal gang, the man without feelings, cool and collected, with a dry, biting wit, and boundless confidence in the might of his own muscles. The more conscious he was that mentally he was still a boy, the more fanatically he acted his role of the iron superman, the more he strove to parade him in front of us.

But was this the first time I had come up against one of these adolescent fakes? At the time of my interrogation about the postcard affair I was only twenty, and my interrogators were at the most a year or two older. They too were adolescents, concealing their immature faces behind the mask they thought most appropriate, that of the hard, ascetic revolutionary. What about Marketa? Hadn't she simply imitated the girl saviour in some banal bestseller or film? And what about Zemanek, suddenly imbued with a sentimental morality? Weren't these just masks? And what about myself? Didn't my troubles stem from my having several masks and turning in confusion from one to the other?

Youth is a terrible thing: it is a stage peopled by supposedly innocent children, who stride about on stilts and in the most varied costumes, pronouncing speeches they have learned by rote and only half understand, but which they regard with fanatical reverence. History too is a terrible thing, because so often it becomes the playground for adolescents: the youthful Nero, the youthful Napoleon, the frenzied mobs of children whose simulated passions and primitive poses are suddenly transformed into catastrophic reality. When I think of this, the whole scale of values is reversed in my mind, and I feel a deep hatred towards youth – coupled, paradoxically, with a measure of forgiveness for the criminals of history, in whose delinquency I now see only the terrible irresponsibility of adolescence.

As I recall these youngsters, I think also of Alexej, who also was attempting to act a part, one which extended beyond the bounds of his ability and experience. He had something in common with the C.O.: he too looked younger than his years, though his boyishness, in contrast with the C.O.'s, had nothing attractive about it. His body was skinny, his eyes myopic under the thick glass of his spectacles, his skin covered with the pimples of eternal puberty. As a national serviceman he had begun by attending a college for infantry officers, but was suddenly deprived of his rank and transferred to us. The notorious political trials were brewing up, and in Party buildings, courtrooms and police stations all over the country hands were constantly being raised, stripping the accused of trust, honour and liberty; and Alexej was the son of a senior Communist official who had been arrested shortly before.

Alexej appeared one day in our company and was allotted Stana's orphaned bunk. He regarded us much as I had first regarded my companions, with great reserve; and when the others in turn learned that he was a Party member (his expulsion had not yet come through) they started to guard their tongues when he was around. As soon as he discovered that I was a former Party member he opened up towards me, and confided that whatever happened he was determined to pass this supreme test of his life and never to betray the Party. He read me a poem he had written – apparently his first venture in this direction – when he learned he was to be transferred to our regiment. It consisted of exactly four lines:

> You may put me in the stocks, comrades,
> And spit and throw filth at me.
> Even so, I shall remain Comrades,
> Within your own ranks faithfully.

I understood his feelings because I had felt just the same a year before. But by now I felt it much less painfully: Lucie had guided me back to the everyday world, out of those regions where the Alexejs of this world dwell in such desperate torment.

11

While the boy commander was busy establishing his new regime I was beginning to worry about whether I would manage to get some time off before Lucie's room-mates returned from their work party. It was a month since I had last been allowed out of camp. The C.O. had taken careful note of my face and name, and in the army that is the worst thing that can happen to you. He lost no chance of letting me know that every hour of my life was dependent on his whim. And as regards leave the situation was particularly bad: at the outset he had announced that leave would only be granted once a month, and then only to those who regularly took part in the voluntary Sunday shifts. This being so, we all took part in them; but it was a miserable sort of life, for we had a whole month on end without a day away from the pit, and when one of us actually got a Saturday free till two in the morning he would set off for the Sunday shift still tired, and creep about the mine like a ghost.

I started working the Sunday shifts too, but there was no guarantee that I would get a day off, since the merit of working a Sunday shift could easily be offset by a badly made bed or some other transgression. Arbitrary power, however, manifests itself, not only in cruelty, but occasionally also in mercy. After several weeks had passed, the boy commander felt in the mood to show me some mercy, and at the last moment before Lucie's girl friends returned I was granted two days' leave.

It was an exciting moment when the bespectacled old concierge signed me in and allowed me to go upstairs to the fourth floor, where I knocked on a door at the far end of a long passage. The door opened but Lucie stayed hidden behind it, so that all I could see was the room, which at first sight bore no resemblance whatever to a hostel room; it looked more like a room made ready for some religious celebration. There was a glorious golden bunch of dahlias on the table and two big creepers climbing round the window, and the entire room – the table, the beds, the floor, even the pictures – was festooned with green sprays (of asparagus fern, as I later discovered), as if Jesus Christ himself was expected to ride in on his donkey.

I pulled Lucie (still hiding behind the open door) towards me and kissed her. She was in the black evening dress and high-heeled shoes that I had bought her, that day when I fitted her out, and she stood in the midst of that festive greenery like a high priestess.

We closed the door behind us, and it was only then that I recognized the room for what it was, an ordinary hostel room, and realized that under that green garland there were just four iron beds, four chipped bedside tables, a larger table and three chairs. But nothing could diminish the delight I had felt the moment Lucie opened the door. For the first time in a month, I was out of camp for a few hours. But not only that: for the first time in a year I was in a small room again, and this intoxicating breath of intimacy almost overcame me. Whenever I had been out with Lucie the temporary freedom and spaciousness had helped to reconcile me to the barracks and my lot there; but the ever-present air circulating around me had kept me chained with an invisible chain to the camp gate with its inscription WE SERVE THE PEOPLE until it seemed there was no place where I could ever for an instant stop 'serving the people'. For a whole year I had not been inside a small private room.

And now all at once there was a completely new situation. For three hours I was absolutely free; I could, for instance, against all military regulations but without fear, throw off not just cap and belt, but shirt, trousers, boots, everything, and I could even give them a kick if I felt like it. I could do what I liked, and there was no observation post from which I could be seen doing it. In addition, it was deliciously warm in the room, and the warmth and my new sense of freedom went to my head like alcohol. I seized Lucie, hugged her, kissed her, and carried her over to her green-bedecked bed. I must admit I was unsettled by the green sprays covering the cheap grey blanket. They could hardly be interpreted except as symbols of wedlock; and I fancied that in Lucie's rather touching simplicity I could hear the unconscious strains of time-honoured popular custom, and that she wanted to surrender her virginity with due ritual and ceremony.

It was some time before I realized that although Lucie was responding to my kisses and embraces she was also preserving an element of restraint. Even when her lips were kissing me hungrily they still remained closed; she clung to me with her entire body, but when I put my hand under her skirt to feel her thighs she twisted away from me. I realized that my desire to be carried blindly away with her was not reciprocated; and at that moment, scarcely five minutes after I had entered the room, I remember feeling tears of disappointment in my eyes.

We sat down side by side, crushing the unfortunate sprays, and started making desultory conversation. Presently I tried again to take Lucie in my arms, and again she resisted. I began struggling with her, only to realize that this was no fine amorous contest but a real fight which was turning our affectionate relationship into something ugly. Lucie was resisting in good earnest, furiously, almost desperately, and I soon gave up the battle.

Next I tried to persuade her with words. I turned on all my charm, telling her that I loved her and that loving means giving yourself to the other with everything you have. The argument was no more original than my aims; but if it was unoriginal it was also irrefutable, nor did Lucie try to refute it. Instead she kept silent or merely said 'Don't, please; don't, please' or 'Not today, not today' or attempted, with a rather touching lack of skill, to turn the conversation to other topics.

I tried another line: 'You can't be one of those girls who lead a man on and then laugh at him, you can't be so cruel and heartless ...' Then I took her in my arms again and we had another brief struggle, the ugliness of which again filled me with depression. It was in earnest, and there was not a trace of love in it; it was as if Lucie had in that instant forgotten who she was with, as if I had been transformed into a total stranger.

Suddenly I thought I understood why Lucie was resisting; God, why hadn't I realized it at once? She was only a child, she was still afraid of love; she was a virgin, and she was frightened, frightened of the unknown. I decided I must camouflage my urgency, must be gentle and kind so that the act of love should seem no different from our other caresses, should only *be* one of those caresses. So I stopped insisting and started gently fondling her. For what seemed an age I kissed her and stroked her, insincerely and without pleasure – these preliminaries had become, in Party jargon, a mere *means to an end* – and tried as surreptitiously as possible to get her lying down. At last I managed this. I stroked her breasts, something she had never resisted, and told her I wanted to be nice to the whole of her body, because her body was *her* and I wanted to be nice to all of her. I even managed to lift her skirt a little and kiss her four, then eight, inches above the knee. But that was the furthest I got; I tried to lay my head in her lap but she sprang away from me in terror and jumped off the bed. I looked at her and saw her face convulsed in some sort of struggle, an expression I had never seen on it before.

'Lucie, Lucie, is it the light that makes you embarrassed? Would you rather be in the dark?' I asked, and she clutched at my question like a straw and admitted she was embarrassed by the light. So I went over to the window and was just going to draw the blinds when she said: 'No, don't do it! Don't draw the blinds!' 'Why not?' I asked. Instead of answering she burst into tears.

Her resistance had aroused no sympathy in me whatever. I considered it senseless, wrong and unfair; it worried and puzzled me. I asked her if she resisted because she was a virgin, whether she was afraid of the pain. She meekly answered yes to this, and to every question which seemed to be offering her a loophole. I told her what a fine thing it was that she was a virgin and that she would find out everything with me, the man who loved her. 'Don't you look forward to being my wife, and everything that goes with it?' Yes, she said, she was looking forward to it. I embraced her again and again she resisted.

It was with some difficulty that I kept my temper: 'Why are you fighting me?'

'Please, next time, I do want it, but please, next time, another time, not today.'

'And why not today?'

'Not today.'

'But why?'

'Please not today, please.'

'When then? You know very well this is our last chance of being alone together, tomorrow your room-mates are coming back. Where else can we be alone together?'

'You'll find somewhere.'

'All right, so I might find somewhere. But promise me you'll come with me, because I very much doubt if it will be as nice a room as this one.'

'It doesn't matter, it doesn't matter, it can be wherever you like.'

'All right, but promise me that you'll be my girl when we go there, that you won't fight me.'

'All right.'

'Promise?'

'Yes.'

I realized that this promise was the most I would get out of Lucie that day. It wasn't much but it was something. I suppressed my indignation and we spent the rest of the time talking. When I went I shook the bits of asparagus fern out of my uniform, stroked Lucie's face and told her I would be thinking of nothing else but the next time – and I wasn't lying either.

12

A few days after my last meeting with Lucie (it was a rainy autumn day), we were returning by companies from the mines to the barracks; the road was rutted with deep puddles; we were grimy, tired and soaked through, and we longed for a rest. Most of us had not had a free Sunday for a month. But immediately after lunch the boy commander had us all lined up before him and informed us that an afternoon inspection of our quarters had uncovered certain irregularities. He then handed us over to the N.C.O.s and ordered them to drill us for an extra two hours as a punishment.

As we were soldiers without weapons our square-bashing was particularly nonsensical; it had, indeed, no other purpose than to waste our time. I remember that under the Boy's command we once spent an entire afternoon humping heavy beams from one end of the camp to the other, and the next afternoon humping them back again; and this went on for ten whole days. This time it was our bodies which had to be lumbered around; we turned them eyes right, eyes forward, wheeled right, flung them on the ground and lifted them up again, ran with them, now here, now there, and dragged them along the ground. After three hours of this the C.O. appeared, and motioned the N.C.O.s to lead us off for P.T.

Behind the hut blocks there was a smallish yard for football and other forms of exercise; and here the N.C.O.s decided to stage a relay race. Our company had nine sections of ten men each; and so, since the N.C.O.s were mostly lads of eighteen to twenty who wanted to pit a team against us and show their superiority, there were ten teams of ten men each.

It took a considerable time before the N.C.O.s managed to get their intentions across to us: the first ten runners had to sprint from one side of the yard to the other, where another row of runners would be waiting for them. These in turn would race back to the starting-line, where by now there would be a third row waiting; and so on. The N.C.O.s laboriously counted us and despatched us to opposite ends of the yard.

We were dog-tired after a day in the pits and the subsequent square-bashing, and furious at the idea of having to run on top of it all. A somewhat crude idea came to me, which I confided to two of the lads: why not run dead slow? The idea caught on at once and was passed from mouth to mouth, until the tired mass of soldiers began to stir contentedly with stifled laughter.

At last we all stood at our posts ready for the start of a race utterly foolish in its conception: even in our uniforms and heavy boots, we were made to kneel under starter's orders; and although we had to hand over the relay in an unprecedented way, with the next runner *facing* us, we were given proper batons and started off with the conventional pistol shot. The lance-corporal in the tenth lane sprinted off at a tremendous pace; the other nine, including myself, straightened up and moved off at a slow jog-trot. After twenty yards we were hard put to it to stop laughing, as the lance-corporal was already approaching the other end of the yard, while we had hardly started, jogging along in improbable formation, puffing and blowing to simulate unaccustomed exertion. The soldiers crowded at each end of the yard began egging us on: 'Faster, faster, faster ...' Half way across we passed the second runner in the corporals' team as he sprinted towards us, making for the line we had left. At last we reached the end of the yard and handed on our batons, but behind us the third N.C.O. was already away, baton in hand.

Today I look back on that race as the last big parade of my partners in crime. Those lads had a tremendous inventiveness. Honza fell, picked himself up, and continued on one leg, heroically reaching the change-over point, to tumultuous applause, two paces in front of the rest. Gypsy Matlos fell to the ground half a dozen times or more; Cenek ran along lifting his knees absurdly up to his chin – a more exhausting procedure than any normal form of racing. No one let the side down: even Bedrich, law-abiding and resigned writer of peace manifestos, ran his slow trot with solemn dignity like the rest. Simple-minded Josef; Pavel Pakny, who disliked me; old Ambrose, who ran bolt upright with his hands clasped behind his back; red-haired Petran with his high-pitched yell; Varga the Hungarian shouting his 'Hurras' as he ran – not one of them spoilt this superb parody, which had all the onlookers holding their sides.

Then we saw the Boy coming towards the yard from the huts. One of the corporals saw him first and went over to report. The captain heard him out and then came as far as the edge of the arena to watch the race. The N.C.O.s, whose team had long since sped victoriously past the winning-post, became nervous and started shouting 'Faster! Move yourselves! Get on with it!'; but their words of encouragement were drowned by our mighty roars. The N.C.O.s were completely at a loss, wondering whether to stop the race, running to and fro to confer, and looking at the C.O. out of the corners of their eyes. The C.O. did not even glance at them, but stood watching the race with icy calm.

It was the turn of the last ten. Alexej was one of them. I was curious to see how he would behave, and I was not mistaken: he wanted to spoil the fun. He ran ahead with all his might and gained several yards in the first twenty. But then something peculiar happened: his pace slowed down and he ceased to gain on the others. At once I realized that Alexej couldn't spoil the game even if he wanted to – this sickly young man who had had to be given lighter work after only two days with us; he had neither the muscles nor the wind. This realization turned his sprint into the highlight of the entire farce. However hard Alexej flogged himself, he was indistinguishable from the lads idling along at the same pace five yards behind, and the N.C.O.s and the captain must have been convinced that his prestissimo opening and subsequent slow movement were as much a part of the comedy as Honza's feigned limping, Matlos's tumbling about, and our ironic cheers. The only difference between Alexej and the others, running with fists clenched and making a great display of panting and puffing, was that Alexej's stitch was real – his efforts to overcome it even brought real sweat running down his face. Half way across the yard he slowed down even more, until he was overtaken by the line of rogues behind; twenty yards from the end he stopped running altogether and hobbled the rest of the way with his hand on his groin.

The C.O. made us all fall in. Then he asked us why we had been running so slowly.

'We were tired, Comrade Captain.'

He told everyone who was tired to raise his hand. Every hand went up – except Alexej's. The C.O. appeared not to notice him. He said: 'I see. In other words, all of you.'

'No, sir,' came the reply.

'Who was not tired?'

Alexej replied: 'I wasn't, sir.'

'You?' asked the C.O., looking at him. 'How is it you were not tired?'

'I am a Communist,' answered Alexej, and the whole company hooted with laughter.

'Are you the one who finished last?' asked the C.O.

'Yes, sir,' said Alexej.

'If you weren't tired then you must have sabotaged the race deliberately. Take fourteen days for attempted mutiny. The rest of you were tired, so you're excused. As your output in the colliery is insignificant it is evidently your days off which are tiring you out. In the interests of your own health all leave for this company is stopped for two months.'

Before Alexej left for the glasshouse we had a conversation in which he reproached me for not behaving like a Communist and asked me sternly whether I was for Socialism or against it. I told him I was for Socialism but that in this camp the distinction was totally irrelevant: here the only valid difference was between the men who had lost control over their destinies and those who had not. Alexej would not admit this, maintaining that the line between Socialism and reaction holds everywhere, and that our barracks were simply a means to defend ourselves against the enemies of Socialism. I asked him how the Boy was defending Socialism against its enemies by sending him, Alexej, to the glasshouse for fourteen days, and generally carrying on as if he wanted to turn the men into Socialism's most confirmed enemies; and Alexej admitted he disliked the C.O. But when I told him that if there had been a dividing line in the barracks between Socialism and reaction then he, Alexej, would not have been here in the first place, he replied sharply that he was here with perfect justice. 'My father was arrested for espionage. Do you understand what that means? How can the Party trust me? It's the Party's *duty* not to trust me!'

After that I had a chat with Honza, in which I complained, thinking of Lucie, of how we could not get outside for two months. 'Don't be daft,' he said. 'What are you afraid of? There'll be more going out than ever.'

The good-humoured sabotaging of that race strengthened our feeling of solidarity and led to considerable activity. Honza organized a sort of miniature council which made a rapid review of the possibilities for going absent without leave. In two days it was all arranged: a secret bribery fund was set up, the two corporals in our quarters were suborned, and several strands of wire were cut at a well-chosen point in the perimeter fence. This spot was right at one end of the camp, where there was only the sick bay, and where the nearest cottages were no more than five yards beyond the wire. The nearest cottage was occupied by a miner whom we knew from down the pit, and with whom a speedy agreement was reached whereby he was to leave his back gate unlocked. The escaping soldier would only have to make his way cautiously to the fence, crawl quickly under, and sprint the few yards to the cottage gate. Once past that, he was safe: he would simply walk through the house and emerge onto the suburban street on the other side.

The exit was thus relatively safe. It was important, however, that it should not be abused – if too many men left the barracks on the same day, their absence could easily be spotted. Honza's informal council had therefore to regulate the escapes and determine a rota.

But before my turn came round the entire enterprise came to grief. The Commanding Officer made a personal inspection of the quarters one night and discovered three men missing. He turned on the N.C.O. in charge of the room, who had not reported the men's absence, and asked, with a knowing air, how much he had got for it. The corporal, dazed by the C.O. being apparently in full possession of the facts, made no attempt to deny them. Honza was summoned before the C.O. and in the subsequent confrontation the corporal admitted taking money from him.

The C.O. had us checkmated. The corporal, Honza, and the three men on french leave were all sent for court-martial. I did not even have time to say good-bye to my best friend, since everything happened during a single morning, while we were at work; it was not until much later that I learned they had all been sentenced, Honza to a full year's jail. The C.O. announced to the assembled company that the ban on leave was extended for a further two months and that the entire company would come under a correctional training routine. And he asked the authorities for two watch towers with searchlights to be placed at opposite corners of the camp, and two dog patrols.

The Captain's swoop was so sudden and so successful that we all believed Honza's scheme had been betrayed. I would not say that informing was particularly common in our regiment; indeed we were unanimous in despising it, and the great majority refrained from practising it. But we all knew that it was an ever-present possibility, being the most effective means at our disposal for improving our conditions, getting home on time, receiving good character references and ensuring ourselves some kind of future. We (the great majority) abstained from this lowest of all evils, but we were too ready to suspect others of it.

On this occasion, although it was not necessary to assume the existence of an informer in order to account for the C.O.'s raid, suspicion ripened rapidly and universally into certainty, and fastened unhesitatingly on Alexej. At the time he still had to serve another two days inside; but he still went to work with us every day, and everyone asserted that he had had ample opportunity, with his nark's ears, of overhearing something about Honza's scheme.

On emerging from the glasshouse, the poor bespectacled

student found there were even worse things in store for him. The shift foreman, one of us, started allotting him the most unpleasant pieces of work. He regularly lost his tools, which he then had to replace out of his pay. He was forced to listen to insinuations and insults and to put up with hundreds of minor inconveniences. On the wooden wall over his bed someone had written, in great black letters and with bicycle oil, BEWARE OF THE RAT.

A few days after Honza and the others had been led off under escort, I looked into our platoon bunkroom late one afternoon. It was empty except for Alexej, who was moving around by his bed, making it up. I asked him why he had to remake it, and he told me the lads rumpled his sheets several times a day. I told him they were all convinced that he had informed on Honza. He protested almost tearfully that he knew nothing about it and would never inform on anyone.

'Why do you say you wouldn't inform?' I said. 'You regard yourself as an ally of the C.O. It's only logical that you would give him information.'

'I'm *not* the C.O.'s ally. The C.O. is a saboteur!' he said, with a break in his voice. Then he told me the conclusions he had reached during his long hours in solitary confinement. The 'black' regiments were run by the Party for men it could not trust with arms but whom it wished to re-educate. The class enemy, however, was not asleep and wished at all costs to prevent the re-education process from being successful; it wanted the 'black' troops sustained in their violent hatred of Communism, as a reserve force for the counter-revolution. The C.O.'s treatment of the men was an obvious part of this plan. One never knew where the Party might have enemies, and the C.O. was definitely an enemy agent. Alexej knew his duty and had written a detailed account of the C.O.'s activities.

I was flabbergasted. 'You wrote what? And who did you send it to?' He replied that he had sent a complaint about the C.O. to the Party.

As we left the hut, he asked me if I wasn't afraid of being seen with him by the others. I told him he was a fool for asking and a bigger one if he thought his letter would ever reach its destination. He replied that it was his duty as a Communist to act in all situations in a way he need not be ashamed of. Then he reminded me again that I too was a Communist, even after being expelled from the Party, and that I ought not to behave as I did: 'As Communists we are responsible for everything that happens here.' I thought this ridiculous, and told him that responsibility was unthinkable without freedom. He replied that he felt sufficiently free to act like a Communist; that he must and would prove that he was a Communist. As he said this his jaw was trembling; today, after all these years, I can still recall the incident, and am more aware now than I was then that Alexej was not much over twenty, that he was an adolescent, a boy, and that his destiny hung on him like a giant's suit on a dwarf.

Shortly after my conversation with Alexej I was asked by Cenek, just as Alexej had feared, what I had been talking to 'that rat' about. I told him that Alexej might be a fool but he was no rat; and I repeated Alexej's account of his complaining about the Commanding Officer. Cenek was not impressed: 'I don't know if he's a fool or not,' he said, 'but a rat he most certainly is. Anyone who can publicly denounce his own dad must be a rat.' He was surprised by my not understanding this allusion; apparently the Political Officer himself had shown them newspapers from a few months back in which a statement by Alexej had been printed: he had denounced his father for 'betraying and dirtying the most sacred things his son knew'.

That evening the searchlights which had been constructed during the last few days made their first appearance on the watch towers, and illuminated the darkened camp, while a guard with dogs patrolled the barbed wire. I suddenly felt terribly lonely: I missed Lucie and knew I would not see her for a good two months. The same evening I wrote her a long letter; I told her that I wouldn't be seeing her for some time, that we were not allowed out of camp, and that I was sorry she had denied me what I had longed for and what would, in memory, have helped me to live through those gloomy weeks.

The day after I posted this letter we were doing our compulsory afternoon drill, about-turning, forward-marching and hurling ourselves to the ground. I was following the prescribed movements quite automatically and hardly noticed the corporal's orders or my colleagues marching about and dropping to the ground. I paid no attention to my surroundings: huts on three sides, barbed wire on the fourth, and beyond it the road. Every now and again someone would walk past outside the wire; occasionally someone would stop – mainly children, alone or with their parents, who would explain to them that the men over the wire were soldiers and that they were drilling. For me everything the other side of the wire had become a lifeless backcloth, so many pictures on the wall. That is why I was scarcely even conscious of the wire until someone called softly in that direction: 'Hey girl, what are you looking at?'

Then I saw her. It was Lucie, wearing her shabby old brown overcoat – it occurred to me that when buying clothes in the summer we had forgotten that the summer would end and the cold weather come – and the fashionable black high-heeled shoes which I had given her, and which just did not go with the shabby coat. She was standing motionless outside the wire and watching us seriously. The men, more earnestly still, commented on her strange, patient air, packing their remarks with all the sexual desperation of men kept in enforced celibacy. The corporal in charge noticed that the men's attention was wandering, and soon realized the cause. He was evidently enraged at his powerlessness to order the girl away from the wire; outside the wire was the land of relative freedom over which his jurisdiction did not extend. Instead, after warning the men to keep their mouths shut, he stepped up the volume of his voice and the tempo of the drill.

For a few moments Lucie walked up and down, at times disappearing from my view altogether, before returning to her vantage point. When the drill period finally ended, I was unable to go and talk to her, as we were marched off to an hour of political instruction, full of talk about the camp of peace and about the imperialists; and it was only after the lesson, when it was already getting dark, that I was able to slip out and see if Lucie was still waiting by the wire. She was, and I ran over to her.

She told me not to be angry with her, that she loved me, and that it worried her if she made me unhappy. I said I didn't know when I would see her again. She told me that it didn't matter and that she would come here for me. At this point some of the men went past shouting vulgar comments at us, and I asked her whether she wouldn't mind the soldiers shouting at her. She said she wouldn't mind that because she loved me. She handed me a rose through the fence – at that moment a bugle sounded, calling us on parade – and we kissed through a gap in the barbed wire.

13

From now on Lucie came to the perimeter wire almost every day. At each visit I received a bunch of flowers (once during a kit inspection the sergeant threw the lot on the floor) and on each occasion we exchanged a few words – utterly stereotyped words, for we had no ideas or information to exchange, and only wanted to reassure each other of the one constantly reiterated truth. At the same time I maintained my flow of almost daily letters to her. This was the time when we were most intensely in love. The searchlights on the watch towers, the barking dogs, the strutting young officer who had ordered them into existence – for all this there was very little room in my mind, which was totally concentrated on Lucie's visits.

In a way I was happy within those barracks with their dog patrols, and down the mines where I leaned on my shuddering drill. I was happy and confident because in Lucie I possessed a prize not shared by any of my companions or even by the officers: I was loved, publicly and demonstratively loved. Even though Lucie was not my companions' idea of the perfect woman, and even though they regarded her way of showing her affection as decidedly eccentric, it was still the love of a woman, and as such it gave rise to wonder, nostalgia and envy.

The longer we were severed from the world of women, the more we talked about them and about their minutest details. Birthmarks were brought to mind, the lines of breasts and backsides were sketched in pencil, with a pickaxe in the mud, or with fingers in the sand; there were arguments about the relative shapeliness of various women's buttocks; words and murmurings during intercourse were evoked with great precision. All this became more and more garbled and embroidered with constant repetition. Naturally enough I too came under fire, and the lads were all the more curious for my reports as the subject of them was on view every day, so that they could visualize her clearly and associate her concrete presence with what I had to narrate. There was no putting them off; I was obliged to tell them about Lucie's nakedness, which I had never seen, and about making love to her, which I had never done; and immediately a precise and detailed picture of her quiet passion rose before my eyes.

What was it like then when I loved her for the first time?

In my narrative I saw this as the quintessence of reality. It happened in her room at the hostel. She stripped off in front of me, loyally but with a certain modesty, since she was after all a country girl and I was the first man to see her in the nude. And it was this obedience mingled with shyness which excited me so insanely, and when I went over to her she shrank away and covered her crutch with her hands . . .

Why does she always wear those black high-heeled shoes?

I told them I had bought them so that she could wear them for me when she was naked; she was shy about it but did everything I wanted her to; I always stayed fully dressed as long as possible and she would walk around naked except for those shoes (how I loved seeing her naked when I was dressed!) and she would go to the cupboard where she kept the wine and, still in the nude, would pour some out for me . . .

And so when Lucie came to the wire she was gazed at not only by myself but by at least a dozen of my companions, all of whom knew precisely what she was like when she made love, what she said in those moments and how she moaned; and they would make innuendoes about how she was still wearing her black high-heeled shoes, and would picture her walking naked round her tiny room.

Each one of the lads had some woman he could think back on and share with the others, but I was the only one who could go beyond the narrative and offer them a *look* at the woman; only my woman was real, alive, and at hand. The feeling of comradely solidarity which had induced me to paint such a detailed picture of Lucie's nakedness and her way of making love had the effect of intensifying painfully my desire for her. I was not in the least indignant at the vile comments with which my companions celebrated Lucie's visits, and which, far from taking my Lucie away from me (she was protected against all of them, and against me, by the barbed wire and the dogs), actually gave her to me in still greater measure: they brought my blurred impression of her into sharper focus, and by depicting her together with myself gave the picture a terrible seductiveness. I surrendered to my companions and we all of us surrendered to desire for Lucie. When I went over to her at the wire I felt myself trembling. I was unable to speak for desire, or to understand how I could have gone out with her for six months like a timid student and not seen the woman in her.

I was willing to give anything for a single night in bed with Lucie. I do not mean by this that my attitude to her grew more violent or coarse, or that it lost any of its affection. I would even say that this is the only time in my life when I have felt a total desire for a woman, in which everything was involved: body and soul, lust and tenderness, loneliness and frenzied vitality, desire for the vile and desire for consolation, desire for momentary pleasure and desire for eternal possession. I was totally involved, totally in suspense, totally concentrated, and today, at the age when one feels one's desire moulting away, I look back on those moments like a paradise lost – a strange paradise with a dog patrol encircling it and a corporal's commands roaring through it.

I was ready to do anything for the chance to see Lucie outside the barracks; I had her promise that next time she would not put up a fight and that she would see me whenever I wanted, a promise which she had confirmed many times during our brief conversations across the wire. All it needed on my side was one bold, perilous stroke.

It was not long before my plans were hatched. Honza's precise escape plan had never been discovered: the wire remained inconspicuously severed, and the arrangement with the miner who lived opposite the barracks merely needed renewing. The camp's security arrangements were so perfect that escape by day was impossible, and even in the dark there were the circling dog patrols and the glare of the lights; but all this was evidently designed more to gratify the C.O.'s love of effect than from any real suspicion of a break-out on our part. Attempted escape carried a court-martial and was normally far too great a risk to take; and precisely for this reason I told myself that my project had a good chance of succeeding.

It only remained to find a suitable refuge for Lucie and myself, preferably not too far from the camp. The area around the camp was inhabited largely by miners who worked in the same colliery as ourselves, and with one of these, a fifty-year-old widower, I soon managed to negotiate the use of his flat. The single-storey grey cottage where he lived could be seen from the camp; I pointed it out to Lucie through the wire and expounded my plan. She was not exactly effusive, and she begged me not to take any risks for her sake. In the end she agreed only because she was no good at resisting.

The appointed day arrived, and brought with it an unexpected incident. Immediately after our return from the pit the Boy made us fall in and treated us to one of his frequent addresses. Usually he threatened us with the war which was liable to break out any day, and the fate in store for reactionaries – by which he meant first and foremost ourselves. On this occasion he introduced some new ideas. Apparently the class enemy had wormed his way into the Communist Party itself; but let spies and traitors take note that hidden enemies would be dealt with a hundred times more severely than open ones, because the hidden enemy was no better than a mangy dog.

'And we have one of these in our midst,' said the Boy. Then he made Alexej take two paces forward, pulled a document from his pocket and thrust it at him.

'Have you seen this letter before?'

'Yes, sir,' said Alexej.

'You're a mangy dog and you're also an informer and a sneak. But a dog's voice can't reach as far as heaven.' He tore the letter to shreds. 'I have another letter for you,' he added, giving Alexej an unsealed envelope. 'Read it aloud!'

Alexej drew a paper from the envelope and looked it over. He said nothing.

'Read it!' repeated the C.O.

Alexej still said nothing.

'Are you going to read it or not?' asked the captain again, and when Alexej still remained silent he barked out an order for him to lie flat on the ground. Alexej threw himself flat in the mud. The Boy stood over him for a moment and we all expected a torrent of commands: 'Stand up! Lie down! Stand up! Lie down!' Instead the captain turned away from Alexej and began to stroll along the front rank, running a regulation eye over their equipment as he went. When he had reached the end of the rank he strolled back to where Alexej still lay on the ground.

'Right. Read it aloud!' he said, and Alexej lifted his muddy chin off the ground, stretched out his right hand in which he had been clutching the letter all this time, and still lying flat on his belly read:

We have to inform you that on 15 September 1951 you were expelled from the Communist Party of Czechoslovakia.

p.p. Regional Committee . . .

After which the C.O. ordered Alexej to fall in again and handed us over to the corporal for drill.

After drill there was political instruction, and by the time this ended it was already dark. Lucie was standing by the wire and nodded to show that everything was all right; then she left. After that there was supper, roll-call and lights out. I waited for the corporal in charge of our room to go to sleep;

then I pulled on my boots and went out just as I was, in my long white underpants and nightshirt. I walked down the passage and out into the yard, feeling distinctly chilly in my night attire. My objective, the place where I hoped to crawl through the wire, was behind the sick bay, which meant that if I met anyone I could say I felt ill and was going to wake the M.O. But I reached the sick bay without mishap and crouched in the shadow of its wall. The sentry on the watch tower had evidently stopped taking his job too seriously, the searchlight was lazily directed on a single spot, and the yard I had to cross was in darkness. I crossed successfully to the sick bay and squeezed in close to its wall; now it was just a matter of not bumping into the dog patrol, as the guard spent the entire night circling the wire with his wolfhound. It was quiet – dangerously quiet, and this upset my sense of direction. I waited for about ten minutes until I heard a dog bark, somewhere over the other side of the camp. Then I dashed across to the wire where, thanks to Honza's management, it stood a little way off the ground. There was no wavering now: I crawled under the wire and covered the few yards to the miner's garden fence. Everything was going well: the gate was open and I found myself in the small back yard of a single-storey cottage with all the lights blazing, and the blinds drawn back. I tapped on this, and within seconds an enormous man appeared in the doorway and noisily invited me in. I almost took fright at the volume of his voice; I couldn't forget that I was barely five yards from the camp.

The door led straight into a room. I stopped short in the doorway: there was a table with an open bottle on it and five other men sitting round it drinking. When they saw me they burst out laughing at my attire; they said I must be cold in my nightshirt, and poured me out a glass. I tasted it: it was a dilution of pure spirit. They told me to drink up, and I tossed the glass down and coughed; this provoked a fresh burst of friendly laughter and they offered me a chair. They asked me how I had managed the 'border crossing', laughed anew at my ridiculous garb and called me 'the escaping underpants'. They were all coalminers in their thirties and they probably met here quite often; they were drinking but they were not drunk, and after my initial surprise, mixed with an element of alarm, their friendly, carefree presence put me completely at ease, and I let them pour me another glass of their strong, pungent liquor.

Meanwhile the owner of the house had gone into another room and now came back carrying a dark suit. 'Will this fit you?' he asked. I could see he was at least five inches taller than me and considerably broader, but I said: 'It'll *have* to fit me.' I pulled the trousers on over my underpants, but it was no good: I had to hold on to them to keep them from falling. 'Has anyone got a belt?' I asked my benefactor. No one had. Eventually we found a piece of string, which just about kept the trousers up. When I put the jacket on the men decided for some reason that I looked like Charlie Chaplin, and all I needed was the bowler and the stick, so to humour them I walked about with my heels together and my toes pointed outwards. The dark trousers flopped around the insteps of my boots; they all liked this and said that no woman would be able to resist what she saw in the twinkle of my eye. They poured me a third glass of spirits and saw me out, the owner assuring me I could knock at the window any hour of the night when I wanted to change back again.

I stepped out into an ill-lit suburban street. To reach the house where Lucie was waiting for me I had actually to walk the length of the barracks – at least ten minutes' walk – and pass the well-lit gates; but any twinge of alarm I may have felt proved quite unnecessary, my civilian dress constituting a disguise far beyond the sentry's powers of penetration. I reached the appointed house safely, opened the door, which was lit by a solitary street lamp, and faithfully followed the miner's directions (I had never been in the house and knew it only from his description): up the stairs on the left to the first floor, first door at the top of the stairs. I knocked. The key turned in the lock, Lucie opened the door, and I took her in my arms.

She asked me if I'd been drinking; I said I had and told her how I had got there. She said she had arrived around six, when the owner had left for his night shift, and had been waiting for me ever since, in fear and trembling lest anything should happen to me. She was indeed actually trembling. I told her how much I had been looking forward to seeing her, and felt her shaking even more violently. 'What's the matter?' I asked.

'Nothing.'

'What are you shaking for then?'

'I was afraid for you,' she said, and twisted lightly away.

I looked round me. It was a small, austerely appointed room: a table, a chair, a bed made with slightly soiled sheets, a religious picture over the bed, a cupboard on the opposite wall full of bottled fruit – the only cheerful thing in the room. A naked bulb shone from the ceiling, glaring disagreeably in my eyes and throwing me into a sharp profile whose melancholy clownishness I realized all too painfully at that moment: the enormous jacket, the trousers fastened with a piece of string and, peeping from under them, the black insteps of my army boots; the *tout ensemble* being crowned by my bare shaven skull which must have shone like a pallid moon in the glare of the electric light.

'Lucie, please don't take any notice of how I look,' I said and explained once again the necessity for my change of clothes. Lucie assured me that it didn't matter, but with alcoholic impetuosity I swore I was not going to stand there in front of her like that and threw off the jacket and trousers – forgetting that under the jacket I was wearing my nightshirt and those terrible army-issue bum-fuggers, an even more ludicrous costume than the one I had just shed. I switched off the light but no concealing darkness came to my rescue, as the street lamp shone straight into the room. I was much more ashamed of looking ridiculous than of being seen naked, so I threw off my shirt and pants and stood naked before Lucie. I took her in my arms; and again I felt her trembling. I told her to undress, to remove everything that stood between us, I ran my hands all over her, I repeated my pleas again and again; but Lucie only told me to wait a bit, said she couldn't, she couldn't straight away, she couldn't so quickly.

I took her by the hand and we sat down on the bed. I put

my head in her lap and stayed there quietly for a moment. Then I realized the full incongruity of my nakedness – faintly illuminated by the murky glare of the rustic lamp – and noted the ironic contrast between the dream and the reality: instead of the naked girl serving drinks to the fully clothed man, a naked man with his head in the lap of a fully clothed woman. Suddenly I had a vision of the naked Christ taken from the cross and lying in the arms of a sorrowing Mary, and the vision horrified me, for I had not come for compassion and sympathy but for something entirely different; and again I began urging Lucie on, kissing her face and clothes, and trying surreptitiously to undo her buttons.

I met with no success: once again Lucie twisted away from me. I had lost my original confident impatience, and had exhausted at one go my repertoire of words and physical contacts; so I remained stretched out on the bed, naked and motionless, while Lucie sat over me and ran her rough fingers over my face. Gradually my accumulated anger and frustration uncoiled inside me: in my thoughts I reminded Lucie of all the risks I had taken in order to see her today, and of all the penalties the excursion might cost me. But these silent reproaches touched only the tip of the iceberg. The real reason for my resentment, the reason I would have been ashamed to admit, was much deeper: I was thinking of my own misery, the miserable failure of my youth, the miserable endless cheerless weeks, the degrading eternity of unfulfilled desire; I was remembering the fruitless courting of Marketa, the abomination of the blonde on the grass-cutter, and again the fruitless attempt on Lucie. And I wanted to cry out aloud: 'Why must I be an adult in everything, sentenced as an adult, expelled, branded as a Trotskyite, sent down the mines as an adult, why is it only in love that I'm not allowed to be an adult, that I have to swallow the full humiliation of my own immaturity?' I hated Lucie and I hated her all the more for the knowledge that she was in love with me, because that made her resistance all the more incomprehensible, unnecessary and infuriating. And so, after half an hour of sullen silence, I launched a fresh attack.

I rolled over on to her; I used all my strength and managed to pull up her skirt, tear off her bra and put my hands on her naked breasts, but Lucie resisted all the more furiously, fighting with the same blind strength as myself; finally she broke free, jumped from the bed and ran over to the cupboard.

'Why are you fighting me?' I shouted at her. She told me not to be angry, said she was sorry, but offered no explanation, nothing rational. 'Why are you fighting me? Can't you see I love you? You're insane!' I shouted. 'Throw me out then,' she said, still clinging to the cupboard. 'I'm going to, I'm going to throw you out. Because you don't love me. Because you're making a monkey of me!' And I screamed an ultimatum at her: either she gave herself or I never wanted to see her again.

I went over to her again and took her in my arms. This time she did not resist, but lay there in my arms as if paralysed. 'What's so special about your virginity? Who are you saving it for?' No answer. 'Why don't you answer me?'

'You don't love me,' she said.

'*I* don't love you?'

'No, you don't. I thought you did but you don't' – and she burst into tears.

I knelt down in front of her, I kissed her feet, I begged and implored her. Still she went on crying and saying I didn't love her.

Suddenly I was seized by a lunatic fury. I felt there was some supernatural force barring my path, tearing from my hands everything that I wanted to live for, everything I desired, everything which by rights was mine. It was this force which had taken away my Party, my Comrades, my studies at the university, everything, and always senselessly and for no reason. Now it was fighting me again in the person of Lucie, and I hated her for having become the instrument of this supernatural power. I hit her across the face – for it wasn't her, it was that hostile force. I shouted that I hated her, that I never wanted to see her again, never, never in my life again.

I threw her brown overcoat at her and yelled at her to get out.

She put on her coat and went.

And I lay on the bed and felt an aching void in my soul, and I wanted to call her back because from the moment I had driven her out I knew it was a thousand times better to have a Lucie who was fully dressed and reluctant than not to have any Lucie at all; because to have no Lucie at all meant living in utter desolation.

All this I knew; but I did not call her back.

I lay for some time on the bed in that borrowed room, because in this frame of mind I could not face meeting people, turning up at the house outside the camp, joking with the miners and replying to their cheerfully lewd questions.

Finally, very late at night, I got up and went. The street lamp still shone opposite the house I had left. I walked the length of the barracks, knocked on the darkened window of the cottage, took off the clothes with the miner yawning away in front of me, made some noncommittal answer to his inquiry about the success of my venture and, back in my night-shirt and underpants, set off for camp. I was in a state of despair and total indifference. I didn't bother to look where the dog patrol was, or which way the searchlight was trained. I crawled through the wire and began walking quietly towards my hut. I had just reached the wall of the sick bay when I heard: 'Halt! Who goes there?' I stopped. A torch was flashed on me, and I heard the snarling of a dog. 'What are you doing here?'

'Being sick, Comrade Sergeant,' I replied, leaning my hand on the wall.

'Get on with it then, man, get on with it!' said the sergeant, and he and the dog continued their patrol.

14

I paused after the last sentence, with the break I use to separate my reminiscences into individual chapters. I am not certain whether this is correct, since the rapid chain of events did not end with my encounter with the patrol sergeant but reached its climax the following morning.

I got to bed that night without any further complications. The corporal was fast asleep; but my own attempts to get any sleep were totally unsuccessful, and I was glad when the odious voice of the corporal bawling 'Wakey, wakey!' brought an end to a miserable night. I slipped into my boots and ran to the washroom to splash some cold, refreshing water over myself. When I got back there was a bunch of half-clad squaddies clustered round Alexej's bed with much muffled sniggering. I saw straight away what was going on: Alexej was sleeping like a log, on his stomach, with his head on the pillow and covered with a blanket. I was reminded at once of Franta Petrasek of C Company who to spite his company commander had one morning feigned a sleep so deep that he was shaken by three consecutive superiors without any effect; it was only when he was carried out into the yard and a fire hose was turned on him that he began lazily rubbing his eyes. But with Alexej any sort of insubordination was inconceivable, so his heavy sleeping could only be a consequence of his physical weakness. At this point the corporal in charge of the room came in from the passage carrying an enormous jug of water in his arms, and attended by a few of the lads who had evidently been egging him on to play this immemorial stupid prank, so dear to the typical non-com mentality of all ages and regimes.

I was irritated now by this pathetic accord between the men and the corporal, who at other times was so detested – irritated that a common hatred for Alexej had wiped clean all the old scores between the corporal and them. The C.O.'s little speech yesterday about Alexej's informing had obviously been interpreted to fit their own suspicions, and they had felt a sudden upsurge of heartfelt agreement with the C.O.'s brutality. In any case, is it not easier to join the powerful Communist in hating the powerless one than vice versa? I felt a blinding rage at everybody there, at their unthinking ability to believe every accusation, at their eagerness for the brutality with which they wished to re-assert their downtrodden self-esteem – and I got in front of the corporal and his gang, went up to the bed and said loudly: 'Alexej, you bloody idiot, get up!'

At this someone twisted my arm from behind and forced me to my knees. I looked round and saw it was Pavel Pekny. 'Bloody commie, trying to spoil everything!' he hissed at me. I tore myself away and hit him across the face. There would certainly have been a fight if the others hadn't quickly quietened us down in case Alexej should wake prematurely. Meanwhile the corporal was there with his jug. He stepped up to Alexej, bawled out 'Wakey, wakey!' and poured the entire contents of the jug over him – there must have been a good two gallons there.

But a strange thing happened: Alexej remained lying exactly as before. For a moment the corporal was at a loss, then he bawled out: 'On your feet, attenshun!' But Private Alexej never stirred. The corporal bent down and shook him – the entire bed was soaked through, and pools of water were forming on the floor. He managed to turn Alexej's body over so that we could see his face; it was sunken, pale, immobile.

The corporal shouted: 'Get the M.O.!' No one moved, we were all looking at Alexej in his soaking wet nightshirt, and the corporal yelled again, 'Get the M.O.!', pointing at one of the men, who raced off immediately.

Alexej lay there motionless, smaller and frailer than ever before, and much younger, like a child (only his lips were locked firmly together, as children's never are), and still the water dripped off him. Someone said 'It's raining.'

The Medical Officer arrived, took Alexej by the wrist and said: 'Hmmm!' Then he removed the wet blanket so that Alexej lay before us in his entire inconsiderable length and we could see his soaking wet long white underpants with the bare feet sticking out at the end. The doctor looked around, picked up two capsules from the bedside table, examined them – they were empty – and said: 'There'd be enough for two men there.' Then he pulled a sheet from the nearest bed and covered Alexej with it.

All this had held things up so that we had to eat breakfast at the double, and in three quarters of an hour we were already going below ground. Then came the end of the shift, square-bashing, political instruction and compulsory singing, then cleaning duties, supper, lights out and bed. I thought of how Stana had gone, and my best friend Honza had gone (I never saw him again and only heard reports that after completing military service he escaped across the frontier to Austria), and now Alexej was gone too. He had assumed his Herculean role blindly but courageously, and it was not his fault if he had suddenly been unable to go on with it, to go on humbly and patiently playing his part as the laughing-stock of them all; it was not his fault that he simply lacked the strength. He was not my friend, he was alien to me in the toughness of his convictions, but in his life story he was the closest to me of them all. I felt that even in his death he had continued to reproach me, as if wanting to inform me that the moment the Party discards a man from its ranks that man has no reason to live. I immediately felt guilty that I had not liked him, because now he was dead and would not come back, and I had never done anything for him, although I was the only one there who could have helped him at all.

But I had not only lost Alexej and the irrecoverable opportunity of offering a man my protection; as I see it today, it was at this point that I lost my feeling of companionship and solidarity with my fellow 'politicals', and with it any chance of resurrecting and reinvigorating my tenuous faith in men. I began to have doubts about the value of a solidarity which had been forged by mere force of circumstances and the urge for mutual self-protection. And I began to realize that our 'black' collective was just as capable of bullying another man, of casting him out and sending him to his death, as was the collective of men who raised unanimous hands in vote, or perhaps as any other collective of men.

During those days I felt a great void within me; I felt utterly empty and desolate and I wanted to call to Lucie. Suddenly I could not understand why I had desired her body so insanely; now it seemed to me that she was not a corporeal woman at all, only a transparent pillar of warmth striding

115

through a land of unending chill, a pillar of warmth striding away from me, driven away by myself.

One evening, after a day down the mine and a drill period spent with my eyes on the wire, waiting in vain to see if she would come (the only person to stop by our fence was an old woman who pointed us out to a slovenly-looking child), I wrote a long and sorrowful letter in which I begged Lucie to come back. I said I had to see her, that I did not want anything from her, only that she should be there, so that I could see her and know that she was with me, know she was there, that she was there at all . . .

As if to mock me the days grew suddenly warmer, the sky was blue and we had a glorious October. The leaves on the trees were a blaze of colour as nature, that miserable Ostrava nature, celebrated the farewells of autumn with crazy delight. I could not consider this as anything but mockery, for no reply came to my despairing letters, and the only people to stop by our wire, under the challenging sun, were all utter strangers. About a fortnight later one of my letters came back; the address had been crossed out and a message added in ink: 'gone away'.

I panicked. A thousand times since my last meeting with Lucie I had mentally reviewed everything I had said to her and she to me, a hundred times I had cursed myself, and a hundred times justified myself, a hundred times I had assured myself that I had driven her away for ever, and a hundred times convinced myself that she would understand and would forgive me. But that message on the envelope had the ring of a final verdict.

I could not contain my disquiet, and the very next day I made another mad excursion. I say 'mad', but it was no more dangerous than my last escape from the barracks, so that the epithet emphasizes in retrospect its lack of success rather than the risks involved. I knew that Honza had done the same thing several times when he had had a Bulgarian woman in the summer, with a husband who spent the mornings at work. I took a leaf from his book: I arrived at the pit early in the morning with the others, collected my number and safety lamp, smudged my face with coaldust – and quietly got lost. I ran to Lucie's hostel and questioned the concierge. I learned that Lucie had left a fortnight before with her suitcase and all her worldly possessions; no one knew where she had gone as she had said nothing to anybody. I was beside myself: had anything happened? The concierge looked at me, and said airily with a wave of the hand: 'What do you expect from these temporary girls? They come and go with never a word to anyone.' I went to her place of work and made inquiries in the personnel department; but I learned nothing more there. I wandered all over Ostrava and returned to the face at the end of the shift to mingle with the others who had been down all morning. But evidently I had missed something in Honza's escape techniques; they were waiting for me and came down on me like a ton of bricks. In a fortnight's time I was up before a court-martial and got ten months' jail for desertion.

Yes, it was here, at the moment when I lost Lucie, that the whole long period of hopelessness and barrenness began, that period whose image I had glimpsed in the dreary provincial scenery of my home town, to which I had returned for a particular purpose. Yes, it was from this moment that it all began. During the ten months I was inside, my mother died, and I could not even go to the funeral. Then I went back to Ostrava, to the same regiment, and served another full year as a 'political'. During this period I signed an undertaking to work for another three years in the mines after completing my military service, for word was going round that those who didn't sign would stay on for an extra year or so in the camp. So I spent another three years hewing coal as a civilian.

I take no pleasure in calling this to mind or talking about it, and I would go so far as to say that I detest it when today I hear men cast out like myself from the movement they believed in boasting of their experiences. Admittedly, I did at one time regard my own outcast fate as something heroic, but this was only false pride. From time to time I have had mercilessly to remind myself that I was not assigned to the penal corps for my bravery, for my resistance in action or on the battleground of ideological warfare; no heroic drama preceded my fall, I was more the object than the subject of the whole story, and unless one considers trials, heartaches or sheer futility as virtues I have nothing whatever to boast about.

Lucie? Oh yes: for the whole of those five years I never once set eyes on her, and it was a long time before I had any news of her either. After being demobbed I heard that she was somewhere in Western Bohemia. But by that time I had ceased inquiring after her.

Part IV: Jaroslav

1

I see a road winding through the field. I see the mud of the track, rutted by the wheels of rustic carts. And I see the verges flanking the road, grassy verges so green that I cannot help caressing their smooth slopes with my hand.

The fields around are small, they are not collective fields. How is this? Are they not of today, these lands I am passing through? What sort of land then is this?

I walk on and a briar bush appears before me on the grass verge. It is full of small wild roses. I stop beside them and am happy. I sit down on the grass under the bush and in a while I lie down. I sense my back touching the grassy earth. I feel it with my back. I hold it on my back and beg it not to be afraid of being heavy, of lying on me with all its weight.

Then I hear the clattering of hooves. In the distance a small cloud of dust appears. It comes nearer, becoming more transparent and sparse. Horsemen emerge from it. Astride the horses sit young men in white uniforms. But the nearer they come the more evident is the negligent array of their uniforms. Some coats are buttoned and their gold buttons gleam, some are unbuttoned, and some of the young men are in shirtsleeves only. Some have caps on their heads and some are bareheaded. No, this is no army, these are deserters, turncoats, bandits! They are *our* cavalry! I raise myself from the ground and watch them approach. The leading horseman unsheathes his sabre and holds it erect. The cavalry come to a halt.

The man with drawn sabre leans across the horse's neck and looks his fill upon me.

'Yes, it is I,' I say.

'The King!' says the man in wonderment. 'Now do I recognize thee.'

I incline my head, happy at being recognized. Centuries they have ridden thus and still they know me.

'How farest thou, King?' asks the man.

'I go in fear, my friends,' I say.

'Do they hunt for thee?'

'No. Yet it is worse than any hunting. Something is being prepared against me. I do not know those that are around me. I enter my house and within is a different room, and a different wife and all things different. I think I have made a mistake, I rush out, but it is in truth my house! Without it is mine, within it is a stranger's. And so it is where I am going. Something is afoot, my friends, which puts me in great fear.'

The man says: 'Thou hast not forgotten how to ride?' Only then do I notice that by his steed there stands a saddled and riderless horse. The man indicates it. I put my foot in the stirrup and leap on. The horse starts but I am already firmly in the saddle and gripping his back with my knees in great delight. The man takes a red veil from his pocket and gives it to me: 'Veil thy face, that they may not know thee!' I veil my face and become at once as blind. 'Thy horse will lead thee,' I hear the man's voice.

The whole column sets off at a trot and I feel the riders jogging along on both sides of me. Their calves touch mine and I hear the snorting of their horses. For about an hour we ride thus, body close to body. Then we halt. The same man's voice addresses me again: 'We are arrived, O King!'

'Where?' I ask.

'Dost thou not hear the murmuring of the mighty river? We stand on the banks of the Danube. Here thou art safe, King.'

'Yes,' I say, 'I feel that I am safe. But I should like to cast off this cloak.'

'Thou must not, King. Thou needest not thine eyes. Thine eyes would but deceive thee.'

'But I wish to see the river Danube. It is my river, my mother river. I wish to see it.'

'Thou needest not thine eyes, King. Everything there is I shall relate to thee. It is better thus. Around us are plains stretching far out of sight. Pastures. Here and there are bushes, here a wooden stake or well-pump juts forth. But we are on the grass by the banks. Not far from us the grass goes into sand, for the river in these parts has a sandy bed. But now do thou dismount, King.'

We dismount and sit down upon the ground.

'The men are making fire,' I hear the man's voice say. 'The sun already merges with the distant horizon and soon it will be cold.'

'I should like to see Vlasta,' I say suddenly.

'Thou shalt see her.'

'Where is she?'

'Not far from here. Thou shalt ride for her. Thy horse shall take thee to her.'

I jump up and beg that I may go for her at once. But the man's hand seizes me by the arm and pulls me to the ground. 'Sit, King. Thou must rest and eat thy fill. All the while I shall relate to thee of her.'

'Where is she, tell me that?'

'An hour's ride from here there is a wooden cottage with a thatched roof. It is encircled by a wooden fence.'

'Yes, yes,' I affirm and feel a joyous weight upon my heart. 'Everything is of wood. Thus it must be. In her cottage there must be not one metal nail.'

'Indeed,' the voice continues, 'the fence is of wooden stakes made ready so hurriedly that one may see the original shape of the branch upon them.'

'All things of wood are like to a cat or dog,' I say. 'They are beings rather than things. I love the world of wood. Only there am I at home.'

'Beyond the fence grow sunflowers, marigolds and dahlias, and there too grows an old apple tree. While we yet speak Vlasta stands upon the threshold of this house.'

'How is she arrayed?'

'She has a skirt of linen, somewhat stained, for she has just returned from the cowshed. In her hand she has a wooden pail. She wears no shoes. But she is beautiful because she is young.'

'She is poor,' I say. 'She is a poor man's daughter.'

'Even so, and yet she is a queen. And because she is a queen she must be hidden. Even thou darest not go to her lest she be revealed. Thou canst go to her only under thy veil. Thy horse will lead thee to her.'

So fine is the man's narration that I feel myself falling prey to a sweet languor. I lie upon the grass and hear the voice, and then the voice falls silent, and I hear only the murmuring of the water and the crackling of the fire. It is so beautiful that I dare not open my eyes. But there is no help for it. I know it is already time and that they must be opened.

2

Underneath me there were three cushions on the polished wood. I do not like polished wood. Neither do I like the curved iron legs on which the divan stands. There is a pink glass globe encircled with three white bands hanging above me on the ceiling. I do not like the globe either, or the china cabinet opposite with so much miscellaneous and useless glass displayed within it. The only thing made of wood is the black harmonium in the corner. It is the only thing in the room I like. It was father's. Father died a year ago.

I got up from the couch. I did not feel rested. It was Friday afternoon, two days before Sunday's Ride of the Kings. Everything depended on me. In our district everything connected with folklore depends on me. A good fortnight I had been kept awake by all sorts of worries, finding things, arguing things, arranging things.

Then Vlasta came into the room. I keep telling myself that she ought to get fatter. Fat wives are usually jolly ones. Vlasta is skinny and already has a number of small wrinkles on her face. She asked me if I had remembered to stop at the laundry for our washing on the way home from school. I had forgotten. 'I might have known,' she said, and asked me if I would be at home at all today. I had to tell her I wouldn't as I had a meeting in town very soon. A district meeting.

'You promised you'd do Vladimir's homework with him today.'

I shrugged my shoulders.

'And who is going to be at this meeting?'

I named those who would be taking part and Vlasta interrupted me: 'Will Mrs Hanzlik be there?'

'Yes,' I said.

Vlasta assumed her outraged expression, and I knew that I was in bad odour. Mrs Hanzlik had a bad reputation. Everyone knew she slept around. It wasn't that Vlasta suspected me of having a relationship with her, but she was always irritated at the very mention of her. She scorned any meetings Mrs Hanzlik attended. It was no use arguing about it – I preferred just to slip out of the house.

At the meeting we discussed the final preparations for the Ride of the Kings. The whole thing was in a mess. The local council had begun cutting down on us. A few years ago the council had supported folk celebrations with big grants. Today we had to support the council. The League of Youth held no attraction for youth these days, so why shouldn't they be given the job of arranging the Ride, to make it more of a draw! The proceeds from the Ride used to support other less profitable folklore concerns, but this time it was argued that they should go to the League of Youth to use as they wanted. We had requested the police to close the road for the duration of the Ride. That very day we had had a refusal from them. They said it was impossible to disrupt the traffic for the sake of the Ride. But what will the Ride be like with the horses stampeding about among the cars? The whole thing was one big headache.

It was around eight when I left the meeting. I saw Ludvik in the square. He was walking along the other side of the pavement in the opposite direction to me. I almost stopped dead in my tracks. What was he doing here? Then I caught his glance, which rested on me for a second and shifted quickly away. He pretended not to know me. Two old friends like us. Eight years at the same school bench. And he pretends not to know me!

Ludvik was the first crack to appear in my life. Nowadays

I'm used to the idea of my life being none too secure. Not long ago I was in Prague and I went to one of those little theatres which sprang up like mushrooms in the sixties and gained quick popularity, as they were run by young people in an undergraduate sort of way. They did a piece with very little action in it but there were satirical songs and good jazz. All of a sudden the jazz musicians put on feathered hats like the ones we wear in our folk costume and began doing a take-off of a cymbalo band. They wailed and squealed, imitated our dance steps and our typical mime gestures with the hands. It only lasted a few minutes but it had the audience rolling in the aisles. I couldn't believe my eyes. Five years ago no one would have dared to make clowns of us. And no one would have laughed at the joke. Now we are made to look ridiculous. Why are we suddenly ridiculous?

And Vladimir, I've had trouble with him the last few weeks. The district council dropped a hint to the League of Youth that he should be chosen as this year's King. There is an age-old tradition that the election of the King means honouring the father. This year they were to honour me. They wanted through my son to reward me for everything I had done for folk culture. But Vladimir tried to get out of it, using every conceivable excuse. He said he had to be in Brno on the Sunday for the motor cycle races. He even said he was afraid of horses. Finally he said he did not want to be King if it was going to be arranged from above. He said he did not want any favours.

I've spent a lot of time worrying about this. It was as if he wanted to remove from his life everything which might remind him of mine. He never wanted to go to the children's song and dance group which had been set up at my suggestion in conjunction with our ensemble. He was already making excuses then. He said he had no musical talent. Yet he played the guitar quite well and used to go round to his friends to sing American songs.

Of course Vladimir is fifteen now. And he's fond enough of me. He's a sensitive lad. A few days ago we had a little private chat together and perhaps he saw what I was getting at.

3

I remember it vividly. I was sitting in the rocking chair and Vladimir was sitting opposite me on the divan. I leaned my elbow on the closed lid of the harmonium, my favourite instrument. I have heard its strains since I was a child. Father played it every day. Mainly folk songs in simple harmonies. To me it sounded like the distant babbling of springs. I only wish Vladimir would think of it like that. I only wish he would try to understand.

All nations have their popular art. But for the most part one can imagine their cultures without it. Ours one cannot. Every western European nation has had at least since the Middle Ages an unbroken cultural development. Debussy could refer back to the rococo music of Couperin and Rameau, while Couperin and Rameau could hark back to the medieval troubadours. Max Reger could refer to Bach and Bach to the old German polyphonic school. Thomas Mann can calmly reach back through several centuries to the medieval Faust.

But in the seventeenth and eighteenth centuries the Czech nation almost ceased to exist. In the nineteenth century it was virtually reborn. Among the older European nations it was a child. It had its past, and a rich culture too, but these were separated from it by a moat of two hundred years during which neither nobleman nor burgher had spoken Czech. The Czech language retreated from the towns to the countryside and became the exclusive property of the illiterate. Among them, however, it never ceased to continue creating its own culture. A humble culture, completely hidden from the eyes of Europe. A culture of songs, fairy tales, ancient rites and customs, proverbs and sayings. And this was the only narrow bridge which led across the two-hundred-year ditch.

The only bridge, the only crossing point. The only seed of an unbroken tradition. And so the men who began at the turn of the nineteenth century to create a new Czech literature and music used this culture to graft it upon. This is why the first

125

Czech poets and musicians spent so much time collecting fairy tales and songs. This is why their early poetic and musical efforts were often only a paraphrase of folk poetry and folk melodies.

Vladimir, if only you would understand this. Your father is not just a crackpot folklore addict. Maybe he is something of an addict but he goes deeper than that. He hears in popular art the sap without which Czech culture would have dried up. He is in love with the sound of its flowing.

This love of mine arose during the war. They wanted to show us that we had no right to exist, that we were only Germans who spoke a Slavonic tongue. We had to reassure ourselves that we had existed before and that we still existed. We all made a pilgrimage to the source. *Ad fontes*. Even the greatest modernists, Halas and Holan, Martinu and Emil Filla, they all made their humble pilgrimage to popular art.

And my turn came as well. At the time I was playing bass in a small student jazz band. My father was a hard taskmaster in music and I could play all the stringed instruments. One day I had a visit from a Dr Blaha, chairman of a local patriotic organization. He said we should resurrect the cymbalo bands, that this was our patriotic duty. To show that we were Slavs. That we had an ancient popular culture.

Who at that time could have turned this offer down? I joined them and played the violin.

We awoke folk song from its deathly slumbers. Those nineteenth-century patriots had transferred popular art to the songbooks only just in time. Urban civilization began rapidly to displace the popular traditions. So at the turn of the century we had folklore societies springing up, taking the folk art out of the songbooks and restoring it to life again. This happened in the towns first. Then in the country. And particularly in our region. Popular feastdays were arranged, the Ride of the Kings and the folk music groups were supported. It was a great effort to stop all this going for nothing. The folklorists could not revive as rapidly as civilization had been able to bury. That is, until the war inspired us with fresh strength.

There are certain merits in having one's back to the wall.

One can see right to the heart of matters where previously one saw merely opaque shells. A war was on and the life of a nation was at stake. We heard the folk songs and we suddenly saw that they were the most essential of essentials. I consecrated my life to them. Through them I merge with the stream which flows deep below. I am a wave of this stream. I am both the wave and the river. And I like it.

During the war we lived everything more intensely. It was the last year of the occupation, and the Ride of the Kings was staged in our village. There was an army camp in our village and there were German officers jostling with the public on the pavements. Our Ride became a demonstration. A host of colourful men on horseback and with sabres. An invincible Czech horde. A deputation from the depths of history. I was fifteen then and I was chosen to be King. I rode between two pages and had my face veiled. And I was proud. And my father was proud, for he knew I had been chosen King as a mark of respect for him. He was a village schoolmaster and a patriot and liked by everyone.

I believe, Vladimir, that things have their own meaning. I believe that the fates of men are interconnected by a cement of wisdom. I see a sign in the fact that it was you they chose to be King this year. I am as proud as I was twenty years ago. Prouder. Because they want to honour me by choosing you. And I appreciate this honour – why should I deny it? I wish to hand over my kingdom to you. I want you to accept it from me.

Perhaps he understood me. He promised to accept his election as King. To take part in the Ride.

4

If only he would try and understand how interesting it is. I can imagine nothing more interesting. Or exciting.

Let me give an example. The musicologists have long been of the opinion that European folk songs date from the baroque age. Village musicians played and sang in castle orchestras and brought the musical part of the castle culture back to the life of the people. In this way folk song is not an art form which arose of itself. It was taken from a synthetic form of music.

In Bohemia, folk songs are indeed related to the artificial baroque music. But which came first? The chicken or the egg? I don't know why the folk song alone should be made to look like the debtor.

But, however things were in Bohemia, the songs we sing in Southern Moravia cannot by any stretch of the imagination be explained as deriving from artificial music. This is clear at first glance. Take tonality, for instance. Artificial baroque music was written in majors and minors. Our songs, however are written in modes undreamed of by the castle minstrels.

Take the Lydian. This is the one with the augmented fourth. It always makes me pine for the ancient pastoral idylls. I see the pagan Pan and I hear his pipes playing. Rather like this:

Baroque and classical music paid devout homage to the orderliness of the major seventh. They knew how to reach the tonic only via a disciplined leading note. They were horrified at the minor seventh, which stepped up to the tonic over a major second. And it is precisely this minor seventh which I love in our folk songs, whether it sounds as Aeolian, Dorian or Mixolydian. I like it for its melancholy and pensiveness. And because it abjures the foolish scamper towards the key note with which everything, song and life, finishes:

But there are also songs in modes so extraordinary that it is impossible to label them as any of the so-called ecclesiastical modes. They take my breath away:

Moravian songs are, in terms of tonality, unimaginably varied. Their thinking can be mysterious. They may begin in the minor and end in the major, they may waver between different keys. Often when I have to harmonize them I just do not know how I am to understand their tonality.

And they are as variegated rhythmically as they are in tonality. Especially the long-drawn-out ones which are not used for dancing to. Bartok labelled them parlando. Their rhythm just cannot be written down in our notation system. Or to put it another way: from the standpoint of our musical notation all folk singers sing their songs in a rhythm which is imprecise and wrong.

How are we to explain this? Janacek said that the complexity and indefinable quality of the rhythm was caused by the varied and transient moods of the singers. It depended on where they were singing, when they were singing, how they felt when they were singing. The folk singer uses his song to react to the colour of flowers, to the weather and the countryside around.

But isn't this a rather over-poetic interpretation? It was during my first year at university that our lecturer acquainted us with an experiment of his. He got several different interpreters of folk song to sing, independently of each other, the same rhythmically indefinable song. By using very precise electronic equipment he ascertained that their singing was exactly the same.

The rhythmic complexity of the songs is therefore not due to any imprecision or imperfection or to the mood of the singer. It has its own secret laws. In a certain type of Moravian dance song, for example, the second half of a bar is always a fraction of a second longer than the first half. How is such rhythmic complexity to be incorporated in musical notation? The metrical system of art music is based on symmetry. A whole note is divided into two halves, the half into two quarters, and the bar divided into one, two, three or four beats of equal length. But what about the bar which is divided into two unequal halves? For us today the problem of writing down the original rhythm of Moravian songs is an extremely tough nut to crack.

But an even knottier problem is the actual origin of all this complex rhythmic thought. One scholar proposed the theory that the long-drawn-out chants were originally sung by riders on horseback. The horses' and riders' movements remained imprinted in the strange rhythms of the chants. Others saw the most likely prototype of these songs in the slow swinging step with which the young people used to stroll around the village green in the evenings. Others saw in it the slow rhythm of the villagers as they scythed grass.

Perhaps all this is merely guesswork. One thing, however, is clear. Our songs cannot be derived from baroque music. Czech songs possibly can. Possibly. Ours certainly cannot. Our country is composed of three lands, Bohemia, Moravia and Slovakia, but the frontiers of folk culture divide it into two halves: Bohemia with Western Moravia, and Slovakia with Eastern Moravia, where my home is. Bohemia had a higher level of civilization, greater contact between town and village, and between villagers and the castle. The East had its castles as well. But the countryside was far more remote from them by reason of its sheer primitiveness. No country folk went to play in any castle orchestras. Here, within the Hungarian cultural sphere, the functions of the Czech castle bands were taken over by the gypsies. But these did not play minuets and Italian sarabandes to the yeomen and barons. They played their csardas and dumkas, and these, again, were folk songs only slightly modified in their sentimental and ornate Romany interpretations.

In these conditions it was possible for folk songs in our parts to be preserved from the earliest times on. This explains why they are so enormously varied. They date from different phases of our long slow history. And so, when you stand face to face with the whole of our musical folk culture, it is like having a woman from the Thousand and One Nights dancing before you and gradually throwing off veil after veil.

Veil number one! It is of coarse material and printed with trite designs. These are the most youthful songs, dating from the last fifty or seventy years. They came to us from the West, from Bohemia. They were brought by the brass bands. The schoolmasters taught our children to sing them in the schools. For the most part they are songs in major keys, of a common European type, and only slightly adapted to our rhythms.

Veil number two! This one is a lot more colourful. These are songs of Hungarian origin. They accompanied the encroachment of the Magyar language into the Slavonic regions of the Hungarian empire. Gypsy bands spread them throughout Hungary during the nineteenth century. Everybody knows them. The csardas and recruiting songs with their characteristic syncopation in the cadence.

As the dancer throws off this veil we see the next one. These are the songs of the local Slavonic populace dating from the seventeenth and eighteenth centuries.

But the fourth veil is more beautiful still. These are even older songs. They go back as far as the fourteenth century. This was when the Wallachian shepherds journeyed across the Carpathians from the east and south-east. Their shepherd and brigand songs know nothing of chords or harmonies. They are purely melodic compositions in archaic tonal systems. The fife and the larger fujara lent a special character to their melodies.

And when this veil falls there is no other beneath it. The dancer is dancing completely naked. These are the oldest songs of all. They stretch back in origin to ancient pagan times. They are based on the oldest musical thinking. On the four-note system, the tetrachordal system. Mowing songs. Reaping songs. Songs that are intimately connected with the rites of the patriarchal village community.

Bela Bartok showed that at this most ancient level the Slovak, South Moravian, Magyar and Croatian songs were similar to the point of being indistinguishable. When you imagine this geographical territory, before your eyes there rises the first Slavonic empire, from the ninth century. Its frontiers were dismantled a thousand years ago but they have remained imprinted to this day in this most ancient stratum of folk songs.

The folk song or the folk rite is the tunnel through history in which has been preserved much of what, above ground, has been destroyed by war, revolution and a heedless civilization. It is a tunnel through which I can see far back into the past. I see Rostislav and Svatopluk, the first dukes of Moravia. I see the ancient Slavonic world.

But why go on speaking about the Slavonic world? That period had its internationalism too! For long we were puzzled by the mysterious text of one of the folk songs. It sang about hops in some unclear connexion with a wagon and a goat. Someone was riding the goat, and someone else on the wagon. Hops were praised for making brides of virgins. Even the singers who interpreted this song did not understand the text. Only the inertia of ancient tradition had preserved in this song a cluster of words which had long ago lost all intelligibility. Suddenly one possible explanation occurred: the ancient Greek festival of Dionysus. The satyr on his goat and the god grasping a hyrsus entwined with hops.

Antiquity! I could not believe it. But afterwards, at the university, I studied the history of musical thought. The musical structure of our oldest folk songs is indeed similar to the musical structure of antique music. The Lydian, Phrygian and Dorian tetrachord. The descending concept of the scale which takes the upper note rather than the lower as the tonic; this latter happens the moment music starts to think harmonically. Our oldest songs, then, belong to the same epoch of musical thinking as the songs sung in ancient Greece. In them the antique age has been preserved for us.

The Moravian painter Uprka once invited the sculptor Rodin to Moravia some time at the beginning of the century. He showed him among other things the Ride of the Kings. Rodin was apparently in ecstasy over this magnificent show and exclaimed: 'Hellas!' No one here knows a thing about

Rodin's sculpture but this one utterance of his everybody knows. Everyone sees in it merely an expression of admiration. But I know that his remark had a very precise meaning.

5

At supper tonight I kept seeing Ludvik's eyes shifting away from me. And I felt myself clinging all the more to Vladimir. Suddenly I was afraid that perhaps I had been neglecting him. Perhaps I had never tried hard enough to draw him into my world. After supper Vlasta stayed in the kitchen and I went into the sitting-room with Vladimir. I tried to tell him something about Moravian folk song. How interesting it all was. And how exciting. But somehow I was unsuccessful. I felt rather like a schoolmaster. I was afraid I might be boring him. Of course he just sat there saying nothing and looking as if he was listening. He's a good boy. He's always been a good boy to me. But how do I know what goes on inside that head of his?

When I had tormented him enough with my talk Vlasta put her head in the room and said it was time for bed. There was nothing I could do, no resistance I could offer. She is the household's heart and soul, its calendar and its clock. Off you go, Vladimir, good night.

I left him in the room with the harmonium. He sleeps there on the divan with the metal legs. I sleep in the bedroom next door, beside Vlasta on the marriage bed. I won't go to bed yet. I'd be sure to sleep badly. I would roll around the bed and wake Vlasta. Presently I'll go and have a look at the garden. It's a warm night and you can see the stars. The garden of the old single-storey cottage where we live is full of old-time rural aromas. There is a bench under the pear tree. It was made by my paternal grandfather out of coarse, hardly processed wood. From planks and four logs.

Damn Ludvik. Why did he have to turn up today? I'm afraid it may be a bad omen. My oldest friend! This was the very bench we used to sit on so often when we were boys. I used to like him. Right from the first form in the high school when I first met him. He had more brains in one finger than the rest of us had in the whole of our bodies, but he never made much use of them. He had a poor opinion of the school and the teacher, and he used to love doing anything that went against school regulations.

Why did we two become such friends? The finger of destiny must have had something to do with it. We were both half orphans. My mother died when I was born. Ludvik's father was sent to the concentration camp when he was thirteen and he never saw him again.

Why the Germans locked up old Jahn no one really knows. Some said with a sneer that it was for profiteering and other shady deals. He was employed by a German firm as bricklayer foreman and by some irregular means or other he managed to get hold of a mass of groceries. Ludvik said he used to give them to some hungry Jewish family. Maybe he did. The Jews never came back to confirm it.

Ludvik was the eldest son. He was also the only one, because his younger brother died. After his father's arrest he and his mother were left on their own. They suffered considerable hardship. The high school cost a fair amount of money. It looked as if Ludvik would have to leave. Then at the last minute came salvation.

It was a salvation Ludvik hated. His father had a sister who some time before the war had married a rich local builder. After that she had lost almost all contact with her bricklayer brother. But when he was arrested her patriotic heart was stirred. She proposed to her sister-in-law that she should take on Ludvik as her responsibility. She herself had only a cretinous daughter, and the talented Ludvik made her very envious. Not only did she support him financially, but he was invited to their place every day. For dinner and for supper. He was introduced to the cream of local society which used to gather at her place. Ludvik had to appear grateful to them as his studies depended upon their support.

But at the same time he liked them about as much as he

liked water in his shoes. They were called Koutecky and from that time on we regarded the name as synonymous with pompous ass. Builder Koutecky was a great Maecenas. He bought up masses of paintings by landscape artists in our neighbourhood. The ones who were well known. These, God knows, were the most utter charlatans. Mrs Koutecky would stand in front of a picture and sigh admiringly: 'Ah, the perspective!' Her one and only criterion for judging a picture was its perspective.

Mrs Koutecky's opinion of her sister-in-law was not very high. She had held it against her brother that he had made a poor marriage. And even after his arrest her attitude remained the same. The heavy guns of her charity were trained on Ludvik. She saw in him a descendant of her own flesh and blood and she longed to make him her son. The existence of her sister-in-law she regarded as a regrettable mistake. She never even invited her to the house. Ludvik saw all this and just gritted his teeth. He doted on his mother. Many a time he wanted to show his defiance. But his mother always begged him with tears to be reasonable and show all possible gratitude to the Kouteckys.

Ludvik much preferred coming to our place. We were like twins. Father was almost as fond of him as he was of me. When I became active in the student jazz band Ludvik wanted to join too. He bought a cheap clarinet at the bazaar and in no time learned to play it quite well. We played in the band together, and when Dr Blaha came round and appealed to our sense of patriotism we joined the cymbalo band together.

Towards the end of the war Koutecky's cretinous daughter got married. Mrs Koutecky decided that the wedding was to be a big one. She wanted to have five pairs of bridesmaids and pages behind the bride and groom. This duty fell upon Ludvik and gave him the eleven-year-old daughter of the local chemist as partner for the wedding. Ludvik lost all sense of humour. He felt ashamed in front of us for having to play the fool at a toffee-nosed wedding. He wanted to be taken for an adult and felt bitterly insulted at having to take the arm of some chit of eleven. He was furious with the Kouteckys for putting him on

135

display as proof of their charity, and furious at having to kiss the cross during the ceremony after everybody else had slobbered over it. That evening he deserted the festivities and came to see us in the back room of the inn. We played, had a few drinks and poked fun at him. He lost his temper and said he hated the bourgeoisie. Then he cursed the church rites and said he spat at the Church and would leave it.

We didn't take this too seriously, but a few days after the end of the war Ludvik actually carried out his threat. Of course by doing so he mortally offended the Kouteckys. This didn't bother him. He was glad to part ways with them. He began to get madly pro-Communist. He used to go to their lectures and buy up their literature. Our area was solidly Catholic and our high school particularly so. This meant we didn't have very much sympathy for Ludvik's communistic views. But we were quite ready to forgive them as an interesting eccentricity. We recognized his rights and privileges.

In 1947 we took our final exams. The very same day Ludvik, to celebrate his maturity, applied at the local secretariat to join the Party. That autumn we all went our various ways out into the world. Ludvik went to study in Prague, I in Brno. We left two poor lonely people at home, Ludvik a mother and myself a father. Luckily Brno is only two hours by train. I used to go home at week-ends. To see father and to play in the group. Ludvik I didn't see for a whole year after he matriculated from high school.

6

It was 1948. Everything was being turned upside down. When Ludvik joined our group during the vacations we were at a loss how to greet him. None of us were Communists. In the February coup we saw the coming of dictatorship. Ludvik brought his clarinet but never needed it. We spent the entire night in debate.

Was it then that the disharmony between us began? I do

not think so. That night Ludvik almost entirely won me over. He avoided political arguments as much as possible and spoke about our group. He said we ought to have a more elevated understanding of the meaning of our work than we had had up till then. What was the sense in merely reviving a lost past? He who looks backwards will end up like Lot's wife.

We shouted at him: 'So what do you want us to do?'

Of course, he replied, we must cherish our heritage of folk art but that alone was not enough. We were in a new age now. There were wide horizons opening up for our work. We must take the ordinary everyday musical culture and purge from it the hackneyed hit songs and empty trumpery with which the bourgeois fed the people. Their place must be taken by the real original popular art, from which we would create a modern style of art and living.

Strange. What Ludvik was saying was merely the old utopia of the most conservative Moravian patriots. They were always fulminating against the godless depravity of city culture. In the melodies of the Charleston they heard the pipes of the Devil. But that is by the by. It only made Ludvik's words all the more intelligible to us.

The rest of his argument sounded rather more original. He was talking about jazz. Now jazz had grown from a negro folk music to conquer the whole of the western world. Forget the fact that jazz had gradually become a commercial commodity. It might serve us as a rousing demonstration of the miraculous power of folk music. The general musical style of an entire era had stemmed from it.

We listened to Ludvik and our surprise was mingled with aversion. We were irritated by his certainty. He was behaving the way all the Communists behaved at that time. As if he had made a secret pact with the future and had the right to act in its name. Perhaps too he left a bad taste in our mouths because he had suddenly changed from the Ludvik we had known. With us he had always been one of the lads, a joker. Now he was talking in deadly earnest and was not ashamed of using long and high-sounding words. And of course he also annoyed us by the unhesitating way in which he linked the fate of our band with the fate of the Communist Party, even though not one of us was a Communist.

On the other hand, his words did have a kind of attraction for us. His way of thinking corresponded to our most secret dreams. Suddenly they elevated us to a historic greatness. They were too flattering to our love of Moravian song for us to be able to turn them down flat. And I personally couldn't on two counts. I liked Ludvik. I liked my father as well and he had no use for Communists at all. Ludvik's talk built a bridge across this ravine.

In my mind I call him the Pied Piper. He blew on his flute and we all flocked after him. Whenever his ideas were too sketchy we ran to his aid. I remember my own arguments. I was talking about European music and how it had developed from baroque times. After the impressionist era it was already growing stale. It had exhausted almost all its store of energy for popular songs as well as for sonatas and symphonies. That was why jazz had had such a miraculous effect on it. From its thousand-year roots it had begun greedily to suck up the fresh sap. Jazz had not only charmed the wine bars and dance halls of Europe. It had also charmed Stravinsky, Honegger, Milhaud and Martinu and they had drawn on its rhythms in their compositions. But at this point we must beware. At the same time, indeed a whole decade earlier, East European folk music had poured its fresh, vigorous blood into the veins of European music. The young Stravinsky, Janacek, Bartok and Enescu had all taken something from it. Thus the development of European music had put folk music and jazz on a par. Their contribution to the shaping of serious European music of the twentieth century was of equal worth. With the music of the masses, however, it was different. The folk music of Eastern Europe had hardly made any impression on it at all. Here jazz remained in complete command of the field. And here was where our mission began. *Hic Rhodus, hic salta!*

He was quite right, we confirmed. There was the same strength concealed in the roots of our folk music as there was in the roots of jazz. Jazz had its own unique melody in which the original six-tone scale of the old negro chants wa still apparent. But our folk song too had its own special melody, one which had even greater melodic variety. Jazz had an original rhythm whose fabulous complexity arose from a thousand-year culture of African drums and tomtoms. But our music also was, in rhythmical terms, virtually self-sufficient. Finally jazz grew from the principle of improvization. But the astonishing knack of playing together that we found with folk musicians who had never had any knowledge of notation also rested upon improvization.

Only one thing differentiated us from jazz, he resumed. Jazz was quick to develop and change. Its entire style was on the move. It was a steep road indeed from the primitive beginnings of New Orleans through hot jazz, swing, to cool jazz and so on. New Orleans jazz could have no idea of the harmonies used in the jazz of today. On the other hand our folk music was a motionless sleeping princess from bygone centuries. We must awaken her. She must merge with the life of today and develop alongside it. Folk music must develop as jazz had developed – only without ceasing to be itself, without losing its melody and rhythm. It must create its own new and changing phases of style. It must speak about our twentieth century. It must become its musical mirror. This was not easy. It was an enormous task. And it was a task which could only be carried through under Socialism.

'What's it got to do with Socialism?' we protested.

He expounded his point. The old countryside had lived a collective life. Communal rites were observed throughout the rural year. Folk art knew no life outside these rites. The romantics imagined the girl cutting grass as being suddenly inspired and pouring forth song like a stream from the mountainside. In fact the folk song originated in a different way from the artificial poem. The poet created to express himself, his uniqueness and his diversity. In the folk song man did not stand out from the others but joined in with them. The folk song grew like a stalactite. Drop by drop it acquired fresh motifs and fresh variants. The songs were passed on from generation to generation and everyone who sang them added something new. Each song had a number of authors, who all disappeared modestly with their creation. No folk song existed just for its own sake. It had its function. There were songs sung at weddings, songs sung at harvest time, songs sung at shrovetide, songs for Christmas, for haymaking, for dancing and for funerals. Even love songs did not exist outside certain habitual festivities. The evening rural promenade, the singing under maidens' windows, courtship, everything had its own collective rite and in that rite the songs had their established place.

Capitalism broke up this old collective life. Folk art lost its base, its sense of being, its functions. It would be useless to try to resurrect it while there still existed the social conditions in which man lived cut off from man, every one for himself. Socialism, however, liberated man from the yoke of his isolation. People would be living in a new collective system. They would be linked together by the common cause. Their private life would become merged with their public. Again they would be united by dozens of communal rites and would create their new collective customs. Some they would take from the past: harvest-time, shrovetide, dancing, work songs. Others they would create as new – the First of May, meetings, celebrations of the Liberation, rallies. In all of these folk art would find its place. Here it would develop, change and be renewed. Could we see this now?

I remember the day when there were field horses tied to the trees in our streets. A few days earlier the Red Army had broken through to our township. We all put on ceremonial costume, took our instruments and went out to play in the park. We drank and played nonstop for hours on end. The Russian soldiers responded with their own songs. At the time I had said to myself that a new era was on its way. A Slavonic era. Just like the Roman Empire and the German Empire, we too were the heirs to an antique age. We had slumbered for many centuries. But we had slept well. We were refreshed. We were at the ready! At the ready!

This feeling came back to me again. Again and again I thought it over. Jazz had its roots in Africa and its stem in America. Our music had its living roots in the music of an

140

tique Europe. We were the guardians of an ancient and rare treasure. Everything was so logical. Every thought fell into place. The Slavs had brought revolution. With it they had brought a new collective and fraternal way of life. With it a new art which would live in the people and with the people, just like the old peasant songs. Unbelievable and at the same time unbelievably logical was the great mission entrusted by history to us, a bunch of young men standing round a cymbalo.

And presently the unbelievable began to come true. No one had ever done a fraction as much for our folk art as the Communist government did. It devoted enormous funds to the setting up of ensembles. Folk music with violin and cymbalo resounded daily from the radio. The universities were inundated with Moravian and Slovak songs. There were the May-day celebrations, young people's festivities, dances. Not only did jazz disappear entirely from the face of the land but it became the symbol of western capitalism and its decadence. Young people stopped dancing the tango and boogie-woogie when they had a party or celebration. Instead they took each other round the shoulders and danced in a circle to the Slavonic chorovod. The Communist Party was devoting all its efforts to creating a new way of life. Just as it had done in the Soviet Union. It based itself on Stalin's famous definition of the new art: Socialist content in national form. Only our folk art was capable of giving our music, dance and poetry this national form.

Our group sailed buoyantly upon the tide of this policy. It soon gained national fame. It added singers and dancers and became a great ensemble which performed on hundreds of platforms and did an annual tour abroad. We did not confine ourselves to the traditional songs, we wrote new ones for ourselves, things like 'How good it is there are no masters now', or the Song of Stalin, songs about ploughed fields and harvests on cooperative farms. No longer were our songs just a memory of the past. They were alive. They belonged to the most contemporary history. They accompanied this history.

The Communist Party gave us its enthusiastic support. In this way our political reservations soon melted away. I joined the Party myself at the beginning of '49. And the others in the ensemble soon followed me.

7

So we still remained friends. When then did the first shadow fall between us?

I know the answer of course. I know it only too well. It was at my wedding.

I had been studying the violin at the Academy of Music in Brno and attending lectures on musical theory at the university. When I went up for my third year at Brno I began feeling badly out of sorts. At home Father was going from bad to worse. He had suffered a stroke. He had recovered all right, but still had to take great care of himself. I kept worrying about his being at home on his own and thinking that if anything were to happen to him he would not even be able to send me a telegram. Every Saturday I would come home in a state of apprehension, and every Monday morning I would leave for Brno with a new load on my mind. There came a point when I could no longer stand the anxiety. It had been oppressing me on the Monday and even more strongly on the Tuesday. On the Wednesday I threw all my clothes into my bag, paid the landlady and said I was not coming back.

I remember to this day my walk home from the station. The way to our village, which borders on the town, lies across the fields. It was autumn and just before dusk. There was a wind blowing and there were boys in the fields flying paper kites in the sky at the end of long pieces of string. Father had once made me a kite like that. Then he took me into the field, threw the kite into the air and ran with it so that the wind would blow into the paper and carry it up. It didn't amuse me much. It amused Father a lot more. I was touched now by the recollection and started walking faster. It occurred to me that

Father had been sending his kite up to heaven to look for my mother.

The thing was that ever since I was very small I have always imagined my mother being in heaven. Not that I believe in the Lord, or have done for a long time, or in the life ever after and so on. I am not talking about faith. I am talking about fantasy. And fantasies surround me and people my solitude. I do not know why I should give them up. Without them I should be all alone in the world. Vlasta tells me I am a dreamer. That I don't see things the way they are. I do see things the way they are, but in addition to these visible things I also see the invisible. Inventions of the imagination do not exist on this earth without good reason for them. They have good grounds for being here. They feel at home with us. And we with them. It is they that make our houses into homes.

I learned about my mother only when she had been gone a long time. And so I had never wept for her. I comforted myself rather with the thought that my mother was young and beautiful and in heaven. The other children never had a mother as young as mine was.

I like to imagine Saint Peter sitting on his stool by the window through which he can see down to earth. My mother often joins him at this window. Peter will do anything for her because she is beautiful. He lets her look down. And Mother sees us. Myself and Father.

Mother's face was never sad. Just the opposite. When she looked at us through the window of Peter's lodge she often used to laugh down at us. Anybody who lives in eternity is spared despondence. And impatience. He knows that human life lasts a second and that reunion is not far off. But when I was living in Brno and leaving my father on his own I always imagined my mother's face as sad and reproachful. And I wanted to live in peace with my mother.

So I hurried home and saw the kites flying into the sky and staying up under the heavens. I was happy. I had no regrets about what I was leaving behind. Of course I liked my violin. I liked my musical theory. But I had no career ambitions. Not even the most sensational rise could replace for me the joy of

143

coming home and being once again surrounded by the things a man has when he is born: the horizons of his native land, the intimacy of his own few walls, his mother and his father. I came home with a great sense of relief.

When I told Father that I wouldn't be returning to Brno he was extremely angry. He didn't want me to ruin my life for his sake. I changed my tactics and managed to persuade him that I had been thrown out of the college for lack of progress. He finally believed this and was even more angry with me. Not that that worried me too much. I hadn't come home to waste my time. I went on playing first fiddle in our band. I found a job as violin teacher in the music school. I could devote myself to the things I loved.

One of these things was Vlasta. She lived in the next village, which today – like my own village – is a suburb. She danced with our ensemble. I had met her while studying in Brno and I was glad that after my return I was able to see her almost every day. But real love came somewhat later – suddenly, during a rehearsal when she fell so awkwardly that she broke her leg. I carried her in my arms to the ambulance which had been hastily summoned. I felt her frail, brittle body in my arms. Suddenly I realized with astonishment that I was six foot three and weighed nearly sixteen stone, that I could have been a lumberjack, while she was a pathetic little waif of a thing. I sobbed with sympathy and it made me feel so good that I wished the moment would never end. That it would last for ever. That it would percolate into everything between us.

It was a moment of revelation. In Vlasta's injured frame I suddenly saw another, more familiar figure. How was it that I hadn't seen it before? Vlasta was the 'poor man's daughter', the heroine of so many folk songs! The poor girl who has nothing on this earth but her honour, the poor girl who is injured, the poor girl in rags, the poor orphan girl.

Literally, of course, this was not the case. She did have parents and they were anything but poor. And precisely because they were a well-to-do farming family the New Age began pushing them to the wall. Vlasta often came to rehearsals in tears. They had levied heavy dues on the family. They had proclaimed her father a kulak. They had requisitioned his tractor and implements. They had threatened him with arrest. I was sorry for her and comforted myself with the idea that I would take her part. The part of the poor man's daughter.

From the time I came to regard her in this light, hallowed by the phrase from folk song, I felt as if I were reliving a love I had lived through a thousand times. As if I were playing it from ancient music. As if it was being sung to me from folk songs. Carried away by this melodious stream, I dreamed of my wedding and looked eagerly forward to it.

Two days before the ceremony Ludvik appeared out of the blue. I greeted him warmly. I at once told him the great news of my marriage and that as my best friend he must be there as a witness. He promised to come. And he did.

My friends in the group laid on a real Moravian wedding for me. They came for us early in the morning with music and in costume. Fifty-year-old Vondracek, the group's cymbalo player, had the duty of starosvat, of giving away. First of all my father regaled everyone with slivovitz, bread and bacon. The giver then signalled for silence and recited in a loud voice:

'Well beloved young men and maidens,
Lords and ladies,
I have summoned you to this abode,
Because this young man hath made a request
That we might make the journey with him to the abode of the father of one Vlasta Netahal,
Because he has chosen his daughter, a gentle maid, for his bride.'

The giver, starosvat, or chief speechmaker is the head, the soul, the director of the entire ceremony. That is the way it has always been. The groom was never the subject of the wedding. He was its object. He was not marrying. He was being married. Someone was using the marriage to possess him and he sailed along on it as if on the crest of a great wave. He was not the one to act or speak. The giver acted and spoke for him. But it was not even the giver. It was the age-old tradition, handed down from man to man, which steered him into its

honeyed stream. In that stream everybody became like everybody else, became merged into mankind.

We set off, the giver leading, to the next village. We walked
across the fields, and my friends played as we went. In front of
Vlasta's house we were already awaited by a throng of people
in folk costume from the bride's side of the family. The giver
intoned:

> 'We are weary travellers,
> And we beseech
> That we might gain entrance into this honest abode,
> For we are thirsty and hungry.'

An elderly man in costume detached himself from the
crowd standing in front of the gate. 'Be ye honest people,
then be ye welcome here.' And he invited us in. Silently we
crowded into the passage way. We were, as the giver had
introduced us, just weary travellers and so we did not at
first reveal our true intent. The old man in the costume, who
was the speaker on the bride's side, challenged us: 'If ye
have anything which weighs upon your hearts, speak it
now.'

The giver began to speak, at first obliquely and in riddles,
and the man in costume answered him in like manner. Only
after much circumlocution did the giver reveal why we had
come. Now the old man asked him this question:

'I ask thee, friend,
Why does this honest groom wish to take this honest maid as his
   wife?
Is it for the flower or for the fruit?

And the giver replied:

'To each it is well known that the flower advanceth in beauty and
   grace so that it is a pleasure to the heart.
But the flower fadeth
And the fruit ripeneth
Thus we take not this bride for the flower but for the fruit, for from
   the fruit there cometh goodness.'

146

The responses continued for a while until the spokesman for the bride concluded: 'Let us all call the bride and let her say whether she chooses aye or nay.' He went to the next room and presently returned leading by the hand a woman in national costume. She was tall, thin and bony, and her face was veiled with a scarf. 'Here is thy bride.'

But the giver shook his head and with loud murmurs we all corroborated his disagreement. The old man spent a little while trying to prevail upon us but finally had to lead the veiled woman away. Only then did he bring in Vlasta. She was wearing black boots, a red pinafore and brightly coloured bodice. She had a garland of flowers on her head. She looked beautiful. I took her hand in mine.

Then the old man turned to the bride's mother and called in a doleful voice: 'Alas, the mother!'

At these words the bride tore herself from my grasp, knelt on the ground before her mother and hung her head. The old man went on:

'Mother, dear mother, forgive me wherein I have done thee wrong!
Mother, dearest mother, I beg thee before God to be forgiven where-
    in I have done thee wrong!
Mother, beloved mother, I beg thee by the five wounds of God to
    forgive me wherein I have done thee wrong!'

We were actors thrown into a play which has been performed for ages past. And the text was beautiful and striking and true in every word. Then our band started to play and we proceeded to the town. The ceremony was in the Guildhall and there was music playing for us there as well. Then came the dinner, and after dinner we all went to the local buda or folk hall. There was music and dancing.

In the evening Vlasta's bridesmaids took her garland of rosemary from her head and ceremonially handed it to me. From her free-hanging hair they made a pigtail which they wound round her head, and her head they tied up in a bonnet. This was the ceremony which symbolized her step from virginity into womanhood. It was a long time since Vlasta had been a virgin, so she was not really entitled to the symbol of the garland. However, I did not consider this important. At some higher and more binding level she lost her virginity now, and only now, as the bridesmaids handed me her garland of flowers.

God, why is it that the memory of that garland of rosemary affects me more than our first real love, than Vlasta's real virgin blood? I do not know why but it does. The women used to sing songs in which the garland floated off across the water and the waves weaved it into ribbons of red. I felt like weeping. I was drunk. I saw before my eyes the floating flowers, I saw the brook handing them on to the stream, the stream to the river, the river to the Danube and the Danube to the sea. It was in this irrevocability that the essence of the whole thing lay. All basic situations in life happen only once and are then beyond recall. To be a real man, a man must go through to the end with full knowledge of what he is doing. He must drink to the dregs. He must not cheat. He must not pretend he does not see what he is doing. The modern man cheats. He tried to get round all the turning points and walk on aimlessly through life till death. The man of the people is more honest. He sings himself to the bottom of every basic situation. When Vlasta stained with blood the towel I had placed beneath her I had no idea that something had been done which was beyond recall. Now there was no escaping it. Women sing a song about parting:

> 'Stay, stay, my little boy,
> Whilst I take leave of my dear mother.
> Stay, stay, do not lash with thy whip
> Whilst I take leave of my dear father.
> Stay, stay, do not spur the horses,
> I have a sister and cannot leave her.
> Farewell, my dear friends,
> I am being taken from you and will not be allowed
> to return.'

Then it was night and the guests accompanied us home. There we stopped and all Vlasta's friends sang to us about how we should not harm the poor *penniless* girl in her new abode, that as at home she had been loved, even so let us love her here.

I opened the gate. Vlasta stopped on the threshold and then turned again to the cluster of her friends gathered in front of the house. Then one of them intoned the final song:

> 'She stood on the threshold,
> Lovely she looked then,
> Fair as a rose.
> She stepped from the threshold,
> Lost all her beauty,
> My fine young maid.'

Then they closed the door after us and we were alone. Vlasta was twenty and I was a little older. But I was thinking of how she had crossed the threshold and how from this magic moment onwards her beauty would fade from her like the leaves of a tree. I saw that fading in her which lay in the future. That fading which had now begun. For this very reason I loved her now more than anything else in the world. I thought of how she was not just the flower but that in this moment the fruit was already present in her. I felt in the whole thing an unyielding order, an order with which I had merged myself and with which I profoundly agreed. In that moment I was thinking of Vladimir, whom at that moment I could not know, whose existence I could have no idea of. Yet I thought of him and looked through him far into the distance of the generations of his children. I lay down with Vlasta in the high piled bed and it seemed to me to be the wise eternity of human generation which took us into its soft embrace.

8

What did Ludvik do to me at that wedding? Nothing really. He looked sour round the mouth and he was in a strange mood. In the afternoon, when the music and dancing began, my friends offered him the clarinet. They wanted him to sit in with them. He refused. Not long afterwards he left altogether. Luckily I had plenty to think about and didn't pay any special attention to the incident. The next day, however, I saw that his departure had left a small stain on the day's proceedings. The alcohol circulating in my blood increased this stain to considerable proportions. And Vlasta helped in this even more than the alcohol. She had never liked Ludvik. Women instinctively classify their husbands' friends into the harmless and the dangerous. Vlasta had filed Ludvik into the second category and was always glad that he lived in Prague.

When I told her Ludvik would be coming as a witness, she had not been very pleased. On the day after the wedding she saw fit to remind me of his behaviour. She said he had gone around all day as if we were all putting him to considerable inconvenience. He was conceited and difficult and he kept his nose so high in the air it was a wonder he didn't drill a hole in the sky.

However, Ludvik paid us a call that very same evening. He brought some presents for Vlasta and made his apologies. Would we please forgive him for acting so strangely the day before? He told us what had happened to him: he had been kicked out of the Party and the university. He didn't know what would happen to him next.

I couldn't believe my ears and hardly knew what to say. Anyway Ludvik didn't want anyone to feel sorry for him and quickly turned the conversation. In a fortnight's time our ensemble was due to leave on a big foreign tour. We provincials were really looking forward to this. Ludvik knew this well and began asking me about our trip. I realized at once that he had longed to go abroad ever since he was a child and now the chances of his ever getting out were very slim. At that time, and for a number of years after, people with any political blemish were not allowed abroad. I saw that we were on opposite sides of the fence and I tried to avoid saying so. This meant I couldn't talk openly about our tour, as this would have illuminated the gulf between our two selves. I wanted to shroud this gulf in darkness and was afraid of every word which might throw light on it. But I could not find a single word which did not do this in some way. Every sentence which had anything to do with our lives charged us with having taken two completely different roads. Told us that our opportunities and our futures were very different. That we were being carried away in opposite directions. I tried to talk about trivial and indifferent matters in an attempt to conceal what strangers we were. But this was worse still. The artificial irrelevance of the conversation was in itself unbearably painful.

Ludvik soon took his leave and went. He volunteered for a labour gang somewhere outside our town, and I went abroad with the ensemble. From then on I did not see him for several years. I sent him a letter or two when he was in the army. After I had posted them they always left me with the same feeling of dissatisfaction as I had had after our last conversation. I was unable to face up squarely to the fact of Ludvik's failure. I was embarrassed at the success of my own life. It was unthinkable to be doling out words of encouragement or sympathy to Ludvik from the heights of my own contentment. Instead I tried to pretend that nothing had changed between us. I recounted what we were doing, the news of the ensemble, about the new cymbalo player and so on. I acted as if my world was still one which we shared. Even as I did so I felt what a hateful pretence it was.

Then one day my father received an obituary announcement. Ludvik's mother had died. None of us had known she was ill. When Ludvik had dropped out of my life, she had dropped with him. I held the obituary in my hand and became aware of my indifference towards people who had, however slightly, withdrawn from my life. My successful life. Even though I had done nothing wrong, I felt guilty. And then I noticed something which shocked me beyond measure. The obituary notice had been signed on behalf of the next of kin by Mr and Mrs Koutecky. There was no mention at all of Ludvik.

The day of the funeral arrived. I felt rather nervous at the prospect of meeting Ludvik again. But he never came. Only a handful of people trudged after the coffin. I asked the

151

Kouteckys where Ludvik was. They shrugged their shoulders and said they did not know. The coffin-bearers stopped by a great marble vault with a white statue of an angel.

This rich builder's family had had everything taken from them and were living on a meagre allowance. All they had left was this great family vault with its white angel. I knew all this but had no idea why the coffin was to be placed here. Only later did I learn that Ludvik was at that time in prison. His mother was the only person in town who had known. She had kept it dark from everybody. She lived completely alone with her illness, which had finally brought her to the infirmary and so to the cemetery.

Once she was dead the flame of family affection burst forth again in Mr and Mrs Koutecky. They took charge of the body of a sister-in-law they had never loved and proclaimed it as their own. At last they were avenged upon their ungrateful nephew. They had robbed him of his mother. They covered her with the heavy marble stone over which stood the white angel with his curly hair and his spray of flowers. I have always remembered that angel. A curly-haired angel with his false garland of peace. Soaring above the ravaged life of my friend from whom even the bodies of his parents had been stolen. An angel of robbery.

9

Vlasta hates any form of extravagance. For her sitting out in the garden at night just because you feel like it is an extravagance. I heard her banging vigorously on the window. Behind the pane loomed the severe shadow of a woman's figure in a nightdress. I have an obedient nature. I can never say no to those weaker than myself. And because I stand six foot three and can pick up a hundredweight sack with one hand, in all my life I have never yet found anyone I could resist.

So I went in and got into bed beside Vlasta. To break the silence I mentioned that I had seen Ludvik today. 'Oh?' she said, with a display of indifference. There was no denying it: he had got right under her skin. To this day she can't stand the sight of him. I don't see what she has to complain about. Since our wedding she has had to see him precisely once. That was in 1956. And on that occasion I was unable to gloss over the gulf that divided us, even to myself.

Ludvik had behind him his military service, prison, and a few years down the mines. He had arranged in Prague to resume his studies and had only come to the town to see about a few legal formalities. Again I was nervous at the prospect of meeting him. However, when I did meet him he was no whimpering wreck. Anything but. Ludvik had changed greatly. He was rough, touchy and perhaps a little quieter than I had known him. There was nothing in him which called for sympathy. It seemed we would quickly vault over the gulf which I had feared so much. To make some sort of contact I invited him to a rehearsal of our band. I still thought of it as his band too. What did it matter that we had different players on cymbalo, bass and clarinet, and that I was the only one left out of the old crowd? Time flies, but this must not throw us off balance. What matters is that all our names are inscribed upon that fugitive time.

Ludvik sat in a chair by the cymbalo player and listened to us rehearsing. First we played all his favourite songs, the ones we used to play at school. Then some new ones we had unearthed in some remote mountain communities. Finally we reached the songs which form the mainstay of our repertoire. These are not real folk songs but songs which we ourselves composed in the folk song spirit. We sang about fields which were to be ploughed up so as to make a single big collective from the many small private fields, songs about the poor who no longer have to be slaves but who are masters in their own land, the song about the tractor driver who does so well at the tractor station. These were all songs whose music was indistinguishable from that of older folk songs but whose words were more up-to-date than any newspaper. Of them all, our favourite was the one about Julius Fucik, the hero tortured by the Nazis during the occupation.

153

Ludvik sat on his chair and watched the musicians' fingers racing over the strings of the cymbalo. Every now and again he poured himself a small glass of wine from the bottle. I watched him across the bridge of my violin. He sat there pensively and never once raised his eyes in my direction.

At this point people's wives began to trickle into the room – an indication that the rehearsal would soon be over. I invited Ludvik round to our place. Vlasta made us some supper and then went to bed, leaving us alone. Ludvik started to talk about everything under the sun. But I felt he was being so talkative only because he didn't want to have to talk about the things I wanted to talk about. But how was I to be silent with my best friend on the subject which had been our greatest shared possession? I interrupted his flow of banalities. What did he think of our songs? He told me without any hesitation that he liked them. But I wasn't going to let him get away with cheap politeness. I asked him what he thought of the new songs we had unearthed in those remote villages. And what did he think of the new songs we had composed ourselves?

Ludvik didn't want to enter into a debate. But step by step I drew him out until finally he started talking. Those few old folk songs he thought were really beautiful. Otherwise he did not care for our repertoire at all. We were accommodating ourselves too much to prevailing tastes. This was hardly surprising. We were performing before the widest possible public and wanted to be popular, so we stripped our songs of everything which was unique to them. We scrapped their inimitable rhythm and adapted it to conventional rhythmic patterns. We chose our songs from the most recent chronological layer, the csardas and so on, because these were the easiest to understand and the easiest to like.

I reminded him that we were only at the beginning of our career. We wanted folk song to spread as widely as possible. Therefore we must make some concessions to popular taste. The really important thing was that we should create a *modern* folk art form, new folk songs, which would have something to say about the life we live today.

He disagreed. It was these new songs which jarred on his ears most of all. What a wretched imitation! What an absolute fake!

To this day it depresses me to recall his words. Who was it that warned us that if we went on looking backwards we would end up like Lot's wife? Who was it who painted such a rosy picture of folk music giving rise to the new style of the age? Who challenged us to set folk music in motion and make it stride forward side by side with history?

'It was a utopia,' said Ludvik.

'Utopia? But we have the songs. They exist!'

He laughed in my face. 'You sing them in your ensemble. But show me one single person outside the group who sings them. Show me one collective farm worker who sings your collective farm songs to himself for his own enjoyment. They're so unnatural and false, they would make his voice crack as he sang them! The propaganda text sticks out from the pseudo-folk music like a badly sewn-on collar. A pseudo-Moravian song about Fucik! What utter nonsense! Fucik was a Prague journalist. What had he in common with Moravian Slovakia?'

I objected that Fucik belonged to us all and that we had just as much right to sing our own kind of song about him as anyone else.

'Our *own* kind of song? You don't sing them our way – you sing them the way Agitprop lays down. Just think of the words. Why a song about Fucik anyway? Was he the only one in the underground? Was he the only one to be tortured?'

'He's the most famous.'

'Of course he is. The propaganda machine wants a hierarchy in its dead heroes' gallery. They want to have a chief hero among heroes so that when the occasion arises they can dredge him up for their own purposes.'

'Why poke fun at it? Every age has its symbolic figures.'

'True enough, but the really interesting point is – who becomes the symbolic figure? There were hundreds of people just as courageous at the time and now they are forgotten. And some of those who fell were famous men – politicians,

155

writers, scientists, artists. None of them became symbols. You don't see their photographs hanging in Party offices and schools. They often have some major achievement to their credit. That is precisely what debars them. What they did is hard to correct or trim or obliterate. Whatever they did is a hindrance to their getting into the hall of fame.'

'None of them wrote *Notes from the Gallows*.'

'That's just it! What about the hero who keeps his mouth shut? What about the hero who does not need to make his last moments an opportunity for theatrical performance? For a pedagogical lecture? Fucik, though far from famous, seemed to think that it was of immense importance to inform the world how *he* thought and felt in prison, what *he* was going through and what messages and recommendations *he* had for mankind. He wrote them on little scraps of paper and he risked the lives of other people who smuggled them out of prison and kept them safe. He had a high opinion of his own views and impressions with a vengeance – an overweeningly high opinion of himself.'

This was more than I could take. Was Fucik nothing but a conceited egoist?

But Ludvik was not to be stopped. It wasn't conceit so much that made Fucik write. The main thing was his weakness. Because he was brave in solitude, without witnesses, without the reward of others' approbation, all alone with himself, he needed great pride and strength. He needed the help of an audience. In the solitude of his cell he could at least create a fictitious public for himself. He needed to be seen! He needed to gain strength from applause. Even if the applause was only fictitious. He needed to turn the prison into a stage and make his lot bearable by not only living through it, but performing and acting it as well. He preened himself on the beauty of his own words and gestures.

I had been prepared for Ludvik to be despondent, even bitter. But I had not expected this viciousness, this ironic malice. What had Fucik the martyr done to hurt him? I know Ludvik was unjustly punished. But this only made it worse: the motive for his change of views was all too transparent. Is a man to abandon the position he has held all his life just because he was once wronged?

I said as much to Ludvik's face. At that something rather unexpected happened. Ludvik did not answer. It was as if his feverish anger had left him. He gave me a quizzical glance and then told me very quietly not to be angry: perhaps he was wrong. He said it in such a strange cold voice that I knew very well it was not meant sincerely. I had no wish to let our conversation end on this note of insincerity. Despite my annoyance I was still guided by my original desire: I wanted to come to terms with Ludvik and renew our old friendship. However sharply we had clashed I still hoped that at the end of the long argument we might find some corner of the common ground which we had once shared and upon which we might be able to coexist again. But my attempts to continue the discussion were in vain. Ludvik apologized, saying that he had a tendency to exaggerate and that unfortunately he had allowed himself to be carried away. He asked me to forget what he had said.

Forget? Why should we forget a serious discussion? Would it not be preferable to continue with it? It was not until the next day that I worked out the real meaning behind this request. Ludvik slept at our place and had breakfast there. After breakfast we had another half an hour in which to talk. He told me what a job he had had getting permission to complete his last two years at the university. He told me how his expulsion from the Party had branded him for life. How nobody trusted him. Only with the help of a few of his friends from before the February take-over was he able to gain readmission to the university. Then he talked about a few of his other friends who found themselves in the same situation as himself. He told me how they were followed around and how everything they said was carefully noted down. How people around them had been interrogated and how some officious or spiteful testimony could easily blight their lives for another few years. Then he digressed again to some trivial topic, and when we said good-bye he said he was glad he had seen me, and that I should forget what he had said the evening before.

157

The connexion between this request and the references to what had happened to some of his friends was only too clear. I was shocked. Ludvik had stopped talking because he was afraid! He was afraid that our conversation might not remain a secret between us. He was afraid I would give him away! He was afraid of me! This was a terrible and again completely unexpected blow. The gulf between us was much deeper than I had thought. It was so deep that it could not even permit us to go through with our arguments.

10

Vlasta's asleep, poor girl, and snoring fitfully. They are all asleep. And I am lying here in my vast bulk and thinking how powerless I am. That last meeting with Ludvik brought this home to me. Until then I had confidently supposed that the whole thing was well within my grasp. Ludvik and I had never done anything to injure each other. Why shouldn't we be friends again in all good will?

It turned out that this was not within my power. Neither our estrangement nor our rapprochement was within my power. I resigned myself to hoping they were in time's hands. Time slipped by. Since our last meeting nine years have passed. Meanwhile Ludvik has graduated and got an excellent job as a scientist in a field which interests him. I follow his life's story from across a gulf. I watch it with affection. I can never regard Ludvik either as my enemy or as a stranger. He is my friend, even though he is under a curse. It is rather like the fairy tale of the prince's bride being changed into a snake or a toad. In the fairy tales everything was always saved by the prince's loyalty and patience.

But time has not yet awakened my friend from his spell. Several times during this period I learned that he had paid a visit to the town. Yet he never came round to see me. Today I saw him and he avoided me. Ludvik is as one of the damned.

It all began the time we had that conversation. Year after

year I have felt the loneliness gathering round me and anxiety sprouting within me. The longer it lasted the more weariness there was and the less joy and success. The ensemble used to go on a foreign tour every year, but then the number of invitations began to fall off and now we hardly get invited anywhere. We are still working, working harder than ever, but everything round us is silent. I am standing in a deserted hall. And it seems as if it were Ludvik who gave the order that I should be alone here. For it is not their enemies who condemn men to solitude. It is their friends.

Since that time I have taken refuge more and more in that track across the fields with the lone briar bush growing on the verge. There I meet with the last of my loyal friends. There is the deserter with his men. There is the wandering minstrel. There is the wooden cottage over the horizon and in it Vlasta – the poor man's daughter.

The deserter calls me King and promises me that at any time I may take refuge in his protection. All I need do is go as far as the briar bush, and there we will always meet.

It would be so easy to find peace in the world of fantasy. But I have always tried to live in the two worlds at the same time and not to abandon one for the other. I must not abandon the real world even if I am losing everything I have in it. In the long run it will be enough if I manage to do just one thing. One last thing: to present my life as my clear and distinct message to the one person who will understand it and carry it on. Before that I must not join the deserter on his ride to the Danube.

The one person I am thinking of, my one hope after all my defeats, is separated from me by no more than a wall, and he is sleeping. Tomorrow he will mount his brown steed. He will wear ribbons across his face. They will be calling him King. Come, my son. I am slipping away into sleep. They will be calling you by my name. Time to sleep. I will dream of you on your horse.

Part V: Ludvik

1

I slept long and fairly well; the bitter memories I had indulged
so freely the evening before, and far into the night, had failed
to disrupt the rhythm of my physical life, drilled as it is to the
strict routine I imposed on myself when it first occurred to me,
on passing thirty, that I was not immune to the process of
growing old. I woke up some time after eight and could not
remember having dreamed. I had no headache but equally I
had no desire to get up, and I have never fought this reluctance, which from a certain time onwards I have viewed less
as a bad habit than as a blessed symptom of indolent youth.

I just lay there; sleep had erected a sort of wall or wind-
break between myself and yesterday's encounter, and behind
this I felt, for the moment at least, secure. It was not so much,
perhaps, that Lucie had that morning dropped out of my consciousness; she had merely returned to her former state of
abstraction.

Abstraction? Yes: when Lucie disappeared from Ostrava
so mysteriously and cruelly, I had no practical opportunity to
start looking for her. And later, after my release from military
service, I found that over the years I had gradually lost the
desire for such a search. I told myself that Lucie, however
much I had once been in love with her, and however much
she remained the *only* girl, was completely unthinkable outside the context in which we met and fell in love. It struck me
as illogical for a man to abstract the one he loved from the
situation in which he met her and in which she lived, and to
try, with dogged inner concentration, to purify her of everything which was not *herself*, of the events they lived through
together and which helped to shape their love.

For what I love in a woman is not what she is in herself and

161

for herself, but the side of her I see turned to me, what she is *for me*. I love her as a character in adventures we have lived through together. What would Hamlet be without the castle at Elsinore, without Ophelia, without all the concrete situations he experiences, what would he be without the *text* of his part? What would remain of the character but an empty, dumb, illusory substance? And so Lucie, stripped of the shanty town of Ostrava, of the roses handed through the barbed wire, of her shabby clothes, stripped of my own endless weeks of despair, would probably cease to be the Lucie I loved.

Yes, this is how I saw it, and as year followed year I was almost afraid of bumping into her again; for I knew that we would meet in a place where Lucie would no longer be Lucie, and that I would lack the resources to mend the severed thread. By this, of course, I do not mean that I stopped loving her, that I had forgotten her, or that her image had in some way palled. On the contrary, she remained within me constantly in the form of a gentle nostalgia; I longed for her as we long for things which are definitively lost. And precisely because Lucie had become for me something belonging definitively to the past (something which as the past lives on, but which as the present is dead), she gradually lost, in my thoughts, all corporeal, material and concrete qualities and became more and more a legend, a myth inscribed on an old parchment and laid in a metal casket in the very foundations of my life.

Perhaps that was why the incredible could happen, why, as I sat in the barber's chair, I could not be sure whether it was her or not. Certainly it was the reason why the next morning, duped by an interval of sleep, I was able to feel that yesterday's encounter was not even real; that it too was something which took place at the level of legends, oracles and riddles. If on Friday evening I had been struck by Lucie's actual presence and abruptly transported to a distant period over which she had held sway, then this Saturday morning I asked with a calm heart, and after a good sleep: *why* did I see her? Was the whole Lucie affair to have some continuation? What did this encounter mean and what was it trying to tell me?

162

Do events really have anything to say beyond the fact that they occur, that they are happening? I do not, perhaps, need to emphasize that I am a thoroughly sober sort of man. But perhaps some trace of irrational superstition did survive in me; for instance this strange conviction that all the events in my life have some additional significance, that they all *mean* something, that life, as it unfolds, is saying something about itself, that it gradually reveals some of its secrets to us, that it stands before us like a puzzle whose meaning must be deciphered, that the incidents we experience during our life are the mythology of life and that in this mythology lies the key to the truth and to the mystery. Is this an illusion? Possibly, indeed probably; yet I cannot rid myself of the need to be continually *deciphering* my own life, as if there were some sense, meaning or truth concealed in it, I cannot escape this need, even though it is merely the need to play some kind of game, like the solving of puzzles.

So I lay on the creaky bed, letting thoughts of Lucie pass through my mind, and by now she had been transformed into a mere idea, a mere question. The hotel bed was indeed, as I characterized it in the preceding sentence, creaky, and as I became conscious of this property again it evoked with sudden excitement the thought of Helena. As if that creaking bed was a voice summoning me to duty, I heaved a sigh, threw my feet off the bed, sat down on the edge, stretched, scratched my scalp, looked at the sky through the window, and finally stood up. My encounter with Lucie, however insubstantial it seemed in the clear light of morning, had only served to muffle my interest in Helena, an interest which a few days before had been so intense. At this moment all that was left of it was the *knowledge* that I was interested; an interest translated into the language of memory, accompanied by a sense of duty towards the lost interest, which my reason assured me would most certainly return with all its former intensity.

I went over to the wash basin, threw off my pyjama jacket and turned the tap full on. I put my hands under the flow of water and almost scrambled to splash great handfuls of it on my neck, shoulders and body. I scrubbed myself down with the towel; I wanted to send the blood coursing round my limbs. Suddenly I realized with a shock that I was completely indifferent to the fact of Helena's coming, and I was alarmed lest this momentary indifference should spoil an opportunity which was hardly likely to come again. I told myself I would have a hearty breakfast and after breakfast a drop of vodka.

I went downstairs to the coffee lounge, but all I found there was a host of chairs lying mournfully, legs in the air, on the unwiped tables, and an old woman in a dirty apron creeping about in their midst.

I went to reception and asked the porter, sitting behind his desk immersed in a much-cushioned chair and a profound unconcern, whether there was any chance of my getting breakfast there. Without moving he said that the coffee lounge was closed today. I went out into the street. It was a pleasant day, with the clouds scudding across the sky and a gentle wind raising the dust from the pavement. I hurried to the main square. There was a crowd of women, young and old, queuing outside the butcher's; they had shopping bags and string baskets in their hands and were patiently and apathetically waiting for their turn inside the shop. Among the pedestrians strolling or hurrying along the street my eye was soon caught by those bearing ice-cream cornets in their hands like miniature torches and licking their red caps. I was already in the main square. There stood a sprawling single-storey structure with a turret on each side of the roof. At the front of the building were four shops, each with a glass sign above: on one was painted three men in costume with their arms round each other and their mouths open, on another a man and woman (also in country costume), on the third a sunflower, and on the fourth a barrel of wine. It was a self-service cafeteria.

I went inside. It was a large hall with a tiled floor and tables on long legs, where people were standing eating sandwiches and drinking coffee or beer.

I didn't feel like having breakfast in this place. All morning I had pictured a substantial breakfast with eggs, bacon, and a tot of spirits to restore my lost vitality. I recalled that a little

164

further on, in the other square with its garden and the monument commemorating the plague, there was another restaurant. It was not exactly alluring, but it was enough for me if it had tables and chairs and just one single waiter whom I might cajole into telling me what there was to eat.

I passed the monument commemorating the plague; the plinth supported a saint, the saint supported a cloud, the cloud supported an angel, the angel supported a second cloud, and on this second cloud sat a second and final angel. It was quite early in the morning; I took in this self-evident detail again as I gazed at the memorial column, that impressive pyramid of saints, clouds and angels which simulated in heavy stone the heavens and their ethereal heights, while the real heavens were a wan matutinal blue and hopelessly remote from this dusty section of the earth.

I crossed the garden with its neat lawns and benches (though it was still sufficiently bare not to break the general atmosphere of empty dustiness), and tried the door of the restaurant. It was closed. I began to realize that my longing for breakfast would remain just that, and this alarmed me, for with childish obstinacy I had made up my mind that a substantial breakfast was to be the decisive factor for the success of the entire day. I realized that provincial towns take no account of eccentrics who wish to eat their breakfast sitting down and that they only open their hostelries considerably later in the day. I made no attempt to find any other place of refreshment, but turned round and walked back through the park in the opposite direction.

Again I kept running into people carrying red-crowned ice-cream cornets, and it struck me that the cornets looked like torches and that there might be a symbolic meaning in their shape, because these torches were not torches, but travesties of torches, and the pink token of delight carried triumphantly in the hand was not real pleasure, but a travesty of pleasure – which would doubtless accord with the inescapably travestied nature of all torches and pleasures in this dusty little township. And then I told myself that since I was walking in the opposite direction to these licking torch-bearers

165

they would probably lead me to a candy store where there might be a table and chairs and perhaps even black coffee and some kind of snack.

They led me, not to a candy store but to a milk bar. There was a long queue of people waiting for cocoa or milk and rolls with butter, and again there were those high tables with people eating and drinking from them; in a back room there were tables and chairs as well, but these were all taken. I joined the queue and eventually bought a glass of cocoa and two rolls with butter, took my stand by a table on which stood six or eight used glasses, found a place with nothing spilt on it, and set my glass down.

I ate with sorry haste, and in three minutes or so I was out in the street again. It was nine o'clock. Helena had taken the first flight from Prague, and from Brno was to take a bus which would get her here around eleven. I could see that these two hours would be utterly empty and utterly wasted.

Of course I could have spent the time having a look round my childhood haunts, pausing in sentimental meditation by the old family house in which my mother had lived to the end of her days. I often think of her; but in this town, where her remains have been plundered and hidden under alien marble, it is as if all my thoughts of her were poisoned. If I had indulged them now, they would have been mingled with feelings of my powerlessness at that time and with a venomous bitterness – and this was what I was trying to fight.

So there was nothing for it but to sit on a bench in the square. I sat down, but almost immediately got up again, went over to the shop windows, glanced at the titles of the books in the bookshop, then finally had the salutary idea of buying a *Rude Pravo* at the news stand. I ran my eye over the unprepossessing headlines, read a couple of interesting reports from the foreign news section, got up from the bench again, folded the *Rude Pravo* and put it almost untouched into the waste paper receptacle. Then I sauntered over to the church, stopped in front of it, gazed up at its twin towers, climbed the wide cathedral steps and went through the porch into the church, a little apprehensive about the indignation that people might display, quite needlessly, at someone entering without crossing himself, and just coming in to stroll about as if in a park or a deserted high street.

Presently some more people crowded into the church, and I began to look like an interloper, ignorant of the correct way to stand, bow his head, or join his hands; so I came out again, looked at the clock and discovered my period of waiting was still fairly lengthy. I tried to focus my thoughts on Helena, to think of her so as to put the long moments to some use; but the thoughts just wouldn't come, and the most I could do was conjure up a visual image of her. This is in fact a well known phenomenon: when a man is waiting for a woman, he finds it difficult to think of her, and can only walk up and down, calmly or otherwise, with an unmoving picture of her suspended before his eyes.

And so I walked up and down. Opposite the church I was puzzled by the sight of some dozen empty prams standing outside the old Guildhall (today the municipal council building). Then a breathless young man pushed another pram in among the others, while the rather nervous woman accompanying him pulled a bundle of white lacy material from the pram, and they both hurried into the Guildhall. Mindful of the hour and a half I still had to kill, I followed them in.

On the broad staircase there was already quite a crowd of idle bystanders, and as I went up the stairs there were more and more of them, especially in the first-floor corridor, while the stairs leading to the second floor were empty. The event all these people were gathered for was apparently to take place on the first floor, most probably in a room off the corridor which had its doors wide open and was packed with people. I went in and found myself in a smallish hall with some seven rows of chairs, most of them already occupied as if in expectation of some performance. At the front, on a raised rostrum, was a long table covered with a red cloth, and on the table a vase with a big bouquet in it. On the wall behind the rostrum was draped the national flag. About three yards from the first row of chairs, in front and rather to one side, were eight other chairs in a semi-circle facing the platform. On the other side

167

of the hall, at the back, stood a small harmonium at which sat a bald-headed old gentleman with bowed head and glasses.

There were a few unoccupied chairs in the auditorium; I sat down on one of them. For a long time nothing happened, but there was no sign of boredom; the people sat or stood in whispering huddles, evidently full of anticipation. Meanwhile those who had been standing in groups in the passage had gradually filled the hall, occupying the few remaining chairs and standing against the walls.

At last the long-awaited action began: a door near the platform opened, a bespectacled woman dressed in brown and with a long thin nose appeared, glanced round the hall and raised her right hand. The people round me grew quiet. Then the woman turned back towards the room she had come from as if making a sign to someone there, but at once she was back, pressing herself against the wall and wearing a fixed and ceremonial smile. Everything appeared to be perfectly synchronized, for at the very instant when the smile appeared the harmonium started up behind my back.

A few seconds later a flaxen-haired young woman appeared in the door by the platform, very red in the face, with expensive hair-do and make-up, a petrified expression on her face and a white bundle of infancy in her arms. The bespectacled woman pressed back even further against the wall so as not to block the way; her smile was evidently meant to beckon the young mother forward. The latter advanced uncertainly, clutching her infant; another woman with a babe in arms emerged behind her, and after her, in single file, came a whole little troop of them. I kept my eyes on the first one: she was looking somewhere up at the ceiling – then her gaze dropped and her eyes must have met those of someone in the audience, and this put her off her stroke, for she tore her gaze away and smiled, but the smile (and one could readily tell the effort she had to put into it) quickly vanished and only a fixed grimace remained. All this facial activity took place in the space of a few seconds – the time it took her to cover the not quite six yards from the door. She was walking in too straight a line and failed to wheel in time past the semi-circle of chairs, so that the bespectacled woman had quickly and frowningly to detach herself from the wall, go up to her, tap her gently on the shoulder, and remind her which way she should be going. The mother quickly corrected her deviation and walked along in front of the semi-circle of chairs, followed by the other women and their babies; there were eight of them altogether. Finally, having covered their prescribed paths, they stood with their backs to the audience, each one in front of a chair. The woman in brown pointed downwards; the women gradually got the message and, still with their backs to the audience, sat down with their infant bundles on the chairs.

The shadow of dissatisfaction vanished from the face of the bespectacled woman, and she was smiling again as she went back to the half-open door near the platform. For a while she stood there, then again she backed a few brisk steps into the hall and pressed herself up against the wall. A man of about twenty, dressed in a black suit and white shirt, the collar of which, adorned by a gaudy tie, was cutting into his neck, appeared in the doorway. He had his head down and swayed as he walked. A further seven men followed, of varying ages but all in dark suits and best shirts. They walked past the chairs where the women were sitting with their children and came to a halt. At this point some of them manifested a certain unrest and began looking around as if searching for something. The bespectacled woman, on whose face the now familiar shadow of dissatisfaction immediately appeared, at once ran up, and when one of the men whispered something she nodded her head in assent, and the embarrassed husbands quickly exchanged places.

Reassuming her smile, the woman in brown returned once more to the door by the platform. This time she did not need to nod or make any sign. A new troop came in through the door, and I am bound to say that this was a disciplined and expert bunch, striding forth without hesitation and with an almost professional elegance. It comprised eight children of about ten, boys and girls alternately, each carrying a bouquet of roses, and each dressed in the national colours: dark blue trousers or skirt, white shirt or blouse, and red kerchiefs folded diagonally, with one corner hanging down their backs and two others tied in a knot at their throats. They came forward, as I said, with certitude and confidence, and instead of passing along the semi-circle of chairs like their predecessors they wheeled right, in front of the semi-circle and along the platform, halted, and executed a left turn, so that they stood in a line before the platform, covering the whole of its length and facing the semi-circle of seated women and the rows of chairs behind.

Several minutes passed; then the door by the platform admitted a final figure: a man of middle age, completely bald, who made straight for the platform, mounting the steps and passing behind the long table covered with a red cloth. He walked erect and with dignity and wore a black suit; in his hand he held a book bound in red. Half way along the length of the table he stopped and turned to face the audience, bowing to them slightly as he did so. One could now see the obesity of his face and a broad red, white and blue ribbon round his neck, its two ends linked by a large gold medallion which hung in the vicinity of his stomach and bounced gently on the table several times as he bent forward.

At this point one of the small boys standing below the platform suddenly, and without first requesting permission, started to speak in a very loud voice. He said that spring had come and that mums and dads were full of joy, that the whole country was full of joy. He spoke in this vein for a while and was then interrupted by one of the girls, who made a similar speech, with no clear meaning but with frequent repetitions of the words *mum, dad* and *spring*, and in addition the word *rose*. Then she was cut short by another of the boys and he in turn by another of the girls, but one could hardly say that they were in any disagreement, as they were all more or less saying the same thing. One little boy proclaimed that children were Peace. The girl who followed said that children were Flowers; whereupon all the children were united on this idea, repeating it in unison and striding forward with the bouquets in their outstretched hands. As there were eight of them, this meant there was a bouquet for each of the women sitting in the

170

semi-circle of chairs. Then the children returned to their place below the platform, where they remained quietly.

Next, the man standing above them on the platform opened his red book and began reading from it. He too spoke about the spring, and flowers and mums and dads, about love, and about love bearing fruit. Then all of a sudden his vocabulary was transformed and in it appeared the words Duty, Responsibility, the State, the Citizen; also there was no more mum and dad, but only Father and Mother. He gave the assembled fathers and mothers a catalogue of all the State offered them (as fathers and mothers), and told them it was their duty to bring up their children as model citizens of the State. Then he announced that all parents present should ceremonially confirm this with their signatures, and indicated a large, leather-bound volume lying on a corner of the table.

Meanwhile the woman in brown had approached the mother sitting at one end of the semi-circle from behind and touched her on the shoulder, the mother had turned around and the woman had taken the baby from her arms. Next, the mother stood up and went over to the table. The man with the ribbon round his neck opened the book and gave the mother a pen. The mother signed and went back to her chair, where the woman in brown gave her back her baby. Then the appropriate husband went over to the table and signed the book; the woman in brown held the child for the next mother in line and despatched her to the table; the corresponding husband signed after her, then the next mother, the next husband, and so on to the end of the line. Finally the strains of the harmonium burst forth again and the people round me poured forward to the mothers and fathers and began grasping them by the hand. I too went forward, as if wanting to shake someone's hand – and suddenly the man with the ribbon round his neck called me by name and asked me if I recognized him.

Of course I did not do so, even though I had been watching him all the time he had been speaking. Not wishing to answer his rather tricky question in the negative, I feigned surprise and asked how he was. He said things were not too bad, and then suddenly I knew him: of course, it was Kovalik, a class-mate from the high school, and I recognized all the features which in his rather fuller face had now become blurred. In any case Kovalik had been one of the less memorable pupils, being neither very diligent nor very mischievous, neither very friendly nor too much of the lone wolf. He had been mediocre at his studies – in short a nonentity. In those days he had had a shock of hair across his brow and this was now missing – so I could have offered a number of excuses for not having recognized him straight away.

He asked me what I was doing there and whether I had any relatives among these mothers. I told him I had no relatives here and had come out of idle curiosity. He gave me a contented smile and began to explain that the local council had done a lot to imbue civil ceremonies with dignity, adding with modest pride that he, as officer responsible for citizen affairs, took most of the credit for this, and that he had been commended for it at district level. I asked him whether this was a christening that had just taken place. He told me it was not a christening, but the *welcoming of new citizens into life*. He was obviously glad to have a chance of expatiating on the subject. He said that there were two great opposing institutions concerned: the Catholic Church with its ceremonies and thousand-year-old traditions, and the civil institutions which must displace these ancient traditions with new ones of their own. He said that people would stop going to church to have their children christened or to be married only when our civil ceremonies had as much dignity and beauty as the church ones.

I said that this was evidently not entirely easy. He agreed and said he was glad that the officers for citizen affairs, of whom he was one, were at last finding a measure of support among our artists, who had perhaps realized that it was their task of honour to give our people really Socialist funerals, weddings and christenings – here he corrected himself and said 'welcomings of new citizens to life'. He added that the verses the young pioneers had recited today were truly beautiful. I acknowledged this and asked if it might not be a more effective way of educating people away from the religious ceremonies if we gave them a chance to avoid any sort of ceremony whatsoever. Didn't he think that the distinguishing feature of the modern man was a dislike for ceremonies and ritual occasions, and that if there was one thing which should be supported it was this general dislike?

He told me that people would never let their weddings and funerals be taken away from them. And that from our point of view – he emphasized the word *our* as if to let me know that he too had joined the Communist Party, several years after their coming to power – it would be a pity not to use these ceremonies to lead people to our ideology and State.

I asked this old classmate of mine what he did with people who did not want to take part in this sort of ceremony, and whether there were any who refused. He said that of course there were, since not everybody had yet begun to think in the new way, and that if they did not turn up they kept receiving more and more invitations, so that most of them came sooner or later. I asked him whether attendance at the ceremony was compulsory. He replied with a smile that it wasn't, but that the national committee adjudged people's sense of citizenship and attitude towards the State according to their attendance at these ceremonies, and that in the end every citizen would realize this and come.

I said this meant that the national committee was just as strict with their believers as the Church was with theirs. Kovalik laughed and said this could not be helped. Then he invited me to come and sit in his office. I said that unfortunately I was a little pressed for time as I had to meet someone off a bus. He asked me if I had seen any of the 'boys', meaning our friends from school. I said that unfortunately I hadn't, but that I was glad I had seen him at least, and that whenever I had a child to christen I would come straight to him. He laughed and clapped me on the shoulder. We shook hands and I emerged into the square again in the knowledge that there was another quarter of an hour before the bus arrived.

A quarter of an hour is not a long time. I crossed the square, went past the barber's shop, peered through the window (although I knew that Lucie would not be there till the afternoon), and strolled over in the direction of the bus station. I imagined Helena to myself: her face hidden under a layer of dark powder, her reddish, obviously dyed hair, her figure far from slim, though retaining the modicum of proportion necessary for our acceptance of a woman as a woman, and I rehearsed to myself all the features which placed her on the provocative borderline between the repellent and the attractive: her voice, louder than one would wish, her exaggerated gesticulations which involuntarily betrayed a febrile desire to continue being liked by men.

I had only seen Helena three times in my life, which is not quite enough for keeping anybody's appearance accurately in one's mind, and whenever I had wanted to recall her my memory had emphasized one of her points so much that for me she had gone through a continuous transformation into a caricature of herself. But however inaccurate my impressions might be they had doubtless managed to catch some essential feature, something hidden beneath the outward form.

This time in particular I could not rid my imagination of an image of Helena's bodily unclarity and blurriness, which I felt to be a characteristic not just of her age, her motherhood, but in particular of some psychological and erotic defencelessness, helplessness almost, which was unsuccessfully concealed beneath a confident manner of talking. Was this in fact an essential part of Helena, or was it rather a symptom of my own attitude towards her? Who knows? The bus was due in a moment and I longed to see Helena just as my imagination had interpreted her to me. I hid in the doorway of one of the houses on the square which enclosed the bus station; I wanted to stand there a moment and watch her looking *defencelessly* round and suddenly thinking she had wasted her time coming, since I was not there.

A large long-distance coach drew up in the square. Helena was one of the first to descend. She was dressed in a blue Italian raincoat of the type which was then being sold in the foreign-currency stores and which give their wearers a youthful, open-air appearance. Even Helena, with her collar turned up and belt drawn in, looked excellent in it. She surveyed the square, she even took a few steps forward to see the areas obscured by the bus, but instead of standing there helplessly she turned on her heel without hesitation and made for the hotel where I was staying, and where she had a room booked for the night as well.

I was convinced once again that my imagination had offered me Helena only in a distorted form (which was at times stimulating but which deformed Helena into an often undesirable and even repulsive shape). Luckily she was always more attractive in the flesh than in my imagination, as I realized afresh when I saw her from behind, striding towards the hotel on her high heels. I started off in pursuit.

She was already in the vestibule, leaning her elbow on the reception desk while a listless clerk signed her in. She was spelling out her name to him: Helena Zemankova, ZE-MAN-KO-VA. I stood behind her and listened as she gave her particulars. When the clerk had signed her in she asked: 'Is there a Comrade Jahn staying here?' The receptionist mumbled that there wasn't. I went up to Helena from behind and put my hand on her shoulder.

2

Everything that occurred between myself and Helena was part of a precise and deliberate plan. Helena, of course, had not entered into the relationship without designs of her own, but these barely went beyond a vague female desire to remain spontaneous and sentimentally poetical, and stopped short at any attempt to arrange or stage-manage events. I, on the other hand, had from the very beginning acted as meticulous stage-manager of the episode on which I was embarked, and had left to chance inspiration my choice neither of words and proposals nor of the room in which I intended to be alone with Helena. Nonetheless I was afraid of letting slip the proffered opportunity, an opportunity which meant so much to me, not because Helena was particularly young, or particularly amiable, or particularly attractive, but for one reason and one reason only: that she had the surname she had, that her husband, Zemanek, was a man I hated.

The day at the institute when I was informed that a Comrade Zemankova from the broadcasting corporation was coming to see me and that I was to give her some information on our research, I thought of my former student friend for a moment, but quickly dismissed this coincidence of names as a mere trick of chance; and if I took unkindly to her being sent to me it was for other reasons entirely.

It had become an invariable custom in our institute that all journalists were routed to me, and that I was the one who was always sent to lecture on behalf of the institute when we were requested to do so by various educational bodies. This apparent honour was a matter of some sadness for me. I had begun my own research almost ten years later than my colleagues – I had still been an undergraduate in my thirties. For a few years I had tried desperately hard to bridge this gap but had then realized the futility of devoting the second half of my life to a pathetic chasing after lost years, and so I resigned myself to it. Luckily this resignedness had its compensations: the less I chased after success in my own narrow field, the more I could allow myself the luxury of looking out from this field onto other areas of research, onto man's being and the existence of the world, and could experience the joys (among the sweetest there are) of speculation and reflection. My colleagues, however, knew full well that if such contemplation gives a man personal pleasure then it is of little use for a modern scientific career, which demands that the scientist burrow zealously in his own field or sub-field like a blind mole and should not waste time lamenting lost horizons. For this reason my colleagues half envied me my resignation and half despised me for it, as they gave me to know with gentle irony, calling me the institute's 'philosopher', and sending me journalists and news editors from the broadcasting corporation.

Perhaps for this reason and certainly because they are for the most part shallow, loud-mouthed and insolent, I do not like journalists. The fact that Helena was a features editor for the radio and not for a newspaper only heightened my aversion. In my eyes newspapers have one extenuating feature; they make no noise. When they are tedious, they are at least quiet about it. They do not intrude; they can be put aside, thrown in the waste paper basket or added to a pile of other papers. The radio, when tedious, does not even have this one extenuating feature: it persecutes us in coffee bars, restaurants, trains, even when we visit friends; for there are people who cannot live without this continual fodder for the ears.

I was put off still further by Helena's manner of speaking. It was clear that she had her feature fully thought out even before she came to the institute, and that now she was only looking for some concrete data and examples to go with all the usual clichés. I tried to complicate her job for her as much as I could; I deliberately spoke in an involved and unintelligible fashion and tried to upset all her preconceived views. Whenever there was any danger of her actually understanding anything I tried to sidestep it by becoming familiar: I told her how much red hair suited her (though I thought the exact opposite), I asked her how she liked her work in radio and what sort of books she enjoyed reading. And in the quiet calculation of probabilities that I was making, far below the surface of our conversation, I came to the conclusion that her surname could not be a mere coincidence. This garrulous, loud-mouthed, prosperous woman journalist seemed to me decidedly akin to the man whom I had also known as garrulous, loud-mouthed and prosperous. In the light, almost flirtatious tone which the conversation had assumed, I asked her about her husband. The clues all fitted into position, and a few further questions identified Pavel Zemanek with absolute certainty.

I cannot, of course, say that it occurred to me at that moment to become as intimate with her as I later became. On the contrary: the revulsion I had felt for her the moment she came in only deepened with this discovery. At first I even began to look for a pretext to break off my interview with this unwelcome guest and hand her over to some other member of the staff. I even thought what a pleasure it would be to take

177

her with her smiles and her air of sagacity and throw her out of my office, and I regretted that this was not possible.

However, at the very moment when I was most filled with dislike, Helena, stirred by my increasingly familiar questions and comments, whose purely investigatory function she was unable to perceive, gave expression to a few completely natural feminine gestures, and my hatred suddenly assumed a new cast: behind the veil of this pantomime journalist I saw in Helena the *woman*, the flesh-and-blood woman, capable of functioning as a woman. Sneering to myself, I had thought this was exactly the woman Zemanek deserved, and she was no doubt quite adequate punishment for him. Now suddenly I had to amend this hasty contemptuous judgement as being too subjective, too involuntary; clearly this woman had once been very pretty, and there was no reason to suppose that Pavel Zemanek should not be enjoying her as a wife to this very day. I sustained the lighter tone of the conversation without giving any indication of what I was thinking. Something was forcing me to learn more about this journalist woman sitting opposite me, especially about her feminine characteristics, and this compulsion automatically governed the direction taken by the conversation.

When a woman comes into the picture, hatred can become endued with certain qualities more symptomatic of affection: curiosity, for instance, the desire for togetherness, the urge to cross the threshold of intimacy. I was in raptures: I imagined Zemanek, Helena and the whole of their alien world, and with exquisite delight I indulged in my hatred, my attentive, almost tender hatred, for Helena's appearance, hatred for her red hair, hatred for her blue eyes, hatred for her short bristling lashes, hatred for her round face, hatred for her upturned sensuous nostrils, hatred for the gap between her two front teeth, hatred for the ripe chubbiness of her body. I was watching her as if watching a woman I loved, as if I wanted everything about her to become embedded in my memory; and in order that she might not notice the spiteful nature of my interest I chose my words in an ever lighter, ever more familiar vein, so that Helena became more and more feminine.

kept reminding myself that her mouth, breasts, eyes and hair belonged to Zemanek; in my mind's eye I took them all in my hands, weighed them up and balanced them, testing them to see whether they would be better crushed in my fist or shattered against the wall, and then I carefully re-examined them and tried to see them first with Zemanek's eyes and then again with my own.

Perhaps I did have the fleeting, utterly impractical and platonic idea that it might be possible to move this woman from the plane of our coquettish conversation further and further towards the target area of a bed. But that was only one thought, one of many which flash through the mind like a spark and are then extinguished. Helena announced that she thanked me for the information I had put at her disposal, and that she would not take up any more of my time. We said good-bye and I was glad to see her gone. My strange elation had passed, leaving only a sense of utter distaste; and I felt uncomfortable for having acted towards her with such confidential interest and simulated friendliness.

This meeting of ours would certainly have remained without a sequel had not Helena herself telephoned a few days later and asked whether she might see me. Perhaps she really did need me to check the text of her feature, but at the time it seemed to me more like a pretext, and the tone she used harmonized more with the familiar and lighter part of our last conversation than with the technical and serious part. I had adopted this tone quickly and without thinking, nor did I now abandon it. We met in a coffee bar. With deliberate provocation I ignored everything connected with Helena's feature; shamelessly I made light of her interests as a journalist. I could see that these tactics were upsetting her equilibrium, and that I was beginning to gain control over her. I invited her to come out into the country with me. She protested and reminded me that she was a married woman. No words could have given me greater pleasure. I lingered on this objection of hers which I found so appealing, I played with it, I kept returning to it, I joked about it. Finally she was glad of the opportunity to turn the conversation and quickly acceded to my proposal. After that everything went precisely according to plan. I had worked it out with the force of fifteen years of hatred, and I felt unaccountably confident of its success.

And certainly things were moving now. I took Helena's small travelling bag from her at reception and accompanied her upstairs to her room, which was just as hideous as my own. Even Helena, who had a rare capacity for euphemism, had to admit it. I told her that there was nothing to be done about it, that we would work things out between us. She gave me a glance full of meaning. Then she said she wanted to have a wash, and I said I would wait for her in the hotel lobby.

She came downstairs – under her unbuttoned coat she was wearing a black skirt and pink cardigan – and I was able to assure myself again of how elegant she was. I said we would have lunch at the People's House – an indifferent restaurant, but the best there was in this place. She said that since I came from these parts she put herself entirely in my hands, and that she would offer no resistance to anything I proposed. It looked as if she was trying to choose her words for the sake of *double entendre* – a ridiculous but gratifying attempt on her part. We followed the route I had taken that morning in my vain quest for a decent breakfast, and Helena kept reiterating how glad she was to be seeing my home town for the first time. She did not, however, bother to look around her or to ask about the various buildings, or in any way to behave like a visitor who is seeing an unfamiliar town for the first time. I wondered whether this lack of interest resulted from that form of spiritual decay which causes normal curiosity towards the outside world to atrophy, or whether it meant that Helena had all her attention on me and none left for anything else; I favoured the second possibility.

Again we walked past the memorial to the plague: the saint supporting his cloud, the cloud supporting the angel, the angel another cloud and the other cloud another angel. The sky was bluer now than it had been earlier. Helena took off her coat, threw it over her arm, and said how warm it was. The warmth merely increased the intrusive effect of dusty emptiness; the group of sculpture jutted up in the middle of the square like a piece broken off the sky which could not be put back. I told myself that the two of us had been cast irrevocably into this strangely deserted square with its park and restaurant; that we too had been broken off something; that mankind was wasting his time imitating the heavens and the heights above, that no one was fooled by it; that our thoughts and words were wasting their time clambering up aloft when our deeds were as low as the earth itself.

Yes, it was a feeling of my own *lowness* which had taken me by surprise; but what surprised me even more was that I was not shocked by this lowness, but accepted it with a certain pleasure, if not with joy or relief, and that this pleasure was increased by the certainty that the woman walking by my side was driven to the dubious hours of this afternoon by motives not much higher than my own.

The People's House was already open, though still empty, since it was only just a quarter to twelve. The tables were laid; opposite every chair there was a soup bowl covered by a paper napkin on which lay knife, fork and spoon. The place was deserted. We sat down, picked up our napkins and implements, put them by our plates, and waited. A few minutes later a waiter appeared in the kitchen doorway, surveyed the dining-hall wearily, and was about to go back into the kitchen.

'Waiter!' I called.

He turned back into the room and took a few steps in the direction of our table. 'Did you want anything?' he asked, when he was still about fifteen feet away.

'We should like to have lunch,' I said.

'Twelve o'clock for lunch,' he replied and turned to go back to the kitchen.

'Waiter!' I called him again. He turned round. 'Have you got any vodka, please?' I had to shout, as he was some distance away.

'No, no vodka.'

'What have you got?'

'We have,' he replied from the distance, 'rye whisky or rum.'

'I don't think much of that,' I shouted, 'but give us two ryes anyway.'

'I didn't even ask you if you drank rye whisky,' I said to Helena.

Helena laughed. 'No, I'm not all that used to rye.'

'No matter,' I said, 'you'll get used to it. You're in Moravia now and rye whisky is the Moravian's favourite spirit.'

'Excellent,' said Helena delightedly. 'That's what I like best of all, just an ordinary sort of bar where lorry drivers and mechanics go and where there's just ordinary things to eat and drink.'

'Have you ever, say, put rum in your beer?'

'Never,' said Helena.

'But you said you liked these proletarian sort of places.'

'I do,' she said; 'I just can't stand those posh places with a dozen waiters circling round you and serving you from a dozen dishes ...'

'Of course, there's nothing like those old taverns where the waiter doesn't even see you for smoke and fug. And there's nothing better than rye spirit. That's what I drank when I was a student. I didn't have the money for anything else.'

'And I like simple food too, like potato pancakes or liver sausage and onions, I can't think of anything better ...'

I have become so jaded with mistrust that when anyone, especially a woman, starts telling me what he or she likes or dislikes I am unable to take it seriously, or, to put it more precisely, I accept it only as indicating what might be called their self-stylization. I didn't believe for one instant that Helena breathed more freely in dirty ill-ventilated dives (of which there is no shortage in this country) than in clean, well-aired restaurants, or that she liked raw alcohol and cheap food better than titbits from a choice cuisine. However, this statement of hers was not entirely without value, as it revealed her predilection for a certain type of pose, a pose which had long become outmoded, a pose dating from the years when revolutionary snobbery delighted in anything which was 'common', 'proletarian', 'ordinary' or 'raw', just as it loved to despise everything which was 'refined' or 'pampered', or which was suspiciously associated with the idea of the dinner jacket and exaggerated good manners. In Helena's pose I recognized the period of my youth, and in Helena I recognized, more than anything else – Zemanek's wife. My preoccupations of the morning vanished and I began to concentrate.

The waiter brought us two glasses of rye whisky on a tray, set them down, and then placed before us on the table a sheet of paper on which was typed, evidently through several carbons, an illegible blurred copy of the menu for the day.

I raised my glass and said: 'Let's drink to rye, the common man's rye!'

She laughed and we touched glasses, and then she said: 'I've always longed for a man who was simple and direct. Unaffected. Straightforward.'

We took a swig of the stuff and I said: 'There are not many like that.'

'They do exist,' said Helena. 'And you're one of them.'

'I wouldn't have thought so,' I said.

'You are.'

Again I was filled with horror at the incredible human capacity to convert reality into a likeness of our own desires or ideals, but I accepted unfalteringly Helena's characterization of myself.

'Who knows – perhaps I am plain and straightforward,' I said. 'But what is plain and straightforward? It's all a question of a man being what he is, not being ashamed to want what he wants or to have the aspirations he has. People are often the slaves of convention. Someone tells them what they ought to be like and they try to be like it, and to the day they die they don't even find out who they were and who they are. They are nobody and they are nothing, they live a double, confused, mixed up life. First and foremost a man must have the courage to be himself. I want to tell you, Helena, from the outset that I like you, and that I desire you, even though you're a married woman. I can't put it any other way, and I can't let it remain unsaid.'

It was a fairly ticklish sort of thing to say – although

Helena, who had lowered her head as I spoke, failed to notice my embarrassment – but it had to be done. The conquest of a woman's mind has its own inflexible rules; anyone who decides to talk the woman round or confound her with rational argument is hardly likely to get anywhere. It is much wiser to discover the desired woman's basic self-stylization – her basic principles, ideals and convictions – and then to try, with the aid of sophistry, illogical rhetoric, etcetera, to steer her behaviour into a harmonic relationship with this self-stylization. Helena, for instance, had raved about 'simplicity', 'unaffectedness', straightforwardness'. These ideals of hers had their origin, no doubt, in the revolutionary puritanism of the early days, and were associated with the idea of the 'pure', 'unsullied', high-principled and strictly moral man. But since Helena's principles, like most people's, were based, not on rational thought but on irrational suggestion, nothing was simpler than to enlist the aid of crude rhetoric in combining the idea of the 'straightforward man' with behaviour which was altogether unpuritanical, immoral, and adulterous, and to prevent Helena's desired, i.e. adulterous, behaviour from subsequently finding itself in neurotic conflict with her inward ideals. A man can ask anything of a woman but, unless he wants to act like a brute, he must make it possible for her to act in accordance with her own most profound self-deceptions.

Meanwhile people had been trickling into the restaurant, and by now most of the tables were occupied. The waiter came out of the kitchen and began taking orders. I handed Helena the menu. She said I would know more about Moravian cuisine than she did, and handed it back to me.

One did not, of course, need to be an expert on Moravian cuisine, since the menu was exactly the same as in all eating-houses of this type and comprised a narrow selection of stereotyped dishes among which choice was difficult, as they were all equally unalluring. I gazed glumly at the illegibly typed sheet of paper. The waiter was already standing over me, waiting impatiently for our order.

'Just a moment,' I said.

'You wanted your lunch a quarter of an hour ago and you haven't even decided what you want yet,' he reminded me and left.

To my relief he came back fairly soon, and we ventured to choose the Spanish fowl and two more ryes with soda. The spirits had had a beneficial effect on Helena and she announced that life was good in spite of all the inequalities which were still with us. In any case it was up to people themselves what sort of life they made for themselves. I chewed at the stringy Spanish fowl and sour gherkins and proclaimed, with my mouth full, that this place became really beautiful when I was able to sit here with her.

Helena's cheeks were flushed (clearly as a result of the spirits), which emphasized their roundness and detracted from her elegance; but I (clearly as a result of the spirits) magnanimously ignored this, telling myself with malicious glee that it was a mercy of the fates that Helena was at least as presentable as she was, since even if she had been hideous, hunchbacked or legless I would still have made an attempt on her and tried to get her into my power.

Helena remarked, chewing at the fowl, how splendid (a favourite word) it was that we were here, sitting in a strange place of which she had dreamed so much when she had been in the ensemble and sung the songs which originated in this region. Then she said that it was probably wrong of her but that she felt happy with me and that she couldn't help it; it was against her will, but it was stronger than her will and that was that. I told her that it was a most deplorable thing to be ashamed of one's own feelings. Then I called the waiter and asked for the bill.

As we left the restaurant there was the memorial to the plague jutting up in front of us again. It looked so ridiculous that I pointed it out. 'Look, Helena, look at those saints clambering up there. Look at them fighting their way up! How they would love to get to heaven! And heaven couldn't care less about them. Heaven knows nothing about them, those winged yokels!'

'True,' said Helena, in whom the fresh air was reinforcing

185

the good work wrought by the alcohol. 'Why are these statues of saints here at all, why don't they put something here to celebrate life instead of this mysticism?' She was not quite sure of herself and added: 'Or is that nonsense? Am I talking nonsense?'

'No, Helena, you're quite right. Life is a beautiful thing and we can never celebrate it enough.'

'Yes,' said Helena. 'Let them say what they like, life is a splendid thing. I hate pessimists; even if I have plenty to complain about, still I don't complain. Why should I complain, tell me, why should I complain, when life can bring a day like this? It's so splendid – a strange town and me here with you ...'

I let Helena ramble on, and whenever there was a pause in her lucubrations I said something to set her going again. Soon we were standing in front of the new block of flats where Kostka lived.

'Where are we?' asked Helena.

'I'll tell you what,' I said. 'Those public bars are completely useless. In this house I have a small private bar. Come on in.'

'Where are you taking me?' Helena protested, following me into the block.

'A genuine Moravian wine bar; haven't you ever been in one?'

'Never,' said Helena.

On the third floor I unlocked the door and we went inside.

3

'This isn't a bar – it's an ordinary flat,' said Helena, when she had gone in and seen from the passage into Kostka's room.

'It's not an ordinary flat. It would be an ordinary flat if you or I lived in it. The special thing about this flat is that it is neither mine nor yours; there is none of my washing lying around here, or of yours, or my memories or your memories, it doesn't have the air of my home or of your home. It's a stranger's flat, and because of that it's *pure* as far as both of us are concerned and because of that we can both feel free in it.'

I had managed to propound a rather remarkable defence of the very principle of the borrowed flat; but my eloquence was quite superfluous. Helena had no objection to my leading her into a strange flat and needed no such apologia. On the contrary, it appeared that from the moment she had crossed the threshold she was determined to proceed from flirtation, which speaks in *double entendre* and pretends to be a game, to that act which has only one meaning and significance and which creates the illusion that it is not a game, but life itself. She stopped in the middle of Kostka's room to look back at me, and I could read in her eyes that she was already waiting for me to go up to her, kiss her and take her in my arms. In that moment when she looked back at me she was precisely the Helena I had imagined to myself: a Helena defenceless and utterly helpless.

I went up to her; she lifted her face. But instead of kissing her as she expected I smiled and took the sleeves of her blue mackintosh in my fingers. She understood and unbuttoned it. I carried it to the hanger in the vestibule. At this stage, when everything was ready – my desire and her willingness – I did not want to proceed too fast and risk missing in my haste a single nuance of what I wanted. I started a meaningless conversation; I told her to sit down, I drew her attention to all the details of Kostka's flat, I opened the cupboard with the bottle of vodka inside, the one Kostka had pointed out the day before, and pretended to be surprised. I opened the bottle, put two small glasses on the table and poured some out.

'I shall be drunk,' she said.

'We'll both be drunk,' I said, though I knew that *I* would *not* be drunk, that I had no intention of being drunk, because I wanted my memory of this encounter to be preserved intact.

Helena did not smile. She took a drink and said seriously: 'Ludvik, you know, I would be terribly unhappy if you thought I was just one of those bored married women who long for any adventure. I'm not so naïve as not to realize that you've known a good few women and that women themselves have taught you to take them in your stride. But I would be so unhappy ...'

'I would be unhappy too,' I said, 'if you were just one of those married women who take in their stride any romantic adventure that diverts them from their marriage. If you were one of those then our meeting would have had no meaning for me at all.'

'Do you really mean that?'

'Yes, Helena, I do. You're right when you say that I've known a lot of women and that they've taught me not to be afraid to keep moving from one to another, but my meeting you is something different altogether.'

'You're not just saying that?'

'No. The moment I met you I realized I'd been waiting for years, literally years, just for you.'

'You're not one of those smooth talkers. You wouldn't have said that if you didn't feel it.'

'No, I wouldn't. I can never conceal my real feelings from women, that's the one thing they've never taught me. So I'm not lying to you, Helena, even if it doesn't sound very convincing: the moment I met you I realized I'd been waiting for you for years, waiting for you without knowing you. And I knew that now you had to be mine. That it was as inevitable as fate.'

'God,' said Helena and closed her eyes; her face was flecked with red, perhaps from the alcohol, perhaps from excitement, and now she was even more the Helena I had imagined: defenceless and utterly helpless.

'If only you knew, Ludvik, I felt just like that as well. From the first moment I knew that meeting you like this was no mere flirtation, and that was what I was afraid of, because I'm a married woman and I knew that this with you was true, that you are my truth and there is nothing I can do about it.'

'Yes, Helena, and you are my truth too,' I said.

She was sitting on the divan, with her big eyes looking at me without seeing me, and I was sitting in the chair opposite her and watched her greedily. I put my hands on her knees and slowly turned up her skirt until her stocking tops and suspenders appeared, and these on Helena's deteriorating legs made a somewhat sorry impression. Helena sat there, not reacting to my touch with either word or movement.

'If only you knew . . .'

'Knew what?'

'About me. The way I live. The way I've been living.'

'How have you been living?'

She smiled bitterly.

Suddenly I was afraid Helena was going to have recourse to that banal expedient of all unfaithful wives and begin to make light of her marriage, thus robbing me of its value at the very moment when it had become my prey: 'For God's sake don't tell me you have an unhappy marriage, that your husband doesn't understand you.'

'I didn't want to say it,' said Helena, rather confused by this attack, 'even though . . .'

'Even though at this moment that's what you're thinking. Every woman starts to think that way when she's alone with another man, but that's where all the untruthfulness begins, and you want to stay truthful, Helena, don't you? You certainly must have loved your husband, you're not a woman to give yourself without love.'

'No,' said Helena quietly.

'Who is your husband?' I asked.

She shrugged her shoulders and smiled: 'Just a husband.'

'How long have you known each other?'

'We've been married thirteen years and we knew each other before that.'

'You must have been a student then.'

'Yes. I was in the first year.'

She wanted to pull her skirt down but I caught her hand and prevented her. I asked again: 'Tell me about him, where did you meet him?'

'In the ensemble.'

'The ensemble? Did your husband sing then?'

'Yes. Like all of us.'

189

'So you met in a musical ensemble.... What an excellent setting for falling in love.'

'Yes.'

'That was a good time.'

'Do you have nice memories of it too?'

'It was the best time of my life. Was your husband your first love?'

'I don't want to think of my husband just now,' she said.

'I want to get to know you, Helena. I want to know everything about you. The more I know you the more you will be mine. Did you have anyone before him?'

Helena nodded: 'Yes.'

I felt almost disappointed that Helena knew some other man, and that the significance of her attachment to Pavel Zemanek was thus diminished. 'Was it serious?'

She shook her head: 'Just silly curiosity.'

'So your first real love was your husband.'

She nodded. 'But that was a long time ago.'

'What did he look like then?' I asked quietly.

'Why do you want to know?'

'I want you to be mine with everything in you, everything in this head ...' and I stroked her hair.

If there is something which prevents a woman telling her lover about her husband then it is rarely refinement or tact or genuine bashfulness, it is simply the fear that this might somehow hurt the lover. Once the lover has dispelled this fear the woman is deeply grateful to him and feels more free: she has something to talk about, because topics of conversation are not unlimited, and for a woman her husband is the most thankful of topics, because it is the only one on which she feels secure, on which she feels an *expert*; and everyone is happy when he can display how much of an expert he is about something, and boast about it. So as soon as I had assured Helena that this did not put me off, she started speaking with complete freedom about Pavel Zemanek, letting herself be so carried away by her memories that she did not add a single shadow to this portrait, telling me in an earnest and matter-of-fact way how she had fallen in love with him, that straight-backed fair-haired youth, how she had looked at him with respect when he became political head of their ensemble (he was none of those dry-as-dust officials, in fact he was a thousand times livelier than any of these young people today!), how she and all her girl friends looked up to him (he had the most charming way of talking), and how their affair was in complete harmony with the whole era, in whose praise also she had a few things to say (how were *we* to know that Stalin was having loyal Communists shot?) – not, perhaps, because she wanted to divert the conversation into political channels, but because she felt herself to be personally concerned in this matter. Her emphatic defence of the period of her youth and the way she identified herself with this period, as if it had been her home, a home she had since lost, was almost a sort of minor demonstration, as if to say: 'Take me as I am and with no conditions save this one: you must let me be the way I am, you must take my opinions with me.' This opinionistic exhibitionism in a situation where opinions do not matter, where only the body matters, had an element of the abnormal in it, suggesting that it is opinions which make women neurotic: either she was afraid I might suspect her of having no opinion at all and so was hastily inventing one, or, in Helena's case the more probable explanation, she had secret gnawing doubts about her views and wanted to regain her certainty at all costs, even if she had to gamble for it with what was for her an indisputable value, the act of love itself – perhaps with the cowardly subconscious certainty that her lover would set more store by her lovemaking than her polemics. This demonstration of Helena's was not unpleasing to me, since it brought me nearer to the core of my passion.

'The young people of today are different from us,' she said. They have had everything free, everything was handed to them on a platter and they can't understand why even to this day I am moved when I hear a Russian chastushka.'

'But you had everything handed to you on a platter as well. You were only fourteen at the end of the war and seventeen in February '48.'

'I know, but even so all that is a part of my life. Do you

see that?' She pointed to a small silver disc she kept attached to her wrist watch by a short chain. I leaned over to see it and Helena explained to me that the design carved on it represented the Kremlin. 'I had that from Pavel,' she said, and she told me the whole story of the ornament. Apparently a love-sick Russian girl had given it years and years ago to a Russian boy called Sasha who had gone off to fight in the war, at the end of which he found himself in Prague, which he protected against destruction, but which destroyed him. In the villa where Pavel Zemanek lived with his parents, on the floor above, the Red Army had set up a small hospital; and here a badly wounded Russian lieutenant by the name of Sasha had spent the last days of his life. Pavel became friendly with him and spent whole days by his bedside. When he was dying Sasha gave Pavel as a keepsake the ornament with the sketch of the Kremlin on it which he had carried right through the war on a piece of string round his neck. Pavel kept this gift as a treasured memento. Once – when they were still only engaged – Helena and Pavel had had a row and thought they were going to split up; but then Pavel had come round to her and given her this cheap ornament and treasured keepsake as a peace offering, and from that time on Helena had never taken it off her wrist because the tiny object semed like a mission (I asked her what sort of a mission and she said 'a mission of joy') or like a baton which she must bear to the finishing post.

She sat facing me, with her skirt turned up, revealing suspenders attached to fashionable black stretch panties, and her face slightly flushed with the alcohol, and perhaps with the excitement of the moment – but for me the moment had caused her image to disappear behind that of another person. Helena's story about the locket and how it changed hands three times had suddenly, even violently, evoked the entire existence of Pavel Zemanek.

I had no faith at all in the existence of any Red Army officer called Sasha; in any case, even if he had existed his real existence would have completely vanished behind the grand gesture Pavel Zemanek had used to transform him into a character in his own legend, a sacred statue, an instrument to touch the heart strings, a sentimental argument and an article of religion which his wife, evidently more constant than himself, would worship, devoutly and defiantly, till the day of her death. It was as if Pavel Zemanek's vilely exhibitionistic heart was with us in the room. At once I was in the midst of that scene of fifteen years ago: the great lecture theatre of the Natural Sciences Faculty, on the rostrum Zemanek sitting behind a long table, at his side a fat girl with a round face, pigtail and hideous sweater, on the other side a youth representing the district committee. Behind the platform there was a large blackboard and to the left of it a framed portrait of Julius Fucik. Opposite the long table were the benches of the lecture hall rising in tiers, myself sitting among them; and now, fifteen years later, looking with my eyes of those days, I saw Zemanek in front of me announcing that 'the case of Comrade Jahn is up for discussion. . . . I shall read you letters written by two Communists.' After these words he made a light pause, picked up a slim volume, ran his fingers through his long, wavy hair, and began reading in an ingratiating, almost tender voice.

'Death, you have been a long time coming. Yet it had been my hope that I would meet you many years from now, that I would continue living as a free man, would continue to work and to love, to sing and to travel the world . . .' I recognized Fucik's *Notes from the Gallows*. '. . . I have loved life and for the sake of its beauty I went to war. People, I have loved you and was happy when this love was returned, and I suffered when you did not understand me . . .' This text, written secretly in prison, and illuminated by the glow of the man's heroism, was at that time perhaps the most widely read book in the country; Zemanek had just read us the most famous passages, the ones everyone knew by heart. 'Let sadness never be linked with my name. That is my last will and testament to you, father, mother and sisters, to you, my Gustina, to you, Comrades, to everyone I have loved . . .' Fucik's portrait hung on the wall. It was a reproduction of the famous etch by Max Svabinsky, that old *Jugendstil* painter and virtuoso imitator of symbolic allegories, buxom women, butterflies and anything you might care to mention; after the war, apparently, the Communists had approached him and requested him to do a portrait of Fucik from surviving photographs, and Svabinsky had done a profile sketch of him in his best pretty-pretty style. He had made him almost girlish, eager, pure, and so handsome that perhaps even those who had known Fucik personally preferred the graceful sketch to the real face.

Zemanek continued by reading out how Fucik and his fellow prisoner Pesek sang songs in cell 267; at this his voice took on a clear, joyous tone. 'The sun! So generously does that circular musician throw his glow, so many miracles he performs before the eyes of men.... Father, father, I should like to see the sun go down one last time ...' Zemanek read on, and everyone in the hall was quiet and attentive, and the fat girl behind the table never took her admiring eyes off him, and then all at once his voice became hard and sounded almost menacing. He was reading about Mirek, who was the prison informer: 'He used to be a man with a backbone: he never dodged the bullets when fighting on the Spanish front, and he remained unbroken by the gruelling test of the French concentration camp. Now he turned pale before the Gestapo guards and gave information to save his own skin. How shallow was this courage of his which could be broken by a few blows. It was as shallow as his convictions.... He lost everything because he began to think of himself. He sacrificed his friends to save his own skin. He succumbed to cowardice and out of cowardice he betrayed his comrades ...' Fucik's handsome face hung on the wall just as it hung in a thousand other public places in our country, and it was so handsome that when I looked at it I felt inferior, not just because of my guilt but because of my appearance as well. Zemanek read on: 'They can take our lives, Gustina, as you see, but our honour and love, these they cannot take away from us. Oh, people can you imagine the way we would live if we met again after all this suffering, met again in a free life, a life made beautiful by liberty and creation? The life that will come into being when all that we have yearned for, fought for, and that I now die for, takes place?' Zemanek read these last sentences with feeling, and stopped.

Then he said. 'That was a letter written by a Communist in the shadow of the gallows. Now I shall read you another letter.' And he read out the three brief, stupid, ghastly sentences from my postcard. Then he fell silent, there was a general hush, and I knew that I was lost. Zemanek, that great showman, deliberately allowed the silence to last some time before calling on me to speak. I knew I had no defence; it had never been strong, and what chance did I have now, when Zemanek had put my postcard in the scales against the absolute weight of Fucik's agony? Of course I had no other course open but to stand up and say my piece. Once again I said that the message was meant as a joke. I condemned the unsuitability and crudity of the joke, spoke of my individualism, intellectualism, isolation from the people, even uncovered in myself complacency, scepticism and cynicism, but vowed outright that in spite of it all I was still a devoted Party man and not its enemy.

Next came the discussion, in which the Comrades held me guilty of inconsistency: how could a man be devoted to the Party when he admitted himself that he was a cynic? One woman member reminded me of my frivolous pronouncements about women and asked me whether that was the way a Communist should talk. Others of them made general remarks about the petty bourgeois, which they illustrated by insinuating me into their number. There was general agreement that my self-criticism had been superficial and insincere. Then the girl with the pigtail sitting next to Zemanek at the table asked: 'What do you think would be the reaction to your words on the part of those Comrades who were tortured by the Gestapo and who did not survive?' I realized they were all pretending not to know how my father died. I said nothing. She repeated her question and urged me to answer. I said: 'I don't know.' 'Think,' she insisted; 'perhaps you may think of something.' She wanted me to pass severe sentence on myself from the imaginary lips of dead Comrades. But I suddenly felt a wave of anger wash over me, completely unforeseen and unexpected anger, and reversing my self-critical statements of many weeks I said: 'They stood between life and death. There could be no question of their being so small-minded. If they had read my postcard it would quite possibly have made them laugh.'

A moment previously the pigtail had given me a last chance to save at least something from the wreck: to understand the criticism of my Comrades, to identify myself with it, to accept it, and on the basis of this identification to gain in turn a measure of understanding from them. But my unexpected reply had suddenly excluded me from the sphere of their thinking. I had refused to play the part which was generally played at many hundreds of meetings, hundreds of disciplinary proceedings, and not long after at hundreds of trials in a court of law: the part of the accused who is also the accuser and who, by the very ardour of his self-accusation, his absolute identification with the accusers, asks that mercy may be granted him.

There was another moment of silence. Then Zemanek spoke again. He said he was unable to imagine what could possibly be funny about my anti-Party pronouncements. He referred again to Fucik's words and said that in critical situations wavering and scepticism were commonly transformed into treachery, and that the Party was a stronghold in which no traitor was permitted. Then he said that my answer clearly proved that I had failed to learn anything, that not only was I unfit to be in the Party, but also I did not deserve that the working class should continue to expend their funds on my studies. He proposed a motion that I be excluded from the Party and expelled from the university. The people in the room all raised their hands, and Zemanek told me I was to surrender my Party card and leave.

I stood up and placed my Party card in front of Zemanek. Zemanek didn't even look at me; he no longer saw me. But I can see his wife now; she is sitting right in front of me, drunk with her face red and her skirt wound up round her waist. Her heavy legs are topped by the black of her stretch panties, those legs whose opening and closing became the rhythm which pulsated its way through a decade of Zemanek's life.

196

On these legs I now put the palms of my hands, and it was as if I had Zemanek's very life in my grasp. I looked at Helena's face, into her eyes, which reacted to my touch by closing ever so slightly.

4

'Get undressed, Helena,' I said quietly.

She got up off the couch, and the hem of her skirt slipped back down to her knees. She gazed fixedly into my eyes and then without a word, and without taking her eyes off me, began to unbutton her skirt down the side. Thus released, the skirt slid down her legs onto the floor; she stepped out of it with her left foot and with her right passed it up to her hand and laid it on the chair. She was now standing in her cardigan and slip. Then she pulled the cardigan over her head and threw it over to join the skirt.

'Don't watch,' she said.

'I want to see you,' I said.

'I don't want you to see me undressing.'

I went over to her. I took her from both sides under the armpits and as I let my hands go down to her hips I felt her soft strong body under the silk of the slip, now somewhat damp with sweat. She bent her head down and her lips opened slightly in the habit (a bad one) of many years, ready for a kiss. But I didn't want to kiss her, I wanted to go on looking at her for as long as I could.

'Get undressed, Helena,' I said again and I stepped back and took off my own jacket.

'Too much light here,' she said.

'That's all right,' I said and hung my jacket over the back of the chair.

She pulled the slip over her head and threw it across to the cardigan and skirt. She unfastened her stockings and slid them off her legs one after the other; but instead of throwing the stockings she took two steps towards the chair and placed them carefully on it. Next she strained her chest forward and put her hands behind her back; it took a few seconds and then her arms, which had been stretched behind her back as if to launch herself forward, came free and fell forward and with them fell her bra, sliding off her breasts, which were pressed into one another, big, full, pale, and naturally somewhat heavy and fallen.

'Get undressed, Helena,' I repeated for the last time. Helena looked me in the eyes and then pulled off the black stretch panties; these she threw on top of the pile on the chair. She was naked.

I am not dragging out the individual details of the scene from any special predilection for the process of female undressing, but because I took careful note of each one of these details. This was not a case of achieving quick pleasure with a woman (*any* woman) but of mastering a very particular alien intimate world in the space of a single afternoon, in the course of a single act of love in which I was to be not just a man carried away by the process of lovemaking, but a man who is ravaging and guarding a fleeting prey and for this reason must be absolutely on the alert.

So far I had gained mastery of Helena just by looking at her. Now again I remained a step or two away from her, while she longed for the speedy application of warm caresses which would conceal her body from the frank coldness of my stare. I felt from my distance of those few paces the moisture of her mouth and the sensual impatience of her tongue. Another second, two, and I went up to her. We held each other close, standing in the middle of the room between the two chairs which stood covered in our clothes.

'Ludvik, Ludvik, Ludvik ...' she whispered. I took her to the divan. I laid her on it. 'Come,' she said, 'come, come to me, come to me.'

Physical love very rarely merges with spiritual. What is the soul to do as the body, in a movement age-old, universal and invariable, combines with another body? What a wealth of invention it can find in those moments as it again makes apparent its superiority over the inert monotony of physical life! How it can scorn the body and use it (and its opposite number) as pretexts for insane fantasies a thousand times more corporeal than both the bodies themselves! Or the reverse: how it can belittle the body by leaving it to its see-saw motions, at the same time turning its meditations, now worn out by the caprices of the body, in a completely different direction: to chess, to recollections of dinner or of a favourite book ...

There is nothing uncommon about the union of two strange bodies. Occasionally, perhaps, we may also find the union of souls. What is a thousand times more rare is for the body to unite with its own soul and be at one with it in a shared passion. But sometimes it does happen, when a man is really in love. Perhaps; I believe it does; I want to go on believing it.

But what was my soul doing during the moments my body spent in physical lovemaking with Helena?

My soul had seen a female body. It was indifferent to this body. It knew this body had meaning for it only as a body which had been seen and loved in just the same way by a third party who was not present; and therefore the soul tried to look at this body with the eyes of this third, absent person, to become this person's medium. The naked body, the bend of the legs, the curve of the belly and breasts: all this gained significance only in the moments when my eyes were transformed into the eyes of the third, absent, person. In these moments my soul suddenly entered into, and became, this alien; it not only mastered the bend of the legs, the curve of the belly and breasts, it mastered them in the way that they were seen by the third party.

Not only did my soul become the medium for this third, absent person but it urged my body to become the medium for his body; then it stood back and watched the squirming struggle of the two bodies, the two conjugal bodies; then it suddenly commanded my body to be itself again, to enter into this conjugal coitus and brutally disturb it.

A vein showed blue on Helena's neck and a convulsion ran through her body; she turned her head to one side and her teeth bit into the pillow.

Then she whispered my name and her eyes begged a few moments' respite.

But my soul commanded me not to stop; to drive her from pleasure to pleasure; to chase her down; to change the position of her body so that not a single look given her by that third, absent party should remain veiled or hidden; no, grant her no respite, repeat that convulsion over and over again, that moment in which she was real and exact, authentic, in which she feigned nothing, in which she was engraved in the memory of this third person, this third man who was not there, like a stamp, a seal, a cipher, a badge. Steal this secret cipher, this royal seal! Ransack Pavel Zemanek's thirteenth bower! Rummage through everything and throw it about! Leave everything in a shambles!

I looked at Helena's face, flushed and disfigured by a grimace. I put the palm of my hand on this face, as one puts one's hand on an object which can be turned over or upside down, smashed or crushed, and I felt that her face accepted my hand in the same way: as something which wants to be turned over and smashed. I turned her head first to one side, then to the other. Several times I turned her head in this way; and then the turning motion was transformed into a first hard slap, then a second and a third. Helena began to sob and scream, not with pain but with excitement. Her chin came up to me, and I hit her and hit her and hit her; then I saw not only her chin but her breasts coming up to me, and hoisting myself slightly over her I beat her on her arms and flanks and breasts . . .

Everything comes to an end; even this delectable devastation was over at last. She lay crosswise over the divan on her stomach, exhausted. I could see the brown round birthmark on her back and below, on her buttocks, the red blotches from my beating.

I got up and lurched across the room; I opened the door and went into the bathroom; I turned on the tap and washed my face, hands and body in the cold water. I raised my head and saw myself in the mirror: my face was smiling. When saw it smiling away, I thought how funny it looked and burs out laughing. Then I dried myself with a towel and sat on the edge of the bath. I wanted to be alone just for a few seconds, to savour the rare delight of sudden solitude.

Yes, I was satisfied; I was even perhaps completely happy. I felt myself the victor. As for the ensuing minutes and hours, they were superfluous and had no interest for me.

Then I went back into the room.

Helena was now lying not on her belly but on her side, looking at me. 'Come here, darling,' she said.

Many people believe, without giving it much thought, that when they are united physically they are united spiritually as well; and so they automatically, and erroneously, feel justified in using a more intimate form of speech. For my part, never having shared this erroneous belief, I viewed Helena's words with embarrassment and distaste. Instead of accepting her invitation I went over to the chair where I had thrown my clothes, and picked up my shirt.

'Don't get dressed,' begged Helena; and she stretched her arm out towards me and repeated: 'Come here.'

I wished for nothing but that the ensuing moments should not, if this was possible, take place at all, but if they had to, then that they should be as unremarkable and insignificant as possible; that they should be of no account, lighter than the dust. I didn't want to touch Helena's body again, I was horrified at the thought of any show of affection; at the same time I was equally horrified at the thought of any tension or dramatics. So I unwillingly renounced my shirt and sat down with Helena on the divan. It was frightful: she pushed up against me and put her head on my leg. Then she began kissing me, and soon my whole leg was wet – but not from her kisses: Helena raised her head and I saw that her face was covered with tears. She wiped them away and said: 'Don't be angry, darling, I can't help crying, I can't,' and she pushed closer again, put her arms round me and burst into sobs.

'What's the matter?' I said.

She shook her head, said 'Nothing, stupid, nothing,' and began ardently kissing me all over my face and body. 'I'm in love,' she said, and when I made no reply, she went on:

'You'll laugh at me but I don't care. I'm in love, I'm in love.' When I still said nothing, she said: 'I'm so happy.' Then she got up and pointed at the table with the unfinished bottle of vodka on it: 'Pour me out a drop of that.'

I didn't feel like pouring any, either for myself or for Helena; I was scared that any further use of alcohol might bring a dangerous sequel to the afternoon's work – the excellence of which was conditional on its being already finished and done with.

'Please, love' – she was still pointing at the table, and added apologetically. 'Don't be angry. I'm just happy. I want to be happy.'

'You don't need vodka for that,' I said.

'Don't be cross, I just feel like it.'

There was no remedy; I poured her a glass of vodka. 'Don't you want any more?' she asked. I shook my head. She gulped the glass down and said: 'Put it down for me over there.' I put the bottle and glass down on the floor by the divan.

She was very quick to recover from her momentary exhaustion; suddenly she had become a little girl, she wanted to enjoy herself, and to make it obvious that she was doing so. She evidently felt completely free and natural in her nakedness – all she was wearing was her wrist watch with the picture of the Kremlin jingling and swinging from it – and she was trying out different positions for comfort. She crossed her legs under her and sat there like a Turk; then she drew them out again and leaned on her elbow; then she lay on her belly and pressed her face into my lap. With the most diverse variations she told me how happy she was; in between she kept wanting to kiss me. This I endured with considerable self-restraint, as her mouth was too wet and she was not content with my shoulders and cheeks but tried to touch my lips as well – and I loathe wet kisses; that is, when I am not blinded by physical desire.

Then she told me that she had never known anything like this before, and I told her, for the sake of saying something, that she was exaggerating. She began to swear that in matters of love she never lied and that I had no reason to disbelieve her. She elaborated her idea and said that the body has its own foolproof instinct; that I had, of course, impressed her with my intelligence and zest (yes, zest – I can't think how she discovered *that* in me), but that she knew (even though she was only now getting sufficiently over her reserve to talk about it) that between our bodies had immediately arisen that secret pact which the human body signs perhaps only once in a lifetime. 'And that's why I'm happy, you see'; and she hung her legs over the edge of the divan, squatted down for the bottle and poured herself another glass. She drank it and said, laughing: 'What am I to do if you don't want any more? I'll have to drink it all by myself!'

Even if I had considered the incident closed I won't deny that I was glad to hear Helena talking like this; it confirmed the success of my project and my satisfaction with it. And because I didn't know what to say, and didn't want to seem too morose, I suggested she was exaggerating when she talked about an experience which comes only once in a lifetime; hadn't she, as she herself had confided, lived through a great love with her husband?

Helena thought seriously about this – she was sitting on the divan with her legs slightly apart and resting on the ground, her elbows on her knees and an empty glass in her hand – and sand quietly. 'Yes.'

Perhaps she thought that the intensity of the experience she had enjoyed a moment before bound her to an equally intense sincerity. She repeated 'Yes' and then said that perhaps it would be unfair and wrong to disparage something which had once been, in the name of the miracle which had happened today. (This was her way of referring to our lovemaking.) She took another swig and went on about how it was the most powerful experiences which were the hardest to compare; and that for a woman there was a great difference between love at twenty and at thirty – was I taking in what she was saying? – physically as well as mentally. And then, illogically and without any connexion, she announced that in any case there was a resemblance between myself and her husband! She said she was not quite sure where it lay; admittedly we looked completely different, but she had a foolproof instinct

203

which enabled her to look more deeply into men, behind their outward appearance.

'I'm curious to know what it is about me that makes me resemble your husband,' I said.

She told me there was no need for me to be angry, that I had been the one who wanted to hear about him, and that was the only reason she had ventured to talk about him at all. But if I wanted to hear the real truth then she must tell me: only twice in her life had she been attracted to anyone so strongly and unconditionally – to her husband, and to myself. What we had in common, she said, was some secret zest for life – the joy which emanated from us – eternal youth – strength.

Helena's attempts to explain my resemblance to Pavel Zemanek may have been incoherent, but there was no denying that she saw and felt, and even *lived*, this resemblance and clung tenaciously to it. Apparently we were so similar that perhaps she had not really been unfaithful in making love with me. I won't say that this hurt or offended me, but I was shocked at the clumsiness and boundless stupidity of the assertion. I went over to the chair with my clothes on it and started slowly to dress.

'Did I say something wrong, love?' Helena had sensed my displeasure, got up off the couch and came over to me; she began stroking my face and begging me not to be angry with her. She tried to stop me dressing; for some mysterious reason she regarded my trousers and shirt as her enemies. She began telling me that she really loved me, that she was not just using empty words, that perhaps she might have an opportunity to prove it, that when I asked her about her husband she had known right away there was no sense in talking about it, that she did not want any man, any stranger, to come between us; yes, stranger, for her husband had for long been a stranger to her. 'But I haven't lived with him for three years, silly. The only reason we don't divorce is because of the children. He has his life and I have mine. Today we're just a pair of strangers. He's simply my past, something that happened a long time ago.'

'Is this true?' I asked.

'Indeed it is.'

'Stop trying to have me on.'

'I'm not. We live in the same flat but we don't live as man and wife. It's years since we lived together as man and wife.'

She was looking at me with the imploring face of a woman miserably in love. Again and again she kept assuring me that what she said was true, that she was not trying to deceive me, that I needn't be jealous of her husband; that her husband was merely the past; that today she hadn't even been unfaithful, because she had no one to be unfaithful *to*; that I needn't be afraid; that our lovemaking was *pure* as well as good.

Suddenly I saw with terrifying clarity that I had no reason to disbelieve her. When she saw this she became more at ease and begged me several times to say in so many words that I believed her. Then she poured herself another glass of vodka and wanted us to drink a toast. I refused. She kissed me. I felt the goose pimples rise but I was incapable of averting my face; I was fascinated by her idiotic blue eyes and her lithe and still-twitching naked body.

But this time I saw her naked body in a completely different light; I saw it as a body which had been *stripped* – stripped of the allurement which till then had blurred over all the faults of age (corpulence, sagging, over-ripeness), in which the whole history and present of Helena seemed to have been concentrated and which had therefore fascinated me. Now that Helena stood before me bare, without a husband or any links binding her to a husband, without marriage vows, just *in herself*, her bodily unloveliness lost all its ability to excite and became merely ugly.

Helena had no idea of the new light in which I was seeing her, and became more and more drunk and contented. She was happy that I believed her assurances of love and hardly knew how to give vent to her happiness. For no apparent reason she decided to switch on the radio, squatting in front of it with her back to me as she twiddled the knob. There was jazz on one station; Helena stood up and her eyes gleamed. She made a clumsy imitation of the undulating movements of the twist; I stared aghast at her breasts as they flew from side to side. 'Is that right?' she laughed. 'Do you know, I've never tried these dances.' She laughed again, very loudly, and came for me with her arms outstretched. She asked me to dance with her and was angry when I refused. She told me that she didn't know the new dances but that she wanted to learn them and I must teach her; she wanted me to teach her a lot of things, she wanted to be young again when she was with me. She begged me to assure her that she was still young (which I did). She realized that I was dressed while she was naked and started to laugh again at that; it seemed to her inconceivably odd. She asked if the owner had a mirror somewhere about the place so that she could see what we looked like. There was no mirror, only a glass-fronted bookcase. She tried to see us in the glass but the image was too indistinct. Then she went to the bookcase and laughed over the titles of the books on their spines: the Bible, Calvin's *Institutes*, *Epistles against the Jesuits*, Jan Hus. Next she took out the Bible, struck a theatrical pose, opened the book at random and began reading from it in an exaggerated clerical voice. She asked me if she made a good priest. Yes, admirable, I told her, but now she must get dressed because Mr Kostka would be arriving any moment. 'What's the time?' she asked. 'Half past six,' I said. She seized my left wrist, looked at my watch and cried: 'Liar! It's only a quarter to six! You want to get rid of me!'

I did indeed wish she was gone; that her wretchedly material body might dematerialize, melt, turn into a river and flow away, into steam and fly out of the window – but her body was *here*, a body I had stolen from no one, in which I had vanquished no one, destroyed no one, a body abandoned, deserted by her husband, a body which I had intended to use, but which had used me and was consequently now in transports of insolent delight, jumping about and playing the fool.

There was no way of cutting short my bizarre torment. It was almost half past six before she started to dress. As she did so she noticed a red mark on her arm where I had hit her, stroked it, and said she would keep it as a memento until such time as she saw me again. Then she quickly corrected herself: she would certainly see me long before the memento had dis appeared. She stood facing me, with one stocking on and the other in her hand, and wanted me to promise we would see each other before then. I nodded. That wasn't enough for her; she wanted me to promise her we would see each other *lots of times* before then.

She took a long time getting dressed. She left a few minutes before seven.

5

I opened the window, because I longed for a wind to waft away all memories of that wasted afternoon, every remnant of odour and emotion. Then I tidied the bottle away, smoothed the cushions on the divan, and when I thought all traces had been removed I slumped in the armchair by the window and waited, almost imploringly, for Kostka. I looked forward to the sound of his masculine voice (I really longed to hear a deep masculine voice), his long skinny frame with its flat chest, his quiet way of talking, eccentric and wise; looked forward to him telling me something about Lucie, who, in contrast to Helena, was so sweetly incorporeal, so abstract, so far removed from all conflicts, tensions and dramas, and yet not without influence on the course of my life – it flashed across my mind that perhaps she had influenced it in the same way that astrologers imagine the stars as influencing the lives of men. As I sat sunk in the armchair, under the open window through which I had banished all scent of Helena, it occurred to me that I knew why Lucie had flashed across the stage during the last few days; it was just so that she could take my revenge and change it to nothing, change into vapour everything I had come here to do. For Lucie, whom I had loved so much and who at the last moment had run away from me so incomprehensibly, was the goddess of escape, the goddess of the race run in vain, the goddess of vapour; and she still held my head in her hands.

Part VI: Kostka

1

It is a good many years now since we last saw each other, and in fact we have only actually met a few times in our lives. This is rather strange, because in my imagination I meet Ludvik Jahn very frequently indeed, and I turn to him in my soliloquies as to my chief adversary. I have become so accustomed to his incorporeal presence that I found myself in some confusion yesterday on suddenly after all these years meeting him again as a real man of flesh and blood.

I called Ludvik Jahn my adversary. Have I the right to do so? By coincidence I have run into him every time I have found myself in real need of assistance and he was the one who always rendered it to me. But beneath this outward alliance there was always a depth of inward disagreement. I do not know whether Ludvik was as fully aware of this as I was. He definitely attached a greater significance to our outward alliance than to our inward difference. He was merciless towards outward adversaries and tolerant towards inward disharmonies. I was not. I am the complete opposite. I do not mean by this that I do not like Ludvik. I love him, as one loves one's adversaries.

2

I first met him in 1947, at one of those stormy meetings with which the institutes of higher education seethed in those days. The future of a nation was being decided upon. Everyone realized this, myself included, and in all the discussions, arguments and ballots I was on the side of the Communist minority against the majority, which in the universities at that time comprised adherents of the People's* and Socialist parties.

Many Christians, both Catholics and Evangelists, bore me a grudge for this. They considered it a betrayal for me to have allied myself with a movement which bore atheism inscribed upon its shield. When I see these people today they imagine that after fifteen years I have at last seen the error of my ways. But I have to disappoint them. To this day I have not changed my position one iota.

Of course the Communist movement is atheistic. But only those Christians who do not wish to see the beam in their own eye can blame Communism for this. I say 'Christians'. But who are they? All around me I see only the most superficial Christians living in exactly the same way as the unbelievers. But being a Christian means living differently. It means taking the path Christ took, *imitating* Christ. It means giving up our private interests, our comfort and power, and turning our face towards the poor, the downtrodden and the suffering. But do the churches do this? My father was a working man, continually unemployed and with a humble faith in God. He turned his pious face towards Him, but the Church never turned its face upon my father. He remained forsaken among those that were near him, forsaken within the Church, alone with his God, until at last he fell ill and died.

The established churches failed to realize that the working-class movement was the movement of the downtrodden and those that groan for justice. Utterly contrary to the spirit of Jesus, the churches turned their backs upon them. They were not interested in striving with them and for them, for a kingdom of God on earth. They allied themselves with the oppressors and thus deprived the working-class movement of God. And now they want to reproach it for being godless. The Pharisees! Yes, the working-class movement is atheistic, but in this I see God's reproach to us, the Christians! A reproach for our hardheartedness towards the poor and the suffering.

And what am I to do in this situation? Am I to feel shocked at the dwindling support for the churches? Am I to feel

* Catholic

shocked at the schools bringing up our children in an anti-religious frame of mind? How silly! True religion does not require the favour of terrestrial power. Secular disfavour only strengthens the faith.

And am I perhaps to fight against Socialism because it is, thanks to us, atheistic? Sillier still! I can only lament the tragic error which led Socialism away from God. All I can do is to explain this error and work for its correction.

And anyway, why this disquiet, brother Christians? Everything is done according to God's will, and I often wonder whether it is God's design not to let mankind know that man cannot with impunity take his seat on His throne and that even the most just disposition of secular conditions will without His participation fail and become corrupt.

I remember those years when people here felt themselves to be but a few steps away from paradise. And they were proud because it was *their* paradise for which they needed no one in Heaven above. And then suddenly it melted away beneath their hands.

3

In any case, until the February coup my being a Christian suited the Communists quite well. They loved to hear me explaining the social content of the Gospel, inveighing against the rottenness of the old world of property and wars, and demonstrating the affinity between Christianity and Communism. It was, after all, their concern to win over to their cause the broadest possible section of the population, and this of course included winning over the believers. Soon after that February, however, things began to change. As a lecturer at the university I took the part of some of my pupils who were due to be expelled from the faculty because of the political convictions of their parents. I protested against this and in doing so clashed with the university. Suddenly it began to be said that a man with such a distinct Christian orientation was

211

not properly capable of educating Socialist youth. It appeared that I would have to fight for my very livelihood. Then I heard that a student by the name of Ludvik Jahn had stood up for me at a plenary meeting of the Party. He said, apparently, that it would be base ingratitude to forget what I had meant to the Party before February. And when they referred to my Christian beliefs he said that they must surely be a passing phase in my life, one which, thanks to my youthful years, I would outgrow.

I went to see him and thanked him for taking my part. I told him, however, that I would not like to disappoint him; and I warned him that I was older than he was and that there was no hope at all of my 'outgrowing' my faith. We then began to debate the existence of God, the finite and the infinite, Descartes's views on religion, whether Spinoza was a materialist, and much else besides. We came to no agreement. Finally I asked Ludvik whether he regretted standing up for me now that he saw how incorrigible I was. He told me my Christian faith was my own private affair and that all in all it was no concern of anyone else.

From that time on I did not see him at the university again. And yet the patterns of our lives became more and more similar. About three months after this conversation of ours Jahn was expelled from the Party and university, and another six months later I too had to leave the faculty. Was I thrown out? Driven out? Impossible for me to say. All I can say for certain is that there were more and more voices raised against me and against my convictions. It is true that some of my colleagues suggested to me that I should make some public statement along atheistic lines. It is also true that I had some unpleasant scenes at lectures with aggressive Communistic students who wanted to insult my faith. The proposal to expel me from the faculty was indeed hanging over my head. Yet it is also true that I still had plenty of friends among the Communists in the faculty and that they respected me for my attitude before the February coup. Perhaps it would have taken very little: I need only have started defending myself and they would certainly have all stood up for me. But this I did not do.

4

'Follow me,' said Jesus to His disciples, and without demur they left their nets, their boats, their homes and their families and followed Him. 'No man having put his hand to the plough and looking back is fit for the Kingdom of God.'

If we hear the voice of Christ's challenge we must follow it unconditionally. This is clear from the Gospel, and yet in modern times the whole thing sounds like something from a fairy tale. Where is the challenge in these prosaic lives of ours, who is there to follow? Whither and with whom are we to leave our nets and go?

And yet the voice can reach us even in this world of ours if our hearing is keen. The challenge does not come to us through the post like a registered letter. It comes disguised. Rarely does it come in rosy or alluring garb. 'Not the deed that thou choosest, but that which befalls thee against thy will, thy thinking and thy desire, this is the path thou must enter upon, this is whither I call, there be thou the disciple, that is thy time, this is the way the Master trod . . .'

I had a number of reasons for clinging to my lectureship. It was reasonably comfortable, it gave me plenty of free time for further studies, and it held promise of a career as a university teacher. Yet I was alarmed when I saw a number of valuable people, both teachers and pupils, being forced in those days to leave the universities. I was alarmed at my attachment to my comfortable life, distancing me as it did with its calm security from the anything but calm fate which befell those near me. I recognized in the proposal that I should leave the faculty a *challenge*. I heard someone calling to me. Someone warning me against the comfortable career which would restrict my mind, my faith and my conscience.

Naturally my wife, by whom I already had a five-year-old child, insisted again and again that I should defend myself and do everything possible to remain at the university. She was thinking of our son and the future of our family. For her nothing else existed. When I looked into her already ageing face I was alarmed at that eternal anxiety, anxiety about to-morrow, about next year, that burdensome anxiety about all tomorrows and all years stretching out beyond count. I was alarmed at the burden of it and in my mind I heard Jesus's words: 'Take therefore no thought for the morrow: for the morrow shall take thought for the things of itself. Sufficient unto the day is the evil thereof.'

My enemies were expecting me to be bowed down with worry, while instead I experienced an unexpected absence of care. They thought I would feel limited in my freedom, while on the contrary I had just discovered for myself the real mean-ing of freedom. I saw that man has nothing to lose and that his place is everywhere, everywhere that Jesus went, which means: everywhere among men.

After my initial surprise and regret I went forward to meet the malice of my adversaries. Their injustice I accepted as a challenge written in code.

5

Communists hold the entirely religious belief that a man who has committed some wrong before his Party may find absolu-tion if he leaves for a period to work among agricultural or industrial labourers. During the years after February a num-ber of intellectuals went off in this way for shorter or longer periods to the mines, factories, building sites and state farms, so that after mysterious purification in these surroundings they might be allowed to return to their offices, their educa-tional or political posts.

When I proposed to the university senate that I would be leaving the university and would not be applying for another scientific post, as I wanted to 'go to the people', preferably as technical adviser to some state farm, the Communists in my institute, both my friends and my enemies, regarded this not by the light of my own faith, but by that of theirs: as the expression of an altogether unusual degree of self-criticism. They applauded this and helped me find a very good post on a state farm in Western Bohemia, under a good manager and in a beautiful part of the country. They sent me on my way with the gift of an uncommonly favourable testimonial.

I was actually happy in my new position. I felt myself reborn. The state farm had been set up in a derelict and under-populated border village from which the Germans had been expelled after the war. There were hills all around, most of them bare pastureland. In the valleys were dotted around at widespread intervals the cottages of exceedingly straggly villages. Frequent mists swirling across the countryside drifted between me and the populated land like a moving screen, so that the world was as it was on the fifth day of creation, when God was perhaps still wavering whether He should hand it over to man.

And people here were much more like original man. They stood face to face with nature, endless pastures, herds of cows and flocks of sheep. I felt at home among them. I soon had a number of ideas about how the vegetation in this hilly country might be better put to use: ideas about manuring, storing the hay, experimental fields of medicinal herbs, a greenhouse. The manager was grateful for my ideas and I was grateful to him for making it possible for me to earn my bread by useful work.

6

It was in 1951. September was cool, but half way through October it suddenly got warmer and there was a superb autumn lasting well into November. The stacks of hay dried on the hilly meadows and their perfume spread far over the land. Delicate little clusters of meadow saffron appeared in the grass. It was then that in the surrounding villages word began to spread about the little lost girl.

Some youngsters from a neighbouring village went out into the flat mown fields. They were talking noisily, shouting at each other, and then apparently they saw a girl crawl out of a stack, tousled and with straw in her hair, a girl none of them had ever seen before. She looked all round in alarm and started running towards the woods. Before they could decide whether to pursue her or not they had lost her.

A farmer's wife from the same village said that one afternoon, when she was busy with something in the yard, suddenly a girl appeared from nowhere, about twenty and dressed in a threadbare coat, and asked her with bowed head for a crust of bread. 'Where are you going, girl?' asked the woman. The girl replied that she had a long way to go. 'And are you going on foot?' 'I have lost all my money,' she replied. The woman asked no more questions and gave her bread and milk.

A shepherd from our estate added his voice to these stories. One day, up in the hills, he had put a piece of bread and butter and a jug of milk in a tree stump. He left for a minute to follow his flock, and when he returned the bread and the jug had mysteriously vanished.

The children immediately seized on these reports and multiplied them with their eager fantasy. They saw the girl in the evenings bathing in the fishing lake beyond the village, although it was the beginning of November and the water was already very chilly. When anyone lost anything the children immediately took it as proof of her existence. At other times, in the evenings, a song, sung in a high female voice, would resound from somewhere in the distance. The adults said that some cottage on the hill had had the radio turned up full, but the children knew it was her, the wild girl, treading the ridge along the hills, her hair hanging free, singing her song.

One evening a fire was made outside the village, and potato stalks and leaves were placed on top of it and potatoes thrown into the glowing ash. Then they looked towards the woods, and one little girl began to shout that she could see her looking at them from the shadows. A small boy picked up a clod of earth and threw it in the direction the girl was pointing. Strangely enough, there was no answering shriek, but something else happened: all the children shouted at the boy and almost beat him up.

Yes, indeed: the customary cruelty of children had never reared its head in the legend of the lost girl, even though there were a number of small thefts associated with the general impression of her. From the beginning she had had their secret sympathies. Perhaps it was the innocent insignificance of the thefts that had won people's hearts. Or was it her tender years? Or was she protected by an angel's hand?

Whichever way it was, the throwing of that lump of earth kindled in those children a feeling of love towards the lost girl. The same day they left a heap of baked potatoes round the embers of the fire, covered them with ashes to keep them warm, and thrust a broken fir branch into the pile. They even found a name for the girl: on a piece of paper torn from an exercise book they wrote in big pencilled letters: 'Little waif, this is for you.' This paper they put up against the mound and weighed it down with earth. Then they left and hid in the surrounding bushes, watching for the timid little girl to appear. Evening became night and still no one came. Finally the children had to desert their hiding-place and go home. At crack of dawn they were back at their posts. It had happened. The pile of potatoes had disappeared and so had the paper and the fir branch.

The girl became the children's own pampered fairy. They left her jugs of milk, bread, potatoes and messages. And they never repeated the same place twice for their gifts. They avoided leaving her provisions in a definite place as if it were put out for the beggars. They were playing a game with her. A game of hidden treasure. They moved from the place they had originally left the pile of potatoes and went further away from the village into the country. They left their treasures by the tree stumps, by the big rock, by the wayside cross, by the briar bush. To nobody did they ever betray the spot where they had hidden their gifts. Never did they violate the spider's-web delicacy of the game, never did they lie in wait for the girl or jump out at her. They allowed her to keep her invisibility.

7

The whole story was shortlived. One day the manager of our estate went on a trip far into the country with the chairman of the local council, to look over some still-uninhabited cottages which had been left behind after the German evacuation, with a view to setting them up as overnight hostels for farm labourers working on a job a long way from the village. On the way there they were overtaken by rain which soon became torrential. Nearby there was a low-lying clump of firs with a greyish barn at the edge – a hay store. They ran over to it, opened the door, which was secured only by a wooden stake, and crawled inside. The light came in through the open door and the holes in the roof. In the straw they saw an area which had been smoothed over. They stretched out on it, listened to the raindrops falling on the roof, breathed the intoxicating scent, and started to gossip about things. Suddenly the chairman felt something hard under the dry straw. It was a suitcase. An old, ugly, cheap suitcase made of vulcanite. How long the two men brooded over the mystery I do not know. One thing is certain, that they opened the case and found in it four sets of girl's clothing, all of them new and pretty. The fineness of the clothes was apparently in strange contrast with the rural drabness of the case, and aroused their suspicions of a theft. Under the clothes there were a few more articles of girl's underwear, and hidden among these a bundle of letters tied up with a blue ribbon. That was all. To this day I know nothing of these letters and do not even know whether the manager and the chairman read them. I only know that the letters helped them to discover the name of their recipient: Lucie Sebetkova.

While they were contemplating their unexpected find the chairman discovered something else in the straw. It was a cracked milk container. The same blue enamel jug whose mysterious loss the shepherd had been relating in the tavern every evening for the past fortnight.

After this the whole thing ran along predictable lines. The chairman hid in the fir trees to wait, and the manager went down to the village and sent the village constable up after the chairman. Towards dusk a girl returned to her perfumed bower. They let her go in, allowed her to close the door, waited half a minute and then went in after her.

8

Both of those who trapped Lucie in the barn were good men. The chairman, a village official under the old regime, honest, father of six, reminded one somehow of the old-time village chroniclers. The policeman was a naïve, coarse, good-natured fellow with an immense moustache. Neither of them would have hurt a fly.

And yet it tore strangely at my heartstrings when I heard of how Lucie was trapped. To this day I feel a twinge in my heart to think of the manager and the chairman rummaging about in her case, taking all her most intimate objects into their hands, the delicate mysteries of her dirty linen, looking into things where it is forbidden to look.

And it hurts to this day when I imagine the little lair made in the straw, from which there is no escape, and whose only doors are blocked by two large men.

When, later, I learned more about Lucie, I realized with astonishment that in both aspects of this agonizing situation the very essence of her fate had been made clear to me. Both were illustrations of her *defilement*.

That night Lucie slept not in the hut of straw but on an iron bed in the shop the police had set up as their daytime office. The next day her case was heard before the council. They learned that up till then she had worked and lived in Ostrava. She had run away because she could not stand it there any longer. When they tried to find out something more specific, they came up against a stubborn silence.

Why run this way, to the west of Bohemia? She said that her parents lived in Cheb. Why didn't she join them? She had got off the train a short distance before her home station because on the way she had begun to feel afraid. All her life her father had done nothing but beat her.

The chairman of the council informed Lucie that they would be sending her back to Ostrava as she had come from there without a proper discharge. Lucie told them she would run away from the train at the first stop. For a while they tried to shout her down but soon saw that this would solve nothing. They asked her if they should send her home, to Cheb. She shook her head furiously. For a while they were severe with her again, and then the chairman succumbed to his own softheartedness. 'What do you want then?' She asked whether she might not be allowed to work here. They shrugged their shoulders and said they would ask at the state farm.

The manager was fighting a constant battle against an acute labour shortage. He accepted the council's proposal with alacrity. Then he told me I would at last be getting the greenhouse assistant I had long been looking for. The same day the council chairman came to present me with Lucie.

I remember that day well. It was the second half of November, and an autumn which had thus far been sunny was for the first time showing its windy and misty aspect. It was drizzling. She stood there in a brown coat with her case, her head bowed and an absent look in her eyes, the tall council chairman by her side. The chairman, holding the blue jug in his hands, announced ceremoniously: 'If you have done anything wrong we have forgiven you and we trust you. We could have sent you back to Ostrava, but we have left you here. The working class requires honest people everywhere. Do not let it down.'

He then went into the office to hand over the jug for the shepherd, and I took Lucie into the greenhouse, introduced her

220

to the two girls she would be working with and explained to her what she would be doing.

10

In my recollections of those days Lucie overshadows everything else. Despite this the figure of the council chairman stands fairly clearly outlined in her shadow. When you were actually sitting opposite me in the armchair, Ludvik, I did not want to offend you. Now at least, now that you are opposite me again in the form in which I know you best, as a figment and a shadow, I shall tell you: this former local official, who had wanted to create a paradise for those near him who were suffering, this honest man, with his enthusiasm and naïvely high-sounding words about forgiveness, trust and the working class, was a lot nearer my heart and my way of thinking than you were, even though he never once showed me any personal favour.

You once stated that Socialism grew from the stem of European rationalism and scepticism, a stem which was non-religious and anti-religious, and that it is otherwise unthinkable. But do you seriously maintain that it is impossible to build a Socialist society without faith in the supremacy of matter? Do you really think that men who believe in God are incapable of nationalizing factories?

I am altogether certain that that line of European thought which stems from the teaching of Jesus leads far more naturally to social equality and Socialism. And as I recall the most ardent Communists from the earlier period of Socialism in this country of mine, the chairman for instance, who delivered Lucie into my care, they seem to me to be much more like religious zealots than Voltairean doubters. The revolutionary era from 1948 to 1956 had little in common with scepticism and rationalism. This was the time of the great collective faith. The man who strode forward in unison with the age had feelings very much akin to religious ones: he renounced himself,

221

his person, his privacy for the benefit of something higher, something more than personal. Marxist teachings were in origin entirely secular, but the significance assigned to them was similar to the significance of the Gospel and the biblical commandments. We saw the formation of a body of thought which was inviolate or, in our terminology, sacred.

This was a cruel religion. It did not elevate you or me among its high priests; perhaps it injured both of us. Yet despite this the age which has just passed was a hundred times nearer my heart than the age which seems to be approaching today: an age of ridicule, scepticism and corrosion, a petty age with the ironic intellectual in the limelight, and behind him the mob of youth, coarse, cynical and bitter, without enthusiasm or ideals, ready to mate or to kill on sight.

The age which is passing, or which has already passed, had something of the spirit of the great religious movements. It is a pity that it was not able to take its religious self-revelations to their conclusion. It had religious ritual and emotion, but it remained empty and godless within. Yet I still believed that God would have mercy, that at last He would sanctify this great secular faith. For this I waited in vain.

This age finally betrayed its religious nature and paid its debt to the rationalistic heritage to which it swore allegiance; and this only because it did not understand its own true nature. This rationalistic scepticism has been corroding Christianity for two millennia. Yet it has not corroded it completely away. But the Communist theory, its own creature, it will destroy in a few decades. In you, Ludvik, it has already done so. You know this full well.

11

When people are able to transport themselves in fantasy to fairytale land they are full of nobility, sympathy and poetry. Unfortunately, in the realm of everyday life they are more prone to caution, mistrust and suspicion. This is exemplified in the way they behaved towards Lucie. As soon as she had left the children's fairy tales and become a real girl, one who worked and lived among people, she immediately became the object of a curiosity which was not without its touch of malice, just as people behave towards angels flung down from paradise and fairies driven from fairyland.

Lucie's being so tightlipped did not help her much either. A month or so later the estate had her file from Ostrava. We found from this that she had started work in Cheb as an apprentice hairdresser. After an immorality charge she had spent a year in a reformatory and then gone to Ostrava. In Ostrava she had proved a good worker. Her behaviour in the hostel was exemplary. Before her flight there had been only one completely unexpected conviction against her: she had been caught stealing flowers in a cemetery.

The reports were fairly bald, and far from unravelling the mystery surrounding Lucie they served to enhance it.

I promised the manager that I would take Lucie into my care. I rather liked her. She worked quietly and with concentration. She was calm in her timidity. I found in her none of the strangeness one would expect in a girl who had lived several weeks as a tramp. She declared several times that she was happy on the farm and didn't want to leave us. She was placid and ready to give way in any argument, and because of this she gradually won over the girls who worked with her. However, there remained something in her taciturnity which betrayed a life of suffering and a wounded soul. I would have liked nothing better than for her to have confided in me, but knew that she had had enough questionings and quizzings in her life and that she probably associated them with police interrogations. So instead of questioning her I began to tell my own story. Every day I used to chat with her. I told her of my plans to start the planting of medicinal herbs on the estate. I told her how in the old days country people used to cure themselves with decoctions and solutions of various herbs. I told her about burnet, with which people used to cure cholera and the plague, and about breakstone, which breaks up stones in the bladder and bile. Lucie would listen. She liked herbs.

But what sainted innocence! She knew nothing about them and could hardly name one.

Winter was already coming on and Lucie had only her pretty summer things. I helped her to budget. I prevailed upon her to buy a waterproof coat and a sweater and other things later: boots, pyjamas, stockings and overcoat ...

One day I asked her whether she believed in God. She answered in a way I thought peculiar. She said neither yes or no. She shrugged her shoulders and said: 'I don't know.' I asked her whether she knew who Jesus Christ was. She said she did. But she knew nothing about Him. In her His name was vaguely associated with the idea of Christmas, which she had somehow muddled up with the crucifixion, in a ragged haze of two or three impressions which came together and made no sense. Up till then Lucie had known neither belief nor unbelief. At that moment I felt a slight dizziness – perhaps something akin to that felt by the lover when he finds that no male body has preceded him in his beloved. 'Do you want me to tell you about him?' I asked, and she nodded. By then the pastures and hills were covered in snow. I began the story Lucie listened ...

12

She had had too much to bear on her slender shoulders. She needed somebody to help her but there had been nobody capable of doing so. Lucie, the help offered by religion is simple. Yield thyself up. Yield thyself up together with the burden under which thou stumblest. This is the greatest relief, to live giving yourself to others. I know that you never had anyone to give yourself to, because you were afraid of people. But God is here. Give yourself to Him. Then you will feel lighter.

To yield oneself up means to lay aside one's past life. To pluck it out of one's soul. To confess. Tell me, Lucie, why did you run away from Ostrava? Was it because of those flowers on the grave?

224

That was part of it.

And why did you take the flowers?

She had felt depressed, so she put them in a vase in her room in the hostel. She picked flowers in the open field, but Ostrava is a black place, with hardly any open fields around it, just dumps and fences and allotments, with here and there a few bushes covered in coaldust. Beautiful flowers were found only in the cemetery. High-flown flowers, flowers for an occasion. Gladioli, roses and lilies. Chrysanthemums too, with their great blooms of fragile florets ...

And how did they catch you?

She often went to the cemetery and liked it there. Not only for the flowers she took but because it was nice and quiet, and the quiet was comforting to her. Every tomb was like a private garden, and she liked to stand by the individual tombstones and read their sad inscriptions. So as not to be disturbed she imitated some of the visitors to the cemetery, especially the older ones, by kneeling with her face to the gravestones. Once she took a fancy to a grave which was almost fresh. The coffin had been buried there only a few days before. The clay on the grave was loose and there were wreaths lying on it, and in front of them in a vase stood a magnificent spray of roses. Lucie knelt, and a weeping willow inclined over her like an intimate, whispering heaven. Lucie dissolved away in unspeakable rapture. It was at this point that an elderly gentleman arrived at the tomb with his wife. Perhaps it was the grave of their son or brother, who knows. They saw an unfamiliar girl kneeling by the tomb and stopped in horror. Who was this girl? To them there must have been something ominous in her appearance, the hint of a family secret – perhaps an unknown relative or an unknown lover of the deceased.... They stopped short, afraid to disturb her, and watched her from a distance. Then they saw the girl stand up, take the fine spray of roses from the vase, the one they had placed there themselves a few days before, turn and leave. At that they set off after her. 'Who are you?' they asked. She became confused and did not know what to say. She began to stutter. When they realized that the unknown girl had not known the deceased at

225

all. They called the cemetery attendant to their aid. They demanded identification. They shouted at her and said there was nothing worse than robbing the dead. The attendant confirmed that this was not the first flower theft in her cemetery. Then they called a policeman and set on her again, and Lucie confessed everything.

13

'Let the dead bury their dead,' said Jesus. Flowers on graves are the property of the living. Lucie, you did not know God but you yearned for Him. It was the unearthly which revealed itself to you in the beauty of earthly flowers. You did not need those flowers for anyone. Only for yourself. To fill the void in your soul. And they caught you and humiliated you. And was that the only reason for your running away from that black town?

She was silent. Then she shook her head.

Someone hurt you?

She nodded.

Tell me, Lucie!

It was a very small room. There was a light bulb in the ceiling, it had no shade and in its lewd nakedness hung crookedly from the fitting. A bed by the wall, a picture hanging over it and in the picture a handsome man in a blue robe, kneeling. It was the Garden of Gethsemane but Lucie was not to know that. This was where he brought her, and she fought and screamed. He wanted to rape her, he ripped off her clothes but she tore away from him and ran away.

Who was he, Lucie?

A soldier.

Did you love him?

No, she did not love him.

Then why did you go with him into that room with nothing but the bare bed?

It was just the emptiness in her soul which drew her to him.

226

All she could find in her misery was an adolescent, a national serviceman.

But there is one thing I still do not understand, Lucie. Since you went with him into the room with just its bare bed, why did you run away from him afterwards?

Because he was nasty and fierce like all of them.

Of whom, Lucie? All of whom?

Silence.

Who did you know before the soldier? Speak, Lucie! Tell me the truth!

14

There were six of them and just the one of her. Six of them between sixteen and twenty. She was sixteen. They were all in the same gang at work and they spoke of their gang with awe, as if it were some pagan sect. On that day they were talking about initiation. They brought along a few bottles of cheap wine. She took part in the drinking with a blind obedience in which she had placed all the unrequited love of a daughter for her father and mother. She drank when they drank and laughed when they laughed. Then they ordered her to strip. She had never done that in front of them before. But when, as she hesitated, the gang's chief took the initiative and undressed first, she saw that the order was not directed at her alone and complied obediently. She trusted them, she trusted their roughness, they were her shield and protection and she could not imagine what there would be if she lost them. They were her father and her mother. They drank and laughed and gave her more instructions. She opened her legs. She was afraid, she knew what it meant, but she obeyed. Then she was screaming and there was blood coming from her. The lads roared and raised their glasses and poured the coarse sparkling wine down the back of the chief, over her body and between their legs; they were shouting some words about christening and initiation, and then the chief got up and the next member of the gang went over to her, and then they all came in order of seniority, with the youngest last, and he was sixteen like her, and Lucie could not stand any more, could not stand any more pain, wanted to rest, wanted to be by herself, and because he was the youngest she dared to thrust him off. But just because he was the youngest he was not going to be humiliated! He was a member of their gang, a fully fledged member! He wanted to prove it and so he hit Lucie across the face, and none of the gang stood up for her because they all knew that the youngest man was in the right and was claiming what was rightly his. Lucie gushed tears but did not have the courage to resist further, and so she opened her legs for the sixth time . . .

Where was this, Lucie?

One of the labourers' flats, his parents were both on night shift, there was a kitchen and one room, in the room a table, a couch and a bed, over the door a framed motto saying GOD GRANT HAPPINESS and over the bed in a frame a beautiful lady in a blue robe holding a child to her breast.

The Virgin Mary?

She did not know.

And then, Lucie, what happened then?

Afterwards it happened again, many times in the flat, and in other flats, and out in the fields. It became a custom with the gang.

And did you like it, Lucie?

She didn't. From that time on they had treated her worse more arrogantly and coarsely, but there was no way out, forward, backward, anywhere.

And how did it end, Lucie?

One evening in one of those empty flats. The police cam and took everyone away. The lads had a few thefts to answe for. Lucie was unaware of this, but it was known that she wen around with the gang and that she gave them everythin which as a young girl she was capable of giving. She was th shame of Cheb and at home she was beaten black and blu The lads got varying sentences and she was sent to a reforma tory. She stayed there a year – until she was seventeen. She di

228

not want to go home again for anything in the world. So she went to the Black City.

15

I was surprised and startled when Ludvik revealed to me on the telephone the day before yesterday that he knew Lucie. Luckily he had only a fleeting knowledge of her. Apparently he had had some superficial relationship in Ostrava with a girl who lived in the hostel with her. When he asked me about her again yesterday I told him the whole story. I had for a long time needed to throw off that burden but until now I had never found a man whom I could trust with the confidence. Ludvik is well disposed towards me and at the same time is sufficiently distant from my life and even more so from Lucie's. I had therefore no need to fear I would be putting her secret in jeopardy.

For what Lucie had told I had related to no one save to Ludvik yesterday. This despite the fact that everybody on the farm knew from her file about her having been in a reformatory and stolen flowers from a cemetery. They were quite affable with her but they constantly reminded her of her past. The manager talked of her as 'the little grave-robber'. He meant it in fun but this sort of talk kept Lucie's past sins constantly alive. She felt continuously and unceasingly guilty. And at the same time she needed nothing other than complete forgiveness. Yes, Ludvik, she needed forgiveness, she needed to go through that mysterious purgatory which to you is unfamiliar and incomprehensible.

For people themselves are not capable of forgiveness. It is not in their power to make as naught the sin which has been. Not within the power of man alone. To deprive a sin of its validity, to undo it, to rub it out of time, to make something into nothing, is a mysterious and supernatural feat. Only God, because He is beyond earthly laws, because He is free, because He can work miracles, may wipe out a sin, turn it to naught, forgive it. Man can forgive man only in so far as he founds himself on God's forgiveness.

Nor can you, Ludvik, forgive, because you do not believe in God. You still remember the plenary meeting when everyone raised their hands against you and agreed that your life should be destroyed. You have never forgiven them that. And not only as individuals. There were about a hundred of them there, and that is a quantity which can become a sort of miniature model of mankind. You have never forgiven mankind. From that time on you have ceased trusting men, and you still feel bitterness towards them. I can understand you in this, but it does not alter the fact that such general bitterness towards people is evil and sinful. It has become your curse. *Because to live in a world in which no one is forgiven, where all are irredeemable, is the same as living in Hell.* You are living in Hell, Ludvik, and I pity you.

16

Everything which on this earth belongs to God may also belong to the Devil. Even the movements of lovers as they make love. For Lucie they had become a thing of disgust. For her they were associated with the faces of the savage adolescents from the work gang and later with the face of the soldier as he forced himself on her. I can see him before me quite clearly as if I knew him. He mingles his banal syrup-sweet words of love with the rough violence of the male caged without women behind the barrack wire. Lucie sees that the tender words are only the mask on a vulgar wolfish face. And for her the whole world tumbles downwards into a pit of loathing.

Here was the source of the disease, here was where I must begin. The man walking along the sea shore and madly waving a lantern in his outstretched hand may be a lunatic. But on night in which a boat has gone astray this man is a rescuer. The land we live in is the borderland between Heaven an

Hell. No act of itself is either good or bad. Even physical love, Lucie, is not of itself good or bad. If it is in accordance with the system created by God, if you love with an eternal love, the loving too will be good and you will be happy. Because God so decreed that 'a man shall leave his father and his mother and shall cleave unto his wife; and the two shall be one flesh.'

I spoke to Lucie every single day, every single day I repeated to her that she was forgiven, that she was not to writhe inwardly, that she must undo the straitjacket of her soul, that she must humbly yield herself up to God's order, in which even the love of the body will find its place.

And so the weeks went by ...

Then came the first days of spring. Apple trees bloomed on the hilly slopes and in the gentle wind their crowns looked like swinging bells. I closed my eyes to hear their velvet tones. Then I opened them and saw Lucie in her blue overalls, with a hoe in her hand. She was looking down the valley and she was smiling.

I saw that smile and drank it eagerly in. For up till then Lucie's soul had been in eternal flight, a flight from both past and future. She was afraid of everything. The past and the future for her were watery depths. With the anxiety of a leaky boat she clung to the present as to a precarious haven.

And now today she was smiling. For no apparent reason. Just like that. And that smile told me she was looking into the future with confidence. And in that instant I felt like a mariner who has spent many months sailing to a longed-for land. I was happy. I leaned on the crooked stem of the apple tree and again for a moment I closed my eyes. I heard the breeze in the white treetops, I heard the trilling of the birds and behind my closed eyes their song was transformed into thousands of lanterns and candles carried by invisible hands towards a great ceremony. I did not see those hands but I heard the high-pitched tones of the voices and I saw them as children, a happy procession of children. ... Then I suddenly felt a hand on my cheek. A voice: 'Mr Kostka, you are so good to me ...' I did not open my eyes. I did not move my hand. I still saw the birds' voices as a throng of lamps, I still heard the ringing of the apple trees. And the voice added more faintly: 'I love you.'

Perhaps I should have waited only for that moment and then quickly left, for now my job was done. But before I could reflect I was seized by a delirium of weakness. We were completely alone in the wide open country between the piteous little apple trees, and I took Lucie in my arms and sank with her into the bower of nature.

17

What should never have happened had happened. When I saw in Lucie's smile the reconciliation of her soul, I had reached my goal and should then have departed. But I did not depart. And what happened was wrong. We went on living together on the same farm. Lucie was happy, she was aglow, she was like the spring which all around us was gradually changing into summer. But instead of being happy myself I was horrified at this exuberant female spring beside me, which I myself had conjured awake and which turned to me with all its blooms opening out, while I knew that these blooms were not and must not be mine. In Prague I had a son and a wife who waited patiently for my infrequent visits home.

I was afraid to break off the intimacies I had entered into with Lucie lest I should hurt her, but neither did I dare continue with them, because I knew I had no right to them. I desired Lucie, yet at the same time I was afraid of her love, because I did not know where to direct it. It was only with the greatest effort that I maintained with her the natural manner in which we had previously conversed. My doubts came between us. It seemed to me that my spiritual assistance to Lucie was a mask which had now been removed. That I had desired Lucie physically from the moment I saw her. That I had acted like a seducer wearing the cowl of comforter and preacher. That all that talk about Jesus and God had been only a veil for the most earthly bodily desire. It seemed to me that in the moment I yielded to my sexuality I had besmirched the purity of my original intentions and had been stripped of my merit before God.

Yet no sooner had I reached this conclusion than my train of thought made an about-turn: what vanity, I mentally shouted at myself, what selfish desire, to want to be worthy, to be pleasing to God! What are the merits of man before Him? Nothing, nothing, nothing! Lucie loves me and her health depends on my love! What if I were to hurl her back into despair just so that I should be pure? Would not then God despise me? And if my love is a sin, which means more, Lucie's life or my own spotlessness? It will be *my* sin, only *I* shall bear it, only *I* shall condemn my own sin!

Suddenly these thoughts and considerations were disturbed by outside intervention. The people at the centre had trumped up some charge against the manager. The manager was defending himself tooth and nail, and to strengthen the case against him his enemies taxed him with being surrounded by suspicious elements. One of these suspicious elements was myself: a man said to have been expelled from the university for anti-state thinking, a cleric. The manager pointed out in vain that I was not in fact a cleric, that I had not been expelled from the university. The more he stood up for me the more he demonstrated his close ties with me and the more he harmed himself. My situation was almost beyond hope.

Injustice, Ludvik? This is the word you use most often when you hear about this or similar incidents. But I do not know what injustice is. If there were nothing else above human affairs and if actions had only the significance ascribed to them by those who performed them, then the concept of injustice would be warranted, and I could speak of injustice when I was more or less thrown out of the state farm where I had been working with such devotion. Perhaps it would have been logical too if I had defended myself against this injustice and fought furiously for my puny human rights.

Yet events for the most part have a different meaning from that which their agents ascribe to them: they are often disguised instructions from above, and those men who have allowed them to occur are only the unwitting messengers of a higher will of which they have no conception.

I was certain that this was how it was in this case too. Therefore I accepted the events on the estate with relief. In them I saw a clear instruction: Leave Lucie before it is too late. You have completed the task that was set you. The fruits of the task are not thine. Thy path leads elsewhere.

And I did the same thing as I had done two years before in the Natural Sciences Faculty. I said good-bye to a weeping and desperate Lucie and went forth to meet apparent disaster. I volunteered the proposal that I should leave the farm. The manager did try to stop me, but I knew that he was only doing so out of decency and that in the depths of his soul he was glad of my departure.

Only this time my voluntary resignation impressed no one. My Communist friends of the pre-February period who had strewn the path of my retirement with good counsel and advice were missing. I left the farm as a man who himself admits that he is unfit to carry out any work of significance in this country. And so I became a bricklayer.

18

It was an autumn day in 1956. I had met Ludvik for the first time in five years, in the restaurant car of the Prague–Bratislava express. I was travelling to work on the construction of some factory in Eastern Moravia. Ludvik had just completed his work quota in the Ostrava mines and had applied to Prague for permission to resume his studies. He was now travelling home to Eastern Moravia. We hardly knew each other. And when we did recognize each other we were astonished at the way each other's lives had turned out.

I remember well the concern with which you, Ludvik, listened when I told you of how I left the university and of the intrigues on the state farm which had led to my becoming a bricklayer. Thank you for that concern. You were enraged, you spoke of injustice, wrong, lack of respect for intellectuals and the absurd policy of personnel-vetting. You were angry with me too: you reproached me for not defending myself, for relinquishing the struggle. You said we should never walk out of anywhere voluntarily. Let our opponents be forced to resort to their very worst! Why make their consciences any easier?

You down the mines, myself on the building site. Our stories have been fairly similar and yet we are so utterly different. I the forgiving, you the implacable, I the humble, you the proud. How outwardly similar we are and how inwardly remote!

You were far less aware of this inward distance between us than I was. When you gave me the full details of why you had been expelled from the Party in 1950, you took it for granted that I would be on your side and just as indignant as you at the bigotry of the Comrades who punished you just for making fun of something they held sacred. Referring to the postcard, you asked in open surprise: What of it?

I shall tell you something. In Geneva, in the days of Calvin's rule there, there was a young man, perhaps somewhat similar to yourself, an intelligent boy greatly given to jokes, on whom was found a notebook full of sneers and attacks on Jesus Christ and the Gospel. What of it? was most probably the thought in the mind of this boy resembling you. He had done nothing wrong, it was all in fun. He hardly knew anything of hatred. He apparently knew only disrespect and indifference. He was executed.

Please don't think I support such cruelties. I only wish to say that no great movement designed to change the world can bear to be laughed at or belittled, because laughter is a rust which corrodes everything.

Carry on thinking as you do, Ludvik. They expelled you from the Party, expelled you from the university, in military service they assigned you to politically unreliable units and then they sent you for another two or three years down the mines. And you? You became bitter to the depths of your soul, convinced of being immensely wronged. This feeling of wrong determines your every attitude to life to this very day. I cannot understand you! Why do you speak of wrong? They posted you among the 'black' divisions, among the enemies of Communism. Granted. And was that a wrong? Was it not more like a great opportunity for you? You could have worked among those enemies. Was that not a more important and greater mission? Did not Jesus send His disciples as 'sheep in the midst of wolves'? 'They that be whole need not a physician, but they that are sick,' Jesus said. 'For I am not come to call the righteous, but sinners to repentance.' But you did not want to go out among the sinful and infirm!

You will retort that my comparison is inept. That Jesus sent His disciples 'in the midst of wolves' with His blessing, whereas you were ostracized and cursed and then sent among the enemies as an enemy yourself, as a wolf among the wolves, as a sinner among the sinning.

But why deny that you were a sinner? Were you utterly blameless before your committee? Where do you derive such arrogance from? The man devoted to his faith is humble and must in humility bear even an unjust punishment. The humiliated will be raised up. The repentant will be purified. Those that are wronged have the opportunity to prove their loyalty. If you become bitter at your group only because too great a burden was placed on your shoulders, then your faith was weak and you failed in the test that was set you.

I am not on your side in your quarrel with your Party, Ludvik, because I know that great things can be done in this world only by a band of men of infinite devotion who humbly lay down their lives for the greater cause. Your devotion, Ludvik, is not infinite. Your faith is feeble. How could it be otherwise when you were eternally appealing only to yourself and your own wretched reason?

I am not ungrateful, Ludvik, I know what you have done for me and for many others who have been injured in some way by today's regime. You make use of your present position and your acquaintance with high-ranking Communists whom you knew before the revolution in order to intercede, intervene and assist. I like you for this. But I shall tell you again for the last time: look into the depths of your soul! Deep down behind your good works the motive is not love but hatred. Hatred towards those who once did you wrong, those who raised their hands against you in that hall! Your soul knows not God and therefore knows not forgiveness. You yearn for retribution. You identify those who wronged you with those who wronged others, and you revenge yourself on them. Yes, revenge! You are full of hatred even when you help people! I feel it oozing from you, I feel it in your every word. But what are the fruits of hatred other than hatred returned and a chain of further hatreds? You are living in Hell, Ludvik, I repeat this again, you are living in Hell and I pity you.

19

If Ludvik had heard this monologue of mine he might have said that I was ungrateful. I know that he has rendered me great assistance. At that time in 1956 when we met on the train, he was distressed at the life I was leading, showed concern for my capabilities and immediately began to think how he might find employment for me which I might like better and in which I would find greater fulfilment. He surprised me then by the speed and drive with which he acted. In his home town he had a few words with a friend of his. He wanted me to teach natural history in the high school. This was an act of courage. Anti-religious propaganda was at that time in full swing, and to accept a Christian teacher in a high school was almost impossible. In any case Ludvik's friend considered the matter and thought of another solution. This was how I came to obtain my post in the virological department of the local hospital, where I have been breeding viruses and bacteria on mice and rabbits for the last eight years.

That is the way it is. If it were not for Ludvik I would not be here, and Lucie would not be living here either.

A few years after my leaving the farm she married. She could not stay on the estate, as her husband was looking for a job in the town. After some uncertainty where they should settle down, she prevailed on her husband to move here, to the town where I was living.

I have never received a greater gift, a greater reward, in all my life. My little lamb, my dove, the child whom I had healed and nurtured with my soul, was returning to me. She wants nothing of me. She has her own husband. But she wants to be near me. She needs me. She needs sometimes to hear my voice. To see me at the service on Sundays. To meet me in the street. I was happy and in that instant I felt that I was no longer young, that I was older than I thought and that Lucie was perhaps the only achievement of my life.

Is that too little, Ludvik? Not at all. It is sufficient and I am happy. I am happy, happy, happy . . .

20

Oh, how I deceive myself! How stubbornly I attempt to re-affirm to myself the righteousness of my life's path! How I boast of my faith before the unbeliever!

Yes, I did manage to bring Lucie to a faith in God. I suc-ceeded in calming and healing her. I rid her of her disgust for physical love. In the end I stepped out of her path. But what good did I bring her by this step?

Her marriage has not turned out well. Her husband is a brute, he is publicly unfaithful to her, and there are rumours that he ill-treats her. Lucie has never admitted as much to me. She knows it would distress me. She presents her life to me as a model of happiness. But we live in a small town where noth-ing remains secret.

How I manage to deceive myself! I interpreted the political intrigues against the manager of the state farm as a coded sign from God that I should leave. But how can God's voice be distinguished from so many others? What if the voice I heard was only the voice of my own cowardice?

I had a wife and child in Prague. I did not exactly dote on them but I was unable to part from them either. I was afraid of an impossible situation. I was afraid of Lucie's love and did not know what I should do with it. I was scared of the complications it might bring me.

I set myself up as the angel bringing her salvation when in fact I was merely another of those who corrupted her. I loved her once and then I turned from her. I acted as if I was bringing her forgiveness, and meanwhile it was she who had call to forgive me. She was desperate, she wept when I left, and yet after a few years she came after me again and settled down here. She had forgiven me. That is absolutely clear. It has not happened to me often in my life, but this girl was in love with me. I held her life in my hands, her happiness in my power. And I ran away. No one ever wronged her as I did.

And now I find myself using supposed challenges from God as mere pretexts to extract myself from my human obligations. I am afraid of women. I am afraid of their warmth. I am afraid of their constant presence. I was terrified of a life with Lucie just as I am terrified at the thought of moving permanently into the teacher's two-roomed flat in the next town.

Why did I volunteer to resign from the university fifteen years ago? I was not in love with my wife, who was six years older than myself. I could not bear either the sound of her voice or the sight of her face. I could not stand the regular tick-tock of the clock at home. I could not live with her, but neither could I inflict on her the injury of a divorce, because she was a good girl and had never done me any wrong. And so I suddenly heard the saving voice of a challenge from above. I heard Jesus calling to me to forsake my nets.

God, is this really so? Am I really so miserably absurd? Say it is not so! Reassure me! Speak, God, speak louder! I cannot hear Thy voice among the babel of tongues!

Part VII

Ludvik

When, late that evening, I got back from Kostka's place to my hotel I was determined to leave for Prague first thing in the morning, since I had nothing left to do here: my ill-conceived mission in this home town of mine had come to an end. Unfortunately my head was in such a whirl that I spent half the night tossing and turning on my creaky bed, quite unable to sleep. When I finally did drop off it was a very fitful sleep, and it was not until the early hours that I achieved anything deeper. Because of this I woke up late, towards nine o'clock, when the morning coaches and trains had already left and there was no means of starting for Prague till around two in the afternoon. I was almost beside myself, like a man who has been shipwrecked; and suddenly I felt a great hunger for Prague, for my work, for the desk in my flat, for my books. There was no help for it; I had to grit my teeth and go down to the restaurant for my breakfast.

I entered with some caution, as I was afraid of bumping into Helena. She wasn't there, however: evidently she was already romping round the next village with her tape recorder over her shoulder, bothering all the passers-by with her microphone and her stupid questions. On the other hand the dining-room was packed with people sitting noisily and smokily over their beers, black coffees, ryes and cognacs. Alas, I could see that on this occasion too my home town even begrudged me a decent breakfast.

I went out into the street. The blue sky, the ragged clouds, the incipient closeness, the dust rising slightly, the street opening onto the wide, level square with its soaring tower (the one which looked like a soldier in a helmet), all this washed over me with the gloom of desolation. From the distance there floated a tipsy chorus of some drawn-out Moravian chant, which seemed to me to have captured for ever the nostalgia of the steppes, the long rides on horseback of the Uhlan mercenaries; and then Lucie emerged in my mind, that incident of long ago which in this moment resembled that dream-like lament, and it spoke to my heart, through which, as through the steppe, so many women had passed without leaving a trace, just as the rising dust leaves no trace on the flat, spacious square, but settles between the cobbles and rises again to float away on a gust of wind.

I strode across the dusty cobbles of the square and felt the oppressive weightlessness of the vacuum which lay over my life. Lucie, goddess of vapour, who had once fled from me, had yesterday turned to naught a carefully calculated vengeance and in no time had turned even my own memories of myself into something pitiful and ridiculous, into a grotesque delusion, because what Kostka had told me testified that in all those years I had never really known who Lucie was.

I had always told myself with satisfaction that for me Lucie was something abstract, a legend and a myth, but now I knew that these would-be poetic terms hid a truth entirely unpoetic, that I had never known her the way she really was, the way she was in and for herself. In my blind egoism I had noticed only those aspects of her being which were turned toward myself – to my loneliness, my captivity, my yearning for tenderness and affection; she had never been anything for me but a function of my own situation; everything which went beyond this concrete situation, everything which was just herself, had escaped me. But if she was in fact only a function of my situation it was entirely logical that the instant the situation altered (when there was a new situation, when I had grown old and changed) my Lucie should vanish with it, because from then on she was only what I had previously missed in her, what had not concerned me, what had transcended my own limitations. And therefore it was entirely logical that after fifteen years I should not even have recognized her. She had long been for me – and I had never thought of her except as 'being for me' – a different person, a stranger.

The message of my defeat had been trailing me for fifteen years and now it had caught up with me. Kostka the eccentric, whom I had never taken more than half seriously, had meant more to her, had done more for her, knew more about her and loved her better (I will not say he loved her *more*, because the strength of my love could hardly have been exceeded), than I had ever done. To him she had confided everything – to me nothing. He had made her happy – I had made her unhappy. He had known her physically – I had never done so. And yet all I had needed in order to possess the body which I so desperately desired was one simple thing: to understand her, to learn how to treat her, to love her, not only for what she was to me, but for everything in her which did not immediately concern me, everything in which she existed as and for herself. I had been unable to do this and had hurt myself and her. A wave of anger against myself washed over me, anger against my age at that time, that silly *lyrical* age when one is too much of a mystery to oneself to turn to the mysteries outside, and when others, even those best loved, are only pocket mirrors in which one follows with horror one's own emotions, one's own impressions, one's own worth. Yes, throughout those fifteen years I had remembered Lucie only as a mirror which preserved the image of myself as I was at that time.

I remembered the bleak room with its single bed, and the street lamp shining into it through the grimy glass; I remembered Lucie's ferocious resistance. It was all like a bad joke: I had taken her for a virgin, and she had fought me because she was not a virgin and was afraid of the moment when I would discover the truth. Or her resistance had another explanation, one which corresponds to Kostka's view of Lucie: her initial drastic sexual experiences had sickened her of the love act and had deprived it of all the significance which most people ascribe to it, had emptied it entirely of affection and love. For this teenage slut the body was something ugly and love was something incorporeal; the soul engaged with the body in a silent and dogged combat.

This interpretation, so melodramatic yet so plausible, spoke to me again of the painful rupture, which I had known so well in many different forms, between the soul and the body, and recalled for me (the painful here continually being shouted down by the ridiculous) an incident which made me laugh out loud. A good friend of mine, a woman of distinctly easy virtue, of which I had myself taken advantage, became engaged to a certain physicist and was determined, this time, really to fall in *love*; but in order to feel this as a *real* love (as distinct from the dozens of amorous relationships she had had) she refused her fiancé any physical contact till the wedding night. She walked with him under the trees in the evening, she squeezed his hand, she kissed him under the street lamps, and so allowed her soul, unburdened by the body, to soar aloft and sink dizzily down again. A month after the wedding she divorced him, complaining bitterly that he had failed to match her great emotion, that he had proved an incompetent, indeed an almost impotent lover.

From the distance the drunken roar of the Moravian lament droned on, mingling with the grotesque aftertaste of the incident I had recalled, with the dusty emptiness of the square, and with my low spirits, which were reinforced by the hunger clamouring more and more loudly from my insides. By now, in any case, I was only a few yards from a milk bar; I tried the door but found it was shut. A passer-by told me: 'The whole milk bar's at the festival today.'

'At the Ride of the Kings?'

'Yes. They've set up a stall there.'

I cursed and set off in the direction of the dirge. My rumbling stomach was leading me towards the folk festival which I had so furiously tried to avoid.

2. Jaroslav

Tired. Tired ever since morning. As if I had been carousing all night. Yet I had slept all night. Except that the way I slept was like a skimmed milk of real sleep. Over breakfast I had to struggle with my yawns. Then people began slowly drifting our way. There were Vladimir's companions and various spectators. A young lad from the farm cooperative brought the horse for Vladimir over to our backyard. Then in the midst of it all Kalasek suddenly appeared, the cultural adviser to the district council. I had been at loggerheads with him for two years. He was dressed in black and wore a ceremonial air. With him was an elegant-looking woman, a features editor from Prague radio. Apparently I was to go with them. The lady wanted to record interviews for a programme about the Ride of the Kings.

Leave me out of it! I'm not going to play the fool. The radio woman was all enthusiasm at meeting me personally and of course Kalasek joined in. He said it was my political obligation to go. Silly fool. I began by resisting. I told them my son was to be King today and that I wanted to be there while he was being dressed. Vlasta then stabbed me in the back. She said it was her job to get my son ready. I was to go and give an interview on the radio.

In the end I went with them obediently. The radio woman was billeted in a room belonging to the rural council. There she had her tape recorder and a young man to run errands for her. She talked nineteen to the dozen and kept laughing all the time. Then she lifted the microphone to her mouth and put the first question to Kalasek.

Kalasek coughed and began. The cultivation of folk art was an inseparable constituent of Communist education. The rural council understood this perfectly. For this reason it lent its full support. It wished them every success and had every sympathy with them. It thanked all those who took part. The enthusiastic organizers and the enthusiastic schoolchildren whom it fully ...

Boring. Boring. Always the same words. For fifteen years I had heard the same old stuff. And now to hear it from Kalasek who had no time at all for folk art. For him folk art is a means to an end. A new charity to boast about. A directive to fulfil. A means of boosting his own prestige. He had not lifted a finger for the Ride of the Kings and had cut down on us by every halfpenny he could. Yet the Ride of the Kings would be a feather in his cap. He was the lord and master of local culture. A former shop assistant who did not know a violin from a guitar.

The interviewer stuck the microphone to her mouth. How well satisfied was I with this year's Ride of the Kings? I felt like laughing at her. The Ride hadn't even started yet! But it was her turn to laugh at me. I was such an experienced folk expert that I was certain to know how it would turn out. Yes, people like me know everything before it happens. The course of future events is known to them. The future happened a long time ago, and for them it will just go on repeating itself.

I had an impulse to tell her exactly what I felt. That the Ride would not be as good as in previous years. That every year folk art loses more supporters. That it was losing even the interest of the institutions it once had. That it was nearly moribund. The fact that some form of folk music was continually being played over the air should not delude us. All those folk instrument bands and folk song and dance ensembles were more like opera or operetta or light music – certainly not folk music. Fancy a folk instrument orchestra with a conductor, a score and music stands! An almost symphonic instrumentation! What desecration! What you know, madame, of the orchestra and ensembles is just stale romantic musical thinking with borrowed folk melodies. Real folk art is dead – yes, madame, dead.

I wanted to gabble all this into the mike, but in the end I said something completely different. The Ride of the Kings was splendid. The strength of folk art. The blaze of colour. Complete sympathy. Thanking all those who took part. The enthusiastic organizers and schoolchildren, whom we fully . . .

I felt ashamed for talking the way they wanted me to. Am I such a coward? Or so well trained? Or so tired?

I was glad to get to the end of my piece, and made a hasty exit. I was looking forward to getting home again. There were quite a few idle spectators standing in the yard and all sorts of assistants decorating the horse with bows and ribbons. I wanted to see Vladimir getting ready. I went into the house, but the door to the living-room, where he was being robed, was locked. I knocked and called out. Vlasta answered from inside. 'You shouldn't be here. The King is being robed!' Why shouldn't I be there, damn it! 'It's against the tradition,' Vlasta's voice answered. I don't know why it should be against the tradition for a father to be present while the King is being robed, but I didn't say so. I heard the concern in her voice and I was pleased that they were concerned with my world. My miserable lonely world!

So I went back into the yard and chatted with the people who were decorating the horse. It was a hefty cart-horse from the farm. Patient and placid.

Then I heard the babel of human voices drifting from the street over the closed gates. There was shouting and banging. My moment had come. I was excited. I opened the gates and went out. The Ride of the Kings was marshalled in front of our house. Horses adorned with ribbons and streamers. Young riders in colourful costumes. It was just like twenty years ago, when they came for me. When they asked my father to give them his son to be King.

Right in front, up against the gates, were two pages on horseback, in women's costumes and with sabres in their hands. They were waiting for Vladimir, to accompany and guard him all day. Now a young man rode out of the band of riders, halted his horse just before me and began with these verses:

— 'Oyez, oyez, oyez!
   Gentle father, we have come hither to ask
   Whether you will give us your son to be King!'

Then he promised that the King would be well guarded. That he would be conducted safely among enemy armies. That he would not be delivered up into enemy hands. That they were armed for the fray. Oyez, oyez!

I looked back. In the dark driveway of our house sat a figure on a beribboned horse, in woman's costume, with puckered sleeves and coloured bands across the face. The King. Vladimir. Suddenly I forgot my weariness and dejection and

247

felt at ease. The old King was sending the young one out into the world. I turned and went over to him. I was standing right by the horse and stepped on tiptoe so that my mouth was as near as possible to the hidden face. 'Good luck, Vladimir,' I whispered to him. He did not reply. He did not move. Vlasta told me with a smile: 'He is not supposed to answer you. He must not say a word till evening.'

3. Ludvik

It took me barely a quarter of an hour before I found myself in the village; in my youth it had been separated from the town by a belt of fields, but now the two were virtually merged into one. The singing I had heard from the town, where it had sounded tipsy and melancholy, now resounded in full force, and proved to be a recorded voice issuing from loudspeakers fastened to houses or telegraph poles. (Like a fool I am constantly being deceived: a short while ago I had allowed myself to be depressed by the melancholy and apparent tipsiness of the voice, and all the time it was only a reproduced voice for which we had the transmitting apparatus at the council house and two well-worn records to thank.) Just outside the village they had erected a triumphal archway with a great paper banner bearing, in red ornamental letters, the inscription: WELCOME.

The people were crowded more thickly here, dressed for the most part in everyday clothes, but with here and there a few old men in folk costume: high boots, white linen trousers and embroidered shirts. Here the street widened into the village green. Between the road and a terrace of cottages there was now a wide swathe of grass with trees dotted about, between which a few stalls had been specially set up for today's festival, selling beer, lemonade, peanuts, chocolate, gingerbread, frankfurters with mustard, and wafer biscuits. In one of the booths the town's milk bar had its stand: they were selling milk, cheese, butter, milk shakes, yogurt and sour cream. The only alcohol being sold was beer, but most of the people appeared to me to be drunk. They were jostling round the stands, getting in each other's way, gaping vacantly; now and then someone would break into loud song, but this was always a senseless straining of the voice (accompanied by a drunken raising of the hand), two or three bars of song which was immediately drowned by the hurly-burly of the market place and the invincible blast of the folk song from the loud-speakers. Although it was early and the Ride had not yet be-gun, the market place was littered with waxed paper beer mugs and paper saucers covered in mustard stains.

The stand with milk and yogurt had an aura of teetotalism about it which put people off, so that I was soon able to get a mug of milk and a buttered roll before moving to a some-what less crowded spot. As I was drinking my milk, there was a commotion from the other end of the green: the Ride of the Kings had entered the village.

Black hats with cockerel feathers, wide frilled sleeves on white shirts, blue waistcoats with red tufts of wool, coloured paper ribbons fluttering from the horses' bodies – all these filled the arena of the green. And now the buzz of people and the song from the loudspeakers were joined by new sounds: the whinnying of horses and the calling of the horse-men:

'Oyez, oyez, oyez,
Ye from up village, down village, here and across the fields,
Ye that are gathered together this saint's day Sunday,
We have a pauper king, but greatly righteous,
A thousand oxen he has had stolen
From an empty farmyard . . .'

Ear and eye alike were assaulted by confusion, in which everything competed for attention with everything else: the folklore from the loudspeakers with the folklore on horse-back; the vivid colours of the costumes and horses with the ugly browns and greys of the badly cut clothes worn by the spectators; the painstaking spontaneity of the fancifully at-tired men on the horses with the painstaking officiousness

249

of the organizers as they ran about in their red armbands among the horses and people, trying to keep the chaos within bounds – by no means a simple task, not only because of the unruliness of the spectators (luckily none too numerous) but more particularly because the road had not been closed to traffic, the organizers merely standing at either end of the troop of riders and signalling the cars to slow down, so that cars and lorries and roaring motor bicycles squeezed their way between the horses, making them uneasy and the riders unsure of themselves.

Quite frankly, in trying so stubbornly to avoid taking part in this (or any other) folk event I had been afraid of something quite different from what I now saw. I had been prepared for lack of taste, for a jejune blend of real folk art and fake, for inaugural addresses by cretinous orators, for all kinds of absurd modernizations – I would not have been surprised to find the Ride of the Kings turned into something like the Ride of the Partisans. I had been prepared for the worst kind of bombast and falsity; but I had not expected this mournful, almost moving, forlornness. It was in everything: in the handful of stalls, in the scanty but exceedingly ill-disciplined and inattentive spectators, in the battle between the everyday traffic and the anachronistic ritual, in the frightened horses, in the loudspeakers inertly bellowing their two unchanging folk songs and mingling with the racket of the motor bikes so as to drown completely the young horsemen as they shouted their lines, the veins standing out on their necks.

I threw away my paper cup, and the Ride of the Kings, which had now sufficiently displayed itself to the spectators on the village green, set off on a lengthy tour of the village. I knew it all well, because once, the last year of the war, I had myself ridden as a page, dressed in ceremonial woman's garb and with sword in hand, at the side of Jaroslav, who was then the King. I had no desire to indulge in sentimental memories, but, as if disarmed by the forlorn quality of the Ride, I was reluctant to tear myself away, and so I slowly made my way in the wake of the riders, who now spread out. In the centre of the road was a cluster of three riders: in the middle the

King and on each side a page, wearing a sword and dressed in women's clothes. Beside them trotted a few other riders from the King's company – the so-called ministers. The rest of the throng split into two independent wings riding on either side of the street, and within each wing the duties of the riders were precisely defined: there were the standard-bearers, with their red flags stuck into their thigh boots and fluttering along the horses' flanks; the criers, calling out before every house their rhymed message about the righteous yet pauper King who had had *three thousand* stolen from an empty *coffer*, and three hundred *oxen* stolen from an empty *farmyard*; and finally the collectors, who called out for gifts ('For the King, old lady, for the King!') and held out their cane baskets for contributions.

4. Helena

Thank you Ludvik, I have known you for just eight days and I love you as I have never loved anyone else, I love you and trust you, I can think of nothing else, and I trust you, because if my mind deceived me, if my emotions deceived me, if my soul deceived me, the body at least is without deceit, the body is more honest than the soul, and my body knows that it has never experienced anything like yesterday – sensuality, affection, cruelty, pleasure, pain, my body never dreamed of anything like it. Yesterday our bodies made their vows, and now let our heads go obediently along with our bodies. I have known you just eight days and I thank you, Ludvik.

I thank you too for coming at the most opportune moment, for protecting me. Today the weather has been fine since early morning, the sky is blue, the blue skies were inside me as well as outside, everything went well in the morning, and we went to the parents' house to record the Ride, the calling upon the King, and then suddenly he came up to me, and I was afraid, I didn't know he was here already, that he would come up from Bratislava so quickly, and I didn't expect he would be so cruel. Imagine, Ludvik, he was mean enough to bring her with him.

And like a fool I had believed to the last that my marriage was not yet completely lost, that it could still be saved, like a fool I would almost have sacrificed even you for that messed-up marriage and would have refused to see you here, like a fool I almost let myself be taken in by that sugary voice of his telling me he would stop off here for me on the way from Bratislava and that he had a lot to say to me, that he wanted a heart-to-heart talk – and then he brought her with him, that kid, that brat, a girl of twenty-two, thirteen years younger than me. It's so degrading to lose simply because I was born earlier, I felt so helpless I could have screamed, but I mustn't scream, I had to smile and shake hands with her politely. Thank you, Ludvik, for giving me the strength.

When we were alone for a moment, he told me that now we had a chance of talking it all over frankly between the three of us and that this would be the most honourable way. Honourable, honourable, I know his idea of honour, two years now he's been angling for a divorce and he knows that with just the two of us he'll achieve nothing, he's relying on my feeling embarrassed face to face with his girl friend, he thinks I won't have the nerve to play the degrading role of the obstinate wife, that I'll break down and give in voluntarily. I hate him, he calmly slips the knife between my ribs when I'm on a job, when I need to be calm and collected, he ought at least to have some respect for my work, to give it some consideration, but this is the way it's been for years and years, I've always been pushed around, I always lose, I'm always humiliated, but now I've learned to show a little spirit, now I've felt you and your love behind me, I felt you still in me and on me and those fine colourful horsemen were all around me shouting and bawling as if crying out that you are here, that life is here, that there *is* a future, and I felt pride within me, the pride I had almost lost, pride washed over me like a flood, and managed to smile sweetly and tell him: 'I don't think there's any need for me to go to Prague with you. I wouldn't want to put you out and anyway I have the company car here. A for the agreement you wanted to discuss, that can be settled very quickly. I can introduce you to the man I want to live with and I'm sure that we can all come to a very amicable arrangement.'

Perhaps this was a crazy thing to do, but if it was, then let it stand. It was worth it for that moment of sweet pride, it was worth it. He immediately became far more amiable, was obviously glad, but was afraid I might not really mean it. He asked me to repeat it and I told him your full name: Ludvik Jahn, Ludvik Jahn, and finally I told him explicitly: 'Don't worry, honestly, I'm not going to put anything in the way of our divorce. Don't worry, I wouldn't want you, even if you wanted me.' He replied that he was sure we would remain good friends. I smiled and said I didn't doubt it.

5. Ludvik

Years ago when I played the clarinet in the band we used to wonder just what the Ride of the Kings meant. Apparently when the defeated Hungarian King Matyas was fleeing from Bohemia to Hungary his cavalry had to hide here, in rural Moravia, from their Czech pursuers, and to maintain him and themselves by begging. The Ride of the Kings is said to be a reminder of this historical event, but one only needs to do a bit of delving into old documents to realize that it is much older than this. Where then did it come from and what does it mean? Does it perhaps date from pagan times and is it a survival of the rites at which boys were accepted as men? And why are the King and his pages in women's attire? Is it a portrayal of how some army (either Matyas's or a much more ancient one) once led their leader through enemy country in disguise, or is it a survival of some old pagan superstition according to which transvestism protects one from evil spirits? Why must the King not speak a word throughout? And why is the event called the Ride of the Kings when there is only one king involved? What does it all mean? There are a number of

253

hypotheses and none of them has been proved. The Ride of the Kings is a mysterious rite; no one quite knows what it means, but just as Egyptian hieroglyphs are the more beautiful for those who cannot read them and accept them as mere fanciful sketchings, the Ride of the Kings is a beautiful thing perhaps for the same reason, that the content of its message has long since been lost, and that gestures, colours, words come into the foreground all the more for that reason, drawing attention to themselves and to their own forms and shapes.

And so, to my astonishment, the initial mistrust with which I watched the Ride as they raggedly set out vanished, and all at once I was completely enthralled by the colourful cavalcade as it slowly moved from house to house. Also the loudspeakers had at last grown silent and I could hear (if I ignored the occasional clatter of vehicles, which I have long since learned to discount from my aural impressions) only the strange music of the verse invocations.

I wanted to remain standing, to close my eyes and just listen; for I realized that here, in the middle of an East Moravian village, I was hearing *verse,* verse in the primeval meaning of the word, verse unlike anything I shall ever hear on radio, screen or stage, verse like a ceremonial rhythmic invocation, something formed on the boundary between speech and song, verse that moved one with its wealth of suggestion and with the pathos of its very rhythm, as it must have moved men when it resounded from the floor of an ancient amphitheatre. It was a splendid, polyphonic music: each of the criers called his lines in a monotone but each chose a different note so that the voices unconsciously blended in a chord; they did not all call at once, but each of them started his invocation at a different time, at a different cottage, so that the voices came from different directions and at different times, reminding one of a round for several voices; one voice would just be finishing, another would be half way through, and a third would begin its invocation at a different pitch.

The Ride of the Kings straggled down the main street, being continually startled by the traffic, and then at a corner it split up, one wing continuing straight ahead while the other turned

254

off right into a little street, at the end of which was a small yellow cottage with a fence and a small front garden ablaze with flowers. The crier broke into humorous improvisations, calling out that there were some fine *pumpkins* growing in the garden of this cottage and that the lady who lived here had a fine *bumpkin* as a son; and a plump woman of forty, obviously amused at the title her son had received, laughed, and handed a banknote to the collector on his horse as he called 'For the King, mother, for the King!' The collector put this in the basket which he had fastened to the saddle and called to the woman that she was as sweet as *candy* but that her plum *brandy* was even sweeter; and he cupped his hand and bending his head back put his hand to his lips. Everyone round was laughing, and the woman ran into her cottage in gratified embarrassment; she had evidently had the plum brandy in readiness, for almost at once she returned with a bottle and a glass, into which she poured some and handed it to the horseman.

While the King's army was drinking and joking the King himself stood motionless and grave a short distance away with his two pages, as if it was part of a king's lot to be swathed in gravity and to stand alone and aloof in the midst of his clamorous troops. The steeds of the two pages stood on either side close to the King's horse, so that the thigh boots of all three horsemen were almost touching; the horses had great gingerbread hearts on their chests, which were also decorated with mirrors and coloured glaze, on their brows they had paper roses, while the hairs of their manes were intermingled with ribbons of coloured crepe paper. All three speechless horsemen were, as I said, in women's clothes; they wore wide skirts and puckered starched sleeves. On their heads the pages wore richly ornamented bonnets, while the King had a brilliant silver tiara, hung with three long wide ribbons, blue at the edges and red in the middle, which completely covered his face and gave him a solemn and mysterious appearance.

I stood enchanted by this solemn trio; twenty years ago I myself had sat on a garlanded horse just like them, but because on that occasion I had seen the Ride from the inside it was only now that I was really seeing it, and I could not tear my eyes away. The King was sitting bolt upright a few yards away, veiled in a flag and looking like a statue under guard, and it suddenly occurred to me that perhaps this was not a king at all, perhaps it was a queen; perhaps it was Queen Lucie who had come to reveal herself to me in her real form, because her real form was her hidden form.

And at the same moment it occurred to me that Kostka was a crank, a blend of the persistent brooder and the ecstatic, and that although everything he had told me might conceivably be true, it was quite uncertain. He knew Lucie, of course, he might even have known a lot about her, but he did not know the vital fact: Lucie had really loved that soldier who had attacked her in the borrowed miner's flat. I could scarcely take seriously Lucie's picking flowers out of some vague religious longing, when I remember that she picked them for me; and if she had kept this hidden from Kostka as an inviolable secret, and also the whole sweet six months of our love together, then even he did not know her. Moreover, it was quite uncertain whether she had really moved to this town because of him; it could have been a mere coincidence. It was also quite possible that she came here because of me, since she did after all know that this was my home town! I felt that the report of her original raping was substantially true but I now doubted the exactness of the details. At times the train of events was evidently coloured by the bloodshot eyes of a man who was disquieted by sin, and at other times it was coloured such an ideal blue as only a man looking up to heaven is capable of seeing; it was clear that in Kostka's narrative truth and fairytale were mixed to produce a new legend – perhaps closer to the truth, perhaps more beautiful, perhaps more profound – which superimposed itself on the old.

I looked at the veiled King and I saw Lucie, unrecognized and unrecognizable, riding ceremoniously and mockingly through my life. Then something caught my attention, and my gaze fell directly on that of a man who had evidently been watching me for some time and smiling. He said 'Hello' and walked up to me. 'Greetings,' I said. He offered his hand and pressed it. Then he turned and called to a girl whom I had n noticed. 'What are you standing there for? Come on, I want to introduce you.' The girl, lanky but goodlooking with dark hair and dark eyes, came up to me and said: 'Brozova.' She gave me her hand and I said: 'Jahn. Pleased to meet you.' 'God, man, it's been years,' said the man genially; it was Zemanek.

6. Jaroslav

Tired. Tired. I could not shake it off. The troupe had set off with the King for the village green, and I strolled slowly after them. I took deep breaths to overcome my fatigue. I stopped with the neighbours who had come out of their cottages to gape. Suddenly I felt I was just another staid, avuncular old neighbour. That I would never think of travelling again, or any form of adventure. That I was hopelessly bound to the two or three streets where I lived.

Before I reached the green when the troupe had already started down the long main street, I wanted to shuffle along after them, but then I saw Ludvik. He was standing by himself on the grass verge, looking thoughtfully at the young fellow on the horse. Damn Ludvik! Why can't he go to hell! Up till now he's been avoiding me, today it's my turn to avoid him. I turned my back on him and went over to a bench on the green under an apple tree. I will sit down there and just listen to the distant invocations of the horsemen.

So I sat there, listening and watching. The Ride of the Kings gradually drifted away. It clung piteously to both sides of the highway along which the cars and motor cycles were continually passing. A bunch of people were walking after it. A miserably small crowd. From year to year fewer people go to the Ride. Though this year Ludvik is here. What *is* he doing here? Damn you, Ludvik! It's too late now. It's too late for everything. You've come like a bad omen. A dark foreboding. even crosses. Now of all times, when my Vladimir is King.

I averted my eyes. There was only a handful of people

standing on the green by the stalls and round the tavern door. Most of them were drunk. Drunkards are the most loyal supporters of revivalist folk ventures. The last supporters. Once in a while at least they have a noble pretext for getting drunk.

Then old man Pechacku came and sat beside me on the bench. He said it was not like old times. I agreed with him. It wasn't. Decades or centuries ago these rides must have been a splendid sight! I dare say they weren't as highly coloured as today. Today it's a bit of a fake, a bit of a masquerade. Gingerbread hearts on the horses' breasts! Tons of paper streamers bought in the department store! The costumes were always colourful, but they used to be simpler. The horses were adorned with just the one red scarf, tied under the neck across the breast. And the king never had a mask of coloured patterned ribbons, just a veil. And he had a rose in his mouth. So that he could not speak. There was nothing circus-like about the Rides. Rather the spirit of tragedy.

Yes, old fellow, it was better centuries ago. No one then had to search laboriously for young men who might graciously condescend to take part in the Ride. No one then had to spend days beforehand holding meetings and arguing who should organize the Ride and who should receive the proceeds. The Ride of the Kings used to gush forth over the life of the village like a spring. And it burst its way out of the village and stormed the neighbouring hamlets to collect for its masked King. Sometimes it would encounter another Ride of the Kings in a strange village and battle would commence. Both sides would defend their kings ferociously. Often there was a flash of knives and swords, and the blood would flow. When a Ride captured someone else's king, it would drink itself unconscious in the inn, at the father's expense.

Old fellow, you are so, so right. It was different when that French sculptor watched the Ride of the Kings. Rodin he was called. Anyway, even when I rode as the King, during the occupation, even then it was different from today. And after the war too it was worth doing. We thought we were about to create a completely new world. That people would live their popular traditions as they had before. That the Ride of the

Kings would continue to gush from the depths of their beings. We wanted to help this spring. We were quick to organize popular festivals. But a spring is not to be organized. Either a spring gushes or it does not. You see, old fellow, now we're just squeezing it out, these songs of ours and the Rides and all that. These are just the final drops.

Ah well. The Ride was no longer in sight. It had probably turned into some side street. But we could still hear the shouting. The invocations were magnificent. I closed my eyes and imagined myself for a moment living in some different time. Another century. A long time ago. Then I opened my eyes and told myself it was good after all that Vladimir was King. He is King of an almost extinct kingdom, but a most magnificent kingdom. A kingdom to which I shall remain loyal to the end.

I got up from the bench. Some one called out a greeting. It was old Koutecky, Ludvik's adoptive father. I hadn't seen him for a long time. He was walking with difficulty, leaning on a stick. I had never liked him but I suddenly felt sorry for his old age. 'Where are you off to?' I asked. He said he took a constitutional every Sunday. 'How did you like the Ride?' I asked him. He gave a flap of the hand. 'Didn't even watch it.' 'Why not?' I asked. Again he flapped his hand in annoyance and it dawned on me then why he didn't watch it. Ludvik was among the spectators. Koutecky didn't want to meet him any more than I did.

'I'm not surprised,' I said. 'My son's in the Ride of the Kings, but even so I don't feel like trailing after it.'

'Your son? What, your Vladimir?'

'Yes,' I said, 'he's riding as the King.'

Koutecky said: 'That's interesting.'

'Why so?' I asked.

'Very interesting,' said Koutecky, and there was a twinkle in his eye.

'Why?' I asked again.

'Vladimir's with our Milos,' said Koutecky. I had no idea which Milos this might be. He explained that this was his grandson, his daughter's son.

'It's impossible,' I said; 'I saw him, I saw him a moment ago riding off on his horse!'

'I saw him too. Milos brought him round from your place on the back of his motor bike,' said Koutecky.

'Nonsense,' I said, but then I asked: 'Where did they go?'

'Well, since you don't know anything about it, I'm not going to be the one to tell you,' said Koutecky and he took his leave of me.

7. Ludvik

I had never expected to meet Zemanek – Helena had told me he would be here, but not until the afternoon – and of course it was extremely unpleasant seeing him. But there was no help for it; there he was standing in front of me, just as he used to be. His yellow hair was as yellow as ever, even though he no longer combed it back in long curls, but had it cut short and brushed fashionably forward; he stood as erect as ever and he still arched his neck back in the same convulsive fashion, always with his head slightly inclined; he was just as jovial and complacent, invulnerable, endowed with the good favour of angels and with a young girl whose beauty immediately trained my recollections on the painful imperfection of the body with which I had spent yesterday afternoon.

Hoping our encounter would be as brief as possible, tried to answer all the trite conversational banalities he heaped on me with trite conversational banalities. He proclaimed again the fact that we had not seen each other for years, and his surprise that after such a long interval we should meet 'in such a godforsaken dump'. I told him I was born here. He asked me to forgive him and said that in that case it was certainly not so forsaken as all that. Miss Broz laughed; I ignored his jest and said I was not surprised to see him here because if I remembered rightly, he had always been a folklore enthusiast. Miss Broz laughed again and said they hadn't come here for the Ride of the Kings. Didn't she like the Ride of th

Kings? I asked. She said it didn't interest her. I asked her why not. She shrugged her shoulders, and Zemanek said: 'Ludvik, old friend, times have changed.'

Meanwhile the Ride of the Kings had moved, and two of the horsemen were struggling with their mounts, which had begun to get badly rattled. One rider was shouting at the other, scolding him for poor control of his mount, and the cries of 'idiot' and 'bloody fool' mingled rather drolly with the ritual of the festival. Miss Broz said: 'Funny if they were to bolt!' Zemanek laughed gaily at this, but by this time the horsemen had managed to calm their horses down, and again 'Oyez, oyez' resounded calmly and majestically through the village.

As we slowly followed the clamorous troupe through a side-street lined with gardens full of flowers I started hunting for some natural and spontaneous pretext for saying good-bye to Zemanek. Meanwhile I had to walk dutifully alongside his pretty companion and continue the desultory conversation. I learned that in Bratislava the weather had been just as fine early that morning as it was here; I learned that they had come in Zemanek's car and that just outside Bratislava they had had to change sparking-plugs; then I learned that Miss Broz was one of Zemanek's pupils. I knew from Helena that he lectured in Marxism-Leninism at the university, but this did not prevent me from asking him what he taught there. He told me he was teaching philosophy, and his use of this word struck me as symptomatic: a few years ago he would have said 'Marxism', but in recent years this subject had declined so much in popularity, especially among the young, that Zemanek, for whom popularity had always been of paramount importance, chastely concealed Marxism behind the more general term. I expressed surprise and said that I thought he had read biology; this was a malicious remark directed against the frequent dilettantism of university teachers of Marxism, many of whom entered this field not so much through aca-demic research, as by serving as propagandists for the state establishment.

Miss Broz now entered the conversation and announced

that most teachers of Marxism had political pamphlets in their heads instead of brains, but that Pavel was different entirely. Her words provided Zemanek with his cue; he protested mildly, thereby demonstrating his modesty and at the same time provoking the young lady to further praise. In this way I learned that Zemanek was one of the most popular teachers in the university and that his pupils worshipped him for not being liked by the university authorities, for always saying what he thought, for being courageous and sticking up for the young. Zemanek continued protesting mildly, and so I learned from the young lady further details of the various battles Zemanek had fought in recent years; how the authorities had even wanted to throw him out for not keeping in his lectures to the rigid, outdated curriculum and for wanting to acquaint the young people with everything taking place in modern philosophy (apparently this had led to a charge of wanting to smuggle 'hostile ideology' into the country); how he had defended a pupil from expulsion for some boyish prank (a fight with a policeman) which the rector, Zemanek's enemy, had characterized as a *political* misdemeanour; how afterwards the girl students in the faculty had held a secret poll to find their favourite teacher, and how he had won it. Zemanek was by now not even attempting to protest against this flood of praise, and I said, with an irony too subtle (alas) to be perceptible, that I could see what Miss Broz meant, as I remembered that Zemanek had been enormously popular back in my own student days. Miss Broz agreed enthusiastically: she was not in the least surprised, as Pavel was a fabulous speaker and could cut any opponent to pieces in debate. 'What of it?' laughed Zemanek. 'Even if I cut them to pieces in debate they can cut *me* to pieces in different and much more effective ways than any debate.'

In the cocksure complacency of this last remark I saw the Zemanek I knew, but the *content* of it staggered me; it was evident that he had completely abandoned his former views and that if today I had anything to do with him I would in any conflict, like it or not, find myself taking his side. This was horrible and quite unexpected, even though such a *volte-face*

262

was nothing miraculous; on the contrary, it was very common and had been performed by many others, while the whole of society was doing the same thing more gradually. It was only in Zemanek that I had not expected such a change; he had become petrified in my memory in the form in which I had last seen him, and I now furiously denied him the right to be any different.

There are people who claim to love humanity, while others hint that one can love only in the singular, only individual people. I agree with this latter view, and would add that what goes for love goes also for hate. Man, pining for equilibrium, balances the weight of the evil which has been piled on his back with the weight of his hatred. But just try directing hatred at mere abstract principles, at injustice, fanaticism, cruelty; or, if you have managed to find the human principle itself hateful, then try to hate mankind! Such hatreds are beyond human capacity; and so man, conscious of his limited power, in the end always seeks to relieve his anger by concentrating it upon a single individual.

This was why Zemanek's *volte-face* had given me such a shock. It suddenly occurred to me that he was capable any minute now of admitting as such the change in himself which he had already shown suspicious haste in demonstrating, and of asking me for forgiveness in its name. This was awful. What was I to say to him? What answer should I give? How was I to explain to him that I could not make my peace with him? That in doing so I would immediately lose my inner balance? That one of the arms of my internal scales would suddenly have shot upwards? That by hating him I was balancing the weight of evil which had crashed on my youth, my life? That in him I saw personified all the evils in my life? How was I to explain to him that I *needed* to hate him?

8. Jaroslav

The narrow street was full of horses. I saw the King from a few yards away. He was sitting on his horse some way from the others. Two other lads on horseback, his pages, were at his side. I was confused. True, he had Vladimir's slightly bent back. He was sitting calmly as if without interest. Is it him? Perhaps. But it might equally well be someone else.

I worked my way closer towards him. I had to recognize him. Didn't I have the way he held himself, his every gesture, inscribed in my memory? Besides, I love him, and love has its own instinct.

I was standing right beside him. I could have spoken to him. It was so simple. But it would have been no use. The King is not supposed to speak.

Then the Ride of the Kings swept on to the next house. Now I would know him! The horse's sudden forward movement was bound to make him move in some way which would betray him. As the horse stepped forward the King did in fact straighten up slightly, but the movement gave me no indication of who was behind the veil. The garish ribbons across his face were hopelessly opaque.

9. Ludvik

The Ride of the Kings had advanced past a few more houses and we continued to follow behind, while our conversation leapt to other topics. Miss Broz had shifted from Zemanek to herself and was holding forth about how much she loved hitch-hiking. She spoke about it with such emphasis (somewhat affected) that I could see at once that she was putting the case for her generation. Every generation has its own set of passions, loves and interests, which it professes with a certain tenacity, to differentiate it from older generations and confirm itself in its uniqueness. I have always disliked kow-towing to the mentality of a whole generation, and as Miss Broz developed her provocative argument, which I have now heard at least ten times from people of her age, about how mankind is divided into those who give lifts (freethinking, adventurous, human people) and those who do not (mon-sters, Socialist bourgeois, inhuman people), I jokingly named her the 'hitch-hiking dogmatist'. She answered sharply that she was no dogmatist, or revisionist or sectarian, or deviation-ist, that she was neither class-conscious nor otherwise, that these were all words which were invented by us, which be-longed to us, and which to *them* were alien.

'Yes,' said Zemanek, 'they are different, I am *glad* to say they are different. Even their vocabulary is different. Neither our successes nor our failures interest them. You wouldn't believe this, but in the entrance exams for the university the young people don't even know what the Trials were. Stalin is just a name to them, and Bukharin, Kamenev, Rajk are not even names. Just imagine, most of them do not even know who Clementis was.'

'That is what seems so dreadful to me,' I said.

'It doesn't reflect on their education. For them this is libera-tion. They have simply not admitted our world into their con-sciousness. They have refused it and everything it stands for.'

'Blindness has given way to blindness.'

'I wouldn't say so. They impress me. I like them *because* they are different. They love their bodies; we neglected them. They love travel; we stayed put in one place. They love ad-venture; we sat our lives out at meetings. They love jazz; we gave an insipid imitation of folk music. They are selfishly devoted to themselves; we wanted to save the world. In fact with our messianism we almost destroyed it. Perhaps they with their selfishness will save it.'

10. Jaroslav

How is it possible? The King! That figure aloft on his mount, veiled in bright colours! How many times have I seen him and imagined him! The most intimate of figures! And now it has changed into reality and all intimacy is gone. Suddenly it is just a coloured larva and I do not know what is inside. What intimacy can there be in this real world if it is not my King?

My son. The nearest person to me. I am standing in front of him and I do not know whether it is him or not. What do I know, if I do not even know this? What certainty can I have in this world if I cannot be certain about this?

11. Ludvik

While Zemanek was eulogizing the younger generation I was watching Miss Broz, finding her to my sorrow a handsome and likable girl, and feeling an envious regret that she wasn't mine. She was walking at Zemanek's side, talking away, taking him by the hand every other moment, turning confidentially towards him; and I was reminded afresh of a truth with which I grow more familiar every year: that since Lucie I had had no girl to love and respect. Life had made mock of me by sending me, in the form of this man's lover, a reminder of the grotesque sexual contest in which only the day before I had mistakenly thought to have defeated him.

The more I liked Miss Broz, the more I realized how completely she typified the outlook of her generation, for whom I and my contemporaries merged into a single amorphous mass, all deformed, as far as they were concerned, with the same incomprehensible jargon, the same ultra-political thinking, the same anxieties (which appeared to them as cowardice) the same strange experiences from a dark and already distant era. In their view it is no longer even worth making the distinction between those of us who contributed to the oppression of that period and those who tried to dislodge it. This has no interest for them, because today the course of history is dislodging it without our help. (Well, yes, it may be an illusion to think that this is without our help, but what of it? Whether with or without our help, the oppression is being dislodged not for *our* sake but for theirs.)

In that moment I suddenly became aware that the similarity between myself and Zemanek did not rest merely in the fact that Zemanek had changed his views and brought them more in line with my own. It was more profound and affected our entire life's destinies; the way Miss Broz and her contemporaries regarded us, we resembled each other even when we were at each other's throats. I suddenly felt that if I were reluctantly forced to tell Miss Broz the story of my expulsion from the Party it would appear too remote, too much like *literature* (oh yes, that theme that has been the subject of so many bad novels), and that in this story both Zemanek and myself would appear as equally unlikable – equally earnest, equally monstrous. I saw the healing waters of time closing over our dispute, which I had felt to be still contemporary and alive; and time, as we all know, can smooth over the difference between entire eras, let alone two miserable individuals. But I fought tooth and nail against accepting the reconciliation proposed by time. I am not living in eternity; I am anchored to the trifling thirty-seven years of my own life, and I have no wish to be detached from them, in the way Zemanek detached himself when he was so quick to embrace the attitudes of his juniors. No, I will not shirk my fate, I will not detach myself from my thirty-seven years even when I see them as a stretch of time that is fleeting and insignificant, already in the process of being forgotten.

And if Zemanek were to lean over to me confidentially and start talking about what has been, and ask for reconciliation, I should refuse that reconciliation; yes, I should refuse that reconciliation, even if it were mediated by Miss Broz, by all her contemporaries, by time itself.

12. Jaroslav

Tired. Suddenly I wanted to say good-bye to the whole thing. To go away and stop worrying about it all. I have no wish to remain in this world of material things, which I do not understand, and which deceive me. There exists another world. A world where I am at home and with which I am familiar. There is the road, the briar bush, the deserter, the wandering minstrel, and Mother.

Then I made an attempt to control myself. I must. I must take to its conclusion my quarrel with the world of material things. I must look into the very abyss of all errors and deceptions.

Should I ask someone? The horsemen from the Ride? Should I make myself a laughing-stock? I remembered this morning. The robing of the King. And at once I knew where I must go.

13. Ludvik

'We have a pauper king, but greatly righteous,' the horsemen were calling from a few houses ahead of us, and we followed them. The richly beribboned backsides of the horses bobbed up and down in front of us, blue, pink, green and violet, and Zemanek suddenly pointed in their direction: 'There's Helena.' I looked but all I could see was the colourful horses' trappings. Zemanek pointed again: 'There.' Then I saw her half concealed behind a horse and felt myself blushing: the way Zemanek had pointed her out – not as 'my wife' but as 'Helena' – showed that he knew that I knew her.

Helena was standing on the edge of the pavement and holding a microphone in her outstretched hand; a wire ran from the microphone to the tape recorder hanging over the shoulder of a young man in leather jacket and jeans and with earphones over his ears. We stopped a short way away from them. Zemanek said, suddenly and out of the blue, that Helena was a grand girl, that she still looked fabulous and was very able as well, and that he was not surprised we got on so well together.

I felt my cheeks hot. Zemanek had not intended his remark as an attack; on the contrary, he had said it in a most affable tone, and I was also left in no doubt as to the real state of affairs by the way Miss Broz was looking at me, giving me significant, smiling glances, as if bent on showing that she was fully informed and perfectly sympathetic, if not directly in alliance.

Meanwhile Zemanek continued his casual references to his wife, trying to make it plain, by hints and innuendoes, that he knew everything but was not going to make trouble, since he was perfectly liberal as far as Helena's private life was concerned. To give his words an air of nonchalance he pointed out the young man carrying the tape recorder and told me that the boy ('Doesn't he look like a great big beetle with those earphones on?') had already been dangerously in love with Helena for two years and that I ought to keep my eye on him. Miss Broz laughed and asked how old he would have been two years ago. Zemanek said seventeen – quite old enough for falling in love. Then he declared jokingly that of course Helena was a virtuous lady, not a baby-snatcher, but that a boy like that would get more and more furious the less successful he was and would be sure to put up a fight. Miss Broz, entering into the spirit of this senseless repartee, observed that I would doubtless know how to handle him.

'I'm not so sure about that,' said Zemanek with a smile.

'Don't forget I've worked down the mines. I've still got a good few muscles from those days.' I had spoken at random and had forgotten that such a reminder would be overstepping the bantering nature of the conversation.

'Have you been down the mines?' asked Miss Broz.

'These twenty-year-olds' – Zemanek stuck doggedly to his topic – 'are really dangerous when they're in a gang. Anyone they don't like they can fix well and truly.'

'How long?' asked Miss Broz.

'Five years.'

'When was that?'

'I came out nine years ago.'

'Oh, that's a long time, your muscles will have gone all flabby by now,' she said, wanting to add her own little quip to the friendly banter. As it happened I was thinking at that moment of how my muscles had certainly not gone flabby, that I was still in the pink of condition, that I could have smashed this blond creature to smithereens, and – most important and most depressing – that my muscles were all I had in case I should want to pay my old debt.

Again I imagined Zemanek turning jovially towards me and asking me to forget everything there ever was between us, and I felt doublecrossed: Zemanek's application for forgiveness would be supported not only by his change of views, not only by time and its bird's-eye view of matters, not only by Miss Broz and her contemporaries, but by Helena too (yes, now they were all on his side!), because if Zemanek forgave me my adultery then this was just a bribe for me to forgive him.

As I visualized his blackmailer's face, cocksure with the certainty of his powerful allies, I felt such a desire to hit him that I found myself visualizing this also: the shouting, whirling horsemen, the sun a splendid gold, Miss Broz making some remark, and before my furious eyes the blood running down his face.

Yes, but this was all imagination: what would I really do if he were to ask me to forgive him?

I realized with a shock that I would do nothing.

Meanwhile we had come abreast of Helena and her technician, who was removing his earphones. 'Have you met already?' Helena looked surprised to see me with Zemanek.

'We've known each other for a long time,' said Zemanek.

'How so?' she asked in astonishment.

'We know each other from our student days, we were in the same faculty,' said Zemanek, and I saw this as one of the last bridges across which he was leading me towards that ignominious, gibbet-like place where he would ask me for my forgiveness.

'Well, there's a coincidence,' said Helena.

'That's the way it is in this world,' said the technician, to demonstrate that he too was in the world.

'I haven't introduced you,' Helena realized and said: 'This is Jindra, Jindra Kadlecka.'

I shook hands with Jindra (an ungainly freckled youth), and Zemanek said to Helena: 'Miss Broz and I had intended taking you back with us but I can see now that this wouldn't suit you, that you'd rather go back with Ludvik . . .'

'Are you coming with us?' asked the young man in jeans, and he did indeed sound none too friendly.

'Is your car here?' Zemanek asked.

'I haven't got a car,' I replied.

'Then come with us, and you'll be comfortable and in the best of company,' he said.

'I can do eighty so don't worry,' said the jeans.

'Jindra!' cried Helena.

'You *could* come with us, that is,' said Zemanek, 'but I fancy you'll be giving your new girlfriend priority over your old friend.' He called me his 'friend' jovially and *en passant*, and I was sure that the dishonourable truce was only a few steps away. Zemanek had grown silent for a while, as if hesitating, and it looked as if any moment now he would turn to me and ask to speak to me alone. I hung my head as if laying it on the block; but I was wrong. Zemanek looked at his watch and said: 'I haven't a great deal of time – we have to be in Prague by five. So I'd better take my leave. Bye, Helena.' He gave Helena his hand, then said good-bye to the technician and myself and shook hands with us all. Miss Broz shook hands with everybody, took Zemanek's arm and they were gone.

They were gone. I couldn't tear my eyes off them. Zemanek was walking erect with his proud, victorious blond head held high and his brunette floating at his side. She was beautiful from the back too, she walked lightly, I liked her – liked her almost painfully, because her departing beauty was icily indifferent to me, just as Zemanek had been indifferent (for all his affability, garrulity, memory and conscience), just as the whole of my past was indifferent, the past I had made a tryst with in my own home town in order to be avenged on it but which had stridden past me unseeing, as if it did not know me.

I was stifled with humiliation and shame. I wanted nothing better than to disappear, isolate myself, wipe out the whole grubby devious incident, the stupid joke, wipe out Helena and Zemanek, wipe out the day before yesterday, yesterday and today, wipe it out, wipe it out so that not a trace remained. 'Do you mind if I speak to Mrs Zemanek alone for a moment?' I asked the technician.

I took Helena to one side. She wanted to explain something, she said something about Zemanek and his girl, she apologized confusedly for having had to tell him everything. Nothing interested me at this moment; I was filled with a single desire, to be out of this place, to be away from here and from the whole affair, to write full stop to it all. I knew I oughtn't to deceive Helena any longer; she was quite innocent towards me and I had acted vilely, because I had turned her into a mere object, into a stone which I had tried, and failed, to throw at someone else. I was stifled by the ridiculous failure of my vengeance and the vileness of my own behaviour and I was determined, even at this late hour, to put an end to it all. However, it was no use trying to explain everything to her; not only would I have hurt her bitterly with the truth, but she would hardly have been able to understand it. So I resorted to merely stating the barest bones of the issue: I repeated to her several times that this was our last time together, that I would not be seeing her again, that I did not love her and that she must understand this.

But it was far worse than I had foreseen: Helena went pale and started shaking, wouldn't believe me, wouldn't let me go. I went through a minor martyrdom before I could finally get rid of her and make my getaway.

4. Helena

All around me there were horses and streamers, and I stood there, just stood there for a long time, and then Jindra came over to me, took my hand and squeezed it and asked me 'What's the matter, what's the matter?' and I let him hold my hand and said 'Nothing, Jindra, there's nothing the matter, why should there be?' and my voice was strange and high and went on in a queer headlong way: 'What else have we got to record? We've got the invocations, we've got two interviews, and I shall have to do a commentary.' So I went on talking about things I was quite unable to give my mind to, and he stood there silent beside me, crushing my hand.

He had never touched me before, he was always too shy, but everyone knew he was in love with me, and now he was standing beside me and squeezing my hand, and I was babbling on about the programme without thinking about it. I was thinking about Jindra and how funny it was, then it occurred to me to wonder what I looked like to Jindra, whether the shock had made me hideous. Maybe not, I wasn't crying, just upset, nothing more . . .

'Jindra, could you please leave me alone for a moment? I'll just go and write a commentary and then we'll record it.' He held me a little longer and kept asking gently 'What's the matter, Helena, what's the matter?' but I twisted away from him and went over to the council offices where we had borrowed a room. I went there and at last I was by myself, in an empty room. I collapsed on the chair and put my head on the table and just stayed like that for a bit. My head hurt horribly. I opened my handbag to see if there was anything I could take, I don't know why I opened it because I knew I had nothing, but then I remembered that Jindra carries all sorts of pills and things round with him, and his lab coat was hanging on the hook. I put my hand in his pockets and, yes, there was a tube of some sort, yes, it was for headaches,

273

toothache, sciatica and neuritis. It was no good for heartache but at least it would ease my head.

I went to the tap in the corner of the next room and poured some water in a mustard glass and took two tablets. Two is enough, that should help, of course aspirin can't help me with heartache unless I were to take the whole tube, because aspirin in large quantities is poisonous and Jindra's tube was nearly full. It should be quite enough.

It was only an idea, a sudden flash, but it kept coming back to me and I couldn't help thinking, why was I alive at all, what was the sense in my living on, but it's not true really, I didn't really think anything of that sort, I was hardly thinking at all, I just imagined myself not living and I suddenly felt such bliss, such strange bliss that I wanted to laugh and I did in fact start laughing.

I put one more tablet on my tongue, I had no intention of poisoning myself, I just squeezed the tube in my hand and told myself that I had my death within my grasp, and I was enthralled by the simplicity of it, I felt I was step by step approaching a deep abyss, not so much to jump into, just to look down. I poured the glass full of water, took the tablet and went back into our room. The window was open and I could still hear 'Oyez, oyez' in the distance, but mixed with the racket of cars, lorries and motor bikes, nasty motor bikes deafening everything beautiful in this world, everything I believed in and lived for. The noise was unbearable and so was the helpless feebleness of the voices, and so I closed the window and again I felt the long, lingering pain in my soul.

All his life Pavel never hurt me as much as you, Ludvik, hurt me in a single minute. Pavel I forgive, him I understand, his flame is quickly consumed and he has to seek fresh pastures and a new audience and a new public. He hurt me, but now through this fresh pain I see him without malice, as his mother might, a showman, a comedian, and I smile at his attempts these last few years to dodge out of my arms. You can go Pavel, you can go, you I understand, but you, Ludvik, I do not understand, you came to me in a mask, you came to resurrect me and, once resurrected, to destroy me. For you I have

274

only curses, I curse you, I curse you, and I ask you to come, to come to me and have mercy.

God, might it not just be some terrible misunderstanding? Maybe Pavel told you something when you were alone together, I just don't know. I asked you about it, I begged you to explain why you don't love me any more, I didn't want to let you go, four times I held you back, but you didn't want to listen, you just said it was all over, finished, definitely, irrevocably. All right, so it's over. In the end I agreed and I had a high soprano voice as if it was someone else talking, some girl before puberty, and I said in my high-pitched voice: 'Have a good trip then.' It's silly, I don't know why I wanted you to have a good trip, but it kept tumbling off my tongue: 'Have a good trip then, have a good trip then . . .'

Maybe you don't know the way I love you, you can't know how much I love you. Maybe you think I'm just another married woman looking for an adventure, and you don't understand that you're my destiny, my life, my everything. . . . Maybe you'll find me here lying under a white sheet and then you'll understand you've killed the most precious thing you ever had in your life . . . or you'll come, oh my God, and I shall still be alive, and you'll be able to save me again and you'll be kneeling and crying, and I shall be stroking your hands, your hair, and I shall forgive you, I shall forgive you everything . . .

5. Ludvik

There was no help for it; I had to undo that whole sorry episode, that bad joke, which, not content with itself, had gone on monstrously multiplying itself into more and more stupid jokes. I wanted to wipe out the entire day, all the events that had only occurred through inadvertence, because I had overslept and been unable to get away. But I also wanted to wipe out everything leading up to that day, the whole stupid, misconceived attempt on Helena.

I hurried away as if I could hear Helena's pursuing footsteps behind me, and I thought: even if I were able to wipe out these few useless days from my life, what good would that do, when the entire course of my life was conceived in error, through the bad joke of the postcard, that accident, that piece of nonsense? I was horrified at the thought that things which occur by mistake are just as real as things which occur by right and of necessity.

How glad I would be to reverse the whole course of my life! Yet how could I do so by my own exertions, when the mistakes it grew from were not only my own? Who was at fault when the stupid joke of my postcard was taken seriously? Who was to blame when Alexej's father – today, incidentally, long since rehabilitated, but none the less dead for that – was arrested and sentenced? The mistakes were so universal that they could not be regarded simply as exceptions or aberrations in the order of things. Who then was at fault? History? Divine reasoning history? Why should it have been a *mistake* on her part? What if history plays jokes? Then I realized how feeble it was to want to annul my own joke when throughout my life I was involved in a joke which was all-embracing, unfathomable and utterly irrevocable.

On the deserted village green (the Ride was now at the other end of the village) I saw a big placard, leaning against a wall and announcing in red letters that today at four in the afternoon a cymbalo band would be giving a concert in the open-air restaurant. Next to the placard was a door into a tavern, and since it was lunch time and I had almost two hours left before my bus was due to leave I went inside.

16. Helena

I wanted so much to move just an inch nearer the precipice, I wanted to bend under the railings and look down into it, as if that could bring me solace and reconciliation, as if down there at least, if nowhere else, down there at the bottom of the pit, we might find each other and be together without misunderstandings, without malicious people, without old age, without sorrow, for evermore ... I went into the other room again, and now I had four tablets inside me, that's nothing, I'm a long way from the precipice yet, I can't even touch the railings. I poured the remaining tablets onto my palm. Then I heard someone opening the outside door, and I took fright and threw the tablets into my mouth and gulped them down. It was too much dry stuff at one go, and I felt them pushing painfully against my gullet, even when I had drunk as much as I could.

It was Jindra. He asked me how the commentary was getting on. All of a sudden I was another person, the confusion had left me, that high-pitched alien voice was gone, and I was purposeful and decisive. 'Oh, Jindra, I'm glad you've come. I'd like you to do something for me.' He blushed and said he would do anything for me and he was glad I felt all right again. 'Yes, I'm all right now. Just wait a moment. I want to write a few words,' and I sat down and took some paper and started writing: 'Ludvik, my dearest, I loved you body and soul, and now my body and soul have got nothing left to live for. Farewell, I love you, good-bye, Helena.' I didn't even re-read what I had written. Jindra was sitting facing me, watching me, unaware of what I was writing. I quickly folded the paper and wanted to put it in an envelope, but there were no envelopes anywhere. 'Jindra, I wonder if you might have an envelope?'

Jindra calmly went over to the cupboard by the table, opened it and began rummaging about. At any other time I would have told him off for rummaging in someone else's things, but at that moment I wanted an envelope, quickly, quickly. He gave me one, it had the local council stamp on it. I put the letter inside, stuck it down, and wrote 'Ludvik Jahn' on the envelope. 'Jindra, do you remember that man who was with us when my husband and the young lady were there, yes, that's right, the dark one. I can't go now and I'd like you to find him and give him this.'

Again he took me by the hand, poor boy, I don't know what he was thinking, how he could have interpreted my excitement. He could never have guessed what it was about, he just sensed there was something bad happening to me. He held my hand again, and all of a sudden it seemed so dreadfully sad, and then he bent down and held me in his arms and pressed his lips against mine. I wanted to stop him, but he held me tight and it went through my head that this was the last man I would ever kiss, and I suddenly felt quite mad and returned his embrace and squeezed him and opened my lips to feel his tongue on my tongue and his hands on my body, and in that moment I had a giddy feeling that now I was completely free and that nothing mattered any more, because I had been deserted by everybody and my world had gone on the rocks and so I was completely free and could do what I liked. I was free like the girl we had sacked from the institute. There was nothing to distinguish her from me, my world was shattered and I would never piece it together again, I no longer had anything to be true for, or anyone to be true to, suddenly I was completely free like that little technician girl, that slut who was in a different bed every night. If I were to live on I too would be in a different bed every night. I felt Jindra's tongue in my mouth. I was free, I knew I could love him, I wanted to love him, love him anywhere, here on the table or on the bare wooden floor, now, at once, without delay, to make love for the last time, to make love before the end. But Jindra was already on his feet, smiling proudly, saying he was off and would soon be back.

17. Ludvik

The waiter dashed about the little room with its five or six tables, thick with smoke and people, bearing on his outstretched arm a large tray, heaped with plates, upon which I could distinguish fried cutlets with potato salad (probably their only Sunday dish); and rudely pushing his way between people and tables he rushed out of the room into the passage. I followed him and ascertained that at the end of the passage the door into the garden was open and dinner was being served

278

out there as well. At the back, under a linden tree, was an un-occupied table; and here I sat down.

A pathetic 'Oyez, oyez' resounded over the village roofs, from such a distance now that by the time it reached the tavern garden it sounded only half real. And this air of unreality made me think that everything around me was not the present but the past, a past fifteen, twenty years old, a past epitomized in the cries of 'Oyez, oyez'. Lucie was the past, Zemanek was the past, and Helena was just a stone I had wanted to throw at the past; the whole of those three days had been nothing but a theatre of shadows.

What? Just those three days? My entire life, it seemed to me, had been overcrowded with shadows and there was nothing particularly remarkable about the present. I saw myself as a man on a moving staircase (time) who runs against the move-ment. The staircase, however, was moving faster than I and was thus slowly taking me further away from my goal, away from the past of the political trials, the past of assembly halls where hands are raised, the past of fear, the past of 'black' divisions and Lucie, the past which had bewitched me, which I was trying to unravel and which prevented me from living as a man should live, with his head facing forward. Day by day, however, the past was becoming more distant (because the pavement was moving quicker than I was) and therefore more insoluble and less susceptible of disentanglement, so that I was running (my eyes trained on the past, my feeling of justice unsatisfied) an utterly futile race.

And the main bond with which I had wanted to tie myself to the past, that past that so hypnotized me, was vengeance; but vengeance, as these three days had demonstrated, was just as futile as my running backwards on the moving staircase of time. Yes, it was when Zemanek was reading from Fucik's *Notes from the Gallows* in the faculty lecture-theatre that I should have gone up to him and punched him in the face, then and only then. With the passing of time vengeance is trans-formed into something deceptive, into a personal religion, into a myth which becomes daily further removed from the people involved, who in the myth remain the same, although in reality (the pavement being in constant motion) they have long become different people. Today we were a different Jahn and a different Zemanek, and the blow which is owed me is irretrievably and definitively lost, so that if I hit out now, years later, my blow would be completely incomprehensible, would attain a completely different, alien significance not intended by myself, and could be deflected in every conceivable direction, in a way I could not even control, let alone justify.

I cut into the great pancake of schnitzel on my plate, and again the 'Oyez, oyez' reached my ears, carrying faintly and mournfully across the village roofs; I imagined the veiled King and his cavalry, and my heart contracted at the incomprehensibility of human gestures.

For many centuries young men have been riding forth in Moravian villages just like today, with strange messages in some unknown language which they pronounce with a moving loyalty and a total lack of comprehension. Some long-dead people certainly had something important to say; and today they are revived in their descendants like deaf and dumb orators speaking to their audiences in fine but incomprehensible gestures. Their message will never be decoded, not only because there is no key to it, but because people have no patience to listen in an age when the accumulation of messages old and new is so relentlessly unending. Today history is no more than a slender cord of things remembered, stretching over an ocean of things forgotten; but time marches on, and the age of five-figure years will come, and the unaided memory of the individual will not be capable of absorbing it; whole centuries and millennia will therefore drop out, centuries of pictures and music, centuries of discoveries, of battles, of books, and this will be bad, because man will cease to have any concept of himself, and his history, unintelligible and unimaginable, will be shrivelled up into a few schematic summaries destitute of all sense. Thousands of deaf and dumb Rides of Kings will set out with their piteous and incomprehensible messages, and no one will have the time to hear them out.

I sat in the corner of the garden restaurant over my empty

plate, having eaten my schnitzel without realizing it, and I saw that I too had been submerged in the inescapable and boundless ocean of human forgetfulness. The waiter came and took my plate, stopping to brush a few crumbs off my tablecloth before hurrying to another table. I was seized with regret for the day, not only because it had been wasted, but because not even its futility would remain; it would be forgotten together with this table, with the fly buzzing round my head, the yellow pollen scattered on the tablecloth by the flowering linden, and the slow and bad service which is so characteristic of the society I live in. Even that society itself would be forgotten; but long before that its mistakes and errors and injustices would have been forgotten, the ones which had hypnotized me, on which I had fed and which I had vainly attempted to punish and redress – vainly, because what had happened had happened and could never be redressed.

Yes, that is how it is: most people deceive themselves doubly: they believe in eternal commemoration (of people, things, deeds, nations) and in redress (of deeds, mistakes, sins, wrongs). Both are false faiths. In reality the opposite is true: everything will be forgotten and nothing will be redressed. The task of obtaining redress (of avengement and forgiveness) is stultified by the fact of oblivion. No one will redress the wrongs which have been done, but all wrongs will be forgotten.

I took another careful glance around me because I knew that the linden tree would be forgotten, and the table, and the people at the table, and the waiter (weary after his last bout of running around), and this tavern which, uninviting enough from the street, was on the garden side pleasantly overgrown with the vine. I looked at the open door of the passage into which the waiter had just vanished, and from which there now emerged a youth in leather jacket and jeans. He stepped into the garden and looked about him. Then he saw me and made in my direction; it was not till several seconds had passed that I recognized him as Helena's technician.

It is a painful situation when a loving but unloved woman threatens to come back, and so when the youth gave me the

envelope ('from Mrs Zemanek') my first wish was somehow
to postpone reading it. I told him to take a seat; he complied,
leaning his elbow on the table and yawning contentedly with
puckered brow towards the sun-bathed linden tree, and I put
the envelope on the table and asked if he would fancy a drink.

He shrugged his shoulders. I suggested vodka, but he refused, saying he was driving; he added that if I wanted one he
would be quite content to watch. I didn't, but since the
envelope was lying on the table in front of me, and I didn't want
to open it, any alternative activity seemed welcome. So I
asked the waiter as he went past to bring me a vodka.

'You don't happen to know what Helena wants, do you?' I
asked.

'How should I know? Read the letter.'

'Anything urgent?'

'Do you think she made me learn it by heart in case I was
attacked?'

I took the envelope between my fingers – it was office
stationery with the printed heading of the local council – then
put it back on the table in front of me and, not knowing what
to say, remarked: 'Pity you don't drink.'

'It's a case of *your own* safety,' he said. I took this as a hint:
clearly the youth wanted to clarify his return journey and his
chances of being alone with Helena. He was a not unpleasant
lad; on his irredeemably childish face – abnormally small,
pale and freckled with a short turned-up nose, the sort of features that become not a jot more manly with age, and turn
even an old man's face into the face of an aged child – you
could see everything that went on inside him. This childish
appearance could hardly be pleasing to a young man of
twenty, because at that age it was a sort of disqualification
which, like (endless hall of mirrors!) the boy officer in our
camp, he felt obliged to disguise in every possible way: by
his dress (his leather jacket was broad-shouldered, a good fit
and well sewn) and by his behaviour (he acted with self-
assurance, a trifle rudely, at times with an exaggerated super-
cilious indifference). Unfortunately for him, in this disguise
he was continually being betrayed by himself: he blushed, he

could not quite control his voice, which at the slighest excitement tended to break (as I had noticed when we first met), he could not even control his eyes and his gestures (he had wanted to indicate his unconcern about whether I was going to Prague with them or not, but when I now assured him I would be staying here his eyes gleamed openly).

A moment later, when the waiter by mistake brought to our table two vodkas instead of one, the youth gave a flap of the hand and said there was no need for the waiter to take it away again, as he would drink it after all. 'I wouldn't leave you to drink on your own,' he said, and raised his glass. 'Your health then!'

'And yours!' I said and we clinked glasses.

We started talking and I learned that the young man was expecting to leave in about two hours' time, as Helena wanted to go over the material they had recorded on the spot, adding her own commentary where necessary, so that the whole thing could be broadcast tomorrow. I asked what it was like working with Helena. He again blushed gently and answered that Helena knew what she was doing but was too tough on her colleagues, as she was always ready to work overtime and disregarded the fact that others might be in a hurry to get home. I asked him if he was in a hurry to get home. He said he wasn't; that for his part he was quite enjoying himself here. Then, taking advantage of the fact that I had started talking about Helena, he asked with a casual air: 'How do you know Helena then?' I told him and he went on pumping me: 'Helena's really nice, isn't she?'

Particularly when the conversation was about Helena he assumed a self-satisfied air which I again put down to his wish for a disguise, since his hopeless adoration of Helena was evidently common knowledge and he had to fight tooth and nail against being labelled as the unhappy lover, which everyone knows to be a most ignominious title. Although I did not take his confidence altogether seriously, nevertheless it did something to lighten the load of the letter lying before me, so that I finally picked it up and opened it: 'My body and soul . . have nothing to live for. . . . Good-bye . . .'

283

I saw the waiter at the other end of the garden and shouted: 'Bill, please!' The waiter nodded but did not allow himself to be deflected from his orbit and vanished into the passageway again.

'Come on – we've no time to lose,' I said to the boy. I got up and hurried across the garden; the boy followed me. We went through the passageway and reached the exit, so that the waiter had, willy nilly, to run after us.

'Schnitzel, soup, two vodkas,' I dictated.

'What's going on?' asked the boy in a subdued voice.

I paid the waiter and asked the boy to take me quickly to Helena. We set off at a fast walk.

'What's happened?' he asked.

'How far is it?' I asked.

He pointed some way ahead of us and I changed from a walk to a run; we were both running now and presently we were in front of the council building, a single-storey structure whitewashed, with a gate and a couple of windows facing the street. We went inside. From the dark passageway there was a door on the right. The boy opened it and we found ourselves in an uninviting sort of office. Under the window two desks were drawn up close together; on one of them lay the tape recorder, open, with a pad of paper and a lady's handbag (yes, it was Helena's); there were chairs by both desks and in the corner of the room a metal clothes tree. Two coats were hanging from it: Helena's blue mac and a dirty gent's raincoat.

'This is it,' said the young man.

'Is this where she gave you the letter?'

'Yes.'

But the office was now hopelessly empty. I called out 'Helena!' and was alarmed to hear how uneasy my voice sounded. There was no reply. I called again: 'Helena!' and the boy asked:

'Has she done something to herself?'

'Looks like it,' I said.

'Is that what the letter was about?'

'Yes,' I said. 'You weren't given any other room?'

'No.'

'What about the hotel?'

'We checked out this morning.'

'She must be here then,' I said, and now I heard the boy's voice break as he called anxiously 'Helena!'

I opened the door into the adjoining room. It was another office: desk, waste paper basket, three chairs, cupboard and clothes tree. (The clothes tree was the same as in the first office: a metal pole standing on three legs and diverging symmetrically upwards into three metal branches; because there were no coats hanging from this tree it stood there looking human and forlorn, and I felt sorry for its green nakedness and ridiculously outstretched arms.) There was a window over the desk and otherwise just the bare walls. There was no other door leading out anywhere; the two offices were evidently the only rooms in the building.

We went back to the first room. I took the pad off the desk and thumbed through it; there were some almost illegible notes concerning, to judge from the few words I managed to read, the Ride of the Kings, but no message, no further parting words. I opened the handbag: there was a handkerchief, purses, lipstick, powder, two leaking cigarettes, a lighter. There was no medicine tube or poison bottle. I tried feverishly to think what Helena could have done, and the likeliest thing seemed to be poison; but in that case there should have been a bottle or tube somewhere. I went to the clothes tree and rummaged in the pockets of the raincoat: they were empty.

'Is she out at the back?' the young man said suddenly, and impatiently, as my search of the room, although it lasted only a few seconds, evidently struck him as aimless. We ran into the passage and saw two doors: one was glazed at the top and commanded an indistinct view of a back yard; we opened the other one, the nearer one, behind which appeared a stairway, stone-built, dark and covered with a layer of dust and soot. We ran upstairs; we were enveloped in darkness, as there was only a single dormer window in the roof (with poor quality glass at that), through which came a dull grey light. All round us we could make out the shapes of every kind of junk (trunks, garden implements, hoes, spades, rakes, even heaps of documents and an old broken chair); we kept stumbling over it.

I wanted to call out 'Helena!' but was stopped by fear; I was afraid of the silence that would follow. The boy did not call out either. We threw the junk around and groped in silence in the dark corners; I could sense how agitated we both were. The worst source of fear was our own silence, by which we were admitting that we no longer expected any answer from Helena, that we were now looking for her body, whether hanging or lying.

We found nothing, however, and went back down into the office. I checked the entire inventory again: desks, chairs, the clothes tree with her raincoat held in its outstretched arm, and, in the other room, the table, chairs, the clothes tree with its desperately outstretched empty arms. The boy called (to no effect) 'Helena!' and I (to no effect) opened the cupboard, revealing shelves full of documents, writing materials, adhesive tape, and rulers.

'There must be somewhere else! A toilet! Or a cellar!' I said, and we went out into the passageway again. The boy opened the door onto the yard, a small one. There was a cage of rabbits in one corner; beyond the yard was an overgrown garden with fruit trees rising from the thick uncut grass. (In some remote corner of my mind I was just capable of taking in the fact that it was a fine-looking garden: a piece of blue sky hanging between the green of the branches, the trunks of the trees rough and crooked, and a few bright yellow sunbeams shining between them.) At the end of the garden, in the idyllic shadow of an apple tree, I saw a wooden shack – clearly a rustic lavatory. I ran towards it.

A revolving plank fastened with a single nail to the narrow post (so that the door could be closed from the outside with the plank in a horizontal position) was hanging down vertically. I inserted my fingers in the gap between the door and the frame and ascertained by a slight pressure that the toilet was locked from the inside. This could mean only one thing. Helena must be inside. I said quietly: 'Helena, Helena!' Then was no reply; only the apple tree, stirring in the gentle breeze, rustled its branches against the wooden wall of the shack.

I knew that the silence from the locked latrine meant the worst and that the only course was to rip the door off; and I was the one who had to do it. I inserted my fingers again in the gap between doorpost and door and pulled with all my might. The door, fastened as it was by a mere piece of string instead of a hook (as is often the case in the country), gave way at once and swung wide open. Opposite me on a wooden seat in the stench of the latrine sat Helena. She was pale but alive. She looked at me with shocked eyes and instinctively pulled at her turned-up skirt, which even with the greatest effort hardly came half way down her thigh; she gripped the hem with both hands and closed her legs. 'Go away, for God's sake!' she implored.

'What's the matter?' I shouted at her. 'What have you taken?'

'Go away! Leave me alone!' she screamed.

At this point the boy appeared behind my back and Helena shouted 'Go away, Jindra, go away!' She lifted herself off the wooden seat and reached out a hand for the door, but I stepped in between her and the door so that she was forced to totter back onto the round seat of the latrine.

The next moment she lifted herself off it again and hurled herself at me with a desperate strength (really desperate, as this was evidently all that remained of her strength after some great effort). She gripped the lapels of my jacket with both hands and pushed me out. 'You beast, beast, beast!' she shouted (in so far as you could call the frantic efforts of an enfeebled voice a shout). She shook me once or twice, then she suddenly let go and started to run across the grass towards the yard. She wanted to run, that is, but was stopped short: she had rushed from the latrine without having had a chance to tidy herself up, so that her panties, the same stretch panties whose acquaintance I had made yesterday, and which did double duty as a suspender belt, were still twisted round her knees and impeded her running (her skirt was down but the black stockings on her legs were turned down so that their darker upper fringe with their suspenders reached down below her knees and could be seen below the hem of her skirt). She took a few little steps or jumps in her high-heeled shoes, covered scarcely three yards and fell heavily on the sun-washed lawn, under the branch of a tree near the tall gaudy sunflowers. I took her by the hand and tried to help her up, but she tore away from me, and when I made a second attempt she started laying about her insanely so that I caught several blows before I was able to seize her with all my might, pull her to me, pick her up, and constrict her in my arms like a straitjacket. 'Beast, beast, beast, beast!' she gasped as she pummelled me in the back with her free hand; and when I said, as gently as possible, 'Quiet, Helena,' she spat in my face.

I still did not relax my grip and I said: 'I'm not letting you go until you tell me what you took.'

'Go away, go away,' she repeated frantically; but then she suddenly went quiet, ceased all resistance and said 'Let me go!' in such a different voice, quietly and in a tone of utter weariness, that I set her down and looked at her, when I saw with horror her face lined with some terrible effort, her jaws clamped shut, her eyes unseeing and her body crouching slightly and bending forward.

'What's the matter?' I asked; but she turned without a word and made her way back to the latrine. I shall never forget the way she walked: it was only three or four yards, but more than once she broke off her restricted, irregular, slow-fast progress, and in these pauses one could sense from the creasing up of her body the struggle raging inside her. Finally she reached the latrine, took the door, which had remained wide open, and pulled it shut.

I stayed in the spot where I had picked her up; and when a loud plaintive moan came from the latrine I retreated even further. Then I realized for the first time that the boy was standing beside me. 'Stay here,' I told him. 'I'll have to call doctor.'

I went into the office; the telephone was standing on the desk. Finding the telephone book was harder; I couldn't see anywhere. I took the middle drawer of the desk by the handle but it was locked, as were all the little side drawers; the second

288

desk was locked as well. I went into the other room; there the desk had only one drawer; it was open, but there was nothing in it beyond a few photographs and a paperknife. I didn't know what to do, and now that I knew that Helena was alive and that her life was hardly in danger I was overcome with fatigue. I stood there for a while, staring stupidly at the clothes tree, that lanky metal clothes tree with its arms stretched upwards as if submitting to our approval or disapproval. Then, in confusion more than anything else, I opened the cupboard; there on a pile of documents was a blue-green telephone book for the Brno district. I took it over to the telephone and thumbed through for the hospital. I had already dialled and heard the ringing tone when the boy rushed into the room.

'Don't phone anyone – there's no need,' he shouted.

I didn't see why.

He tore the receiver from my hand and put it back on the hook. 'There's no need, I tell you!' I asked him to explain what was going on. 'It's not poison at all,' he said and went over to the clothes tree. He rummaged in the pockets of the gent's raincoat and took out a tube which he opened and turned upside down; it was empty.

'Is that what she took?' I asked.

He nodded.

'How do you know?'

'She told me.'

'Is that your tube?'

He nodded. I took it from him; it was an empty aspirin tube. 'Do you think aspirin is harmless in a dose like that?' I shouted at him.

'There wasn't any aspirin in it,' he said.

'What was there then?' I shouted.

'Laxatives,' he snapped.

I yelled at him to stop trying to make a monkey of me, that must know what had happened and that I didn't care for his solence. I ordered him to give me a proper answer at once.

When he heard me shouting he started shouting back: 'I've told you. There were laxatives in it! Has the whole world got know there's something wrong with my bowels?' I saw then that what I had taken for a stupid joke was the literal truth.

I looked at his ruddy face and snub nose, small but sufficiently large to accommodate a considerable quantity of freckles, and the meaning of the whole thing became clear to me: the aspirin tube was a disguise for his ludicrous ailment, just as his jeans and leather jacket were a disguise for his ludicrous, childish features, he was acutely self-conscious and he carried his immaturity through life with great difficulty. In that moment I liked him; with his boyish bashfulness he had saved Helena's life and saved me from several years of sleepless nights. With imbecile gratitude I looked at his projecting ears. Yes, he had saved Helena's life; but at the expense of an extremely hurtful and utterly purposeless degradation, meaningless and unjustifiable, a new link in a whole chain of deeds for which there could be no atonement. Suddenly I felt a guilty and urgent, if unformulated, need to run after her, raise her up out of her degradation, humiliate myself before her, assume all the blame and all the responsibility for the whole senselessly cruel incident.

'What are you staring at?' barked the boy. I didn't answer and walked past him into the passage; then I turned toward the door into the yard.

'What are you going out there for?' He caught me from behind by the shoulder of my jacket and tried to pull me towards him. For a second we looked into each other's eyes, then I grabbed his wrist and detached his hand from my shoulder. He pushed past me and stood blocking my way. I went up to him, intending to push him aside, and he punched me in the chest.

It was a feeble blow but the boy jumped back and stood in front of me again in an amateurish boxer's stance; his expression was a blend of apprehension and rash courage.

'She doesn't need you out there!' he shouted. I stayed where I was. I thought that maybe the boy was right: that there was nothing I could do to redress the irredressible. And the boy, seeing me standing there and not putting up any defence, went on shouting: 'She detests you! She hates your guts! She said so! She hates your guts!'

Nervous tension makes one defenceless against tears, and also against laughter; the absurd poetic justice of the boy's reference to guts made the corners of my mouth twitch. This maddened him: this time he hit me in the mouth. Then he stood back and again put his fists up in front of his face in boxing style, so that only his pink ears were visible projecting behind them.

I said: 'Stop that. I'm going.'

He shouted after me: 'You bastard! You bastard! I know you had something to do with this! I'll get you. You swine! You swine!'

I went out into the street. By now it was empty, with the emptiness of any street after a festival. Only a gentle breeze raised the dust, driving it over the flat ground which was as vacant as my own stunned head; for a long time I was incapable of a single thought ...

It was only later that I suddenly found I had the empty aspirin tube in my hand. I looked at it: it was badly scratched, and had evidently seen long service as a permanent disguise for the youth's laxatives.

Later still the tube reminded me of two other tubes, the tubes full of Alexej's sleeping tablets. Then I began to think that the boy had not really saved Helena's life after all: even if it had been aspirin in the tube it could hardly have caused Helena more harm than a certain discomfort in the stomach, with the boy and myself so close at hand. Helena's desperation had settled its account with life at a safe distance from the jaws of death.

8. Jaroslav

She was standing in the kitchen over the stove. Standing with her back to me. As if there was nothing wrong. 'Vladimir?' she replied, without turning. 'You saw him yourself, didn't you? Why ask?'

'No,' I said, 'Vladimir went off this morning with

Koutecky's grandson on his motor bike. I've come to tell you that I know all about it. I know why you were pleased that silly journalist woman came this morning. I know why I wasn't supposed to be there for the robing of the King. I know why the King kept silent even before the Ride. It was all very well thought out.'

My certainty confused Vlasta. But she soon regained her presence of mind and tried to defend herself by attacking in turn. It was a strange attack. Strange, because the protagonists were not facing one another. She was standing with her back to me, her face turned towards the gurgling soup. Her voice was not raised. It was almost indifferent. It was as if what she was saying was some ancient self-evident truth which only my eccentricity and lack of understanding obliged her to repeat. If I had to hear it, then this was it. From the beginning Vladimir had not wanted to be King. Vlasta was not surprised. There was a time when the lads used to do the Ride of the Kings by themselves. Now they were organized by a dozen organizations, and even the regional Party committee had a meeting about it. Nowadays there was nothing people could do by themselves and off their own bat. Everything was arranged from above. Before, they used to elect the King themselves; now they had Vladimir 'suggested' to them from above to gratify his father, and everyone had to obey. Vladimir was ashamed to be a privileged child. No one likes specially privileged children.

'Do you mean Vladimir is ashamed of me?'

'He doesn't want to seem like someone with special privileges,' Vlasta repeated.

'Is that why he makes friends with the Kouteckys? Those bourgeois? Those toffee-nosed idiots?' I asked.

'Yes, that's why,' said Vlasta. 'Milos isn't allowed to study just because of his grandfather. Just because his grandfather ran a building firm. Vladimir had his way paved with roses. Just because you're his father. Vladimir finds it hard to take. Can't you see that?'

For the first time in my life I felt angry with her. They had tricked me. All the time they had been coolly observing me anticipation of the event. My sentimental, emotional anticipation. They had calmly deceived me and watched me being deceived. 'Was there really any need to deceive me like that?'

Vlasta poured salt over the noodles and said I made things difficult. I was living in another world. I was a dreamer. They didn't want to take my ideals from me, but Vladimir was a different person. He had no use for my singing and yodelling. He got no pleasure from it and was bored by it. I would just have to get used to this fact. Vladimir was a modern person. He took after her father in this. Her father was always a great one for progress. He was the first farmer in the village to have a tractor before the war. Then he had everything taken from him. But from the time the fields belonged to the cooperative they had never yielded half as much.

'I'm not interested in your fields. I want to know where Vladimir went. He went to the motor cycle races at Brno, didn't he? Admit it.'

She had her back to me, stirring the noodles, and calmly went on talking. Vladimir took after his grandfather. He had his chin and eyes. Vladimir was not interested in the Ride of the Kings. Yes, if I wanted to hear it, he did go to the races. He went to watch the races. Why shouldn't he? He was more interested in motor bikes than in streamered horses. What of it? Vladimir was a modern person.

Motor bikes, guitars, motor bikes, guitars. A stupid, alien world. I asked: 'Just tell me how you define a modern person?'

She had her back to me, stirring the noodles, and said that even our flat wasn't allowed to be furnished in a modern way. What a fuss I had made about that modern standard lamp! Even the modern chandelier I hadn't liked. And yet anyone could see that the modern standard lamp was good to look at. Lamps like that were being bought everywhere these days.

'Shut up,' I said. But there was no stopping her. She was on her high horse. With her back turned on me. Her small, cross, bony back. This was what irritated me most of all. Her back. The back without eyes. The back so stupidly sure of itself. The back I could not come to terms with. I wanted to make her shut up. Turn her round to face me. But I felt such a distaste for her that I didn't even want to touch her. I'll make her turn round some other way. I opened the cupboard and took out a plate. I dropped it on the floor. She was silent for a moment. But she didn't turn round. Another plate, another and yet another. She still had her back to me. Huddled up within herself. I could see from her back that she was afraid. Yes, she was afraid, but she was defiant and wouldn't give in. She stopped stirring and stood motionless, gripping the wooden spoon in her hand. She was hanging on to it like a refuge. I hated her and she hated me. She didn't move and I never took my eyes off her even as I threw more and more china from the shelves onto the floor. I hated her and the whole of her kitchen. Her modern standard kitchen with its modern kitchen cabinet, modern plates and modern glassware.

I felt no excitement. I looked calmly, sadly, almost wearily at the floor covered in fragments of china, with pots and pans strewn over it. I was throwing my home on the floor. The home which I had loved and to which I had fled from Brno. The home in which I had felt the gentle domination of my pauper girl. The home I had peopled with fairytales, songs and good fairies. Over there on those three chairs we used to sit down to our dinner. Those delicious dinners in which the stupid trusting breadwinner of the family was appeased and bamboozled. I took one chair after another in my hand and broke the legs off. I put the crippled chairs down on the floor with the pots and broken china. I turned the kitchen table upside down. Vlasta was still standing motionless by the stove with her back turned towards me.

I went out of the kitchen into my own room. My room had red globes on the ceiling, a standard lamp and a hideous modern divan. My violin lay in a black case on the harmonium. I picked it up. At four we had to play in the garden restaurant. It was still only one. Where could I go?

I heard sobbing from the kitchen. Vlasta was crying. It was a heart-rending sobbing and somewhere deep inside me I felt a painful regret. Why hadn't she started crying ten minutes ago? I could have let myself be taken in by the old self-delusion and seen her as the little pauper girl again. Now it was too late.

I left the house. The invocations could be heard across the village roofs. We have a pauper but righteous king. Where could I go? The streets belonged to the Ride, home belonged to Vlasta, the taverns belonged to the drunks. Where do I belong? I am an old, deserted, ousted king. A righteous and beggared king. A king without heirs. The last king.

Luckily there are some fields out there beyond the village. There is a road. And ten minutes away is the river Morava. I lay down on the bank. I put the violin case under my head. I lay there for quite a long time. An hour, maybe two. And I thought of how I had come to the end of the road. So suddenly and unexpectedly. And the end was here. I could not imagine any continuation. I had always lived in two worlds at once. I had believed in their mutual harmony. It had been a delusion. Now I had been ousted from one of those worlds. From the real world. Only the make-believe one was left. But I cannot live only in a make-believe world. Even though I am expected there. Even though the deserter is calling for me and has a free horse for me and a red veil to cover my face. Now I knew. Now I understood why he forbade me to take off the scarf and wanted me to know only what he narrated to me! Now I understood why the King must have his face veiled! Not that he should not be seen, but that he should not see!

I couldn't imagine myself getting up and going. I couldn't imagine myself taking a single step. I was expected at four. But I wouldn't have the strength to get up and go. I like it here. Here by the river. Here there is water flowing. It flows slowly and I will lie here long.

Then someone spoke to me. It was Ludvik. I expected another blow. But I was not afraid now. Nothing could shake me now.

He sat down and asked if I would be at the performance that afternoon.

'You're not going?' I asked him.

'I am.'

'Is that why you came?'

295

'No, that's not what I came for. But things turn out dif
ferently from the way we expect.'

'Yes,' I said, 'completely different.'

'I've been wandering about the fields for an hour. I didn'
expect to find you here.'

'Nor did I.'

'I've something to ask you,' he said without looking me i
the eye. Just like Vlasta. But I didn't mind it from him. I like
it from him when he didn't look me in the eye. I could se
his shiftiness was only reserve. And the shyness warmed an
restored me.

'I want to ask you,' he said, 'whether you might let me si
in with the band this afternoon.'

19. Ludvik

There were still a few hours left before the next coach wa
due to leave, so I set off, driven by the disquiet within me, ou
of the village by the side lanes, and across the back yards an
into the fields, trying as I went to drive from my mind al
thoughts of that miserable day. This was not easy. I felt my li
itch where it had been injured by the boy's fist, and again th
vague outline of Lucie emerged to remind me that every at
tempt to redress my wrongs had ended with my wrongin
others. I tried to drive the thoughts away because the message
they kept repeating to me were all too familiar at that mo
ment. I tried to keep my mind blank and to admit into it onl
the distant calls of the horsemen which carried me away some
where beyond my own troubles and offered me relief.

I encircled the entire village along the meadow paths unt
I reached the bank of the Morava and set off along it dowr
stream; on the opposite bank there were a few geese and i
the distance a wood on level ground, otherwise just fields an
more fields. Then in the distance ahead of me I saw a figur
lying on the grassy bank. As I got nearer I recognized him
he was lying on his back with his face turned up to th

heavens, and under his head he had a violin case. All around were fields, flat and extending for miles, just as they had been for centuries, except that in these parts they were perforated by iron pylons carrying the heavy high-voltage cables. Nothing would have been easier than to avoid him. But on this occasion I did not want to avoid him, I would rather have avoided myself and the thoughts which were thrusting in on me, and so I went up to him and addressed him. He looked up at me and his eyes struck me as timid and apprehensive. This was the first time I had seen him at close range for a number of years, and I noticed that only a sparse fringe remained of the thick hair which had once added to his lofty stature by a good couple of inches, and that on the crown of his head there were only a few sad strands covering the bare skin. His lost hair reminded me of the long years in which I had not seen him, and I suddenly regretted those years, when I had avoided him (the calls of the horsemen came, scarcely audible, from the distance), and I felt a sudden guilty love for him. He lay before me, resting on his elbow, and was big and clumsy while the violin case was small and black like a baby's coffin. I knew that his band – what was once *my* band – would be playing that afternoon in the village, and I asked him if I might be allowed to sit in with them.

I made this request before I had had time to think it out fully (as if the words came before the thought) and so I expressed it abruptly, yet completely in accord with the way I was feeling. At that moment I was filled with a sorrowful love for this world I had abandoned years ago, in which horsemen ride around the village with a masked king, in which people walk about in white frilled shirts and sing songs, a world which for me is merged with the images of my home town and of my mother (my poor mother taken and hidden from me) and of my youth. All day long that love had been quietly growing inside me, and now it had burst out almost tearfully; I loved that long-lost world and begged it to offer me sanctuary and to save me.

But how and with what justification? Had I not avoided Jaroslav two days ago precisely because his appearance evoked the hateful music of the folk song? Had I not that very morning approached the folk festival with distaste? What had suddenly destroyed the old barriers which for fifteen years had stopped me from looking back with happy memories on my youth spent in the cymbalo band, stopped me from returning to my home town with affection? Could it be because a few hours ago Zemanek had sneered at the Ride of the Kings? Was he perhaps the one who had made me dislike folk song and had now cleansed me again of this dislike? Was I really only the other end of the compass arrow and he its point? Was I really in such degrading dependence on him? No, it was not just Zemanek's mockery that had made it possible for me to regain my love for the world of folk costumes, songs and cymbalo bands. I could love it because this morning I had found it, unexpectedly, in its misery and abandonment – abandoned by the showmen and publicists, by the political propagandists, by the purveyors of social utopias, by the swarms of cultural officials, abandoned by the sanctimonious exhibitionists among my contemporaries, abandoned even by Zemanek. Its abandonment had purified it, endowed it with the reproachful quality of a dying man, illuminated it with some irresistible ultimate beauty; its abandonment had given it back to me once more.

The band's performance was to take place in the same open-air restaurant in which I had recently dined and where I had read Helena's letter. When Jaroslav and I arrived there were already a few elderly people waiting patiently for their musical afternoon and about the same number of drunks tottering from table to table. At the back, round the wide-branched linden, were a few chairs. A double-bass stood leaning against the tree trunk in its grey shroud, and not far from it a man in a white frilled shirt was sitting at the cymbalo or dulcimer, quietly running the hammers over the strings. The other members of the band stood a few feet away, and Jaroslav introduced them to me. The second fiddle, a tall, dark young man in folk costume, was a doctor from the local hospital; the bespectacled bass player was the educational inspector for the local district council; the clarinettist, who would be good enough to lend me his clarinet and to alternate with me, was a schoolmaster; the cymbalo player, the only one apart from Jaroslav whom I remembered, was a draughtsman from the factory. Jaroslav ceremoniously introduced me as a founder member of the group and a most presentable clarinet player, and we sat on the chairs round the linden tree and started playing.

I had not held a clarinet in my hands for a long time, but I knew the first song well and soon lost my initial reserve, especially when the others voiced their approval at the end of the song, and refused to believe it was such a long time since I had played. Then the waiter (the same one I had paid for my lunch in such desperate haste a few hours before) set a table in front of the tree and put six glasses on it for us and a wickerwork demijohn of wine; and we began to drink, though with moderation. After one of the songs I nodded to the schoolmaster; he took the clarinet from me and said again that my playing was excellent. Happy at this praise, I leaned up against the tree trunk, and while I watched the band, now playing without me, a long-forgotten feeling of warm companionship washed over me and I was thankful for its coming to my assistance at the end of this bitter day.

And now once again Lucie emerged before my eyes, and I thought I now knew why she had appeared to me at the hairdresser's, and then next day in Kostka's account of her, which had been at once both truth and legend. Perhaps she had wanted to tell me that her destiny, that of the corrupted young girl, was close to mine, that, although we had passed each other by and not found understanding, our lifelines were kindred, linked, allied, because they were both stories of *devastation*: just as physical love had been devastated for Lucie, thus depriving her life of its most elementary value, so my life had been robbed of values which were to have provided its foundations, and which were in origin pure and innocent. Yes, innocent: physical love, however much devastated in Lucie's life, is still an innocent thing, just as the songs of this region of mine were and are innocent, just as the cymbalo band is innocent, just as my home, for which I had conceived an intense dislike, was innocent, just as Fucik, whose portrait

I could not look at without loathing, was completely innocent as far as I was concerned, just as the word *Comrade*, though for me it had a menacing ring, was as innocent as the word *you* and the word *future* and many other words. The blame lay elsewhere and was so great that its shadow had fallen far and wide on the whole world of innocent things (and words) and had devastated them. We lived, Lucie and I, in a devastated world; and because we did not know how to show regret for things which had been devastated we turned away from them and in this way injured them and ourselves as well. Lucie, little girl who has known so much love, so much bad love, is this what you have come from across the years to tell me? Have you come to intercede for the world of devastation?

The song came to an end and the schoolmaster handed me the clarinet, saying he would play no more today, as I played better than he did and deserved to play all the more since nobody knew when I would be coming again. I caught Jaroslav's eye and said I would be very glad of a chance to come back and see them as soon as possible. Jaroslav asked me if I really meant it. I said I did and we started playing. Jaroslav had long since abandoned his chair and was standing with his head bent, his violin leaning down his chest against all the rules, and walking about as he played; the second fiddle and I also stood up every now and then, mainly because we wanted to offer as much scope as possible to the free flow of inspiration. In those moments when we plunged into adventurous improvisations demanding inventiveness, precision and great rapport, Jaroslav became the life and soul of us all, and I was amazed at what a good musician this great fellow was, belonging as he did (he especially) to the devastated values of my life; he had been taken from me, and I, to my detriment and shame, had allowed this to happen, although he had been perhaps my most faithful, disinterested and innocent friend.

Meanwhile the character of the audience gathered in the garden was slowly being transformed: to the handful o' mostly elderly people who had initially followed our playin; with warm interest was now added a growing crowd of young sters from the village or more probably the town, who occupied the remaining tables, ordered beer and wine in stentorian tones and very soon, as their alcohol level rose, began demonstrating their exuberant need to be seen, heard and recognized. The atmosphere became noisier and more nervous – the youths were staggering from table to table, shouting at each other and at their girls – until I caught myself ceasing to concentrate on the music and looking too frequently at the tables in the garden, watching the adolescent faces with an undisguised hatred. When I saw those long-haired heads ostentatiously and theatrically spitting out words, and saliva, my old hatred for the age of adolescence flooded back until it seemed to me that all I could see was actors, their faces masked to represent cretinous masculinity, arrogant ruthlessness and brutishness. I could see no mitigating circumstances in the existence, under the masks, of other, more human faces; indeed, the real horror of the whole thing lay in the fact that the faces beneath were themselves fiercely devoted to the inhumanity and vulgarity of the masks.

Jaroslav evidently felt the same, for he suddenly put up his violin and said that he was in no mood for playing before an audience of this kind. He suggested we should leave, taking the roundabout path through the fields, the one we used to take in the old days; it was a fine day, dusk would soon be coming on, it would be a warm starlit evening. At some point we would stop by a briar bush in the fields, and there we would play, just for ourselves, for our own pleasure, as we used to do; we had got into the stupid habit of playing only on formal occasions, and Jaroslav had had enough of it.

At first the others all agreed enthusiastically, because evidently they too felt that their love for folk music needed to be expressed in more intimate surroundings; but then the bass player (the school inspector) reminded us that we had agreed to play until nine, that this was what the district Party committee and the restaurant manager expected, that it had all been arranged, that we had to go through with it once we had pledged ourselves, and that we could play in the open air some other time.

At that moment the lamps which were hanging on long wires stretched from tree to tree all came on; since it was still barely dusk, they spread no light around them, but just stuck there in the greying arena like great motionless tears, milky-white tears which cannot be checked and must not be allowed to fall; there was a sudden and inexplicable melancholy in this that was impossible to resist. Jaroslav repeated almost imploringly that he didn't want to stay here, that he wanted to go out into the fields, to the briar bush, and just play there for his own pleasure; but then he made a gesture of resignation, pressed the violin to his chest, and began to play.

This time we did not allow ourselves to be distracted by our audience, but played with an even greater concentration than before; the more inattentive and rude the atmosphere in the restaurant garden, the more closely we were ringed (like a sort of desert island) by the tumultuous sea of indifference, and the more depressed we felt, the more we turned inwards to each other, playing for ourselves rather than for the audience, so that we managed to forget the noisy drunks and to create a magic circle of music, with ourselves inside, as if in a glass cage dropped into deep cold water.

'If the mountains were made of paper and the water of ink, if the stars were scribes, if the whole wide world was a-writing, it could not write the whole testament of my love,' sang Jaroslav without taking the violin from under his chin; and I felt myself happy inside the glass cage of these songs, in which sorrow is not a jest, laughter is not mockery, love is not ridiculous, and hatred is not restrained, where people love with body and soul (yes, Lucie, with body as well as soul!), where in hatred men reach for knife or sword, where in joy they dance, in despair jump into the Danube, where love is still love and pain is pain, where primal emotion has not yet been distorted and where values are not yet devastated. It seemed to me that among these songs I was at home, that this was where I came from, my home, a home which I had betrayed but which because of this was all the more truly my home — for the home we have wronged has all the more urgent

302

a voice. But then I realized that the home was not of this world (of which world, then, was it?), that what we were singing and playing was only memories, recollections, a pictorial memento of something that no longer was; and I felt the firm ground of this home of mine sinking under my feet, felt myself falling, clarinet in mouth, down into the depths of years, the depths of centuries, those peerless depths where love is love and pain is pain. I told myself with astonishment that my only home was this very falling, this searching, longing fall, and I abandoned myself to it and felt its delicious vertigo.

Then I looked at Jaroslav to see whether I was alone in my exaltation, and I noticed (his face was illuminated by a lamp hung from the top of the tree above us) that he was very pale; he had stopped singing, his lips were tightly clenched, his timorous eyes had become more startled still, he was playing wrong notes, and his violin hand was slowly slipping downwards. Suddenly he stopped playing and sat down. I knelt beside him. 'What's wrong?' I asked. The sweat was running down his forehead and he was holding his left arm near the shoulder. 'It hurts,' he said. The others hadn't realized that Jaroslav was ill and were still caught up in the spell of their own music; the gaps left by the first violin and clarinet gave the cymbalo player a chance to excel, accompanied now only by second fiddle and bass. Remembering the second fiddle was a doctor, I called him over to Jaroslav; only the cymbalo and the bass were playing now. The second fiddle took Jaroslav by the left wrist and held it for what seemed an age; then he lifted up his eyelids and looked at his eyes; then he touched his sweating forehead. 'Heart?' he asked. 'Arm and heart,' said Jaroslav, who looked green. By now the bass player had noticed us; he leaned his bass against the linden tree and came over, so that the cymbalo player was now all on his own, quite unaware of what was going on and thoroughly enjoying his solo.

'I'll phone the hospital,' said the second fiddle.

'What is it?'

'Pulse very slight. Cold sweat. It must be a thrombosis.'

'God,' I said.

303

'Don't worry, he'll get over it,' he consoled me and set off for the restaurant building at a brisk pace. He was held up by people who were by now quite drunk and had noticed nothing, being completely absorbed in themselves, their beers, their boasts and their insults, which in the far corner of the garden had even led to fisticuffs.

Now the cymbalo fell silent too, and we all stood round Jaroslav, who looked at me and said it was all because we had stayed there, that he had not wanted to stay, he had wanted to go out into the fields, especially when I came, especially when I came back to them, that we could have played beautifully out in the open. 'Don't try to talk,' I told him. 'You need complete rest.' I was thinking of how, although he would probably recover as the second fiddle had predicted, it would be a completely different life, a life without passionate devotion, without the ecstatic playing in the band, a life under the aegis of death; and I suddenly had the feeling (though at that time I had no way of assessing its justice) that one's destiny is often completed long before death, that the point at which one's destiny ends is not identical with the point at which one dies, and that Jaroslav's destiny was now fulfilled.

Overwhelmed with grief, I gently rubbed the top of his bald head, where the sad long hairs covered the baldness, and I realized with a shock that my trip home, made in the hope of striking at the hated Zemanek, had ended with me holding my stricken friend in my arms; yes, in that moment I could see myself holding him in my arms, holding him and carrying him, big and heavy as he was, as if I were carrying my own mixed-up guilt, carrying him through the indifferent mob and weeping as I went.

We had stood round him like this for about ten minutes when the second fiddle reappeared and signalled us to help Jaroslav to his feet, and we slowly supported him through the noisy, drunken adolescents into the street where the ambulance was waiting with its lights full on.